Danny Boy

Barry Walsh is a Londoner and a rather late starter.

Danny Boy is his second novel, following *The Pimlico Kid*, a story of first love.

He is proudly associated with St Andrew's Westminster, the world's oldest youth club, and considers Pimlico to be London's finest village.

He is married with two daughters.

www.bjwalsh.com
 @Barry Walsh
 @bjwalsh

Also by Barry Walsh

The Pimlico Kid

Danny Boy

BARRY WALSH

HarperCollins*Publishers*

HarperCollins*Publishers* Ltd
1 London Bridge Street,
London SE1 9GF

www.harpercollins.co.uk

HarperCollins*Publishers*
Macken House,
39/40 Mayor Street Upper,
Dublin 1
D01 C9W8
Ireland

First published by HarperCollins*Publishers* 2023
1

A catalogue record for this book is
available from the British Library

ISBN (PB): 978-0-00-851861-5

This novel is entirely a work of fiction.
The names, characters and incidents portrayed in it are
the work of the author's imagination. Any resemblance to
actual persons, living or dead, events or localities is
entirely coincidental.

Typeset in Sabon by Palimpsest Book Production,
Falkirk, Stirlingshire

Printed and bound in the UK using 100% Renewable
Electricity by CPI Group (UK) Ltd

This book is produced from independently certified FSC™ paper
to ensure responsible forest management.

For more information visit: www.harpercollins.co.uk/green

For my 'very own and golden' daughters,
Megan and Rachel.

The Estate

In an area known as the mucky hem on Westminster's fine robe, the housing estate sat insolently close to a palace, a cathedral, an abbey and two royal parks. On three of its corners stood pubs that didn't serve food; occupying the fourth was a working-man's cafe that did.

Scattered untidily throughout the estate to meet the daily needs of its 1,800 inhabitants were: a newsagent, a grocer, a greengrocer, a hairdresser, a butcher, a cobbler and a laundromat. It was a walk to the market for a fishmonger, but there was always the chip shop.

1

August 1965

Ten o'clock on a balmy Saturday morning. The cafe's door stood open. Danny Byrne waited outside, nose up, like a Bisto Kid, savouring the smell of frying bacon which, once he went inside, would disappear in the dominant but still comforting aroma of warm fat.

Almost seventeen and six feet tall, he wore jeans, basket ball boots and a polo shirt. After a growth spurt during which only his bones had stretched, his muscles had finally caught up, thanks to extra weight training in the boys' club gym. This summer, possessed of visible biceps, long-sleeved shirts were no longer needed to hide skinny arms.

He had recently been spending more time looking in mirrors for what he hoped would soon be good looks. His face, unlike his arms, hadn't firmed up enough to be thought handsome, but he felt he was getting there, although what he considered slightly girly lips remained a worry. After checking himself briefly in the window, he stepped inside.

The cream tiled walls and Formica tabletops hardened the cacophony of cutlery scrape, plate clack and the raucous banter of men who had been at work before Danny had got out of bed. Rising above the noise was the clatter and ding of a pinball machine being taken to its limits.

Nobby Clarke's slender fingers were tapping lightly on the flipper buttons, while his body moved as if a gyroscope generated oiled hip thrusts inside his arse-empty Lee Coopers, and smooth shoulder rolls inside a red Harrington jacket. In this way, he could seduce any pinball machine into giving up its prizes. In the presence of greatness, Danny hung back while Nobby repeatedly sent the silver ball up the sloping table, to be punched around by pulsing rubber bands and illuminated mushrooms. Nobby glanced over his shoulder and through thin lips clamped around a skinny six-strander, said, 'Danny boy! Sweet!'

Another soft shag of his hips and the ball rifled into a clown's face that spun until a buzzer signalled 'replay'. He gave a vain shrug and trapped the returning ball in the armpit of a flipper. With his free hand, he took the roll-up from his lips and held it vertically between thumb and second finger as the Buddha might, if he smoked.

Warm, watchful eyes widened beneath a high forehead that eventually reached thin fair hair. Lighter still were the hairs of a moustache he was trying to grow: lengthy bum fluff that signalled its presence only when fingered to monitor growth, or in a wind.

'All right, Danny?'

'Yes.'

'Want to play.'

'Please.'

'How many games?'

'Three will do, thanks.'

Nobby gave a master's smile for an apprentice who thought three attempts would be enough to score a replay. 'Fancy yourself today, then?'

'Piss off, Nob!'

Three goes for the price of one was excellent value, but such deals required discretion because the cafe's owner, Angelo, had called time on Nobby trading replays for cash. Danny went to slip the sixpence into Nobby's jacket pocket.

'No, tell you what, I'll have a cheesecake instead . . . and a tea.' This would cost more than sixpence. Danny was about to mention it, when Nobby winked and resumed easy thrusting and flipping.

Cordelia Hill was behind the counter, wiping it down. She looked older than sixteen and, in her white coat, reminded him of Westminster Hospital's young radiographers, who occasionally appeared in his night-time fantasies.

'Hello, Danny.'

'When did you start working here again?'

'Last week. . . Hello Danny!'

'Sorry, it's just that I didn't expect to see you, I thought you'd stopped working here.'

She smiled. 'Nice surprise?'

'Oh yes,' he said, with an enthusiasm that surprised him because her smile had beamed with more than familiarity. Dodds and Crockett had recently talked of her as fanciable but, even though he hadn't seen her for a while, he wondered why he hadn't noticed how attractive she'd grown. Probably, he reasoned, because their friendship had never been like that. It began in their primary school. At a time when boys who played with girls were called cissies, Danny had resisted ridicule to spend time with Cordelia because, like him, she

5

often read a book at playtime. Starting with Enid Blyton, they began reading the same books, agreeing and disagreeing.

Unconcerned at first whether they were boys' or girls' books, they later drew lines, either side of which they accepted each other's enthusiasm for the likes of *Little Women* or *The Call of the Wild*, but didn't read them. This had stopped when Danny left for a boys' grammar school but, on the rare occasions they met, they ended up talking about books.

Cordelia's raised eyebrows told him she was waiting.

Danny gave her Nobby's order and returned her smile, at which she pushed both palms over her ears to smooth blonde hair, even though it was already held neatly in a ponytail.

'That's a shilling please, Danny. Had your exam results yet?'

He gave her two sixpences. 'Sometime this week.'

'I'm sure they'll be good.'

Yellow flecks lit her green eyes as they locked on to his, making him feel as if he'd left his curtains open. Extended eye contact bothered Danny: with boys it could lead to confrontation; with girls it was tricky. Her gaze stirred a strange excitement in him, as if they had walked together through a familiar door but into an unfamiliar room.

'Hope so.' He looked away, but not before she had seen in a bit.

Holding the large, chromed teapot with two hands, she filled a white mug, added milk, and popped the cheesecake on a plate. She pushed them towards him with a smile that died when Angelo passed by and prodded her backside.

She wheeled around, hand raised to slap. He held up a tea towel like a matador and grinned at Danny.

Rich from Angelo, who would pull the face off anyone who did that to his own daughter.

Yet, in his natural impulse to please, Danny hadn't been able to stop himself returning Angelo's grin. Cordelia noticed and gave him a look of silent fury. Instantly ashamed, he hoped he had got the brunt of her anger because Angelo paid her wages. She closed her eyes for a few seconds. When she opened them and turned to Angelo, it was with the controlled grimace of pretended tolerance. 'Dirty old bugger.'

Angelo shrugged, disappointed that his bit of fun hadn't been funny. 'Sorry, lovely girl.' He thwacked the towel over his shoulder and disappeared into the kitchen. Cordelia snatched her ponytail out of its rubber band, yanked her hair back through it three times, while glaring at Danny. 'Anything else?'

He shook his head.

No, except he'd like to say sorry.

He hoped this unspoken response had shown in his face, as it was more honest than his smile for Angelo. If it had, Cordelia hadn't noticed. He picked up Nobby's tea and the London cheesecake with its topping of iced-coconut strings that had nothing in common with what non-Londoners call a cheesecake – except that it, too, didn't taste of cheese.

Nobby now sat at a table. Danny gave him his shilling's worth.

'Sweet,' said Nobby, who rose, hand twirling in a Regency courtier's bow to usher Danny to the pinball machine. Four replays had been racked up, and a shilling sat on the glass top. 'A little bonus for you.'

Unsurprised by Nobby's generosity, Danny bridled at being patronised by his oldest friend. 'Thanks.'

As he launched the first ball, he heard the scratch-patter

of a dog's unclipped nails on the quarry tiles. Banger, an overweight black Labrador, made for the counter where he sat and waited with imploring, seal eyes for anyone who might feed him. The noise in the cafe dropped. Behind Danny, the mouth-organ whine of laboured breathing grew louder. Before Danny could turn around, Gasping George had barged him aside in the way only very big men can, while leaving their victims unsure whether they've done it deliberately. Danny bumped into the pinball machine, causing all the lights to go out save for the illuminated 'Tilt' sign that signalled 'game over'.

'All right Pages?' The 'a' in Pages disappeared in a wheezy dash to get it said before taking his next breath.

'Pages' was an old nickname for Danny, because from an early age he had carried a book or its torn-out sections to read whenever he was on his own and, to the irritation of his mother and friends, when he wasn't. His mates no longer used the name, but George kept it going as a put-down for the local bookworm.

'Yes, thanks George. You?'

Apart from being an ignorant, clumsy bastard.

'Would be if there was a bit more oxygen in the world.'

George Kelly was a chronic asthmatic of brick shit-house dimensions, at whose approach people would move to the kerb. In his late forties, ruined lungs and huge bulk had him fighting for air after the slightest exertion. These days he got others to do most of his physical stuff but, under the flab, his muscles remained powerful. It paid to keep clear when he got upset, as he remained capable of three-yard rushes to nab victims and hold them in a crushing grip, while hissing in their ear to, 'Fucking hold still till I get me breath.'

Arthur Reilly, Gasping George's ginger-haired pilot fish, stood in the doorway, turning a matchstick over in his mouth while scanning the cafe like a hood covering his boss's progress through a speakeasy. An unfortunate lack of space between his nose and top lip turned smiles into threatening sneers, but he became less scary every few seconds, when his face crinkled in a squeezed blink, as if everything he saw merited a double take.

Danny started another game. Reilly passed by. His shove was deliberate.

Tilt!

'Oh dear!' said Reilly, laughing, and pushed Danny again to emphasise the fun of it all.

'You really must be . . .' George snatched a shallow breath '. . . more careful, Arthur.'

Reilly stayed close, took the matchstick from his mouth and blinked into Danny's face. 'Well?'

A couple of years older than Danny but no longer bigger, Reilly reminded him of Abraham Lincoln with his loose-limbed strength and visible tendons on freckled forearms that could well have developed from chopping wood. Yet, for the first time, Danny wondered if he could take him. Reilly's street radar picked this up. He blinked and stepped back to give himself room to swing.

'Leave it!' said George.

Reilly swaggered over to the counter. Danny started his third game but, in trying to steady his shaking hands, he gripped the table too tightly.

Tilt! He marvelled again, as everyone else did, how Nobby got away with all those gentle pulls and nudges without turning the lights out.

George raised an arm and in a wheezed command of

low-volume menace, said, 'Nobby, over here, my son!' Tea in hand, shoulders slumped, Nobby got up and followed George as he made his way to a window seat that only strangers made the mistake of using.

He called to Angelo. 'All right about the dog?' A question he asked every time, never expecting an answer. He sat down and the noise level picked up again. Nobby waited. George took his tea away from him. 'Have you drunk from this yet?' Nobby shook his head. 'How many sugars?'

'Two,' said Nobby.

'This'll do. Don't forget your cake.'

Nobby fetched it.

'Cheer up my son, I ain't gonna bite,' said George, and buried his teeth in the cheesecake. 'Why don't you get yourself another one?'

When Nobby turned to go, George slapped the table. 'Money!'

'Oh, sorry, George.'

Nobby pulled an envelope from inside his jacket and handed it over. George waved him away, extracted a slim wad of fivers, dropped the envelope on the table and flicked it to the floor. He counted the notes and tucked them into his 'readies' pocket on the front of his jacket: the top half of a suit that had never been out with the matching trousers. Nobby returned, put down his second mug of tea and remained standing.

'No cake?' said George.

'Not hungry any more.'

George shifted his bulk, stretched out a leg and fiddled in his pocket to make more room for his right bollock. 'What'd he say today?'

'Who?' said Nobby.

'Who d'ya think?'

'Nothing much, except that he was sorry to be a bit late.'

'He didn't have it all when we collared him yesterday. Wonder where he got the rest?'

'Don't know.'

'How was his finger?'

'Didn't notice, George.'

Danny looked up from his game at the wrong moment and caught George's eye.

'Pages, my son! Here a minute.' Danny felt a childish rage at not being allowed to finish and raised a just-a-minute hand. George rasped, 'I ain't got all day!'

At the same time, he shoved Nobby away. 'Why don't you go and finish his game for him.'

As they crossed, Nobby wouldn't look at him and Danny felt a twinge of pity. Gone was the once smug satisfaction at being one of George's crew, and the money that came with it, and the illusory status of driving around in his white Ford Zodiac. He was now a bullied runner for a man who frightened him.

'Have a seat, Danny,' said George.

His proper name: it must be serious.

George bared his teeth – his way of smiling – and rubbed a hand over his head as if hair grew on it, when all he had was a greying monk's-worth circling below. 'Now, my grammar-school boy, I might have a bit of work for you.'

George's eyes narrowed when Danny didn't answer.

Danny swallowed hard. 'What's that then, George?'

'Want you to do a bit of work for me, like what Nobby does. Not so much taking messages or making collections . . . although I ain't sure I can rely on him to do that like I used to.' He shook his head. 'No, something different.'

11

'Oh, Nobby's all right,' said Danny without thinking but, on seeing George's displeasure, added, 'isn't he?'

George closed one eye as if taking aim. 'Not all right enough. Been having trouble finding those who owe me. Makes me look soft. Can't be having that now, can I?'

'No, George.'

'Anyway, I want to make changes to the way I do things, become a little more, you know, professional. Some people reckon that because I'm common I'm also thick.'

You're both, thought Danny, but being scary and cunning was enough to make a living on the estate.

'Well, Danny?'

'Yes, no . . . course you're not, George.'

George enjoyed this flustered response, and the stretch of his smile whitened a crescent scar under his nose: his only visible 'hard man' mark. According to Danny's mother, he got it aged twelve when his nan had lashed out at him and broken the glass of Tizer he was drinking.

'I'm thinking of putting things in writing, just so's no one's in any doubt about what's agreed.' He leaned closer. 'Thought you could give me a hand.'

With effort, Danny resisted the urge to pull away from the bristled chin. George noticed, smiled and sat back. 'I know what I want to say but writing it down's different, ain't it?' He went on, gasping, chopping his sentences into bits. 'I want to get a bit more formal, polite like. I need the bastards, these people, to know exactly what I want – but to be nice about it, at least until . . . know what I mean?'

'Guess so.'

'No guessing about it.' He waggled his index finger close to Danny's face as if writing. 'Written notes. What do you say?'

12

George opened his hands, offering Danny the privilege of being part of his crew with the likes of Reilly, as well as Nobby. He was expecting gratitude. Although more frightened than grateful, Danny felt slightly flattered that, for once, his grammar-school education should have a little status, even if it was with the local thug.

'I don't know, I've a lot of schoolwork this summer . . . then there's the job at the off-licence, and my holiday . . .'

'Won't take much of your precious time, Danny, my son. And you'll earn a few bob.'

'It's just that I wouldn't want to let you down.'

George's lips peeled back from his teeth. 'Oh, I don't think you'll do that.'

'No, George.'

'A few little messages. Nobby can deliver them. Nobby!'

Nobby abandoned his game and came over. 'What's that, George?'

'Talking about you and Danny here working together.'

Nobby checked to ensure George wasn't looking at him before giving Danny a wide-eyed shake of his head. 'Oh yeah? Sweet.'

George leaned closer again. Creamy cobwebs of saliva had appeared at the corners of his mouth. 'Shall we say two bob a note?' Danny earned only ten bob for a whole Saturday at the off-licence. George's head dropped to one side as if checking a picture that needed straightening. 'Easy money, but if you don't think it's worth it . . .' He stopped without saying what Danny wanted to hear: something like, 'you can jack it in'.

The extra money would be welcome; enough, among other things, to buy his mother the hairdryer she'd love. He wanted time to think but George had raised a hand, ready to shake on the deal.

Danny cleared his throat to avoid a squeaky reply. 'OK, let's see how it goes . . . till the end of the summer holidays?'

'Done.' George spat a spray of saliva into the palm of his hand and held it out. Danny noted how big a fist it would make, and winced at the crushing squeeze that followed.

'Right. Breakfast.' George raised an arm and rasped out his order. 'Ready when you are, Angelo, and a couple of bangers for Banger!' He chuckled at his habitual joke and told Nobby to get him another cup of tea. Nobby slouched off.

Danny stood up. 'I'll be getting away now, George.'

'Yeah, see you around, Pages. Welcome on board.'

Nobby was waiting at the counter next to Reilly and rubbing the patient Banger's head. Danny stopped to do the same when he heard Cordelia say, 'No thanks Arthur, sorry. I don't have much time these days, what with covering for my mum and all.'

After a prolonged blink, Reilly switched from nice to nasty. 'What, looking after your drunken old lady?' Cordelia drew back as if she had been struck. He leaned on the counter. 'Don't know who you think you are.'

The hurt in her face triggered anger that surged past Danny's natural caution. 'Too good for you, Reilly!' Shaking at the realisation of what he'd said and not daring to look at Reilly, he said, 'Are you OK, Cordelia?'

His question released her tears and she ran to the kitchen. Reilly grabbed his arm and between blinks said, 'Oh yeah?' He cocked his fist. 'Keep your fucking nose out!'

Danny wondered whether nutting Reilly would take him down and then, what if it didn't? Here was the white knight scene in which he had imagined himself starring. But it hadn't featured his legs starting to buckle. He waited, knowing he was leaving the 'first-in' chance to Reilly. Nobby appeared at Danny's shoulder. Reilly's eyes flicked between the two of them, wondering whom to punch first.

'Arthur!' George was shaking his head.

Reilly let go. Danny yanked his arm away as if Reilly still held it and walked out, while Reilly made loud clucking 'chicken' sounds.

Halfway down the street, Nobby caught up with him. 'For a minute, I thought it would all kick off in there. Boy, have you pissed off the blood-nut blinker.'

'Fuck Reilly,' said Danny.

Nobby grinned. 'Rather you than me! Still, nice of you to stick up for Cordelia.'

And good of you to stick up for me, thought Danny, remembering how Nobby had been ready to throw his frail body into the fray.

'Not the best start to being one of George's crew, though,' said Nobby.

'I'm not one of George's crew. I agreed to help out now and again, that's all.'

'Yeah, like it says in your contract. Know what mine says?' Danny didn't answer. 'It says that I do everything he asks or I get a fucking clump. Yours say something different?'

'Piss off, Nobby. And watch yourself. He reckons you're getting sloppy about finding those who owe him.'

His face stiffened. 'Yeah?'

'Yeah.'

He stopped to light a roll-up and drew deep. 'Shit. I gave Streaky Gordon a couple more days to pay but he ran into me and George yesterday and begged for more time. George agreed but when Gordon went to shake hands, George grabbed his little finger and bent it back till it cracked.'

15

Nobby grimaced. 'When the poor gits were only selling for George, they always found the money. But some, like Gordon, have started taking the stuff, too, and while they're on it they don't care. I went around to his gaff this morning. He was coming down big time and shitting himself at being five quid short. I said I'd take what he had but he freaked out because George wants it all or nothing.'

'And?'

'I subbed him.'

2

The windows of the reading room in the library were wide open but street air failed to penetrate its fetid atmosphere. Danny and half a dozen men sat around a long oak table, fighting off sleep. As usual, most of Danny's fellow readers were from the nearby Salvation Army hostel and, although it was high summer, their attire would have kept them warm in winter. Lumps of varying sizes bulged under macs and coats. Crammed carrier bags and ruined holdalls sat at their feet – each man his own walking larder and wardrobe.

Danny was struggling to focus on *Tess of the d'Urbervilles*, part of his A level English course for the next year. The others, chins or cheekbones propped on elbows, were making a show of reading a variety of newspapers or magazines but their eyes were closed.

A tramp on Danny's right gave in to the heat and draped a filthy herringbone coat over the back of his chair. Whenever he scratched himself or stretched, he revived Danny – as if by smelling salts – with acrid blasts of baked sweat escaping from under two pullovers, a shirt and what appeared to be several vests.

Danny wanted to move to another seat but the ostentation of getting up daunted him. He worried a little about embarrassing his neighbour, and a lot about embarrassing himself. However, he worked out that the only vacant chairs were next to those who looked equally pungent. Although relieved at there being no point in moving, he felt a twinge of shame at knowing he would have stayed put anyway.

On his other side, a grizzled bear of a man with long grey side-whiskers slept soundly, arms straight down at his sides, forehead resting on the *Daily Express* while his dribble darkened the racing pages. At first, Danny had taken him for a tramp who didn't smell, but his blue overalls and the clean white spots on his red kerchief indicated a working man who looked too old to be working.

Soon a librarian would ask the sleeper to leave. Bad smells were unacceptable but hard to deal with when there were multiple sources. Sleep publicly offended the library's purpose as a place for improving the mind. In winter, with the windows closed and the marvellous central heating at full blast, the librarians were less tolerant of smells, yet still allowed even the most fragrant visitors ten minutes to read, or pretend to read, while they got warm. But sleeping remained taboo.

Through the glass-panelled partition, Danny spotted a librarian approaching. Others saw her too and made a show of reading and turning pages. The big man slept on, until Danny leaned over and shoved his shoulder. He came to with a grumpy start. Danny pretended to point at something in his newspaper. The big man looked about him, realised his position and flipped from the soaked racing columns to the dry leader page. The librarian stood in the doorway for a minute to let everyone know she had her eye on them. As she returned to the main desk, the big man winked and held out a huge, calloused paw, inside which Danny struggled to gain a grip. He expected his hand to be crushed, as it had been by Gasping George, but it received only a gentle squeeze.

Everyone settled down and Danny tried again to focus on *Tess of the D'Urbervilles*. Before long, he was dozing and waking with a nod over pages that had to be re-read. He gave up and fell to musing about how he would feel if his girlfriend – if he ever had a girlfriend – were, like Tess, to lose her virginity to someone else. As he daydreamed, sympathy rose in his chest, not for the shitty Angel Clare but for a betrayed Danny Byrne, and anger grew for the imaginary seducer who'd had his way with his girlfriend before he did. These thoughts served only to increase his belief that a lack of sexual experience must be obvious and that girls would be more attracted to boys who weren't virgins. He feared that his own virginity would render him and any future girlfriend vulnerable to sexually experienced interlopers.

His drowsy thoughts drifted around virginity and the ridiculous notion of 'losing' it, like something mislaid or stolen when not paying attention, or even while unconscious. When he considered the erections that greeted him on waking each morning, the idea of having sex while he slept seemed at least possible, and only marginally more likely to disrupt his sleep than the turbulent, vivid dreams in which he enjoyed sex with girls he knew, or film stars like Sophia Loren or – a bit of a worry this – the school caretaker's fat wife. He hoped that once he had enjoyed the real thing, it would relieve the daily groin-ache for which he found only one form of temporary relief. He wondered, though, if finally having sex would put an end to his Technicolor dreams, or if they would only revert to black and white?

Dodds and Crockett claimed they had already done it with Barbara Gethin, a girl who had worn a sizeable bra since she was eleven. Danny had had his chance the day they'd sat together on the bench outside Jones's grocer shop. She had rubbed his thigh and looked into his eyes which, Dodds had assured him, would lead to him being invited to her flat. Sure enough, the invitation came but, despite the arrival of an eager erection, he became flustered and declined. When Dodds asked how he'd got on, Danny claimed that he didn't fancy her. This was true, but also true was the fact that – in the face of Barbara's fully fleshed, full-bodied come-on – he'd bottled it.

Dodds shook his head. 'Didn't fancy her? All you had to do was give her one. It's not as if she fancies you either! Who do you think you are, Steve McQueen?'

Embarrassed and miffed at not being fancied, Danny was also shocked to realise that some girls could be just like Dodds.

Danny's never-ending virginity continued to keep him low in the pecking order whenever mates talked of girls. He recalled how late he'd been reaching an earlier maturity milestone. While friends were sounding like Paul Robeson, his voice had remained stubbornly falsetto. In school assembly, he had mimed to hymns rather than sound like a choirboy, and coughed in search of a lower octave before speaking. With the arrival of his first deep croaks, responses of family and friends included, 'finally', or 'at last'. Happily, they hadn't been monitoring his equally slow-developing dick.

Danny had thought of pretending he'd had sex but was deterred by the fear of being exposed as a liar. And exposure was all too possible, because when anyone claimed to have had sex with a local girl, Dodds made a point of asking her whether it was true. None confessed, although Judy Graham was betrayed by her short temper, 'the big-mouthed bastard! . . .' she'd said, followed by hopelessly late denials. Dodds claimed he could tell if a girl was a virgin by the way, when questioned, she said, 'maybe', or 'mind your own business', or 'fuck off'.

Danny wondered whether it was his sexual frustration that was making things physically tricky. Erections had started catching him off guard by rising spontaneously during the day. He could only guess that this was a response to juicier, subconscious images in his brain while he was thinking of mundane stuff. One morning, while heading to the Oval to watch cricket, he been surprised by a stirring in his crotch every bit as vigorous as if he'd been thinking of Brigitte Bardot jiggling out of her underwear. Practised at keeping a newspaper or a tray over his lap when watching Sandy Sarjeant dancing on *Ready Steady Go*, he could be shocked by his increasingly independent member wanting to come out to play during the *Nine O'Clock News*. He'd have been happy to co-operate, but only when his mind was on the job. He did find time, in private, to relieve these urges, but he'd found that relief and satisfaction were different things – like enjoying a trailer but never getting to see the main feature.

Despite his failure with the willing Barbara Gethin, Danny continued to harbour the hope that when he finally got to enjoy actual sex, it would be with a special girl, a co-star. Trouble was, he knew no one special. There were girls who might oblige, but it would mean having to go out with them, and to fib into faces like Barbara's that he didn't want to kiss. And those who were special probably wouldn't do it, anyway.

'Maybe it's best to wait for someone special,' he had said to Dodds.

'Bollocks,' said Dodds, 'that's what birds say. And they don't all mean it.'

Perhaps Dodds was right, better to focus on the sex rather than the kind of girl to have sex with. Until then, Danny would equate virginity with immaturity and believed that, once he'd lost it, his face would firm up; his gaze become more direct; his demeanour altogether more confident. And girls, consciously or unconsciously, would sense that here was a sexually experienced boy, a caresser, not a fumbler, someone who knew that girls don't like to rush things. Crockett had told him this. He'd got it from his girlfriend the day she dumped him.

3

Dodds and Crockett sat side by side on the wall outside Jones's grocer shop. Dodds's legs reached the ground and stretched his jeans over muscular thighs. Crockett's jeans contained more slack than leg and his feet dangled. Not quite an *Of Mice and Men* pairing; Dodds wasn't slow, but Crockett could make him feel it.

Dodds stood up eagerly at Danny's arrival, as if being relieved of a shift with his little partner. 'So, what's new, Danny?'

'Not much.'

Crockett slipped down from the wall. He made an 'O' with his mouth to receive an invisible cigar, which he lit with an invisible lighter and puffed imaginary smoke into Dodds's face.

'What's with him?' said Danny

'He's had some news,' said Dodds.

Crockett turned Danny's wrist over and pretended to tap ash into his upturned palm 'I've passed all my O level, grade A.'

'Great! Told you it would be worth it, Croc.'

Crockett had left school at Easter, but his art teacher had encouraged him not to give up and to do a final term at night school.

Dodds smiled. 'O level Art, it's gonna change his life.'

'Might do,' said Crockett.

'What are you gonna do with it?'

Crockett winked at Danny. 'Become an electrician.'

Dodds clipped him around the head, an easier response than trying to keep up with his friend's fast mouth.

Dodds, too, had left school early to work as a butcher with his father. He lived off the estate, above the shop that his parents owned. This set him apart, a status that came to the fore during occasional fallouts and fights, but he'd spent his childhood with the estate boys and had become a friend. Daily load-up trips at Smithfield Market had broadened his shoulders and given him arms like Bluto. His hard, square face was almost war-comic German soldier, but he was beginning to resemble Charles Bronson, which put him ahead of Danny in the good-looks stakes.

'See how butchers behave with people more qualified than them,' said Crockett, rubbing the back of his head.

Matthew Murphy had been 'Crockett' since he was eight years old, when he had worn his Davy Crockett hat day and night, and driven everyone nuts with endless renditions of the song from the TV series. He had refused to answer to his own name and every kid's game, whether it featured Roy Rogers, Dan Dare or Robin Hood, had to include Davy Crockett – and his hat.

He stood five feet three in his socks and rose to normal height only when wearing his size five-and-a-half Cuban-heeled Chelsea boots. He was waiting for a long-promised growing spurt his parents swore would come before he reached eighteen, but he had the cast of a small man.

At Easter, he had accepted a job as a sewer man, one of the few occupations for which being short was an advantage. He ignored with aplomb any 'shit-shovelling' comments and references to his smell, because he was easily the cleanest person the boys knew, thanks to powerful daily showers at the depot that put to shame once-a-week baths or feeble sprays from hand-held hoses in estate bathrooms.

What Crockett lacked in height he made up with front. He had a hundred ways of saying, 'Oh yeah?' that could turn conversations into rows. It took time to get used to him, something that few strangers were prepared to give. Although undeterred by the threat of violence, the real thing sometimes surprised him and left him in a bad way. Even Dodds and Reilly tailored what they said according to the size of an opponent; not Crockett, whose dial had two settings: 'on' when you got him in full, piss-taking glory, or 'off' when he was asleep.

'And what about Brains then?' said Dodds. 'How many?'

Danny shrugged. O levels were no big deal on the estate, where piss-take imposed procrustean limits on status, and respect was largely unspoken. Being known as a clever dick was a handicap, a bit like being ginger.

He had opened the envelope while his mother watched. When he read out the results, she had lifted her pinny to her eyes. 'Oh Danny! I'm . . . your dad, he . . .' she said, relating, as usual, her son's achievement to the certain joy of his dead father.

'I know, Mum.'

'My clever, handsome boy!'

The less relevant 'handsome' pleased him most. Unable

to handle her tears, he'd grabbed her hands and danced her around the kitchen, changing the *West Side Story* song to, 'I'm so clever, I'm so clever . . .' until she was laughing and begging him to stop.

'Well?' said Dodds.

'A few,' said Danny.

Dodds's face came closer. 'How many?'

'Eight.'

'Well, haven't you been the little swot.'

'Terrible thing, envy,' said Crockett. Dodds gauged the distance to his head.

'Where've you been?' said Dodds.

'Library, holiday homework for next year.'

'So, you're gonna stay a schoolboy?'

'Grammar schoolboy, please,' said Crockett.

'So?' said Danny.

'So, skint for another year!' said Dodds.

A familiar jibe from Dodds, the wage earner who had enough money to go out every day of the week.

'Not exactly,' said Danny.

'No?' said Dodds.

'There's the job at the off-licence.'

'Biking bottles of stout to old dears?'

'It's more than that.'

'Yeah, right.'

Sod you, thought Danny, and your old man's shop, and his Rover, and especially the Ford fucking Anglia you'll be getting this summer.

Danny's pride in his results dissolved in anger and envy as he considered, for the umpteenth time, giving up school, getting a job, and having money to hold his own with mates.

Since he'd passed the eleven-plus, his mother had banged on about there being no merit in leaving school early; that passing exams meant not having to go to work while he was a kid, like she and his dad had to; that with qualifications he'd eventually earn more. This didn't wash with Dodds and, most of the time, it didn't wash with Danny.

'Anyway, all the butchers' jobs have been taken,' said Danny.

Dodds's face stiffened, and in a second they were facing each other, fists clenched, on the boundary between verbal and physical conflict.

Crockett stepped between them. 'Not long now till our trip to Devon.'

Dodds accepted the chance to ease up. 'I've only a quid left to pay.'

'I'm paid up,' said Crockett, 'now, what we should be thinking about, instead of careers, is how we're going to absolutely cream this holiday.'

Dodds lifted Crockett and pulled him face to face. 'That, my half-pint friend, is exactly what I'm going to do. Trust me.'

Crockett looked closely at Dodds's nose. 'This spot of yours is nice and ripe, soon be a real mirror-cracker.'

'Catch!' said Dodds and threw him at Danny, who stepped back. Crockett tumbled against his legs.

'Oops,' said Dodds.

Crockett got up. 'You're a dick, Dodds. I wouldn't trust you as far as you could throw me.'

'I wonder if Nobby will go?' said Danny.

Nobby was a member of the boys' club but he didn't belong. Playing pinball took him to self-imposed sporting limits and he scorned any activity that got him out of breath.

Danny admired Nobby's outspoken contempt for those who mocked his lack of sporting prowess.

'Who cares?' said Dodds.

'I do!' said Danny.

The tension between them returned. Crockett held up his hands. 'Easy, chaps. What do you think, Danny? It's not as if the hiking and canoeing stuff is compulsory.'

'And not as if he hasn't got the dosh,' said Dodds.

'Up to him, I guess,' said Crockett.

Danny recalled that morning in the cafe. 'Except it isn't up to him any more.'

Dodds and Crockett knew what this meant. Crockett locked his fingers and pushed out his palms. 'Well, poor bastard's got himself so far up George's arse, he needs a torch.'

'Up himself more like,' said Dodds, 'and not so cocky now George treats him like shit.'

Crockett crossed himself. 'Yeah, but it's Nobby for fuck's sake. Our mate, one of God's children your old man goes on about.'

Dodds grinned. 'Be still and know that I am Dodds!'

His butcher father was a lay Methodist preacher, who promoted his life-saving product as if it were soap to help Dodds and his friends lead clean lives. Dodds continued to attend chapel, but swore it was only until he was given his promised car when, he had assured Crockett and Danny, Sundays would be for the open road.

'Nobby's a child all right,' said Dodds.

Crockett's eyes rolled up under their lids. 'Speaking of children.'

'Hi gang!'

Jinx, Crockett's younger brother, approached, toes scraping,

28

heels lifting, jerking each leg as if it dragged a small ball and chain. He grinned pre-emptively against Crockett's irritation and lurched to a shy halt. Pencil-thin and much taller than Crockett, he carried his arms at scarecrow angles. With a gormless smile, he cupped an elbow in one hand, leaving the other to wander over his face, to pick his nose or knuckle sleep from the corners of his eyes. Deep brown curls wrapped a head that in repose, with mouth closed, was beautiful. Jinx looked straight in the eyes of those he spoke to but turned away the moment they replied, a habit developed from years of dealing with reprimands. But it took only a smile, a benign question, a gentle hand on his arm to release him to jerk around, to ask questions, and to suggest how others might play with him. He knew he wasn't 'right' and spoke with a grin about his 'bang on the head'.

Jimmy Murphy had been 'Jinx' long before the accident that stalled his brain and slackened limbs that would never work together again. As a baby, he'd fallen out of his pram and dislocated a shoulder; he'd suffered a fractured leg when a car beat him to an escaping football, and a scaffold coupling had dropped from three floors up to break his collar bone. There had been regular visits to casualty for suspected concussion, cuts and – his speciality – fingers mangled by closing doors. At ten years old, he'd done the job properly and fallen from a narrow wall into a bombsite, missing a discarded mattress by inches to land on unforgiving stone.

He made life hard for Crockett, in whom love competed with anger at never-ending responsibility for his troublesome, string puppet of a brother. The harsh words and clouts of Crockett's fraternal guard duty no longer bothered Jinx. He had worked out his brother, and his friends. On meeting strangers, he stayed mute, watchful, waiting for them to be kind. If they weren't, he'd slink away.

'What do you want?' said Crockett.

Jinx shrugged, more by pulling his head down than raising his shoulders. 'What you doing?'

'What does it look like?'

After thinking for a moment, his large, blue eyes lit up. 'You're leaning against the wall!'

'For Christ's sake!' said Crockett. 'Get to the bloody playground and leave us alone.'

Jinx ignored him and took Danny's hand. 'Danny?'

'Yes, Jinxy.'

'Wanna play football?'

'No thanks. Anyway, there's no ball.'

'Can't we pretend we've got one, like last time?'

'Hah!' said Dodds. 'Imaginary football. Sounds about your mark, Danny, bet you're quite good.'

Danny took a deep breath. 'Not now, Jinxy, but how about a game of Would Ya?'

Jinx gave a dribbling smile. 'OK, Danny, if I can go first.'

'Jesus, just tell him to sod off,' said Crockett.

Danny held on to Jinx's hand. 'It's OK, it won't take long.'

Dodds punched Crockett's arm. 'I'm off, coming?'

'Yeah,' said Crockett. As he left, he pulled Jinx's hand away from his face. 'And you get home soon, right?'

'I'll watch him,' said Danny.

'See, Danny will watch me!'

'I don't know, Croc, anyone would think Jinx was his brother, not yours,' said Dodds.

'Except that he doesn't have to live with him,' said Crockett.

'Tall like him, though, and your dad's a short-arse.'

'Fuck off,' said Crockett.

Dodds smirked. 'And dark-haired like you, Danny. Wasn't your dad dark, too?'

This was the kind of innuendo – born of assumptions, accurate or false, and augmented by mischief – that flourished and sometimes endured among the estate's inhabitants. Even though Crockett's mother was reassuringly tall, and dark, the suggestion stung Danny.

'Fuck off Dodds.'

'Yeah, don't be a dick, Dodds. See you later, Danny,' said Crockett.'

When they left, Jinx tugged Danny's hand. 'Would ya like to sit in a big bowl of custard, Danny?'

Danny made a horrified face. 'Cold or hot?'

Jinx clapped his hands. 'Cold!'

'Euch, no thanks.'

'Your turn, Danny.'

'OK, would ya like to find a caterpillar in your ear?'

Jinx shrieked, 'No, not in my ear.' He thought for a moment. 'I'd like to keep one in a matchbox though.'

'Would ya?'

'Yes.'

Danny drew him close. 'Well, maybe you can keep this great big one, if we can winkle him out of your ear.'

Giggling and panicking, Jinx tried to pull away. 'There isn't one in there, there isn't!'

'Oh, I think there is.'

Jinx screamed. Danny held him tight till he grew calm, then led him to a bench near the playground. After sitting down, Jinx put an arm around Danny's neck and waited, head down, content; minutes passed.

'How do you like your summer school?' said Danny.

31

Jinx shifted in his seat.

'Come on Jinxy, you can tell me.'

'I like the bus, and I like the bus driver.'

The bus came three times a week and took Jinx and a dozen other 'backward' children to a play centre.

'Don't you like it there? Aren't the teachers nice?'

'I like some teachers. I like the ones who don't shout.' He looked up. 'I like Susan.'

'A teacher?'

'No, she's my friend. She gets on the bus too.'

'Is she nice?'

'Yes, she wears glasses. I'd like to wear glasses, Danny.'

'What about the other children, do you like them?'

'They're not kind to Susan. Now they're not kind to me because I told them to shut up.'

'Good for you, Jinxy.'

He grinned. 'Yeah, good for me. Susan's glad I fell off the big wall.'

'Really?'

'Yeah, 'cos if I hadn't hurt my head, I wouldn't be at her school.'

The wall, one brick wide. On one side, the pavement, on the other a twelve-foot drop into the bombsite. The dare: to walk its six yards. Many lost their balance but always jumped down on the pavement side.

'Danny!'

Jinx falling, hands out, pressing down on thin air.

Danny unable to scream.

Jinx on his back, blood spreading like a dark amoeba behind his unmoving head.

Danny, turning this way and that, bending from the waist, finally squeezing out the word, 'Help!'

The woman in a full-length pinny. 'What's the matter?' Looking over the wall. 'Oh, my godfathers!' Rushing to her house.

Danny climbing down. Shouting, wake up, Jinxy! into his unblemished face.

Jinx, eyes half-open, only whites showing. Lacy bubbles of saliva pulsing from his lips and nostrils.

Slipping a hand under his neck to lift his head. Pulling it back, fingers bloody.

Wrists bent at horrible angles.

The ambulance men, 'What happened, son?'

Danny wiping blood on his trousers. 'He fell. He just fell. I couldn't . . .'

'Couldn't what?'

Danny wondering if the man believes him.

'What's your friend's name?'

'Jinx.'

His real name?

'Jimmy Murphy.'

'Where does he live?'

'On the estate. Is he going to die?'

'Not if we can help it. How old are you, son?'

'Twelve.'

Jinx, strapped to the stretcher, white face above a bright red blanket. The ambulance men struggling up ruined basement steps.

The woman in the pinny, 'The estate's around the corner, I'll go.'

The ambulance doors slamming, the bell fading.

The woman taking Danny's hand.

In the courtyard, Crockett playing keepy-uppy, smiling at Danny, then not smiling.

33

The woman, 'Who are you, love?'
'Crockett.'
'Is your mum home?'
Crockett scooting up to the second-floor flat.
Jinx's mother, wild-eyed, hurtling down the stairs, shouting up at Crockett, 'Stay there, tell Dad!'
Danny frightened to leave, frightened to go home.
'He just fell.'

4

'I hear they're demolishing our old street,' said Danny's mother. 'Now there'll be nowhere for a plaque to tell people the Byrnes once lived there!'

'Fancy going back for a last look, Mum?'

'Not me love, said my goodbyes a long time ago, with a song in my heart. Why, do you?'

'Yes.'

A red-and-white pole between concrete-filled oil drums barred entry to the street. Five years after Danny and his mother had left, the houses were finally being knocked down. Delayed slum clearance, according to the local papers.

Had he been born and lived till the age of ten in a slum? When do homes become slums? Is it what their tenants do to them? There had been rough families, who often had the police at their door and were, his mother said, strangers to Jeyes Fluid. He'd thought that slum houses had outside toilets and no bathrooms. In his basement flat, the tin bath hung on a hook outside the kitchen but the lav had been inside, under the stairs up to old Elsie Hoy's flat. According to Elsie, it used to be outside where the shed stood.

Ugly word, slum, but he hadn't thought so when the Pathé Pictorial commentator used it to describe the destruction of similar streets in Stepney. Danny had enjoyed seeing the wrecking balls smash away outside walls, exposing rooms, in their underwear of different wallpapers – and the fireplaces, a series of black holes rising to long-gone chimney stacks. He'd admired the men with pickaxes removing layers of bricks from the very walls on which they stood. Hadn't those cheery Cockney residents been as pleased as he to move to an estate, into flats – with bathrooms and central heating?

Yet it bothered him now to remember the Pathé man's plummy voice, as he lauded demolition as progress, and greeted the future by bidding good riddance to houses that had been homes.

Danny's mother, like Crockett's and Nobby's, had welcomed the council's plan to demolish their street and badgered the rent man weekly for news of when the flats would be ready. Danny never saw his mother happier than the day she secured a top-floor flat, with a bathroom and an extra bedroom, on the estate. Before moving in, they walked around their new home, smiling at each other in the extra space, and at what felt like squandered daylight from an ever-present sky, which would replace the shady view of their basement area's distempered walls and the disembodied legs of passers-by on the pavement above.

It had needed only two trips in burly Mr Bowman's van to move their possessions across Vauxhall Bridge Road and into the estate, where he and his mate moaned about the dining table and couch being too big for the lift. A lift! Nearly as good as having a bathroom!

After they moved out, their street received a stay of execution and other families were moved in 'temporarily' for the next five years. Now they, too, were gone.

Danny ducked under the pole and slipped past the night watchman's hut, a squat half-tube of corrugated iron. A brazier full of unlit coke and a wooden chair sat outside the open end. Inside, a wooden bench ran the length of one wall. Donkey jackets hung along the other above stacked sledgehammers and pickaxes. At the dark end, a large metal trunk stretched the width of the hut.

The houses opposite his old home had been reduced to piles of rubble, laid out in a line by bulldozers that had worked their way up the street and crashed in via the back yards to shove the remains into the road. The pavement, too, was gone, smashed down to fill the voids that were once areas and coal cellars. A fifty-yard gap in the line of spoil heaps showed where German bombers had begun an earlier clearance in 1941, leaving a bombsite that became a playground where, his mother warned, dangers lurked that could maim a child. He'd avoided the perils of rusting bike frames, ruined prams, bedsteads and other unwanted furniture, but suffered regularly from the broken glass that gouged and peppered knees and hands whenever he fell. Every November, the bombsite was lit up by a magnificent Guy Fawkes bonfire. As a small boy, he had danced around it and coughed in smoke that billowed out whenever the fire consumed a damp mattress – and marvelled at tall flames chasing glowing cinders high into the night.

There was smoke today: thin plumes spiralling up from dying fires that had burned since morning to make ashes of doors, floorboards and window frames. The demolition crews had left. Two bulldozers sat idle, their still-warm engines gently plinking and giving off the scent of evaporated diesel. The wrecking balls, scarred and pitted by the houses' futile resistance, lay with their great rusty chains curled around them.

They had made a start on his side of the street, where four terraced houses had been reduced to piles of uneven height as if, although of the same stature, some had had more substance.

Next to his old home, the first of the condemned houses that were yet to be demolished was the roofless, floorless shell that had stood since being firebombed during the war.

For Danny and his friends, this house had been their favourite 'keep out' place. Inside, they had tottered across charred joists, jumped down into the plaster-strewn base-ment, crouched in back-yard dens built from old doors, drunk Tizer, smoked cigarettes, sung songs and scared them-selves with stories of sooty skeletons.

Although not the bravest of the house's intruders, Danny had conquered the most common dare: to climb the creaking remains of the staircase up three floors to open sky and chalk a personal sign on the rendered chimney stack. His had been a simple Chad with an extra-long nose. But this and others' drawings were eclipsed by little Crockett's image, perfected with shading, of a tremendous dick and balls.

Bits of the shaky staircase came away each time it was climbed. It finally collapsed under the extra weight of the Bradshaw twins who, as in everything, insisted on climbing together. They crashed in successive thumps into the base-ment and lay covered in wood and plaster. While they struggled to get free, dust-choked moans alternated with plaintive calls to each other: Johnny? David? Johnny? David? Danny tore at the debris, surprised and relieved that rotten wood could be so light. The twins eventually got to their feet, holding each other, feeling for injuries. Finding none, they hugged for a whole minute. The only danger now was their mother's reaction to what they'd done to their clothes. They left with their arms around each other, leaving Danny with bleeding hands – wishing he had a brother.

The wooden staircase into the basement area of his old flat had partially slipped its moorings. Halfway down it lurched violently, forcing Danny to leap the remaining steps. He waited, watching it settle, wondering if he could risk it on the way back.

The front door was ajar, stuck on chewed, grit-laden lino. He forced it enough to get through and, in the gloomy passage, surprised himself by reaching up for the useless brown Bakelite light switch, when it was now barely chest high.

The front room felt smaller but less crowded, without the heavy, dark furniture that had seemed to begrudge making room for people. And so bright, in light that had been kept out for a hundred years by the now demolished houses opposite. The last tenants had painted over the Asian Grass wallpaper of which his mother had been so proud. The plaid lino remained, scarred and worn through to its mesh backing.

This had been the room kept for 'best'. Here the rent man was received, where he and anyone who saw it might think it typical of the whole flat. Only at Christmas was it changed when a tree was set in the corner, decorations hung and an American cloth of jumbled poinsettias laid over the table.

His nan would join them for Christmas dinner, bringing a bottle of port, which was opened only after she and his mother finished the one left in the sideboard from last year. Soon they'd both be singing and rocking side to side on the couch. It got livelier in the evening when Nobby and his mother, whom Danny knew as Auntie Jean, came bearing a half-bottle of gin, tonics and a bottle of Tizer. When they stacked 45s on the Dansette record player, Nobby and Danny would retreat under the table to show each other their new toys and play board games, while the women sang ever louder and eventually got up to dance around, flipping up their skirts.

Nobby patronised Danny in the way only a boy a whole year older can do. But he was kind and one Christmas left behind his long-awaited main present, a red double-decker bus with battery-driven headlamps, for Danny to play with till Boxing Day.

The front room's special status diminished with the arrival of their first television, when Nobby would be allowed to join him early evenings to watch cowboys like Roy Rogers or Gene Autry. Later, his mother would often keep Danny up beyond his bedtime, snuggled next to her on the couch, long after *Emergency Ward 10* had finished.

Their old bedroom was empty and rubble-strewn.

He'd shared it with his mother until the day they moved out. As a five year old, 'aren't you the big boy now?' comments had been no comfort for having to leave his mother's bed for a small one of his own. Only when unwell was he allowed to return, and his own bed had to be moved from its place in front of the fireplace, as it was the only time the fire was lit.

When he was seven, Nan had taken his bed for the final weeks of her life and her sickness changed the smell of their bedroom. From the made-up bed on the front-room couch, he'd heard his mother weeping the night Nan died and got up to go to her. She hugged him and, as if he already knew she had died, said, 'Nan was old, love, her time has come, don't cry.' As she led him back to the couch, he felt guilty that his tears weren't because of his nan's death but at seeing his mother crying.

In the morning he woke to sounds from the kitchen of his mother and old Elsie from upstairs talking and, to his surprise, laughing. After breakfast, before she went for the doctor, his mother took him in to see Nan. Her child-sized frame barely disturbed the surface of the blankets that were tucked under her chin. He refused to kiss her goodbye but relented when his mother started crying and said he'd regret it one day. He kissed the cold, furrowed forehead, relieved to find her smell had mostly gone, and pleased he was going to get his bed back.

He moved along the passage to the kitchen. The Ascot and the iron fire-surround were gone but the old Belfast sink remained in the corner.

Here he felt his early life most keenly; where he'd spent thousands of hours in his mother's company, reading books while she listened to the wireless and knitted or sewed. Here he took weekly baths in the large tin tub into which hot water was basined across from the Ascot and cold via a hose attached to the kitchen tap. Then, in pyjamas and dressing gown, he'd go to the front room to read his book in front of one bar of a two-bar electric fire, while his mother bathed in the same water.

The back yard was as oppressive as ever under the high, soot-blackened wall that separated it from the yards of the houses that rose behind. Against this wall he had played out an early obsession: throwing a ball against the black bricks and trying to make a hundred catches without dropping it. He recalled his fury at each failure, and his mother laughing from the kitchen window. 'God, isn't ninety-five enough?' And his screams that, 'No it wasn't,' followed by her own anger with 'this kind of nonsense', which included wanting her to take no more than fifteen steps from the front door to the kitchen each time she came home.

'You shouldn't be in here, boy.' A deep Irish voice, which pronounced boy 'by'.

Danny replied like the small boy who once played in the yard. 'I wasn't doing anything.'

'That may be, but ye really oughtn't to be here. This is a demolition site now, and dangerous.'

A large, grey-haired man stood with one hand jammed into the top corner of the doorframe. A life of outdoor labour showed in his weather-beaten face and massive, gnarly hands. Big as Gasping George, he wore faded navy overalls and clenched a clay pipe in his teeth. His bulk filled the doorway but didn't threaten. Danny sensed that if he tried to pass him, he would step aside. He was the sleeper.

The big man took the pipe from his mouth. 'Aren't ye the boy who woke me in the library?'

Danny nodded.

The man grinned. 'Just in time, too. It was kind of ye to wake me.'

'Oh, it was nothing.'

'But it was . . . something. Thanks.'

He said no more and to fill the silence Danny said, 'I used to live here.'

'And did ye like living here?' said the big man.

Had he? Yes. But he'd been pleased to leave, what with the shared bedroom at nearly eleven years old, the tin bath, the absence of daylight. But why had he come back? To bring clarity to fading images of his early years? To check the context of childhood memories? Nostalgia? At his age?

Aware he was taking too long to answer he made it short. 'Yes.'

Before stepping into the yard, the man hesitated, as if it were still Danny's home and permission was needed. Danny pointed to the bedroom window. 'I was born in there.'

'Were ye now? It must be sad to see it like this.'

'A bit, maybe. We were glad to leave, though, for the estate. I just wanted to see it before . . . you know.'

The big man nodded and waited to hear more.

Danny thought of mentioning his surprise at how the visit was giving him a clearer sense of the boy who had lived there. Instead, he said, 'It's smaller than I remember.'

'Yes, 'tis the way.'

'Guess I've got bigger,' said Danny, and instantly regretted stating the obvious. The man peered through the bedroom window and Danny felt an old twinge of embarrassment, even shame, at others seeing inside.

It had been a hard flat to keep tidy. In her defence, his mother had complained of 'no bloody storage space'. A knock at the door would prompt a hurried ritual of hanging coats and jackets behind doors, secreting newspapers, magazines and anything not too bulky under cushions, and the clearing of crockery from the table into the sink.

His mother preferred visitors not to come in and, except for Nobby, he wasn't allowed to have friends around. Cora Byrne's hospitality usually started and finished at the front door, which embarrassed Danny whenever friends, in whose homes he had been welcomed, called around. He wondered then, as he did now, why it took her so long to reward people with a 'come in'. It must have started when his father had been killed, as it was only friends like Jean, whom she had been close to before his death, who made it into their kitchen.

Things hadn't changed in their flat on the estate, where she continued to answer the front door and hold it like a shield.

'How does it feel to be back?' said the big man.

'A bit strange.'

'Fair enough, boy. Have ye seen all yiz need to see?'

'Everything but in there.' He pointed to the timbered shed built onto the kitchen. 'I used to play in it.'

'Who with?'

'No one, on my own mostly.'

'No brothers or sisters then?'

'No.'

The shed had lost its door. Danny went inside.

Along with one of the coal cellars under the pavement, the shed had contained everything his mother wouldn't throw away. It had been the scene of her spectacular failure to make elderflower champagne, using ordinary wine bottles that couldn't take the fermenting pressure. The explosions during a hot June night woke the neighbours and had Elsie complaining, as she vacuumed snuff into her nicotine-stained nostrils, that it had reminded her of the Blitz.

The shed had partly detached from the wall. The big man noticed and once more pushed an Atlas hand up into the corner of the doorframe.

Ruined shelving hung from the walls on ripped-out L brackets. An eviscerated chest lay on its back, surrounded by smashed drawers and the wreckage of other, less recognisable furniture. But in one corner, and roughly intact, was the heavy oak box, which in Victorian times had housed an earth closet.

Inside, Danny had hidden, among other things, a short-bread tin with a kilted Scotsman on the lid. In it he saved pocket money for a train fare to Carlisle, home of his adored Aunt Doris, should anything happen to his mother: the ever-present terror of his childhood. However, unlike some of his friends, he knew that – barring accidents – she would never leave him. As his father had.

'Mrs Byrne? Mrs Cora Byrne?'

'Go inside, Danny.'

Waiting behind his mother. The big policeman, a silhouette at the door.

His mother sinking to her knees before he can tell her.

'The crane's chain, it broke. I'm sorry, Mrs Byrne. Can someone come and sit with you?'

'I want my husband.'

The policeman helping her to her feet

'Are you sure you'll be all right, Mrs Byrne?'

'Yes, thank you. Come here, Danny love.'

Lying on the bed with her, while she cries.

Wondering if he should be crying too.

The crane's chain: the phrase that entered his head whenever his father was mentioned. Michael Byrne had been killed when a chain had snapped as the crane lifted the large steel bucket of clay that he had helped to fill. According to the foreman, it swung back and hit him as he sat on the edge of the trench for a breather.

His favourite image of his father was in a framed black-and-white photo, standing tall behind his wife, white shirtsleeves rolled up arms that were draped around her. She had her hands over his and was laughing. Danny aspired to his father's clear-eyed regard and the strong chin, clefted like that of Kirk Douglas.

His clearest memory was of his father's smell: the damp bits of cement or concrete that got onto his clothes and became stronger the closer he was held. The smell came back to him sometimes when passing building sites. It was absent in the ruined basement in the dryness of destruction.

'Ready to go now?' The big man stood back to let him leave the shed. 'It'll be safer to go up the inside staircase.'

Danny started climbing, deliberately missing out, as he always did, the bottom step. They passed Elsie Hoy's doorless flat. 'I used to run errands for the old lady who lived there. She died one winter while warming her feet in front of her open oven. She fell asleep and didn't notice when the flames went out . . .'

'A power of memories ye have here, boy.'

In the street, a Jack Russell terrier with a red, white-spotted hanky for a collar, trotted over and sat at the big man's feet. Danny had seen the dog on the steps as he left the library.

'This is Finnegan,' said the man. 'And I'm Liam, Liam Marnell, the night watchman here.' He held out his hand.

Danny tried to shake it but, once again, found little purchase inside Liam's leathery mitt. 'I'm Danny Byrne.'

'Pleased to meet ye.'

They walked to the end of the street. Outside his hut, Liam stopped and tapped Danny's shoulder to usher him on his way. 'A good job done, so, Danny Byrne.'

5

The boys' club sat among Peabody Buildings on the corner of an ancient Westminster lane, where the ghost of Purcell, who once lived there, must have shuddered whenever pop music boomed from the club's coffee bar.

Danny and Dodds entered the foyer. At the reception desk, Ernest Penfold's face opened in a welcoming smile that the boys had come to know was genuine, if a little too constant. Ernest's Christianity was always gently on the boil, ready to overflow in concerned frowns or kind acts. He had a habit of glancing behind whomever he was talking to, as if God or maybe an angel was at their shoulder. The boys liked how he listened to them in a way their parents couldn't and thought, mistakenly, that he believed everything they told him.

Anger rarely augmented Ernest's authority and his standard, if exasperated, response to bad behaviour could include an embarrassing promise to pray for the culprit. Danny thought it better to have a good person praying for him than trying, as he did occasionally, to pray for himself.

Only Dodds couldn't take Ernest's Christianity, which he deemed a nicer but only slightly less irritating version of his father's.

Ernest used Brylcreem, which made him look older than his thirty-four years. Beefy, sporting and heterosexual, he had the trust of boys well aware of stories of dodgy youth workers and scout leaders who would check whether showers were working only when boys were in them.

Ernest's fiancée, Valerie, sat behind him with a card-index box on her lap. Although in her late twenties, her flared summer frocks resembled those worn by the boys' mothers. Her bright blonde hair was Doris-Day permed but her figure was decidedly Marilyn Monroe.

Dodds was smitten. Instead of keeping his distance out of respect for Ernest, he engaged Valerie in conversations about faith and life, especially her life. Clever this, as most boys, including Danny, didn't question girls about their lives but waited to be asked about their own. The boys speculated that she was probably a virgin and that – much as Ernest must have wanted to give her one – he was the sort of bloke who'd wait till they were married. Dodds was convinced she was fed up waiting and would be a right goer if she let her hair down.

Like Ernest, Valerie brought her faith into most conversations, albeit on a simpler, Sunday-school level. She had the sexy habit of pulling down her bottom lip with two fingers when trying to think of an appropriate biblical example. Dodds, who claimed that his childhood had been deafened by bible talk, invariably came up with the reference ahead of her. Unaware of his lascivious intentions, she'd raise his temperature by putting the same hand on his to show her approval, at which Dodds would turn around to face the others, eyes up in his head and lips tucked back between clenched teeth.

To the rest of the boys, Valerie was simply Ernest's bird, who rode around on a bike with a basket on the front. She had, for a time, been their pin-up on two wheels, thanks to the practice of letting her dress flop over the saddle and sitting directly on her knickers. When her bike stood outside the club, Dodds would put his palm on the seat to assess temperature and, like Tonto examining the tracks of outlaws' horses, guess how long it had been since she had dismounted. Valerie abandoned this riding style the day Dodds called out, 'Lucky saddle', before turning around to see Ernest shaking his head.

'Good evening, Daniel, Stephen, come to settle up for the trip?' said Ernest, who used full Christian names instead of familiars or abbreviations.

'No, to cancel,' said Dodds.

Ernest's eyebrows rose.

Danny slapped his pound note on the counter. 'Don't listen to him, Ernest, we're all set.'

Ernest took the money and recorded payment in a lined ledger. 'Well, that's you done. Not long now before we're off. We'll have a van full if Alan decides to come. Do you know if he will, Daniel?'

'Don't think so,' said Danny.

'I still have his deposit, could you give him a nudge? I think a break would do him good.'

Danny didn't mind being considered Nobby's best mate but he was tired of being thought his keeper. Nevertheless, Ernest had a point. Nobby's deathly pallor and skinny rounded shoulders could get a passing ambulance to stop. He ate crap food at places that were open when he didn't want to be at home: London cheesecakes or bacon sand-wiches at the cafe during the day, fish and chips or a Wimpy at night. The only regular meals he got were at Danny's, where he often turned up, evenings and Sunday-dinner times, knowing Danny's mother would insist he join them.

As the only sons of women without husbands, this had been the pattern of their lives since they were toddlers. As they grew up, they had witnessed, first-hand, how differently their mothers had coped. After her husband's death, Danny's mother had lifted her chin and set about her different life with vigour and, as far as Danny knew, had not sought another man to take his place. She was using, she had said, the love she had left for her son. She kept some back for Nobby, who basked in the intermittent care of a woman who remained a staunch friend of his mother, when few on the estate had time for her. Much as he cared for his mother, Nobby had come to the painful conclusion that she wasn't up to much. Unlike Danny's father, who'd been killed in an accident, Nobby's was never mentioned, not least because no one knew who he was.

Over the years, Nobby had been obliged to share his home with a series of 'uncles' and a couple of 'almost step-dads', whom his mother introduced as 'our new friend who'll be staying with us for a while'. The 'our' sickened him. There were those on the estate who suspected Jean of being on the game but, even if this wasn't true (and Nobby swore it wasn't), she was always encouraging him to be elsewhere. The only fight Danny remembered Nobby having was a brief and painful one with Dodds, who had suggested it might be easier for Nobby if his mother went on the game full-time, as she might keep more regular hours.

Danny's close friendship had dwindled steadily, as he

spent more time with other friends and played sports in which Nobby had no interest. Although a matter of regret at first, Danny had cared less since Nobby had opted to work with Gasping George and had found new mates up West.

Before Christmas, Danny, Dodds, Crockett and Nobby had put down their deposits for the camping trip in the West Country. Danny had struggled to get the six pounds together from his evening and weekend work at the off-licence, as his mother had promised him spending money, only on condition he paid for the trip himself.

The closer the holiday came, the more Nobby had back-pedalled and taken the piss: 'Why does it have to be Yokel land? All that outdoors stuff and camping in the rain, it's bound to rain. And eating porridge, I fucking hate porridge!'

'It's up to him, Ernest, we've asked him enough times,' said Danny.

'Do your best though, please, won't you Daniel? Let's pray that he changes his mind.'

Danny nodded. 'If I see him.'

Behind Ernest, Valerie was updating the membership cards for the new term in September. Club members were divided by age into under-fourteens, under-seventeens and under-nineteens. After transferring their details to new cards in the index box, the old ones lay haphazardly on the table beside her. Danny itched to put them in order and the right way up. When he was on the point of offering to do so, Valerie crossed her legs. Her floral dress fell back to reveal the top of her thigh. Valerie had yet to engage with tights and there was a momentary flash of bare flesh, suspenders and stocking tops. Dodds, eyes wide, did that thing of whispering a comment while turning sharply to look away. 'S'why Ernest's so happy.'

Valerie gave an embarrassed smile.

Ernest cleared his throat. 'Now Stephen, let's get you signed off.'

While looking at Valerie, Dodds said, 'There you go Ernest', and handed over his pound note.

'How are things at the butcher's shop, Stephen? All well?'

'Yes thanks, Ernest. What are you doing, Valerie?' said Dodds.

'Helping Ernest put everyone in their new age groups for next season. I see you and Danny are seniors now.'

'That's us, Valerie,' said Dodds, winking. 'All grown up . . . and much bigger.'

A frown came and went on Ernest's face.

In these situations, Danny felt anything but grown up. Although he cringed, part of him admired the way Dodds could bring sexual innuendo into conversations with girls, and even women of Valerie's age, like the time he talked to her about Aaron playing with his rod.

Danny had thought that Valerie was either thick, or simply open and trusting. But her embarrassed smile contained a hint that she was only too aware of her attraction, like the women in *Carry On* films who lowered their eyes at references to their figure. He felt a sudden twinge of concern for Ernest.

6

Gasping George drove his white Ford Zodiac through the estate, slowly enough for his glare to be returned with dutiful nods. Reilly rode shotgun in seated swagger, with an arm hanging from his window. In the back, Nobby sat with Banger, staring straight ahead, his days of 'look at me and who I'm with' long gone. The car pulled over to Danny's side of the street.

'Pages, my son,' said George, jerking his head towards the back seat. 'Shift over for him, Nobby.'

Nobby pulled Banger to the middle and mumbled, 'All right?' to Danny, as he squeezed in behind George. Without turning, George dangled a pad of blue Basildon Bond over his shoulder. Banger went to sniff it, but Danny got his hand to it first and the dog's snout banged into his wrist. The subsequent sneezes flicked slobber over Danny and Nobby. Reilly sniggered. George spoke into his rear-view mirror.

'Got someone who needs a polite note, Pages.'

'OK George, when do you need it?'

'Now.'

The roll of fat on the back of George's neck thickened and thinned as he nodded.

Danny took a deep breath. 'And you want me to be polite?'

'Yes, but firm. Nice language instead of what I'd say to a prick who's behind with what he owes me.'

'What would that be then, George?'

George wheezed through an explanation. 'Something like, "Look, you little shitbag. Just because you've been avoiding me, it don't mean I've forgotten how much you owe. If you don't come across, plus a week's interest of ten per cent, I'm going to break ten per cent of your fingers." Now, put that nicely so's anyone else reading it would think it was reasonable like.'

He held up a Bic. This time Banger sat back, but Danny didn't take the pen quickly enough for Reilly, who was keen for any walk-on part in George's shows. He swivelled and, with an elbow over the back of his seat, squeezed out a couple of blinks and said, 'What you fucking waiting for?'

Danny's stomach churned at the prospect of an inevitable confrontation with Reilly. He took the pen and flipped up the cover of the writing pad. Under Reilly's enforcer stare, he longed for Crockett's ability to sketch his freckled face with a dick flopping out of his forehead, and hand it to him as a token of esteem.

Elbowing away Banger's interest, Danny began to write, trying to follow the guidelines sheet that showed through the thin blue paper. However, his words jumped the tracks into nonsense. He scrunched the first version in his fist. Reilly, who could barely sign his name, tutted.

In the rear-view mirror, George's eyebrows arched, as if

watching through a letterbox. 'It's OK, Pages, you'll get it right this time, won't you.'

Danny wrote, 'Your loan is overdue. This is to inform you that if you fail to pay it back immediately, plus ten per cent interest, I will have to resort to more serious measures to ensure the return of my money.' Although feeling sympathy for the poor recipient of the threat, Danny was pleased with his effort.

He passed the pad between the front seats but George wouldn't take it.

'Read it out first.'

Danny read it out.

'Just the job, Pages my son.'

Reilly reached over to snatch back the pad, but Danny held on to it. Reilly's face reddened and his next, more violent tug coincided with Danny opening his fingers. The pad and Reilly's hand hit the back of George's head. A startled Banger jumped up, barking, and released a sickening fart. Holding his nose, Nobby reached under Banger's stomach to give Danny a thumbs-up.

Reilly glared at Danny. 'Sorry George, bastard wouldn't let go . . .' He waited, blinking. George's scary long silence signalled 'fucking idiot', but he did nothing.

'I'll be off then, George,' said Danny and, assuming George's silence to be assent, got out.

As if he'd forgotten Danny, George said, 'Nobby, take Banger out for a quick slash, will you.'

Nobby grabbed Banger's collar and, as he opened the door, he gave a small shake of his head that said to Danny, 'Poor bastard, you're in now.'

Danny turned away and saw stunning Linda Bain standing a few yards away, smiling as if she had observed something amusing. He had to pass her to get home and, guessing that he was the source of her amusement, decided not to stop.

She stepped in front of him, head cocked to one side.

'Hello Linda,' he said.

'Mixing with the tough guys now?'

Linda, the new girl on the estate, slender, self-assured, with elfin good looks and short, Mary Quant hair. She had come from Camberwell and soon let it be known her family wouldn't be on the estate long before moving on, and up. He had spoken to her briefly after being introduced by Dodds, who had homed in on her early. He had been a little intimidated by how she talked so confidently, in short, decisive phrases, with a slight Cockney accent that Danny suspected was undergoing removal. She had surprised him by giving him more attention than Dodds, asking questions about his studies and, as the 'swot' – no doubt briefed by Dodds – what he planned to do with his life. She could only have been disappointed by his vague answers that revealed him to have no specific long-term ambitions.

What to say to her mockery? He'd already taken too long to answer, but from experience he knew that saying what he was thinking straight away, rarely came out right.

'Who?'

'Who d'ya think?' she said.

He waited, determined to say nothing stupid; nevertheless, his reply was stupid. 'I don't know, who?'

'Fat Capone over there, and him, ginger bollocks!'

Danny flinched at her lack of volume control, given that George's car hadn't moved and the windows were open. Like Crockett, she said what she was thinking, without filters. As far as Danny could tell, neither ever suffered the 'did-I-really-say-that?' agonies that could rake his stomach for days, while he rephrased what he should have said, and how he'd say it next time.

He slowly nodded his head as if weighing things up, like Steve McQueen in *The Great Escape* which, according to Crockett, wasn't cool and made him look more like a pipe-smoking codger puffing on a pipe before replying.

Linda, too, was unimpressed. She put her hands on her hips. 'Well?'

'Well, what?' he said.

Linda closed her eyes and shook her head.

'Look,' he said, 'I just help him out a bit.'

She sighed. 'Oh yeah?' She waved at George and, while giving him a big smile, said, 'Fat bastard.'

George smiled back.

'Don't worry, he didn't hear me,' she said.

'I'm not worried,' he lied.

'Aren't you supposed to be the bright boy on the estate, the one with prospects, grammar school and all? Why do you need pocket money from the likes of him, like your weird mate, Nobby?'

He liked hearing Linda, someone his own age, thinking his schoolboy potential a good thing, but not hearing money described as 'pocket', the income of schoolboys.

'He doesn't give me pocket money.'

'What then, Liquorice Allsorts?'

Sod this, he thought, and was about to walk away when, with Nobby and Banger back on board, George started up the car and lifted his chin in farewell. Danny responded obediently with a similar gesture. He caught Linda's mocking smile.

'And I'm not, as you say, mixing with him.'

'Really, sitting in his car and nodding like a little boy?'

'He asked me to get in,' he said, then blushed at his little-boy response.

'Oh, that's different?'

'Yes, it is.'

He went to leave.

'Where are you going? she said.

'To play cowboys and Indians.'

'OK, OK,' she said, smiling. She put a hand on his arm and held him with a warm, brown-eyed gaze. She was about to change the subject, and he wanted to listen.

'Anyway, going to the dance Saturday?' she said.

'Dance?'

Her eyes closed. 'Why do you do that? You're not deaf! What's wrong with yes, or no, or I don't fucking know?'

He stayed silent.

'Well, what is it?'

As if wading in water that had suddenly got too deep, he stopped himself saying he didn't like her swearing.

'It's "I don't know". I work Saturday evenings.' Then, in a panic to keep the door open, he said, 'But perhaps later?'

'OK, then maybe we can have a dance?'

A dance with sparky, beautiful Linda Bain? He'd imagined as much and more, privately, as well as publicly with Crockett and Dodds, when she had featured in their 'would ya?' speculations.

'OK, but only for the slow stuff.'

He wasn't up for dancing apart, since the last dance, when Linda had moved around the floor like Sandy Sarjeant. Her silky spins and lithe hip shakes, especially to Tamla Motown, had him abandoning forever his self-conscious jerking around, which preserved too much of the Twist he'd mastered as a small boy, when it hadn't mattered what others thought.

58

She frowned. Had she thought wanting to dance only to slow music was a crude shortcut to intimacy? He had never knowingly tried to be suggestive, unlike Dodds, whose flirting innuendoes with girls Danny found embarrassing but also impressive.

'Don't put yourself out, will you? Fucking hell!'

'No. I meant . . .'

Talking to her was like tugging a shoelace to loosen a knot, only for it to get tighter. Would he want a girlfriend who swore like this? 'Fuck' was in common use among boys but rarely uttered in girls' company. His mother claimed that only common girls used it. Yet, here was lovely Linda Bain: anything but common. So, yes, he would want her as a girlfriend.

'OK, Danny Byrne, the slow stuff.'

'Thanks . . . Anyway, you'll probably be ready for a rest by then.'

'What!'

Heat rose to his face as another inadequate response snagged on her sharp edges. 'I mean you . . . you dance so much.'

'Better than standing around the wall or sliding off to the toilet to swig Dutch courage that only works in time for the last record.'

True, except for Crockett who, drunk or sober, gyrated boldly between girls from one back-turned rejection to another.

She threw up her hands. 'All right, I'll try and save enough energy to dance slowly.'

'Really?'

She came closer. 'Really. And maybe you could see me home . . . if you like.'

59

A breathtaking offer but it felt too much like an instruction and sparked resistance. 'I think we all might be going up West afterwards.'

'Please your fucking self.'

Resistance over, he said, 'Well, maybe we won't.'

'As I said, please yourself.'

Anyway, why on earth would he want to go up West? To find a girlfriend, when the most attractive girl on the estate was making herself bewilderingly available? But he didn't want to back down now. 'I will . . . please myself.'

She gave him a sharp look, followed by a resigned smile and said, 'See you Saturday, maybe.' She set off, hips swinging, as if heading onto the dance floor to the first bars of a Supremes record.

He watched her until she disappeared into her block.

Dancing with Linda Bain on a Saturday night! He walked home, barely tethered to the ground. Later, he wondered whether he had been right to suggest he could take or leave her. Had that been cool, or stupid? A spontaneous groan told him which.

7

Jones's nestled between two blocks, in front of the children's playground. It had been only a newsagent until Mr Jones began selling groceries and erected a new sign: *General Store*. However, in a time when local shops were known by those who ran them, it remained Jones's.

Inside, Cordelia Hill waited behind a woman whose shopping bag sat on the counter while Mr Jones filled it with her orders. Under one arm, Cordelia balanced a box of eggs on the broad side of a packet of cornflakes.

Danny joined the queue. The smell of cigarette smoke rose off Cordelia's yellow cardigan. Her blonde hair hung lank to her shoulders. He wanted to wash it, like he did his mother's. Once dried and brushed, he was sure that it would brighten and shine like a film star's.

As Cordelia kept shifting her weight from one foot to the other, he took in the swell of her bum stretching further her red pedal-pushers. It was less pert than Linda's but more curvaceous and, he imagined, softer.

The woman in front hoisted her bag from the counter.

Cordelia stepped aside to let her pass and saw Danny. Her smile, at first warm, quickly froze: a chilly reminder of his faux pas at the cafe.

As she turned towards the counter, the eggs slid off the cornflake packet. She shrieked. Danny dived forward in what felt like slow motion as he found time to confirm the softness of her bum against his shoulder. He stretched a hand under the egg box before it hit the floor and rolled onto his back like a slip fielder. His head thudded into the chest freezer.

'Well held, sir!' said Mr Jones.

The woman with the bag stood over him. 'Do you expect me to climb over you, young man?' He recognised Linda Bain's mother, who would know him only as one of the boys on the estate, for whom she reserved haughty disapproval. Today she could enjoy actually looking down her nose at one.

He tucked back his legs.

She passed by to reveal Cordelia leaning over him. 'Blimey, Danny, are you OK?'

He nodded.

She held out her free hand. He took it and got to his feet, unsure whether it was he or she who was holding on. They released hands at the same time. He gave her the eggs, while trying to hide how pleased he was with himself, and resisting the need to rub the back of his head.

She put the eggs and cornflakes on the counter and said to Mr Jones, 'That was lucky. I didn't bring enough money to buy replacements.'

'Indeed, it was,' he said, smiling.

Knowing Mr Jones, Danny was sure that he wouldn't have charged her.

'Oh, and ten Rothman's, please,' said Cordelia.

As Cordelia didn't smoke, the cigarettes prompted Mr Jones to ask, 'How's your mam then, Cordelia?'

'Oh, you know . . . OK.' In case this wasn't enough to refute the local view that her mum wasn't up to much, she added, 'She's really well at the moment, thank you.'

'Glad to hear it. That's three and six, please.'

She paid with the exact change and her bum lifted as she rose onto her toes to squeeze the cigarettes into a front pocket. She clamped the cornflakes and eggs together, gave Danny a closed-mouth smile and left.

When Danny came out with his bottle of Coke, he found her sitting in the sun on the bench from which mothers could sit and watch their children in the playground.

He wasn't going to stop but, although no longer smiling, she said, 'Thanks for saving my shopping, Danny.'

He had trouble handling compliments elegantly, and shrugged to signal that it had been nothing. Here was as good an opportunity as any to apologise for smiling at Angelo's bad behaviour. 'Look, about the other day, you know when Angelo . . . well, I'm sorry.'

'It's OK, but you should know I was more angry with you, your smile hurt. I don't care about Angelo so much.'

Her fury had been for him after all, not because she couldn't show it to Angelo. So much for his vain assumptions.

'But thank you for what you said when Reilly . . . you know.'

He knew. Relief at being forgiven was spoiled by the memory of how scared he'd been then, and how worried he was now about probable repercussions.

Cordelia put the cornflakes and eggs to one side. He

noticed the egg box was upside down and turned it the right way up. He remained standing but relented when she patted the place beside her.

'Congratulations, I hear you did really well in your O levels,' she said.

'Thanks, I did all right.'

His self-deprecation elicited only an impatient, eyes-closed shake of her head.

They sat without speaking for a minute until her face brightened. 'I meant to tell you how much I liked the book.'

During Cordelia's earlier stint working for Angelo, he had been in the cafe, finishing *A Stone for Danny Fisher* by Harold Robbins, when she had noticed tears in his eyes.

'That must be a sad story,' she said without mockery as she wiped his table.

Embarrassed, he looked away, blinking as she lifted his mug and plate and stayed to keep wiping.

'I think the table's clean now,' he said.

She frowned. To make amends, he pushed the book across the table and asked if she'd like to read it.

Cordelia leaned against him to emphasise how she'd enjoyed it. She touched readily and naturally. Danny didn't, even when he wanted to. What little physical contact he'd had with girls felt like the start of he-wasn't-sure-what. She shifted closer, as if making space for another person to sit down. He leaned away but grew warm wondering what would have happened if he hadn't.

He thought of all the conversations they'd had about books and how it had occasionally brought them to the point of revealing feelings, at which he would clam up. Then she would carry on talking to fill the space between them and ease him back into the conversation.

'He made me think of you,' she said.

'Who?'

'Danny Fisher . . . had your name.'

'Oh.'

'You know, tall, dark . . .'

He waited for a 'handsome' that didn't come.

Until she'd left her local secondary school at Easter, Cordelia had read the same books as Danny. She'd borrow them from the library, or he'd lend her paperbacks bought from a local shop, where the next book was half-price if you returned the old one in good nick within a week. He got the majority back in time, except those he tore into sections to fit in his back pocket to read when he was out alone or on the move.

She had raced through Danny's O level English set books, even Arthur Grimble's boring *A Pattern of Islands*. He had read none of her set books in return. He couldn't match the speed at which she devoured books and suspected, initially, that she merely skim-read everything. However, all doubt was dispelled by her detailed comments, many of which found their way into his English essays.

Grateful, as well as flattered by her interest, he felt resentment, too, at her sharing so much of his reading. He had not mentioned this ungracious thought, just as he had said nothing to younger hanger-on kids, like Jinx, who wanted to know what he was doing or where he was going. It wasn't that he didn't want to hurt their feelings, but because he didn't want them to stop liking him.

He and Cordelia were friends because of books. Talking about them had established a bond in which conversations could move from what they read to subjects that never featured in the boy–girl banter that dominated on the estate:

the flirting, the sexual innuendoes and piss-take that boys served up to girls, who responded with a mix of outraged pleasure and sharp putdowns at which Linda would be expert. With Cordelia there was no verbal ping-pong. Conversations ended in pauses, not breaks, and laid tracks along which they could travel back or forward next time they met.

'Are you going to the dance at the boys' club on Saturday?'

'Yes, you?' he said.

'All being well.' A reference to her mother, Ellen, and her problems, that Cordelia had to consider whenever she made plans. Ellen's husband had walked out when Cordelia was a baby, leaving his daughter with nothing but a Shakespearean name that had made life tricky on the estate among Janets, Susans and Barbaras.

Her father had been a handsome blond actor who was forever on tour with one repertory company or another. One day her mother received a postcard featuring Liverpool Town Hall. All it said was, 'Terrific opportunity! Going to America. Will write when settled in.' He had never written again. Her mother kept the postcard for years, until Cordelia finally tore it up after finding her mother, yet again, sobbing while holding it. Since her husband had left, Ellen had regularly 'suffered with her nerves' and had recently tried to calm them with alcohol. Before Easter she'd had a break-down and lost her job. When it came to staying on at school or earning money to support her mum, Cordelia hadn't hesitated to leave. She worked mornings at the cafe, except when covering her mother's part-time cleaning job when she was 'unwell'.

Cordelia stood up. 'I'd better be off. Mum will wonder where I am. Thanks again for saving my eggs.'

'See you Saturday,' said Danny.

She smiled and her green eyes contained as clear an invitation to dance as Linda's had.

Here was a second girl who seemed to like him and was prepared to let him know. He was impressed by how they both spoke so easily of what they were thinking, of what they would like to do, while his guarded excitement had him tongue-tied. If only there had been an O level in Girls.

8

Danny walked down the street that bisected the estate, swinging his kit bag and savouring the bicep-ache that followed weight training at the boys' club. On the other side, Ellen Hill was tottering in the same direction, until she decided to cross over. Passing between two parked cars, she tripped and stumbled headlong into the road. To save herself, she thrust out her arms and launched her handbag into the air. On hitting the ground, the bag spewed its contents across the tarmac. She fell to her knees and then, on all fours, began breathing deeply, composing herself before getting back to her feet. Danny marvelled to see a king-size cigarette sticking out, undamaged, between her fingers. She rose shakily to her feet but, instead of attempting to pick up her stuff, she stood still, eyes closed and chin up, as if she were blind and waiting for assistance at a zebra crossing.

When no help came, she hobbled around the wreckage. Blonde hair screened her face as she bent down to point at each of the possessions in turn, but didn't risk bending further to retrieve them. A van braked and waited. She straightened and spread her arms. 'My bag, my things . . .'

The driver stayed put and motioned to her to pick them up, but she flicked back her hair and refused to move.

Danny's heart sank. He was too close to pretend he hadn't seen her, and the van driver had already involved him by shaking his head in comradely disapproval. The man meant no harm, but he was a stranger. The drunk was Cordelia's mum, who wasn't 'really well at the moment'.

Danny stepped into the road and took her by the arm. 'Let me give you a hand.'

The driver stuck his head out of the window. 'Is she all right, son?' When Danny didn't answer, he shook his head. 'How has she lived so long?'

Ellen's hearing remained unimpaired, and she answered the driver with a limp V-sign. He threw up his arms and sat back.

Danny put down his grip and held her hand while he crabbed around refilling her handbag. She kept trying to pull away as he held on, but each tug set her head wobbling as if her neck was a spring. He snapped the handbag shut and hung it in the crook of her arm. She nodded vague gratitude and released a gentle burp of soured alcohol. 'Oh, excuse me, darling.'

Danny cupped her elbow and shuffled her to the kerb. The driver gave a complaining blast of his horn and roared off. Ellen faced the wrong way and aimed another V-sign at the empty street. She dropped her cigarette but, before Danny could pick it up, she staggered forward and stepped on it.

He held her while she swayed, unseeing, helpless, and it wasn't yet nine o'clock. Several buttons on the dark green overall, worn for her office-cleaning job, were undone, revealing her white slip. Danny looked around in vain for other, more appropriate neighbours to take over, but it would have to be him or no one. He let go of her arm, hoping she could make it on her own, but her walk became a stagger that would have ended in another fall if he hadn't caught her.

'Have to get home,' she said.

'I know.'

'Nearly there, though.'

He stooped to grab his own bag.

She squinted over puffy cheekbones to focus. 'Ooh' what a big bag you've got.'

Unsure whether she was flirting, or joking, Danny found himself momentarily flustered but also a little excited. Ellen said no more, closed her eyes and, with Danny to hold on to, felt no need to open them.

In the cool stairwell of her block, she sensed the dark and pulled Danny closer. Along with her bitter, nicotine breath, he recognised the smell of the pan-stick make-up his mother used.

As she lived on the first floor, Danny thought it best to keep going rather than wait for the lift. He dropped behind as they tackled the stairs. After a few unsteady steps, she swivelled around as if to tell him something but fell forward. She slammed against him before rocking backwards. He steadied her with his free hand and paused to take in her breasts: full and, for a moment, available. The idea flared and died in the time it took her to turn and stagger on.

They were close to her landing when she stopped again, turned and began trembling. He put down his bag and steadied her with both hands.

Four floors up, a door closed and someone began clipping down in the one-two, one-two of those on familiar stairs. Time for him to leave. He was about to let go when her body tensed, shuddered, then relaxed. To the sound of urine trickling onto the stone steps, she groaned, 'Oh God no, I'm sorry.'

The neighbour had reached the floor above. Danny stepped away from Ellen, but she toppled backwards. He caught her once more and held her at arm's length, grateful that her eyes remained closed against the foggy realisation of what she had done. He prayed, for both their sakes, she wouldn't remember.

Arthur Reilly arrived on the landing in his crispy-clean Fred Perry and razor-creased mohair trousers. With a packet of cigarettes and a lighter in one hand, he was ready for a couple of hours in the pub, talking bullshit about Chelsea FC and lying about girls he'd been with. In full sneer, he tiptoed theatrically past them to avoid getting piss on his polished loafers.

After a long blink, he pointed to the dark stains on Danny's Hush Puppies 'Hah! Fuck your luck.'

Ellen flinched and pressed her face against Danny's chest.

On reaching the ground floor, Reilly shouted up, 'Leave the slag, you're wasting your time!'

Did Reilly think he was trying it on? Or was it contempt for them both?

Fuck you, thought Danny, and your moron's glee at thinking you've found someone you can look down on.

'Fuck you, Reilly!'

'What did you say?' said Reilly.

'I'm not talking to you!'

'What did you say?' said Ellen.

71

'Nothing, only a couple more steps.'

At her front door, she buckled. Danny held her hand as she slid down onto the coconut mat, knees up, clutching her handbag to her stomach. Tears appeared on her cheeks. She wouldn't look at him but – as he let go – she squeezed his fingers. 'Thank you.'

He rapped hard with the knocker and jogged down the stairs, stooping on the way to lift his kitbag out of a pool of urine. On the ground floor, he waited and listened.

Cordelia opened the door. 'Oh Mum.'

'It's all right, darling . . . just need to . . .'

'You haven't wet yourself?'

''Fraid so.'

'Who was with you? Who banged on the door?'

'There was someone . . . him, on the stairs.'

'Who? Oh, please, not Arthur Reilly!'

'Don't know, maybe.'

'Come on, Mum, you can't stay down there.'

'No, can't, can I darling? I'm so sorry.'

Out in the street, Danny met Dodds.

'Where've you been then?'

Danny nodded to his kit bag as he put it down. 'Training.'

A sly smile appeared on Dodds's face. 'In this block? What kind of training was that then, vertical press-ups?' Dodds was obsessed with knee-trembler sex, which he believed was what top lovers achieved on doorsteps when others got only a kiss goodnight. 'Cordelia, eh?'

'I wasn't with Cordelia. It was her mum.'

'Her mum? You dirty bastard.'

The Dodds routine: talking about sex, getting it, not getting it and, Danny suspected, lying about it.

'I was helping her up the stairs, that's all.'

'Pissed again, was she?'

Danny nodded. Dodds's eyebrows shot up. 'Good chance for a feel of those lovely tits.'

Danny shook his head but, as he recalled the squash of Ellen's breasts on his chest, he could see Dodds's point. Ellen, like Danny's mother, was only in her late thirties and, although she may have been on the slide, she could still turn heads whenever she dressed up and had her hair done.

Dodds shrugged. 'Missed a trick there, mate. Anyway, fancy a light ale? I'll get 'em in.'

This wasn't an offer to pay. Dodds looked old enough to buy drinks: Danny didn't. In the pub he would have to hand Dodds his money and hang back.

'No, I'm starving – chips are what I need.'

Dodds wasn't one for asking twice. 'Suit yourself.'

When Danny picked up his bag, Dodds noticed the wet patch it left on the pavement. 'Looks like you've broken your Old Spice bottle.' He knew it wasn't Old Spice but not what it really was. 'Now how will you pull at the dance on Saturday?'

Danny remembered he would be dancing with Linda Bain.

'I don't need aftershave for that.'

'No? Anyway, stay close to me and no one will know you're not wearing any.'

'Thanks, Dodds, what would I do without you?'

In farewell, Dodds's heavy punch on the arm was that of a friend maintaining a physical pecking order.

73

9

The corridor to the gym was crowded with boys who went to dances but didn't dance, until later, when it was the price they had to pay to get close to a girl. There were risks in waiting too long and the last slow session would trigger a now-or-never stampede towards girls they fancied or, when desperate, those they didn't.

Danny pulled open the gym door whose wired windows were covered in red cellophane. In the smoky dark, a rotating disc threw coloured bubbles on the walls and a spotlight illuminated a revolving mirror ball.

At the far end, Eric Harper bopped behind a desk with a single turntable. On the floor beside him, three cut-down cardboard boxes were crammed with 45s, separated into categories by strips of coloured paper. Eric revelled in the music and, given he could have been Quasimodo's cousin, saw DJ-ing as his best chance of pulling a bird. It worked, and there'd usually be one girl hanging around the desk making requests, offering to get him a Coke, and dancing with him when, eyes closed and top incisors reaching down over his bottom lip, Eric demonstrated his commitment to the music.

Most girls were dancing in groups around their handbags piled on the floor. The boys stood around the walls in their uniforms of Ben Sherman button-downs, mohair trousers and Hush Puppies. The exception was Crockett, in a black polo-neck and jeans, who was moving silkily between the girls in his two-inch Cuban heels. He beckoned Danny to join him, knowing he wouldn't. Danny looked for Linda but she wasn't there.

Back in the corridor, he met Dodds, alcohol shine in his eyes. 'How's it going? Many birds in there?'

'A few,' said Danny.

'Want to come back later when it's warmed up a bit? Royal Oak?'

He remembered Linda's warning about needing Dutch courage. But he didn't feel right yet, not ready to stay and certainly not ready to dance. He followed Dodds, but couldn't help regretting his lack of resolution and thought of what Crockett would say – something like, 'Fuck off, Dodds, I've got a bird to see!'

In the club foyer, Linda, in a black miniskirt, was returning from the ladies with a couple of friends.

'Had enough already?' she said, walking past. 'Or not had enough?'

Annoying, but she had a point. Was the evening panning out as she'd feared? Was he like Dodds and the others, who needed to get pissed before they could enjoy anything but football?

If she had said, 'Hello', instead, he might have told Dodds to leave on his own.

'Just going out for a bit of air.'

'Air, eh?' said Linda. Her smile, cynical and attractive, wasn't enough to make him stay.

'I won't be long,' he said.

'Remember I only dance with boys who are vertical.' She disappeared down the corridor.

'What was that about?' said Dodds.

'Nothing.'

'Fancy her, do you?'

He was about to say, 'Of course not' but he hesitated.

'So, you do!' said Dodds.

'No, no I don't. She's a bit flash, don't you think?'

'No,' said Dodds.

Nor did Danny. Then why had he said it? Why was it easier to impress someone who was with him, rather than be loyal to someone who wasn't?

'She's tasty,' said Dodds. 'I might have a go for her myself.'

Jealousy rose in Danny's chest, fired by frustration at what he'd said, and what he'd failed to say. 'Oh yeah?'

'Yeah,' said Dodds, 'I've been wondering about her for a while. Sharp tongue but I wouldn't mind tasting it.'

But Linda was Danny's date, sort of. He was beginning to feel a little like Angel Clare.

In the pub, Dodds went to get the beers. Sitting at the bar, an off-duty Reilly squinted and shouted at Danny, loud enough for the barman to hear. 'Should you be in here at your age?'

The barman looked over at Danny but said nothing. Dodds returned and gave Danny a half-filled pint glass and a bottle of light ale and smiled. 'Don't mind him.'

'I don't,' said Danny.

But he did. Being reassured by Dodds pissed him off, too.

Danny topped up the bitter with light ale and gulped it down. 'One of these days . . .'

'What? Reilly?' said Dodds.

'A showdown, maybe.'

Had he really said that, and to Dodds of all people. This was the Royal Oak for Christ's sake, not the saloon in *High Noon*.

Dodds, ever to the point when there was friction in the air, said, 'Why not go for him now?'

Like Reilly, Dodds could walk up to someone and start a fight. Danny couldn't; he was an avoider. Unlike those two, he had never been considered one of the local hard nuts. But were they so tough? He'd not seen either of them confront anyone bigger than they were. Whereas Crockett did it regularly; but then, everyone was bigger than Crockett. Danny feared that Reilly's constant hostility wasn't going to stop unless he did something about it. But what?

As if reading his mind, Dodds said, 'Don't worry about Reilly. Want another? Your round.' Danny handed over the money and Dodds went back to the bar.

On his way back, Reilly said, 'Got his lemonade and bag of crisps?'

This time, with his hands holding glasses and bottles, Dodds leaned close. 'That's enough!' he said, and pushed past him.

No one could accuse Dodds of being predictable.

Two-pints confident, Danny opened the gym door to see couples shuffling around in the dark to 'You've Lost That Loving Feeling'. Around the dance floor a few girls and many boys waited and watched. When the Righteous Brothers stopped singing, those who had paired-off stayed close. Everyone else returned to their friends.

Again, Danny couldn't find Linda, but he could see Cordelia standing against the wall, hands behind her back, blonde hair pinned up, revealing more of her face and, extra attractive, her slender neck. Should he ask her to dance? She smiled and looked away.

Dodds nudged him. Linda had returned with a couple of friends. She gave Danny a little wave but became obscured by Dodds crossing the floor towards her. She leaned to one side to smile at Danny, but put her arms out to accept Dodds's offer to dance.

What to do? Leave? Wait? Embarrassment merged with jealousy as Dodds and Linda circled in front of him. When he caught Linda's eye, her smile said, 'See, I'm in demand', while Dodds's defiant raised eyebrow said, 'Well?'

Dodds soon abandoned the 'shall-we-dance' hold and wrapped his arms around her with his hands meeting in the small of her back. Each time they passed sideways on, Danny monitored the gap between their hips. On the other side of the gym, Cordelia turned down a request to dance.

When the song ended, Linda detached herself from Dodds and walked towards Danny. But the lights went up to signal the end of the slow session. Linda's girlfriends started dancing around her. She beckoned Danny to join them but, riled that she was ignoring what he'd said about dancing apart, he shook his head.

With a 'Not even for me?' glance, she turned to dance with the girls.

'Well, that was something.' Dodds was shouting in Danny's ear above the music.

'Yeah?'

'God, there's real heat coming off her.' He pointed to his crotch. 'Especially down there.'

'Really?'

'Really. By the way, have you seen Cordelia Hill over

there? Not bad when she's done up, is she? And tits like her mum's. I think she might be more co-operative than most. Know what I mean?'

'No.'

'Ready to give more than a bit of tit.'

'You don't know that,' said Danny.

Dodds bristled at the challenge and tapped the side of his nose. 'Who says I don't?'

'I do. I think you make it up as you go along.'

'Not jealous, are you?' said Dodds, whose smile had disappeared.

'No!'

But could he be? Danny sighed at the absurdity of being possessive about two girls, neither of whom was his girl-friend.

'I'm going to the pub.'

'Really, on your jack?' said Dodds.

'Yes, on my jack.' The time had come to order his own drinks.

'Please yourself,' said Dodds.

At the Albert, in Victoria Street, Danny took a deep breath and asked for a light and bitter. The barmaid looked doubtful, but served him with the indulgent smile of a big sister. Soon he was enjoying the first pint he'd ever bought himself. He celebrated by drinking two more, and left when the barmaid suggested that a fourth was too many.

He crossed Victoria Street city-dweller fashion, by going halfway and waiting in the middle. From a car passing behind him, someone screamed 'giddaadoutofit'. Startled, Danny stumbled forward into the path of an approaching van. A horn blared and tyres screeched. Danny raised his hand in thanks, hoping to give the impression he'd stepped out deliberately. But any pretence of sobriety disappeared when he tripped up the kerb and sprawled on the pavement. Embarrassed, he leapt to his feet to find Victoria Street was moving as if on water. He set off, weaving his way kerb-to-wall, wall-to-kerb until he reached the boys' club. Before going in, he took a deep breath. Dodds or no Dodds, he would ask Linda to dance and not let her go for the rest of the night.

Ernest greeted him from behind the desk, but his smile soon turned to a frown. 'Are you OK, Daniel?' By now Danny feared that speaking would be tricky. He smiled and gave a nod.

In the corridor, he fended off both walls on his way to the gym. Crockett left off talking to a small girl for whom he needn't have bothered with his Cuban heels. 'Blimey, how much have you had then?'

'What's it to you?' said Danny.

'It's nothing to me that you're pissed.'

'I'm not.'

'Yeah, and I'm six foot six.' Crockett gave up and turned back to his girlfriend.

In the gym, Danny inhaled the heady scent of smoke, warm bodies and, depending on who came closest, whiffs of perfume or Old Spice. Ten past eleven. Any moment now, Ernest would tell Eric to start the last slow session, after which he'd turn up the lights and shout goodnight. Time was running out for boys who had waited to make a move – and for girls who'd been waiting to be moved on.

In the far corner, Linda was talking to Dodds, who acknowledged Danny with a lift of his head. Danny set off towards them but the floor and those on it were rolling, taking Linda in and out of view. He tacked closer, bumping into dancers and receiving retaliatory shoves that sent him further off course.

Dodds stepped forward to bring him close. 'All right?'

'Fine.'

Gerry and the Pacemakers launched gently into 'You'll Never Walk Alone'. Danny shoved Dodds away and held out his hands to Linda, who hesitated before putting hers on his shoulders. Dodds didn't move away. Danny tried dancing Linda towards the middle of the floor, but his feet wouldn't co-operate. All he could do was sway on the spot. Linda shouted in his ear. 'So, you got pissed after all.'

'Pissed? No.'

'Yes!' she said.

'Lin . . . Lin . . .'

He abandoned speech and pulled her close, but his legs couldn't move back to accept her forward momentum. Down he went, pulling her on top of him. With his hands clasped behind her back, he couldn't open them quickly enough to stop her forehead hitting his nose. Before she rolled off, he had a close-up of her startled face, haloed by pulsing disco lights that synced with the stabs of pain in the back of his head. Dodds helped her up. The ceiling revolved ever faster around the mirror ball and became a centrifugal force sucking at the contents of his stomach. He clamped shut his mouth but the rising vomit diverted through his nose and out over his chin. When rough tugs on his arms brought him to a vertical position, the pressure to puke eased.

His two friends swayed in front of him, tall and short. They took an arm each around their necks and steered him towards the door. He leaned heavily on Dodds but when slumping the other way, the extra distance down to Crockett's shoulder shocked like stepping off an unseen kerb. They paused at the front desk, where Danny caught only a blurred image of Ernest's face and imagined his look of disappointment. On looking down to avoid eye contact, he noticed blood among the puke on his shirt and prayed it wasn't Linda's.

'It's OK, Ernest, it wasn't a fight, we've got him,' said Crockett. Outside, they steadied him against the waist-high wall that bounded the club's parking area. The cooler air felt good but the street heaved, and lamp posts scored sparkler trails in the dark.

While Dodds and Crockett said indecipherable, vaguely reassuring things, Danny leaned over the wall, head down, and let the geyser blow, flooding past his teeth and blocking his nostrils. Convulsion followed convulsion, vacuuming his stomach. He stood up, gasping, and wiped his face with the back of his hand.

'Better out than in,' said Crockett. 'But no gold watch yet.'

On the pavement, his sick had formed a frothy comma whose tail reached up the wall. He tried to step back but his legs betrayed him.

Dodds, doing a mate's grudging duty, said: 'Just fucking stay still for a while.' Danny obediently propped himself on the wall with his elbows

'Is he OK?' said Linda.

Danny closed his eyes.

'He'll be all right,' said Crockett.

'Really?' said Linda.

'Yeah, he's only legless.'

'Tell me about it.'

'Are you coming back in, Linda?' said Dodds.

Danny silently begged her to refuse.

'No thanks, that'll do me for the night,' she said.

Grateful, Danny kept his head down and watched her legs skirting his spew as she left.

Crockett helped him over to one of the benches by the club entrance and sat beside him. 'Quite a performance. So, you fancy Linda? Boy did you fuck that up. And you've pissed off Dodds. Not to mention upsetting our Ernest. Thought I'd let you have a list, in case you want to apologise.'

'Fuck off, Croc.'

'And you can add me. Look, I'm going back in. There's a bird in there who's missing me terribly. Take it easy, you should be fine in a week or two.'

Head in hands and gulping air, Danny watched an elastic cord of bloody snot dribble drop and bounce from his nose until it gathered enough weight to reach the ground.

Someone sat on the bench beside him. 'Here,' said Cordelia, and handed him a couple of tissues.

He wiped and blew his nose. She shifted closer and began rubbing his back. It felt nice but he didn't feel good about it. Even now, he wanted Cordelia to be Linda.

'That's enough, I'm fine.' After a pause, he added, 'Thank you.'

He got up, shrugged off Cordelia's helping hands and lurched away. Once around the corner, he stopped to steady himself against a wall. He heard approaching voices; loudest among them, Reilly's. He should have crossed the street but, piss-brave, decided to press on. As he passed Reilly, he broke under the strain of keeping straight and banged against him.

'Oh dear, has the boy had too much to drink, then?' said Reilly, coming close enough to Danny's face to give him the benefit of his halitosis.

'Fuck you, Reilly.'

Reilly shoved him against the wall. Danny rebounded and was checked by Reilly's forearm. Danny closed his eyes and waited for the first punch, until one of Reilly's companions said, 'Leave it, Arthur, he can barely stand.'

Reilly came close again. 'Go on then, fuck off home, you little shitbag.'

'Little?' said Danny. 'You're the short-arse here.' He was slurring, but as long as Reilly understood, he didn't care.

Reilly went for him and a struggle ensued as his laughing mates held him back. Danny gritted his teeth and reeled away, but an outstretched foot brought him crashing to the ground. He curled up, expecting Reilly to put the boot in, but fading jeers told him it was over. Lying on his back, he relaxed. A couple of stars wobbled in the night sky. He decided to wait until they came to rest but, as he was getting comfortable, the smell of dog shit filled his nostrils. Turning to one side, he made out a couple of fresh turds. He rolled away, retching, but his aching, concave stomach found nothing to eject.

'Danny? It's OK, Danny, come on, let's get you home.' Cordelia helped him up. 'Reilly's a pig,' she said.

Anger flared in him for Reilly and for Dodds, but mostly for himself. Yet he had some to spare for the girl who had witnessed every episode of his disastrous evening. 'Leave me alone! Who are you, my nurse or something? I can get home by myself.'

'Danny, please, don't.'

He pushed her away. Under the streetlight, he saw her face crumple, as it had when Reilly insulted her. His shame was complete. Before he could apologise, she had crossed the road.

Even drunk, he knew his condition would upset his mother. He staggered on towards the river, stopping to pee behind the bins near Jones's.

He crossed the Thames at Lambeth Bridge and came back over Vauxhall. On reaching his block, he rode the lift to his floor and sat at the top of the stairwell. As he inhaled the night air, the night's humiliations played back in a painful clarity: disgrace on the dance floor; Linda, lost now, and Dodds moving in on her; falling foul of Reilly, and rounding off the perfect evening by hurting Cordelia.

Here, then, was the real Danny Byrne, who thought drink would help him play the character he wanted to be, when it had only revealed him as immature, selfish and now, nasty.

10

Sunday passed in a blur of headache, remorse and a need to be horizontal. Danny didn't know how often his mother had stood in the doorway of his bedroom, silent, exasperated, but during the times he knew she was there, he pretended to be asleep. And, as it had been when he was a small boy, he knew that she knew. In another throwback to childhood, he had been aware at one point of his blankets being rearranged and of a kiss on the back of his head.

He groaned as the events at the dance crashed into his aching head. He may not have been blind drunk, as the returning images were all too clear, but he regretted that he hadn't been dead drunk after which, he'd been told, embarrassing memories don't survive.

Around teatime, his mother bustled in, wafting toast and jam. She took the plate and mug of tea from the tray and banged them down, alarm-clock loud, on his bedside cabinet. She opened the curtains and stood over him, clutching the tray to her stomach. She sighed, 'I suppose there had to be a first time to get drunk but I hope you've learned your lesson. You must have been in a sorry state last night.'

Shielding his eyes from the light, he spoke to her silhouette. 'No, I wasn't.'

'No? Maybe only your willy was drunk, as it peed everywhere but in the toilet.'

'For Christ's sake, Mum, use grown-up words, will you?'

'I will, when you behave like a grown-up.'

He needed to pee and tried to sit up, but his head, bowling-ball heavy, thudded back on the pillow and throbbed.

'Eat the toast, it'll help.'

'Later, Mum.'

'Your tea will get cold.'

It did. Later, when peeing could not be postponed, he shuffled to the toilet and aimed ultra-carefully into the bowl. He went into the kitchen, where his mother poured a glass of water and gave him two Aspros and what he recognised as her look of waning disapproval that would eventually become a resigned smile. She asked if he was hungry. He shook his head, hoping the Aspros would soon kick in.

He considered staying up but it would mean an evening on the sofa watching, among other things, *Sunday Night at the London Palladium*. Back in his room, he ate the toast, drank the cold tea and slept.

On Monday morning, his mother came in before leaving for work. 'Is this an off-licence day?'

'No.'

With a smile, both disapproving and forgiving, she asked what he would like for breakfast. This was the pattern of her anger: blistering comments, frosty silence, followed by grudging kindness, a perfect guilt-inducing combination.

She popped home at lunchtime to make him cheese and

pickle sandwiches. 'And there's a bit of sponge cake for later, when you can make your own bloody tea!'

By evening, he banked on a long, hot shower at the boys' club to get him going again. He set off, wary of facing Ernest, who would undoubtedly greet him with concern for his well-being and say something about learning lessons: the limit of a bollocking from Ernest which, as the club members had found, could be every bit as effective as the traditional kind.

Walking through the estate, his shoulders tightened at the sound of clicking heels. Linda was gaining on him. He resisted the urge to turn around. A broadside was coming and, once alongside, he knew she would hold position and blast away. He stared ahead, ready to get it over with, to be dumped or whatever dismissal she considered appropriate to end a relationship they'd nearly had.

Potential responses, which would not include jealousy of Dodds, passed through his head: I'm not used to drinking so much (screamingly obvious); if you hadn't danced with Dodds (pathetically self-pitying); it wasn't the real me (oh *please!*).

Anyway, who was the real Danny Byrne? The grammar-school pupil with university potential (teachers), the good son (Mum), the considerate friend (Jinx), the bright boy (off-licence), the responsible lad (boys' club)? He worked hard at crafting and maintaining these personas. And he had succeeded, in that he could usually call up the appropriate one for whomever he was with. At the dance, all these versions had dissolved in alcohol to reveal, if not the real Danny Byrne, a version he was ashamed of.

If he'd stayed sober, he might have been able to develop a decent boyfriend persona and, today, instead of flinching as a lost girlfriend bore down on him, he could be looking forward to another date. But had that even been a date? Hadn't it been more an agreement to meet, to dance, slowly, to see what happened, maybe to take her home? When talking of them meeting at the dance, Linda had said, 'maybe' a lot.

He would apologise and say no more. He turned to face her indignant glare, which he held until realising he was making things worse. When he walked on, she followed.

She put a hand on his arm to stop him.

He wanted it to be over, for her to just say so and to leave him be. But no such luck.

'That was impressive on Saturday night,' she said.

'Yes, sorry.'

'Is that it then?'

Again, much as he liked her, she had the knack of prompting a sharper form of self-defence than he could normally muster. 'That about sums it up.'

It was the wrong time to be clever.

Frustration tightened her face. 'Really?'

'What more do you want me to say?'

'Lots more.'

He could think of nothing. 'Sorry' would have to do.

'I was humiliated,' she said.

He stopped himself saying that she wasn't the only one, that everyone felt sorry for her, that her humiliation would be temporary, that his embarrassment would last for ages.

'By someone who was supposed to be my date.'

'Look, I'm sorry,' he said.

'Sorry? Hanging on my neck, dragging me to the floor, so that God knows who saw my knickers. And getting myself up, thanks to Dodds, in time to see you puking up over your own face. And you're fucking sorry!'

He thought she might be about to cry and a small, hope-less shrug had him resisting an impulse to hold her.

'What else can I say?' he said.

'Say? What are you going to *do*?'

As he struggled for an answer. Dodds came along, kit bag in hand.

He nodded to Danny and said, 'Hi Linda, how was work?'

'All right,' she said.

Here he was, a schoolboy, in the presence of those who were earning a living.

They started walking. Dodds fell in beside them and with piss-take in the guise of enquiry, he said, 'How's your head, Danny?'

'Fine.'

'Going to the club?'

'Yeah.'

Linda stopped and gave Danny a wide-eyed signal that she hadn't finished. Dodds turned and waited.

'I'll see you there,' said Danny.

Dodds's nod failed to conceal his annoyance. As Dodds left, Danny turned to face his final seconds of most-favoured status with Linda.

'Well?' she said.

Well, what? He took a guess. 'Do you want me to pay to get your clothes cleaned?'

'My clothes?'

'Didn't I muck them up?'

'I got out of the way before you were sick. Why get legless, Danny? It's not as if you needed Dutch courage. Hadn't I promised to dance with you?'

But she had danced with Dodds.

'Look, I'm sorry. How many times do you want me to say it? Now just leave me alone!' he said.

'Do you want me to leave you alone, Danny? Because I will, you know.'

He caught his breath at the idea that he might have a choice.

'No, I don't want you to leave me,' he said, and realised, immediately, how much more it meant than, 'leave me alone'.

Her voice dropped to a whisper. 'I was so embarrassed.'

'Me too!'

'OK, we were both embarrassed.'

'But it's not as if anyone knew you . . . we, were . . .' said Danny.

'Were what?'

'I don't know, together?'

'How do you know?' she said.

Had she told others about their half-date?

'Well, I said nothing to anyone,' he said.

'Why not?'

'Because I wasn't sure that – when it came to it – you'd actually say, yes. And when you danced with Dodds . . .'

'I danced with Dodds, Danny Byrne, because he asked me to dance! Has it occurred to you that one reason I might like you is that you're not like Dodds?'

Disappointed that she'd said 'might', he said, 'But you know what I'd said about dancing only to slow stuff.'

'You could have waited. You should have waited. But oh no, you got drunk which, of course, made you much more attractive than Dodds.'

Danny felt his side of the conversation had run out of steam. 'I think I'll get going now. Sorry.'

She didn't move. 'I'm sorry too.' A softer parting shot than he'd been expecting.

He went to walk around her.

'Look,' she said, 'shall we forget about Saturday?'

Saturday! He was now having a job remembering five minutes ago.

'Forget about Saturday?'

She sighed. 'That's what I said!'

'Sorry, yes, let's.'

They faced each other while he failed to find the right words to say. She cocked her head and came to his rescue. 'Well, how about going out together?'

'Yes, yes, of course.'

'No, Danny, I mean you ask me out.'

'Sorry. Would you like to come out with me?'

She took his hand and kissed his cheek.

Crockett came up behind them. 'Mind out, Linda! If you're not careful, he'll have you on the deck again!' They let their hands drop and stepped back as if halfway through folding a sheet together. 'Teaching him how to dance properly?'

Linda smiled. 'It might take a while. Aren't you going to the club?'

He grinned. 'Nod's as good as a wink . . . See you there, Danny, unless Ernest has barred you.'

'Where were we?' said Linda.

'Would you like to go to the pictures then?'

Why had he said 'then', as if she'd refused an earlier suggestion?

She sighed. 'All right, how about Sunday afternoon, then?'

'Where shall we meet? How about by Jones's?'

'Meet? Aren't you coming to pick me up at home?'

'Pick you up at home?'

'You're doing it again, repeating what I say.'

He did it because it gave him time to think.

'Am I? Sorry. Maybe not, as it's the first time?'

Her eyes closed and she gave an impatient shake of her head. Was she bridling at his assumption there would be another time?

He changed his mind. 'OK, how about two o'clock, at your place, then?'

She shook her head but smiled too. 'Fine, see you there, then.'

He bent to pick up his bag and, as he straightened up, she stepped close enough for an embrace. He should have taken her in his arms, but a warm, confusing heave in his chest got him walking.

'Bye, Danny.'

He waved and kept going. With every step he regretted not kissing her, but maybe he would on Sunday when she might become his girlfriend. The thought had him breaking into a run, as if it had started raining.

11

Danny's mother sat in her slip on a kitchen chair, head down over the sink, clutching its edge with both hands. A blue towel lay over her shoulders like a sailor's collar.

From a large, enamelled jug, Danny emptied warm water over the back of her head. He put the jug on the draining board, laid a green line of Silvikrin shampoo in her hair and began rubbing it in.

'How's that?' he said.

'It's fine, love.'

She liked this part the most. So, did he: the shampoo foaming over his hands as he massaged it into her hair; pulling on the long strands and coiling them onto her head before giving them a squeeze, and even being surprised, each time, by how hard her skull felt under his fingertips. She pushed down on the rim of the sink to sit back, but he resisted and massaged a little longer.

She didn't mind. 'That's nice but take it easy. You're getting stronger, I can feel it.'

Pleased to hear this, he said, 'Is that enough then?'

'Yes, rinse now, please.'

He put the jug underneath the Ascot, half filled it with hot water and topped it up from the cold tap. He poured and rubbed until the jug was empty.

She pulled her hair down in front of her face to check it.

'Thanks, love. That'll do.'

But it wouldn't. One or two spits of white foam remained, and he wanted them gone.

'No, it won't. I'll give it another rinse.'

'Danny, it'll do!'

'No, it won't!'

'Well hurry up then!'

He refilled the jug and emptied it over her head, breaking the water's fall with the back of his hand. He was still seeking more white flecks when she said, 'OK, that really is enough.'

He framed her head with his hands, gathered her thick dark hair and squeezed out the water. 'There you are.'

The towel was soaked where it had lain close to her neck. He wished he'd been more careful, but his mother didn't notice. She pulled it up to rub her hair with her splayed fingers and sat back to coil the towel into a turban.

It would have been simpler to wash her hair in the bathroom with the rubber hand-shower connected to the taps but, since moving to the estate, an unspoken understanding had maintained a weekly ritual that had started in their old home. He had been eight years old and offered to pour the water to rinse her hair. Before long he was shampooing too.

His work was done but there was more for her, more towelling before pouring on Amami lotion and applying it, hand-over-hand, through her straight hair. Then there would be the pinning of large curlers to roll her ends under.

'What are you up to this evening?' she said.

'Off-licence.'

'I know, but after.'

'Seeing the lads. It's Saturday night, Mum.'

'Alan?'

'Maybe.'

'Jean says he's hardly at home and she has no idea what time he gets in.'

'He could say the same about her,' said Danny.

'That's enough, she's his mum.'

'Is that how mums behave?'

She frowned. 'Stop it!'

'I'd better go.'

'Will you be seeing him?'

'Maybe.'

'I know Jean isn't managing too well but look out for Alan, will you? Is it true he's running errands for George?'

'Dunno.'

'Yes, you do. If I know, you must!'

'Why ask me then?'

'Don't be cheeky. Alan needs to keep as far from that one as possible. He's a bully and a taker, like his nasty father, who played around with other women on the estate without caring who knew.'

'I know, Mum, you've told me before.'

But she wouldn't tell him which women.

'George is a chip off a rotten old block. He'll get his come-uppance like his father did. George has done time, too, you know.'

Yes, Danny knew that George senior had died in prison and that Gasping George, far from seeing this as a warning about his own behaviour, believed it enhanced his reputation as a scary rogue. In his twenties, he spent a year in Pentonville Prison after being caught burgling a widow's prefab. Her neighbours had heard George shouting at her to sit down while he jemmied open a cabinet. Not a fast worker, he gave the police enough time to greet him as he left by the back door.

'Please swear you'll have nothing to do with George.'

When Danny didn't answer, she grabbed his arm. 'Hear me?'

It was too late but she spooked him by looking in his eyes as if she knew.

He thought of the hairdryer that he planned to buy her with George's money, but knew she'd throw it at him if she found out who had paid for it.

'Did you hear me, Danny?'

'Yes, yes, Mum.'

A rap on the front door.

'Now who's that, with me like this?' She looked in the mirror to confirm what 'like this' meant. 'Get it, will you?'

Nobby stood, back resting against the balcony wall. 'Watcha, Danny.'

'What's up? It's not dinner time.'

Nobby gave him a V-sign. 'I've eaten.' Then, a smug smile. 'George wants you.'

'Jesus!' Danny stepped outside and pulled the door to.

His mother called from the kitchen, 'Danny?', which meant, 'who is it?'

'It's only Nobby.'

She popped her turbaned head out of the kitchen. Danny pulled the front door wide to let her see. 'Hello Alan, coming in, love?'

'No thanks, Aunt Cora.'

'Say hello to your mum for me, won't you.'

She went back into the kitchen.

'Keep your voice down,' said Danny. 'She'll go bananas if she finds out about me doing stuff for George. What does he want?'

'Dunno, but I know where he wants you – at the Tap House.'

'I don't go in the Tap House; they know I'm underage.'

'I'll come with you and let him know you're outside,' said Nobby.

'But I've got to be at the off-licence.'

'That's how it goes when you work for George, Danny boy.'

'The extra money won't be extra if I lose my job.'

'Still, you'd better see what he wants.'

Danny went back to the kitchen. 'Off now, Mum, see you later.'

'OK love, what's Alan want?'

'Nothing, he didn't realise it was nowhere near teatime.'

'That's enough,' she said in a whisper. 'I want him to come here whenever he wants, especially when he's hungry.'

'I think he knows that, Mum, don't you? Anyway, we're off. See you later.'

'Danny Byrne, there are enough unkind people around here without you adding your two-penn'orth.'

'OK, Mum.'

'Don't be late for work, and don't be out late afterwards.'

His mates were going up West later to a new night club

but he rarely felt like going out after work. He headed down the passage. 'It's Sunday tomorrow, Mum.'

'So what?' she said.

He closed the front door.

12

On their way to see George, Nobby said, 'So, will you be coming up West later tonight? We're going to this club called, La Discotheque. I've been already, it's sweet.'

'It's Saturday.'

'So?'

'Saturday, Nobby. I work at the off-licence.'

'I mean later.'

'No.'

'What's the matter? Under the thumb?'

'Whose?'

'Mummy's? Linda Bain's?'

'Sod off, what's Linda Bain got to do with it?'

'Thought from what I've heard she's got a lot to do with it.'

'Well, you know what thought did.'

'Suit yourself. Anyway, it's in Wardour Street, we're meeting there around ten.'

*

At six o'clock, Danny waited outside the Tap House while Nobby went in. He came back and held open the door. 'It's sweet, in you go.'

'Coming too?' said Danny.

'No, I'm off before he gets me to do anything else.'

Inside, George sat on a bench, legs outstretched, behind a small round table. Banger sat bolt upright beside him. Reilly perched on a stool, holding a pint. George told Danny to bring over a chair and took a gulp from his glass of whisky. 'Pages my son, sit down. Now, want a drink?'

'No thanks, Bill knows I'm underage.'

With the self-satisfied smile of a bully, he said, 'He'll serve you if I ask him.' This ensured Danny's refusal. Bill was not only a decent bloke; he knew Danny's mother.

'No, really, I've got to work this evening.'

Reilly picked up his pint. 'Just as well, handles booze like a five-year-old.'

His grin faded when George said, 'Maybe, but he handles a pen better than you.' George gave Danny the writing pad. 'OK Pages, another note, please.'

Not a threat to a debtor this time, but a character reference for one of George's runners, who'd been nicked for selling purple hearts. Danny jotted down notes of what George wanted to say: knowing this boy to be a good kid; never known him to be in trouble; decent family, blah, blah. None of it true but, for a first known offence, likely to help get him off.

'Get my drift?'

'Got it, George.'

Danny wrote the letter and read it back.

'Just the job, Pages, you're getting the hang of this.'

George beckoned the landlord over. Bill lifted his head to acknowledge the call, but took time to serve a customer and to give the counter a thorough wipe. When he came to the table, he eyed Banger, 'I can't have your dog on seats, George.'

George's displeasure flashed on his face, but he jogged Banger to get down. He gave the letter to Bill and invited him to read and sign it. Twisting a tea towel around his fist, Bill said, 'I don't know this kid.'

George sat back and gave a half-smile. Bill was no softie; you couldn't be if you were a pub landlord on the estate. Since taking over at the Tap House, locals had grown to like and respect him.

'Don't worry about it, Bill. Look at it this way, you're helping a young man avoid serious trouble, and you're helping me.' With a threatening smirk, he said, 'And I appreciate it.'

'I'm not comfortable with this, George, don't ask me again.'

George the grateful disappeared. 'Life does get uncomfortable at times, Bill, but it could get a lot worse, couldn't it?'

Unable to conceal his anger, Bill held George's gaze. Reilly, the alert lieutenant, stood up. The landlord glared at Reilly 'You can sit down, now!' Reilly's blink went into overdrive. He looked to George for a steer. George tugged him down to his seat. 'Easy, Arthur.'

After a slow shake of his head, Bill put the letter down on the table, took a pen from his shirt pocket and, with an elbow close to Reilly's face, signed it.

Before returning to the bar, Bill looked at the three of them in turn with visible contempt. Unflustered, George responded with his smile; Reilly, feeling safe now, sneered, but Bill's hostility left Danny shaken at the realisation that he had crossed a line. Now he was on the wrong side with Gasping George Kelly, who cared for no one but his dog; Reilly, who hated him; and poor Nobby, no longer the friend he used to be. On the other side, everyone else.

George took two florins from his pocket and gave them to Danny. 'There you go, four bob for today and for last time.'

Danny couldn't bring himself to say thank you. George noted this with a shrug.

'Now Arthur, get Nobby in here.'

Reilly checked outside.

'He's gone, George.' Reilly locked his fingers and pushed them out in a stretch. 'Want me to find him?'

'No, Pages will do it, won't you?'

'Can't, George, I'll have to be at my job for half past five.'

George held up the letter. 'But I want this in the solicitor's office in Victoria Street today, so there'll be no doubt that he'll have it first thing Monday morning. Here's the address.'

Nobby was right, George's work came first.

Danny wrote the address on the envelope. George stabbed a stubby finger at its top left corner. 'Put "by hand" on the front too, that's what's done, isn't it?'

Danny had no idea but nodded as if he did. 'Yes, George.'

In Victoria Street, he put the envelope in the solicitor's letterbox and pondered whether it would be quicker to run the short route to the off-licence or go the longer way by bus. Already ten minutes late, he wasted another ten waiting for the number 24 before he started running.

13

Danny arrived breathless at the off-licence. There was no one in sight, but a clink of bottles from under the counter located Ron. He stood up, in his brown shop-coat and weighed in pre-emptively, 'Sorry's no good.'

'Afternoon, Ronald.'

'I'll give you, "Afternoon Ronald". Cut the lip and get to work. That's half an hour you're going to have to make up.' He shook his head and made 'thtup' noises behind his teeth. 'What was the problem, then?'

'I was in Victoria Street on an errand and got held up. I ran all the way here.'

'Well, there's errands and there's employment. You need to sort out which matters most. Now, downstairs and start stocking up.'

Danny set about hauling up crates of beer, cider and stout and slotting the bottles into place under the counter. In the cellar, he stacked full crates nearer the stairs to make room for new stock, and piled crates containing returned empties under the trapdoor to the street above, ready for collection.

When he finally emerged, Ron pointed to the broom, mop and bucket.

'Get the floor swept and swabbed while we're quiet.'

Danny had decided that cheerful acceptance was his best response to Ron's hostility, born, he believed, of resentment at Mr Braden hiring grammar-school boys to work part-time when Ron wanted to take on a full-time apprentice and train him his way. Worse, they were allowed to wear the same brown cotton coat as his.

One evening Mr Braden had taken Danny aside. 'There's a future for you in this trade, lad, and eventually in management, if you've a mind. Let me know if it appeals. Talk to your mother. I'll be happy to see what I can do.'

Mr Braden's interest pleased him, as did the idea of having money to keep up with Dodds and Crockett. But talking to his mother about leaving school? Out of the question.

Ron Brisco was in his late forties. Of slender build and sallow complexion, he had the face of an interrogator below a high forehead bisected by a dark widow's peak. Behind rimless spectacles he could assess, from anywhere in the shop, the number of bottles needed to fill the shelves and how many packets of cigarettes it would take to bring them flush with the shelf edges.

A sotto voce communist, Ron made sure Mr Braden never saw the *Morning Star*, hidden face-down under sandwiches in his lunch box. But he didn't hold back with Danny. 'Grammar schools? Nurturers of class traitors! Once they get their precious GCEs, all they want to do is to join the ranks of the bosses.'

Danny saw some truth in this. Ron's future was bounded by the shop, and a brown coat, yet he clearly had the experience to be a manager. Danny felt a twinge of guilt that having O and A levels, which had nothing to do with the wine trade, could enable him to become a Braden not a Ron.

For now, Ron ensured that this potential manager spent his time hauling crates and stacking shelves. 'You may be Braden's little bum-boy, but with me you'll do the work you should be doing.'

Despite their prickly relationship, Danny loved watching Ron serve customers. Not one for small talk, he would smile at those venturing a word about the weather, politics or Chelsea's last game, and reply, 'Will there be anything else?' He whispered himself through the fulfilment of each order: 'Now, the lady wants twenty Weights and two bottles of Mackeson. Second shelf up for the fags, end bin for the stout. There you are, that will be four shillings and sixpence please, madam.'

This routine worked well unless he was interrupted. Old Louis, who ran the second-hand book shop next door, came in daily for a quarter bottle of Martell and twenty Senior Service. He delighted in remembering something extra while Ron was mid-commentary. This would elicit a snake-like hiss from Ron as he started again, and Louis would wink at Danny.

Ron's peccadillos exasperated Mr Braden but he rarely let it show. Without Ron, the business would struggle, and Mr Braden would have to work much harder – a fact that Ron often imparted to Danny.

An affable fifty-year-old, Mr Braden had a stomach befitting a licensed victualler. When 'on parade', as he called working, he sported a range of suits and silk ties – 'Always done up, Danny, unless you remove your jacket.' Only during stocktaking did he don a brown coat and descend into Ron's domain. Most afternoons, to Mrs Braden's weary disapproval, he nipped out to the local Conservative Club, leaving everything in Ron's capable hands.

At busy times, Danny was allowed to serve behind the counter, another point of friction between Mr Braden and Ron. Danny enjoyed wrapping each bottle in brown paper that was twisted above the neck, lifting cigarette packs in their cellophane wrappers from the racks and, occasionally, opening a glass-fronted box for a cigar in a silver tube. Most satisfying was working the till: a dark beauty, inlaid with swirls of lighter wood. Its ivory keys were laced with tiny cracks and embossed with black symbols. Pressing them down raised pounds-shillings-pence flags in the window at the top, and pulling a knob rang a bell and opened the drawer, whose compartments had curved fronts to make scooping out change easier.

Danny was putting away the mop and bucket when a suited, heavy-set man came in, shod with steel-tipped shoes that resounded on the wooden floor. Before Ron could greet him, he barked a demand for a bottle of Gordon's and half a dozen Schweppes. Repeating the order under his breath, Ron took down the gin, wrapped it, reached for the tonics and placed everything in a carrier bag.

'That'll be—'

Before he could finish, the man grabbed the bag and left, shouting over his shoulder, 'Add it to my account, there's a good chap.'

Ron closed his eyes, curled an invisible rope around his neck and gave it an upward tug. 'There aren't enough lampposts.'

'Lampposts, Ron?'

'A metaphor, lad, for the summary justice of the oppressed

107

working classes. That bastard's been clopping in here like a two-legged horse for months but gives his orders like he's never seen me before.' He noted the sale in the customer accounts ledger, as if it were a list of those the Party would denounce, come the revolution.

'Anyway, what are you hanging about for?' said Ron, thrusting a list into Danny's hand. 'Get that lot to Warwick Square for Lord Armitage-Shanks,' a title with which he ennobled all posh customers, 'and don't expect a tip from the likes of them.'

The order filled at least two boxes. Taken on one trip, they made for high-risk wobbling on the shop's delivery bike, a heavy black beast, ulcerated with rust. Danny set the boxes in the tray over the front wheel and secured them with a rope. Pedalling loaded was hard enough, but there was the ancient saddle to contend with. It reared up like the prow of a Viking longship. Jumping aboard without care could stop a boy maturing and sitting on it risked a pinched arse from the wire frame piercing the worn leather.

Danny kicked away the stand and scooted along till he had enough momentum to swing his leg safely over the saddle. In Warwick Square, he coasted to the kerbside but forgot the old rod brakes had only two positions: on or off. The bike jerked to a stop. The pain inflicted as he passed over the saddle's nose rose through his stomach to take his breath away. As the bike keeled over, he thrust out a leg to save it and the crossbar delivered a second blow. Giddy with pain and close to vomiting, he managed to pull the bike onto its stand and collapsed on the pavement, where he lay, curled up, gasping to concerned passers-by that he'd be 'OK soon.'

He recovered a little and rose on legs like rope to lug the

boxes down to the basement and through the tradesmen's entrance. This branch of the Armitage-Shankses occupied the top floor of a six-storey house, served by a dumb waiter. He pressed the bell. From a smudge of light far up the shaft a woman called down, 'Is thet the orf licence?'

'Yes, madam.'

The flatbed lift sat at the top and, as gravity played no part in the mechanism, hauling down required the same effort as winding up – a daunting prospect in his weakened state. He took the crank handle in both hands and rowed the lift down and swapped sides to wind up the first box.

'OK, wait and I'll orfload', said her ladyship.

Halfway through raising the second box, he stopped for a breather.

'Do get on, I'm rather busy.'

When he finished winding, he sat down to rest.

'I say, delivery boy, are you still down there?'

He got up and shouted into the shaft. 'Yes, madam.'

'There's something for you on the dumb waiter.'

Something? In 'no-tip' Warwick Square? Wait till he told Ron.

He grabbed the handle and, with arms turning to jelly, wound down the lift until his tip came into view. Clearly of top quality and shiny in the dim light, the token of Lady Armitage-Shanks's gratitude was . . . a Granny Smith.

'Hev you got it?'

He didn't answer.

'Hello! Hev you got it?'

He didn't touch the apple.

'Are you down there?'

Yes, he said to himself, I'm down here and you're up there.

Hearing no response, her voice turned shrill. 'Well really!'

Danny reflected on the difference between what he'd been offered and the generous tips he received for less effort from the inhabitants of the Peabody flats. For them, he guessed, giving tips was about knowing that those like them, their own class, appreciated, and often needed, a little extra to augment their wages. But the Armitage-Shankses of the world either didn't know this, or they didn't care. He realised that his understanding of the relationship between rich and poor had been too simple, too accepting.

The ache in his balls had eased a little but he decided to push the bike back to the shop. It was getting dark. Lampposts flickered into life and he smiled at Ron's crazy claim that there weren't enough. But it wasn't crazy to think that something needed to change.

'You took your time,' said Ron. 'What's up? Looks like you've seen a ghost.'

Danny was about to tell him he was right about the Warwick Square people, but Ron pointed to the stairs. 'Time to bring up more stock, now, get to it.'

During his visits to the cellar, Danny cheered himself up by knocking back three Babychams, opened by banging off the tops against a crate edge, as being caught with a bottle-opener downstairs was a sacking offence. He hid the crinkled caps inside an empty cider flagon and popped the little bottles in the empties crate.

At nine p.m., Danny's normal going-home time, Ron surprised him by not insisting on the extra thirty minutes work. 'Don't be late on Monday, or it'll be the last time.'

Danny showed his gratitude by giving Ron what he knew would be an irritating, slightly alcoholic smile.

'Thank you, Ronald.'

Ron's face hardened and Danny left before he could reply. Spirits lifted, Danny decided to meet Nobby and the others up West after all. He ran home to change his clothes.

14

In Wardour Street, Crockett and Dodds were waiting outside La Discotheque. The doorman, in a shiny black dinner jacket, spread his arms in practised welcome. His bowtie, too, was shiny, Danny guessed, from adjusting it after fingering Brylcreemed hair. His switched-on smile bore no relation to his watchful eyes. According to Nobby, this was his mate, Giles.

'Evening lads, coming in?'

They hesitated. 'We're meeting a mate here,' said Dodds, 'Nobby.'

The name meant nothing to Giles. 'Sure he's not inside already?'

'Sure,' said Danny, 'said we'd meet down here.'

They moved aside as Giles welcomed another group of lads, who paid four shillings each and jogged up the steep staircase. At the top, a heavy door opened and treble joined the booming bass to reveal ten seconds of recognisable music.

In the street, crowds of fans were streaming next door to The Flamingo to see Georgie Fame. Giles tried in vain

112

to divert them. 'Evening lads, ladies, great music, cheap drinks, and beautiful people to dance with.'

Danny, Dodds and Crockett drifted down to Leicester Square and killed fifteen minutes in the throng of wide-eyed, uncertain tourists, and Londoners who knew where they were going.

When they returned, Giles said, 'Coming in this time, lads?' The expression on his face added, 'or fucking off?'

'Has Nobby turned up yet?' said Danny.

'Who?' said Giles.

'Nobby, or Alan, he comes here regularly.'

'Never heard of him. Make up your minds, lads, you're in the way.'

'Fuck this,' said Crockett and left.

Half a dozen girls turned up, Saturday-night-ready in short dresses and miniskirts.

'Evening, ladies. Two shillings each, please, some handsome lads up there for you.'

Dodds leaned close to Danny. 'How bad's that? Pay half to get in and still expect you to buy them a drink.'

Danny watched them climb the steep stairs, looking for a flash of underwear. Giles caught his eye. 'They'll soon be snapped up, son. Why wait for this friend of yours?'

At that point, Nobby loped in, wearing his Harrington jacket, even though it was a warm summer's night.

'Where've you been?' said Dodds.

'Sorry, couldn't resist making a few bob selling replays in the arcade. So sweet, like taking candy from a baby. Where's Crockett?'

Crockett jabbed his arse. 'Here. Got bored talking to your good friend Giles.'

Nobby ignored him. 'Evening, Giles.'

113

Giles winced, evidently wearied by punters who considered him a mate.

'Whoever you are, you've been keeping your pals waiting. Four bob each, please.'

Nobby frowned and switched on a hopeless smile, as if this were Giles's little joke. They paid and Nobby led them upstairs.

La Discotheque occupied the whole first floor of a large Victorian house. Through a smoky haze, mirror-ball reflections spattered its black walls. Danny realised he'd been expecting something more sophisticated. In the hot, stuffy dark, suffused with the scent of stale perfume and more adult sweat than he associated with the club dance, he felt more unnerved than excited.

Against one wall, a DJ sat on a tall stool behind two turntables, bookended by large speakers that blasted out 'Little Red Rooster', the one Rolling Stones record Danny hated. A single dull lamp cast no more than a yellow haze over the tiny dance floor, on which four girls danced self-consciously in front of two slender swarthies, who moved like professionals but carefully avoided eye contact with the hostile, non-dancing males who watched them.

'Dagoes,' said Dodds, for whom anyone brilliant at dancing couldn't be British.

Crockett shouted in Danny's ear and pointed, 'How about that then?' Ranged along another wall was a line of mattresses, one already occupied by a snogging couple. He grinned. 'We'd better pull soon or they'll all be occupied.'

'I suppose once you've got a bird horizontal, being a short-arse isn't a problem,' said Dodds.

'I'd sooner be short with a long dick than tall and get asked by a girl if it's in,' said Crockett, and stepped back in case Dodds reacted physically. Dodds tilted his head as if saying 'next time'.

A small bar, backed by a tessellated mirror, stood in one corner. 'Anyone fancy a drink?' said Dodds, looking at each in turn, expecting one of them to offer to pay. Despite his relative wealth, Dodds was unashamedly thrifty, but no one called him by his nickname, 'Scattercash', to his face. Crockett rushed to accept, 'How kind, Dodds, I'll have a light ale, please.'

Danny followed suit. 'Me, too, thanks.'

Nobby shook his head and made for the toilets. Danny and Crockett followed a frowning Dodds to the bar. Above the music they heard him shout, 'What?'

'I've opened them now,' said the barman.

Dodds handed over bottles of Watney's Pale. 'Six bob for three light ales, fuck that!'

Nobby came over.

'You could have mentioned the cost of the beer,' said Dodds.

'Oh yeah, sorry. Anyway, not many people drink here.'

'I wonder why?' said Crockett.

'Because they've got something better, much better.' Nobby opened his hand to reveal half a dozen heart-shaped pills. 'This is what you want, far better than booze – and no hangover.'

'No thanks,' said Dodds. 'I want another beer but not here.'

'Let's go,' said Crockett, 'bastards could show the cavalry how to charge.'

'OK, but if you want to really blow your mind tonight, you should try these,' said Nobby.

'Blow my mind? Get you,' said Crockett.

'Please yourself,' said Nobby.

At the bottom of the stairs, Giles said, 'Leaving so soon, lads?'

'Back later,' said Dodds.

With a pen that had a ball on the end like a roll-on deodorant, Giles drew a circle on the back of their hands that would be luminous under ultra-violet light and permit re-entry.

In a nearby pub, Danny and Crockett gave Dodds their money. He fetched light-and-bitters to the alcove, in which Danny hid his under-age face and Crockett his under-age height. Danny gulped his beer and looked forward to a time when he could relax and enjoy a pint slowly.

After a second pint, Crockett said, 'Right, mattress time!'

'Hello lads, four bob each, please,' said Giles, showing not a trace of recognition after only half an hour.

'We've already paid,' said Dodds.

Giles smiled as they shoved their hands under the bulb.

'OK lads, up you go.'

For twenty minutes, they stood near the dance floor, pretending to ignore the girls. Crockett got tired of waiting and grooved in among them. Unusually, his wild presence didn't bother them. No giggles, no back-turned rejection, only a starey, gum-chewing determination to keep dancing. Only Crockett had a smile on his face. He gave his friends the come-on-in-the-water's-lovely shimmy, and showed them what they were missing with occasional lewd thrusts behind the girls' bums.

Nobby returned. 'You two ever going to dance?'

'Get you, Gene Kelly,' said Dodds.

Nobby, who never danced, began swaying on the spot. While Danny and Dodds exchanged smirks, he stepped on to the dance floor, where Crockett put an arm around his shoulder and, together, they slid clumsily towards the girls.

The DJ announced an interval before the live group came on. The floor emptied and another couple got down on a mattress.

Nobby and Crockett came over, still jiving about although the music had stopped. 'Enjoying yourselves, chaps?' said Nobby.

'What's got into you? said Danny.

'What do you mean?'

'The dancing, you, dancing!'

'Oh that. Just expressing myself to the music.'

Crockett had had enough. '"Expressing yourself" and, what was it earlier, "blowing your mind"? When did you start talking this kind of shit?'

Nobby ignored him and came closer. 'Want to try some dubes?'

'Dubes?' said Danny.

'Purple hearts, blues, the pills I showed you. They make dancing, everything easier. Give you stamina too; the club's open all night, you know. Why not give 'em a try? Or are you two going to stand here for hours watching other blokes get the birds?'

'No thanks,' said Crockett. 'Why would I need them, unless they also make you grow.'

'Anyway, I've no money left. I'm already walking home,' said Danny.

'I can give you a few. Free, an introductory offer.'

Dodds and Danny looked at each other and the desperation of wallflowers kicked in.

'What do you reckon?' said Dodds.

Danny caught the eye of a blonde girl in a short white

dress. When she smiled, he turned to Nobby and put out his hand. 'Sod it, why not.'

'Not here! Let's go to the bog,' said Nobby.

Inside the cramped Gents, Nobby stood back from the urinals and tipped eight purple hearts into his hand from a small brown envelope. Danny grew nervous at this transaction going on in front of others coming in for a piss. But they either didn't notice or considered it normal.

'Four each, should do it. I take more, of course, but you'd better see how you go.'

'Of course,' said Dodds, who palmed them into his mouth and swallowed. Danny took his to the sink and knocked them back with a cupped handful of water.

Two men in their twenties came in and went into a cubicle together.

Dodds winked at Danny. 'Shirt-lifters.'

'No,' whispered Nobby. 'Serious syringe stuff goes on in there. One shot is better than ten dubes.'

'What, needles?' said Dodds.

Nobby flinched and pushed them towards the door. 'Not so loud, they could turn nasty.'

The group started playing and a spotlight highlighted a long-haired singer who sang with the microphone halfway down his throat.

Crockett was dancing again, eyes half-closed, as if in his own world but checking everything, including the two ace dancers who exchanged mocking glances about him. On his next pass, Crockett tripped one of them and pretended to wake up to apologise.

It looked like a fight might start. When it didn't, Dodds looked disappointed and turned to Danny. 'Fucked if I'd actually pay for these pills. With a couple more pints, we'd be feeling great by now.'

Danny agreed. But soon a persistent pressure grew in his head and with it came an impulse to move. Dodds, too, looked edgy, and shifted clumsily on the spot in time with the music while under their feet, the floor vibrated on straining Victorian joists.

Nobby came over, with a satisfied smile. 'All right? How are you feeling?'

They shrugged, unsure of what was happening except that it wasn't the boosting, laughing change that came with alcohol. For Danny it became a driving excitement that picked up the music more acutely and needed movement to deal with it.

Nobby gave them a stick of Wrigley's. 'Stops your mouth getting dry.' The girl in the white dress danced close to Danny and gave him the beginning of a smile, as if her face were too cold to complete it. She chewed gum, too, and stared out of large dark eyes beneath a fringe of blonde hair. Her name was Jackie. She came from Richmond but was staying in Chelsea with her cousin. He asked her to dance and she responded by simply swivelling into his arms. They danced hip-to-hip for half an hour and, still moving, started kissing. They stopped when the band handed back to the DJ.

They were standing by a mattress from which a couple were getting up. They shared a moment's embarrassment until Jackie shrugged and let Danny help her down between other couples who were in varying stages of writhe. From a sitting position, they began to slide down and Jackie struggled against her short dress getting shorter. Instead of finding this exciting, he shared her embarrassment and realised that the last thing he wanted would be to imitate the uninhibited actions under way on either side of them. He settled for hugging her closely enough for them to feel their heartbeats racing each other. Jackie closed her eyes. Had the reason for her getting down on the mattress been to rest? He pillowed her head with his arm and watched the crush of dancers shuffling around. Only a few were trying to match the beat.

Dodds and Crockett had found dance partners and circled regularly to signal to Danny the now pointless, 'Go on, my son.' Dodds's girl was draped around his neck like a satchel and looked more than ready for the mattress.

La Discotheque, he decided, might be somewhere to go to meet girls but not, in a million years, a place to take a girl. At about two a.m., Jackie's cousin kneeled to wake her and say it was time to go. Jackie sat up, half asleep, but more than ready. Danny went to prop himself on an elbow but fell back as his arm had gone to sleep. He struggled to his feet as his useless limb came back to life in agonising pins and needles. On his way to the exit with Jackie, Crockett came alongside. 'You off now? How's it looking?'

Danny shook his head. 'Back in a minute.'

At the bottom of the stairs, Jackie kissed him. 'See you again?'

He wondered if she meant it. 'Next week?' he said, and wondered if he meant it.

She waved as she left but didn't smile. She hadn't smiled all night. Neither had he.

Back upstairs, Dodds was moving around on the edge of the dance floor on his own but his girl was now dancing to '24 Hours from Tulsa' with one of the slick movers.

'What happened?' said Danny. Dodds ignored him, nodded towards his ex-partner and began revving up. When the girl stopped dancing and started kissing, Dodds released his brakes. Danny jumped in front of him, took hold of his arms and gave him the usual: it's not worth it; there are other birds here, don't spoil everything, blah.

Someone dug Danny in the back. He whirled around, thinking the fight was starting. It was Crockett. 'No go with the blonde bird then?'

'No.'

'I could be on for it here.' He pointed towards the 'Ladies' toilets where a Crockett-sized girl gave a little wave.

He looked past Danny at Dodds's expression and twigged straight away.

'Who's in the firing line?'

Danny nodded towards the girl and her dancing smoothie. 'I think she only came on to Dodds to make that bloke jealous.'

'That must have worked a treat, seeing how Dodds is such an ace dancer.' Crockett's grin showed no trace of pill-induced paralysis.

'Time to get him out of here,' said Danny.

'OK,' said Crockett. 'I'm with the mate of the girl who's dumped him. I don't want Dodds spoiling my once-in-a-blue-moon chance of a shag.'

They coaxed Dodds from the dance floor. He let them steer him to the door but didn't unclench his fists.

'So, you're staying, Croc?' said Danny.

'I should coco. You two need to go and get some beauty sleep, you look like shit.'

As Danny told him to piss off, his jaw clicked and began to ache.

Crockett said cheerio with a thumbs up and his hallmark hip-thrust to hint at what was to come.

At the front door, Giles said, 'Cheerio lads. And you, baby-face,' he said to Danny, 'look out for the boys in blue, they're being difficult tonight.'

Giles must have seen the irritation on Danny's face but, with what sounded like genuine concern, added, 'Just be careful, kid.'

15

Danny and Dodds turned into Coventry Street, aiming for the Mall and their route home across St James's Park. From a doorway, a policeman, accompanied by a female officer, stepped in front of them.

The policeman took a firm hold of Dodds and the WPC grabbed Danny's wrist. 'Out late, boys,' she said.

They nodded.

'How old are you?' she asked Danny

'Sevent . . . seventee . . .'

'Pardon?'

His mouth had stopped working.

'Have you been drinking or taking stuff?'

Realising the risk of trying to speak, Danny shook his head.

'You look young for seventeen. Do you have anything on you to prove your age?' Another headshake but it wasn't enough. 'Let's try again. What's your name?'

He had to force his chin down to say Danny and couldn't get past the B in Byrne.

Dodds, eyes what-the-fuck-wide, finished for him, 'It's Byrne, Danny Byrne, and he *is* seventeen.'

Ignoring Dodds, she said, 'Well, Danny Byrne, I don't believe you and I don't think you're old enough to be out all night.'

They turned to Dodds. 'And you, who are you?'

'Dodds.' Her eyebrows rose. 'Stephen Dodds,' he added.

'Age?'

'Seventeen.'

They believed him. 'And where've you been?'

'Just to a club.'

'The Discotheque?'

Dodds gave a 'maybe' shrug.

'Taking pills?'

He shook his head.

'Been chewing gum, too?'

'Since when was Wrigley's illegal?' said Dodds.

'Purple hearts speed things up: heart rate, speech – and chewing, which can lead to a kind of lockjaw. It's why Danny, here, is so eloquent. Are your pupils normally as big as dinner plates?'

'What do you mean?' said Dodds.

'Purple hearts blow them up. I can't tell the colour of your eyes.'

Danny and Dodds looked at each other. She was right.

The policeman tired of his colleague's informative approach. 'OK, you can go.' They both turned to leave but the policewoman held on to Danny. 'Not you, junior.'

'Shall I come with him, then?' said Dodds.

'No,' she said, 'You get home and think twice about going to dumps like the Discotheque again.'

'OK,' said Dodds. 'See you later, Danny. Want me to tell your mum?'

The last thing on earth Danny wanted him to do.

Danny shook his head and they led him to a waiting Black Maria. Inside, he joined two girls and three boys: drugged up, white-faced and silent. How different to the shouting, complaining drunks he'd seen being forced into police vans outside the Tap House.

At Savile Row Police Station, the duty sergeant was either seven feet tall or standing on a raised floor behind the desk.

'Name?' The policewoman answered for Danny. A look from the sergeant told her not to do it again.

'Age?'

Danny's aching jaw had loosened. 'Sixteen, nearly seventeen.'

The policewoman smiled. The desk sergeant loomed over him and took more details. 'Right, you'll be held till we can contact your parents about coming to get you.'

'When?' said Danny.

'The morning. You can't be on the street through the night and we don't want to be waking your parents at this time on a Sunday, do we?'

'There's only my mum. Can you call her early, please? She'll be frantic when she gets up and sees I'm not home.'

'We'll see, lad.'

On his own in the cell, he lay on an oblong of solid foam inside a plastic cover that showed the dried swirls of a disinfected cloth with which it had been wiped. And from the floor, the familiar smell of Jeyes Fluid didn't quite conceal the sour aroma of vomit. He couldn't sleep, thanks to the high-pitched whine in his ears from the loud music, and the shouts and complaints in the corridor as other miscreants were shown unwillingly to their cells. When the shrill noise in his ears died to a hum, his mind became a tumble dryer in which his mother's angry face spun round with those of Jackie, Giles and the desk sergeant.

It had been different the only other time he had been inside a police station. He had been pleased with himself as he stood at the desk with a wallet that he'd found in a phone box. The desk sergeant had taken his details and told him he could go. Danny had waited for a 'well done' that didn't come. The sergeant noticed. 'Look, you did the right thing, son, but it's what you should have done. What's the alternative, keeping it? Praise is for praiseworthy, not for doing what should be done.'

He had felt as ashamed as he would have done if he'd kept the wallet. The rebuke had taught him that expecting praise can lead to disappointment, that coppers can be bastards and that you can be made to feel bad about doing something decent.

At nine a.m., after barely an hour of troubled sleep, a different policeman was holding open the door. 'Wakey wakey, someone here to see you.'

His mother stood at the desk, her face a mix of anger and worry. She looked him up and down, took his face in her hands, turned his head left and right to satisfy herself he was OK.

'I'm all right, Mum.'

She relaxed but her face stayed severe.

The same desk sergeant leaned forward on his elbows. 'I've told your mother why you're here, lad, and why, at your age, you mustn't be out overnight in the West End. You've no idea how dangerous it can be for a young man like you. Now, your mother has told me you're doing well at grammar school.'

Of course she did.

'Well, I hope you keep it up. It's easy to take a wrong turn, lad, but it can be hard to get back on the right road.' Then this imagined route of Danny's life turned downhill. 'There are many slippery slopes, and the kind of muck they take in the dive you were in last night makes them more slippery.'

Danny was tempted to tell him it was upstairs, and therefore not a dive, but decided not to when it became clear that things weren't going to be too serious: no more, he hoped, than an avuncular, long-winded lecture. Danny switched off during the Dixon-of-Dock-Green drone, until a change of tone got his attention. 'Daniel Byrne, this is an official warning. Get caught again in similar circumstances and it will be the magistrates for you.'

His mother flinched. He wanted to put his arm around her, to promise it wouldn't happen again, but not in front of the sergeant.

'Do you understand, lad?'

His mother answered for him. 'Yes, he understands, don't you, Danny?'

The sergeant leaned over Danny. 'Do you?'

'Yes. But I didn't know it was against the law . . .'

'Ignorance of the law is no excuse. I hope never to see you in here again. Now, go home with your mother.'

Danny seethed at the small-boy dismissal, made worse by his mother grabbing his arm to lead him out of the station. On the way out, he thought of the night before: the exhilarating energy, the music, the dancing, and Jackie. Maybe the fatigue, the ringing in his ears and the morning's embarrassment were worth it?

At the bus stop in Trafalgar Square, his mother followed the time-honoured parental practice of seeking out those who were really to blame for their son's predicament.

'Who were you with?'

'Dodds, Crockett.' He hesitated. 'Oh, and Nobby.'

'Nobby, who's now working for that no-good George? I might have guessed. Where were they when you were arrested?'

'I don't know.'

He resisted the chance to offload blame, less to avoid dropping Nobby in it than, at the great age of sixteen, to avoid being the misled innocent.

'It wasn't Nobby, we all wanted to go.'

She ignored him. 'I could've died when the police called.' She took a deep breath. 'I thought they had the wrong Danny, till I checked your bloody room.'

Her first 'bloody'. Now the anger would roll.

'The police, for Christ's sake! Coming to our door, like they do for the bloody ne'er-do-wells on the estate. Tell me, in this dive where they take drugs, did you take any? Did Nobby?'

'No, I didn't . . . we didn't.'

'Look at me. Did you?'

'No, we drank beer.'

'After last week I thought you might have learned your lesson.' She looked at him more closely and took his chin between thumb and forefinger. 'You look strange, not with it.'

'I'm tired, Mum.'

'I'm not surprised.'

He was looking forward to sleep when he remembered his date with Linda that afternoon. He let out an involuntary groan.

'Are you OK?' said his mother.

'Just remembered, I'm going to the pictures this afternoon.'

'So?' She smiled. 'Oh, I see! Nice girl?'

'For God's sake, Mum.' The arrival of the 24 bus saved him from having to answer. They sat opposite each other on the bench seats. Danny massaged his jaw and avoided looking at her. When she first caught his eye, he got a deep squint of disapproval. The next time he looked, she stuck out her tongue! His head dropped with embarrassment. Then she did it again, this time with crossed eyes. He smiled but the pills wouldn't release him into laughter. She began flicking her eyes left and right at their fellow passengers until she lost control and began laughing herself. The man sitting next to Danny started chuckling. Embarrassed, Danny got up and went to ride on the back platform.

At the stop outside the Army and Navy Stores, he held out a hand to help his mother off the bus. She ignored it. On their way home, he was grateful for her silence. Although, every now and then, she gave him a reproving shove, but there was, too, a barely suppressed smile. Finally, she said, 'Danny Byrne, petty criminal! My Danny, a bit of a crook! Oh, and he's got a girlfriend!'

She said no more till they turned into their block, when she put her arm around his waist. 'Ready for a Sunday fry-up?'

16

After breakfast, Danny got into bed and set the alarm for two o'clock. After a couple of hours of fitful sleep, he had a bath and shaved off any visible facial hair and noticed with relief that his pupils had shrunk to normal size.

'A bath, eh? Must be someone special,' said his mother. 'Anyone I know?'

He shrugged.

'I'll find out anyway,' she said. She would. Anyway, he didn't mind her knowing that he had a girlfriend, at last.

'It's that Linda Bain. You know, the one who hasn't lived here for long.'

She smiled. 'Oh, that Linda Bain, not one of the others!'

'We're going to the pictures.'

'Oh, where?'

'Sorry, Mum, no more information.'

'She looks a nice girl, always well dressed, holding down a job too.'

Yes, he thought, I'm a schoolboy going out with a girl who works. This may have bothered Danny but not his mother. Nothing could shake her conviction that he should stay at school. Whenever the subject of leaving came up, her stock answer was, 'Everyone goes to work eventually, but not everyone gets a good education.'

'Her mother seems a bit stuck-up but Linda doesn't. She's a pretty one, too. I hope you're being nice to her.'

'Nice?' said Danny.

'Treating her with respect.'

'Why wouldn't I?'

'Well, you're a teenage boy for a start.'

'Mum, for God's sake!'

'And if she's a nice girl, a girl for you, it's worth . . .'

'Worth what, Mum?'

She hesitated. 'Worth being kind . . . not pushing things, waiting.'

He had her on the run. 'Waiting for what?'

'And you can take that smile off your face, you know bloody well what for.'

'Mum, it's the first time I've been out with her.'

'I know but . . .'

'What?'

'You know what! Having sex too soon can ruin a girl's life.' She looked him in the eye. 'And a boy's, for that matter.'

'Really?'

'Really.'

'Like who?'

'Like some on our estate . . .'

'Oh.'

'Now, your father and me . . .'

'Mum, enough!'

She shook her head, as if acknowledging she'd said too much. 'We waited.'

'I know, till you were married.'

She closed her eyes. 'Not exactly . . . till we both knew absolutely that we loved each other.'

His mother had had sex before marriage.

'Blimey, Mum.'

'Well, I guess you're old enough to know how it was.'

Heat rose into his face. 'Maybe, but please, you don't need to . . .!'

As he moved past her into the hall, she took his hand. 'Danny, I'm trying to say it's better if love comes first. I hope you'll always behave well, like a gentleman.'

'Mum, I haven't been out with her yet!'

'It's never too soon to know how to be decent with girls.'

'I really do have to go now.' He moved towards the front door. She kept hold of his hand. 'Got it, Mum, see you later.'

He squeezed her fingers and pulled away.

17

Outside Linda's flat, Danny reached for the knocker framing the letterbox but, just in time, saw the white bell in its shiny chrome casing. The bing-bong announced him like an Avon Lady. Behind the door's frosted glass panels, one figure approached down the hall and another emerged from the right. They collided. A clumsy dance and a hissing exchange followed until the figure from the right retreated. The one who had prevailed opened the door.

Shirley Bain wore a beige twinset and a tight skirt that she was palming down the sides of her thighs. Beneath her immaculate perm, bright, dark eyes that she'd passed on to Linda scanned him from top to toe

'You must be Daniel Byrne, how nice to see you on your feet this time.'

'Hello, Mrs Bain.'

'You don't mind if I call you Daniel, do you?'

'Not at all, Mrs Bain.'

'I think that a "y" on the end of a young man's name sounds, well, childish, don't you?'

Did he? She was giving him the chance to gain approval by agreeing but he recalled her sour face looking down at him in Jones's and chose not to. 'My mother calls me Danny.'

'All young men are boys to their mothers.' Her last word on the matter. 'And you look so grown-up, Daniel. I suppose you must be six feet tall.'

He liked people referring to his height, but Mrs Bain had made it sound like he should be taller.

As they passed the closed bathroom door, she said, 'Linda's making herself pretty for you. Not that I think she needs to.'

Because Linda was already pretty enough? Or, more likely, that she didn't need to for the likes of him?

'Come into the living room.' Not the front room, as his mother and he inaccurately called theirs; on the estate, 'front' rooms were in the back. 'Albert, here's Daniel Byrne. He's come to take Linda to the cinema.'

Mr Bain stood up and put down his *Sunday Express*. In shirtsleeves, he wore corduroy trousers with braces. In his slippers he stood only slightly taller than his wife; enough, physically at least, to hold his own with her. His thick, dark hair – his contribution to Linda's beauty – was greying at the temples, but the five o'clock stubble on his tanned face was Desperate-Dan dark.

'I know, love, Linda told me about him. I'm Albert, pleased to meet you, Danny.' He proffered a hand, which surprised Danny, as most men did not do this with boys; with this gesture Mr Bain joined Liam and Ernest in a small, admired club. Danny shook it.

Mrs Bain's face stiffened at her husband's lapse into Christian-name terms.

'What is it you're going to see, lad?' said Mr Bain.

'*Moll Flanders*.'

'Bit racy, isn't it?'

'It's what I said to Linda,' said Mrs Bain, 'and I think you'll find that its correct title is, *The Amorous Adventures of Moll Flanders*.'

Mr Bain caught Danny's eye but he didn't give the wink Danny sensed was coming.

'Oh well, they're sixteen now, aren't they?'

'I'm not sure it's the kind of film I'd want to watch at any age,' said Mrs Bain. 'Isn't there anything else on?'

'There's only a foreign film at the Cameo,' said Danny.

Silence. A foreign film, subtitles, sex.

Mr Bain barely concealed another smile. 'Well, I think that settles it, Shirley, don't you?'

Linda came into the room. 'Settles what, Dad?

'Oh, nothing, love. My, don't you look a picture.'

She did. Skinny white polo-neck top, short black mohair skirt and white tights; cream lipstick contrasting seductively with dark eyeliner.

'Shall we go then?' said Linda, but her mother wasn't going to miss a chance to cross-examine.

'I hear you've passed several O levels, Daniel. Congratulations.'

He thought of telling her how many but felt her reply might be 'only eight?'

'Thank you, Mrs Bain.'

'So, what are you going to do with them?' she said, as if they were something he needed to spend or put in a bank.

'It means I can stay on for A levels.'

'You won't be looking for a job then?'

'Mum!' said Linda. 'We need to go.'

'I don't think so, Mrs Bain,' said Danny.

Why hadn't he said 'no, Mrs Bain' instead of 'I don't

think so?' Why sandpaper off the edges of answers to avoid giving offence? Because, he reasoned, he'd been trying to be a 'nice young man'. Yet he regretted a missed opportunity to have appeared sure of himself. He guessed that, if asked, Linda would simply have said 'no'.

He'd noticed that flabby responses encouraged the likes of Mrs Bain to be even more forthright.

'Those who leave with good qualifications at sixteen can get miles ahead of those who join companies later with their A levels.' She made them sound like hoity-toity affectations.

Time to be less accommodating. 'And if I do well, I'll go on to university.'

Satisfaction at seeing Mrs Bain's frown faded when he saw disappointment on her daughter's face. 'Maybe,' he added.

'What? For another three years?' said Mrs Bain.
'And why not, if the lad's bright enough?' said Mr Bain. 'I think it's good for a young man to get into a sound job as soon as he can, to wear a collar and tie. Isn't that so, Albert?'

Mr Bain was one of the few men on the estate who went to work in a suit, collar and tie.

'Depends, love. Main thing is to choose what he wants. Wish I'd had the choice – and the brains.'

This time Danny got the wink. He liked this man from the Pru who, because he couldn't work in his local area, wore his suit and tie when collecting door-to-door in Fulham. Danny imagined Mr Bain dealing affably with all kinds of people, including those who hid behind the door when short of money.

Danny recalled another insurance man whom he and Crockett had found unconscious but breathing on the stairs in Crockett's block.

'Ambulance,' said Crockett, and started loosening the man's tie. Impressed, Danny accepted the instruction and rushed down to Jones's to call 999. When he returned, the man was still unconscious and Crockett was writing something in his collection book. He put it back inside the man's jacket and returned the biro to the front pocket.

'What are you doing?'

Crockett gave a sheepish grin. 'We're a couple of weeks overdue.'

He had deployed his artistic skills to imitate the man's squiggle indicating 'paid' on the line for his family's payments. The stricken man's leather money pouch, attached by a strap around his neck, lay on the step beside him.

Danny looked at Crockett. 'You didn't?'

'Of course not. What do you take me for?'

They heard later that the man had died. Crockett and Danny were thanked by the insurance company for trying to help. And Crockett's parents were, for a time, back in the black.

Linda made for the hall. 'Come on, Danny. Mum, he's here to take me to the pictures, not to get careers advice.'

Her mother followed her. 'Now, have you got your key?' She glanced over Linda's shoulder at Danny. 'Not that we won't be up. Oh, and an umbrella, Linda, it's going to rain.'

While Mrs Bain searched in the hall cupboard, Mr Bain came into the hall and shook Danny's hand again, this time with a tighter grip. In a lowered voice, he said, 'Enjoy the film, Danny. But do remember, won't you, that it's my Linda you're with, not Moll Flanders.'

'Of course,' said Danny.

They walked across the courtyard without touching. Danny hadn't heard the door close after them and assumed that Mrs Bain would be watching from her balcony.

Linda waited till they turned into the street before speaking. 'Sorry about my parents.'

'They were nice. I liked your dad.'

She gave him a sharp look. 'I like them equally. Everyone prefers Dad because he's easy-going, because he doesn't think about being a dad too much, but more about being a man. Mum thinks mostly about being a mum and that makes it harder for her to be nice all the time.'

Danny guessed that he wasn't the first to be chastened in this way. 'Look, your mum, I didn't mean . . .'

'I know, but she's like that because she wants everything to be better than it is now. Anyway, she thinks you're a bit of all right.'

'Really?'

'Yes.'

'She didn't give me that impression.'

'It's her way. I'd told her you were brainy but she was surprised you were handsome, too.'

So, Linda hadn't told her that bit.

'How do you know?'

'Because I know my mum. Anyway, you *are* handsome.'

In the glowing seconds that followed, and for the first time since it had mattered to him, Danny believed he could be good-looking.

She linked her arm through his. 'Do you really not want to leave and get a job?'

'Why do you ask?'

With a softening pre-emptive smile, she said, 'I hope it's not because you'd miss being known as the clever one on the estate.'

He would, a bit.

'No, not at all.'

She squeezed his arm and briefly put her head against his shoulder. 'OK. You don't mind me asking?'

Yes.

'No, but I'm surprised you think I would.'

'I would if I were you,' she said. She stopped to kiss him on the cheek and he remembered he was out with a proper girlfriend. He looked about him, hoping they'd be seen together.

'I'm a bit like my mum, though.'

Not too much, he hoped.

'Really?'

'She's a bit of a snob but being one keeps her at it. You know, trying to better herself, have more. She does overdo the collar-and-tie bit though. It's not as if Dad works in an office.'

'But does it make your mum happy?' Mrs Bain hadn't given the impression of being a happy soul, but he knew that this had sounded pompous.

With the beginning of a glare, Linda said, 'She's as happy as anyone else. Why do you ask?'

'I don't know, people say that money, things, aren't what make you happy.'

'Really?' she said. 'Don't see why not. More money would get me out of this estate sooner rather than later. Wouldn't you be happy to get away as soon as possible?'

He was in no rush to leave. 'Yes, I suppose, one day,' he said, 'but look, if someone told you that you could have either a thousand pounds or happiness, what would you choose?'

Linda didn't pause to think. 'The thousand pounds. If you're not happy, it's your own fault.'

This threw him; he would have chosen the pious answer.

All he could do was shrug and smile; getting to know the spiky, beautiful Linda Bain was going to be tricky.

It started to rain. Linda put up the umbrella, wisely pressed on her by a mother who wanted things to be better.

18

In the foyer of the New Victoria cinema, Danny and Linda shuffled forward in the queue, exchanging smiles but no words, as if their date wouldn't start properly until he had bought the tickets. He fingered the pound note in his pocket. He had enough silver but using a note would be more impressive. At the booth, he bought the most expensive seats, in the royal circle. He checked if Linda had noticed but she had stepped aside to leave it to him. Because she had no intention of paying? Or to ease his embarrassment should he buy cheaper seats?

He groaned at the arrival of the usual speculations on the impact of his words and actions, and feared he'd become tongue-tied in the company of a girl free of such constraints. As they entered the dark auditorium, Linda took his arm and he relaxed – until it came to deciding where to sit.

The usherette didn't lead them to seats but sent a guiding ball of torchlight down the stepped aisle. The back row came too soon. He hesitated. Presumptuous on a first date? Crass even? Wouldn't a 'gentleman' avoid the snogging seats?

He stepped down beside the next row, hoping Linda hadn't sensed his dilemma. 'How about here?'

His heart sank when she glanced at the seats behind. A man on the end of the second row stood to let them in. Danny turned to Linda for a steer but her shrug signalled, 'up to you'.

'Well?' said the man.

Panic rose in Danny's chest. He wanted to say, 'Thank you but we're going to sit back here' but nothing came out after, 'Thank you.' Flustered, he led the way in. Once they were seated, he read into Linda's resigned smile, displeasure at being in the wrong row with a boyfriend showing a lack of ardour. Whatever she thought, he was certain he had blown it, not by choice but by indecision.

'These seats OK?' said Danny.

'They're fine.'

But they weren't the back row and, as if reading his mind, she said, 'Really, they're fine,' which sounded like, 'They'll have to do.'

They settled back to watch a *Look at Life* documentary in which the river police hauled a human dummy out of the water to show how they saved people or, more frequently, retrieved corpses.

A couple sidled along the back row and sat directly behind them. Two hands covered Danny's eyes. 'Guess who?'

Dodds, obviously, but on turning around, he saw Cordelia first. In the raked seats, her knees were at eye level but, unlike Linda, she was wearing slacks, not a miniskirt.

'Fancy seeing you two here,' said Linda, with no hint of a smile.

Cordelia wasn't smiling either. She jogged Dodds. 'Shall we move along a bit?'

'We're all right here, aren't we?' said Dodds. He leaned forward over Danny's shoulder. 'So, *Moll Flanders*, I've heard it's a bit raunchy!'

'Really?' said Danny, hoping a disapproving tone would impress Linda. Her shake of the head would have been fine if it hadn't been accompanied by a smile.

'Yeah, Crockett told me, can't wait,' said Dodds.

He gave Cordelia a hug, as if what happened on the screen might later be imitated in the back row. When Cordelia shoved him away, Danny and Linda decided to find the river police fascinating.

In the break before the main film, the two boys went for ice creams. Danny bought two tubs. So did Dodds but he added a bag of Maltesers. Danny resisted an urge to buy some, too, because it would give Dodds the kind of edge he enjoyed.

Dodds gave him a shove. 'I'll have my eye on you two.'

'Jesus, Dodds, why are you sitting behind us?'

'Would you sooner be sitting where I am?'

Good question.

'Yes.'

Dodds grinned. 'What, next to Cordelia?'

'With Linda, don't be a dick.'

Dodds cocked his head to one side. 'You and Linda getting on OK?'

'What do you mean?'

Dodds gave a leer.

'It's a date, for God's sake, in a cinema, not La Discotheque,' said Danny.

'Still, it's nice and dark. She not keen then?'

Not a question Danny could answer, even if he wanted to.

They made their way back to their respective rows, where Dodds held out his hand to Cordelia. 'Here's your change.'

Danny looked to Linda for at least a collaborative smirk at Dodds's thrift, but she gave a brief smile that was anything but critical and began peeling off the top of her tub.

Moll Flanders proved a film he'd be happy to miss if he was in the back row with an active partner. But Linda seemed to be enjoying it and, as it romped along, Danny forced himself to join her in laughing at scenes that weren't funny. Even the supposedly raunchy bits – Moll losing her clothes or being completely naked, save for a thwarting camera angle – failed to generate sexual excitement strong enough to make it to the last-but-one row of the royal circle.

Danny imagined more would be happening in the row behind but didn't dare turn to look. He stared at the screen, regretting that his only contact with Linda was via touching shoulders. Her hands lay in her lap. Should he reach for them? But they were positioned modestly above what Nobby's mother would call her ha'penny. Rest a hand on her thigh? OK if she were wearing slacks, but not a miniskirt.

Eventually, during a tender on-screen moment, Linda sighed and leaned close. Their temples came together in a gentle friction of hair and bone. He eased her face around for a kiss. She obliged by offering only her cheek and turned back to the film. He decided that putting his arm around her would be less pushy. But as he did, his hand brushed against Cordelia's knee. In the dark, he couldn't tell whether this had annoyed her, but her response was to cross her legs. He pulled back his arm and a disgruntled sigh came from Dodds, for whom crossed legs formed a tougher barrier. He prodded Danny's back. Danny turned around expecting retaliation but, in the low light, Dodds's teeth gleamed in a

144

grin of encouragement as he chopped his hand into the crook of his elbow and raised a lewd fist.

Cordelia looked away in what Danny hoped was disgust. Yet why was she with him? Like everyone who knew Dodds, she was aware how he enjoyed the reactions to his provocative behaviour. Did she really think he'd change for her?

Danny slipped his arm around Linda, carefully this time. No reaction. Disapproval? Or was she waiting for his follow-up move? Which would be what? He gave up guessing and pretended to watch the film, while a familiar feature of his frustrated life stirred in his groin, yet another useless erection.

Once the rustling of the Malteser packet stopped, the sounds from behind changed to those of shifting positions, seat squeaks and sighs from Cordelia – of resistance, or co-operation? Danny risked a quick look and saw her shoving Dodds's hand away from her breast. Undeterred, Dodds tried to kiss her. Before he could see Cordelia's response, Linda's elbow reminded him where his attention should be focused.

To make amends, he tried a kiss on Linda's lips. She tolerated it for a second before pressing a finger on his cheek, as if it were an inkpad in a police station, to direct his gaze at the screen, leaving him with the sickly taste of lipstick, and failure. The film dragged on and he fell to speculating about if and when Linda would dump him.

As the end of Moll's adventures approached, he tried once more for a kiss and Linda surprised him by allowing his other hand to settle on her stomach, but when he lifted it to within a couple of inches of her breasts, she shoved it away and lifted his other arm from her shoulders as if it were a scarf. Dodds snorted.

As Danny spun around to give a V-sign, his hamstring bunched in a ball of pain. Instinctively straightening his leg, he kicked the back of the seat in front and sprang to his feet, trying to catch his breath. The muscle knotted again. He leaned forward to clutch his leg but lightly nutted the head of the woman in front. She shrieked and her husband got up, fist cocked. Danny, in no position to defend himself, waited for the blow.

'All right, Danny?' Dodds had risen to his feet. The husband sat down.

'Sorry,' said Danny and scrambled, stiff-legged along the row, mumbling excuses. He sat on the carpeted aisle and grabbed his toes to stretch out the seized muscle.

The usherette's light darted angrily around him. 'What do you think you're doing?' she whispered.

'Cramp,' he said.

'Cramp or no cramp, you can't stay down here.'

Linda appeared beside her. She put out a hand to him. 'Come on, up you get.'

Standing brought on another stab of pain and, as he bent over to stretch it out, Linda prodded his arse with her little umbrella. 'Come on, you can do that outside.'

He limped up the steps, swinging his stricken leg like Chester in *Gunsmoke*. In the foyer, the pain began to ease.

'Ready to go back in now?' said Linda, more the impatient nurse than girlfriend. Had he missed her asking if he was all right?

'It might happen again. It's called cramp because it gets you in cramped spaces. I'll wait out here,' said Danny.

'No, come in, you'll be OK standing at the back.'

He followed her but, once inside, the usherette hissed, 'You can't stand here.'

146

'I'm having a job standing anywhere,' said Danny.

'Why can't he?' said Linda.

'Because he can't.'

'He's paid for his ticket.'

'He's paid for a seat. This is an aisle.'

The pain was now a dull ache but twitches warned of the spasm's return. Linda kept snatching glances at the screen. He'd had enough of being talked about as if he weren't there and he couldn't care less about Moll Flanders. He turned to go. 'I'll wait outside.'

'You sure?' said Linda.

'Go on, don't let this spoil it for you.'

She returned to her seat.

For the first time, the usherette sounded sympathetic. 'Don't worry, it'll be over soon.'

How true, he thought.

In the foyer, he sat on the floor beside a Coke machine. As he pulled back on his toes, he reflected on the reasons for Linda's transformation from early affection to irritation. His awkwardness when choosing where to sit? The proximity of Dodds and Cordelia? His clumsy attempts at physical affection? Had she really wanted only to watch the film? Whatever the reason, he must have confirmed any doubts she'd had about him since the club dance.

He was still on the floor when she came out.

'Enjoy it?' he said.

'What I saw of it.' The I-don't-mean-it smile that followed was too late.

'Sorry.'

'It doesn't matter.' She leaned down and kissed the top of his head as if he were a child.

Dodds and Cordelia joined them. 'Well, that was quite a

show, Danny!' said Dodds, clearly not referring to the film. His hand fished for Cordelia's but she stepped back. He shrugged and offered it to Danny to pull him to his feet.

'Good film?' said Dodds, looking at each of them in turn, as if needing to be told.

'Yes, what I saw of it,' said Linda. Again, the belated smile couldn't soften what she'd said.

Cordelia offered no opinion but touched Danny on the shoulder. 'Are you OK?'

'He's fine, now,' said Linda.

'Hamstring cramp. Nothing you can do but stretch it out,' said Danny.

'Cramp can be so painful,' said Cordelia.

Linda took Danny's arm. 'Oh, you know, do you?'

Cordelia turned away.

'Look, we're going for a Wimpy, why don't you come too?' said Dodds.

Ignoring Danny's negative headshake, Linda said, 'Why not, it's on the way home.'

In the Wimpy Bar, Danny ushered Linda first into a four-seater booth: what, his mother had told him, a 'gentleman' would do. Dodds dived in ahead of Cordelia to sit opposite Linda and began producing farting noises with the tomato-shaped ketchup holder until a dollop spurted onto the table.

'Please, Stephen, enough!' said Cordelia. As if using his first name would have more impact.

It didn't. While they ate their burgers, Dodds got into his stride by reeling off lewd references to the film's sexy scenes, most of which Danny couldn't remember. Linda responded with mock outrage, leavened with encouraging smiles. At one point, she aimed a flirty cuff close to his head.

Although forced to concede that Dodds could be funny, Danny refused to laugh. So did Cordelia, but she couldn't help the occasional smile. Danny's heart sank further at Linda's fulsome laughter, which made false her claim that she found Danny attractive because he wasn't like Dodds.

Weary and irate at being only part of Dodds's audience, Danny tried to compete. 'There may have been the odd snatch of Moll's tits, but not a single snatch of her snatch.'

Linda's face froze. Cordelia looked away. Dodds's roaring laughter confirmed that he had gone far too far. Face burning, he stood and said to Linda, 'Look, I'd like to go now, ready?'

'But she hasn't finished,' said Dodds.

Danny ignored him. 'Linda?'

Answering Danny but looking at Dodds, she said, 'Yes, coming.'

They walked home in silence. When they reached her doorstep, he started to apologise but she stopped him with a brief kiss on the lips.

'I think you upset Dodds,' she said.

'And you?'

'Not at all.'

'Really?'

He went for a second embrace but she held him at arm's length and gave him an appraising smile, as if the interview had gone quite well but he had fallen a bit short. Was this where she told him it was over?

'See you next weekend?' she said.

'Really?

'Not if you don't want to.'

'Oh, no . . . I mean, yes I'd love to.'

'What would you like to do?'

'Do?'

With a sigh, she hugged her handbag and the umbrella to her chest. 'Yes, *do!*'

An image came into his head of him hanging from her hand over a precipice. He slowed his racing brain and chose. 'Maybe we could go for something to eat? On our own, this time?'

She didn't let go. 'That would be nice.'

'Sunday, then?' he said.

'Give me a call . . . then.' She pecked him on the cheek and put her key in the door, then turned back to him, smiled and went in. On his way home, he agonised over the day's painful episodes, which eased a little when he recalled Linda's beautiful face and her parting smile. But later he wondered whether she had asked him to phone because it would make dumping him easier.

19

Aluminium-coloured clouds lay above the estate like a fire blanket beneath the sun. Danny sat on the bench outside the children's playground. The heat had driven him down from his stuffy flat to seek fresher air but, save for the smell of baked pavement dust, he had found it no different. He was reading the torn-out second half of *Brave New World*, marvelling at 'feelies' and imagining how different it might have been with Linda if they had been available at the cinema during *Moll Flanders*.

'What you doing, Danny?'

Jinx was leaning over him, trying to let go of Crockett's hand.

'How goes?' said Crockett.

'OK, God it's hot.'

Jinx, unhappy at being ignored, closed his eyes and began revolving from the waist, as if being stirred from above.

'Stop that!' said Crockett.

Jinx fell silent, cupped an elbow in one hand and explored his face with the other.

Danny stuffed the half-book in his back pocket. 'No work today, Croc?'

'Yes, but I had to take him to the clinic this morning.'

'Is he OK?'

'He's fine, fine as he'll ever be.' He grabbed the back of Jinx's neck and pulled his head down to his level. 'Now I'm going to leave you here at the playground. OK?'

Jinx nodded several times to encourage his brother to leave and finally broke free to make for the playground.

'Let's go to the playground, Danny.'

'Not now, Jinxy.'

'Please, Danny.'

'I've got to go,' said Crockett. 'See you later, Danny, and don't let him boss you around.'

Jinx toe-scraped to Danny, bright with expectation. 'Coming, Danny?'

'Maybe later, Jinxy.'

'Can we go on the new slide first?'

Danny smiled at Jinx's impressive ability to ignore unwelcome answers to his questions and thought he might try it himself more often.

'Please, please, Danny, please!'

'OK, just for a few minutes.'

It wasn't much of a playground: a roundabout, a rocking horse, a couple of swings and a new slide that stood ten feet high. Jinx made a beeline for it and clambered up the steps. After struggling to get his long legs out from under him, he let go, but enjoyed only four feet of sliding before his feet hit the ground. Disappointed, he scrambled up again. This time, he clutched his knees to his chest to form an imperfect ball before speeding down and off the end. When his curled back thudded on the ground, he cried out but quickly forced an 'I'm OK' grin in case Danny wanted to leave.

He made for the rocking horse, on which he had to tuck his knees up to his chin to get his feet on the running boards. He grabbed the horse's metal ears, but for all his urging it stayed head down, as if feeding, with its arse bobbing in the air.

'Get on the back, Danny, make it work properly!'

Danny obliged and they got the horse rocking while Jinx roared, 'Ride 'em, cowboy!'

Small children ran into the playground but stopped to eye the big boys, while their mothers settled on the bench outside. Danny sensed their disapproval at him being on the kids' rocking horse.

He dismounted. 'Come on, Jinxy, a spin on the roundabout, then I have to go.'

'Go where, Danny?'

'I don't know, somewhere.'

'Great, somewhere!'

Jinx started pushing the roundabout, but its momentum dragged him staggering around it until he tumbled to the ground.

'Just get on, will you!'

'OK. Make me giddy, Danny.'

Jinx lay back and grabbed the bars that divided the top into segments. Danny got the roundabout under way and maintained speed by tugging the handrails as they passed. Jinx squealed as he watched the sky spin.

A minute later, he struggled to raise his head against the centrifugal force. 'Feeling sick, Danny!' Danny stopped the roundabout. Jinx sat up and gave a burp that smelt of cream soda. 'Still spinning, Danny.'

Danny ushered him over to a bench. Jinx closed his eyes and leaned against him. One of the women called over, 'Are you all right, Jinx?'

'He'll be OK in a minute,' said Danny, knowing that if he'd been Crockett she would have asked him.

The woman turned away, unsmiling. Jinx opened his eyes and his face came close, dried saliva around his lips.

'Where we going, Danny?'

'You have to stay around here, Jinxy.'

'But where, Danny, where?'

'We can't go anywhere right now.'

'But you said, you said we'd go "somewhere".'

'Hello Danny, and hello Jinx.' Cordelia stood on the other side of the wire-mesh fence. Under a white cardigan, she wore a yellow cotton frock.

'Hello Cordy!' said Jinx. 'Danny and me are going somewhere.'

'No, we're not, Jinxy.'

She ignored Danny's denial. 'That's nice, Jinxy, where's that then?'

Jinx stood up and turned to her, head down. 'Only Danny calls me Jinxy.'

'Oops, sorry, Jinx.'

She waggled her fingers through the fence and Jinx waved in return.

'Danny, Cordy wants to know where we're going.'

Cordelia's eyes widened and she tilted her head. 'Yes, where, Danny?'

He gave in. 'How about the park?'

Jinx did a Tin-Man lollop over to Cordelia. 'Yes, the park!'

'Which one?' she said, and grabbed the wire mesh, pressing her breasts against it.

154

While thinking he'd like her to press harder, he missed her question. She stepped back as if he had said so out loud. Not for the first time, he'd been looking at breasts, not face, while a girl was speaking.

'I said, which one?'

'Oh, don't know,' said Danny.

'What about St James's? It's not far, and you can feed the ducks.'

'Will you come with us, Cordy?' said Jinx.

Looking at Danny, she said. 'Would you like me to?'

'Oh yes, come with us, Cordy,' said Jinx.

He wanted her to come too but merely shrugged.

She carried on looking at Danny. 'I'd love to.'

'OK, let's go,' said Danny.

As they walked either side of the fence towards the exit, he had a fleeting sense of her as a girlfriend, and when they came together at the gate, he resisted a small impulse to take her hand. At the same time, he remembered the Wimpy Bar and, face burning, he took his chance to mention it.

'Look, about the evening in the Wimpy Bar and what I said. I'm sorry, I don't usually . . .'

'I know you don't,' she said. 'Dodds doesn't bring out the best in people.'

Yes, he had said the wrong thing but it stung that she knew he'd been driven to say it under Dodds's influence.

'Look, let me pop home for some stale bread for the ducks,' she said.

She returned with a few slices in the Lyon's blue-gingham wrapper. She waved them at Jinx. 'Duck food.'

Cordelia reached for Jinx's hand but he hesitated and took Danny's first before holding his hand out to her. They set off as the sun broke through the clouds and the walls of the estate brightened as if floodlit.

The route to the park took them past the Great Smith Street Library, where Liam was coming down the steps. The Jack Russell stayed at the top.

'Good day, Danny Byrne,' said Liam.

He picked up straightaway that Jinx was their special charge. 'And who is this fine young fellow?'

'This is Jinx,' said Danny.

'A fine name. Are yiz off somewhere nice?'

'The park,' said Danny.

'We're going to feed the ducks,' said Jinx, and pointed to the bread in Cordelia's hand.

Liam took a fob watch from a pocket on the front of his overalls. 'Ah, of course, 'tis their dinnertime. Sure, won't they be delighted to see ye.'

'What's your dog's name?' said Jinx.

'Finnegan. Here, boy!'

The dog trotted down the stairs.

'Can I stroke him?' said Jinx.

Liam beckoned him forward. 'Sure, he'd like nothing more.'

Jinx dropped to his knees to pet the willing dog.

Liam smiled at Cordelia and turned to Danny, eyebrows raised.

'Oh, this is Cordelia,' said Danny.

'Ah, Cordelia "too late the beloved".'

She flicked up a hand, child-like, only half sure of her answer. 'That's me.'

Jinx held up his hand too. 'He licked me, he licked me, Danny!'

'Finnegan knows a good fellah when he sees one,' said

Liam, 'and so do ducks – if you don't keep them waiting on their dinner.'

As they left, Liam glanced at Cordelia, then winked at Danny.

Passing through Storey's Gate, a tramp stepped in front of them, face outdoor-burned, eyes struggling to focus. 'D'ya hae a tanner frae a cup o' tea, Jimmy?' When Danny didn't push on past him, he got more polite. 'If ya please, Jimmy.'

'He's not Jimmy, I am,' said Jinx.

The man's head swivelled, uncomprehending, between Jinx and Danny, who took out a sixpence and dropped it into his filthy hand.

The man made a fist around the coin and raised it to his forehead in salute. 'Thanks Jimmy, God bless ya, son.'

Cordelia began to lead Jinx away, but he resisted. 'Why is he calling Danny "Jimmy", Cordy?'

'I think it's a name some Scottish people use for those who are kind.'

'Does that mean I'm kind too?'

'Yes, Jinx, it does.'

Danny savoured a virtuous glow. 'Poor bloke doesn't know what day it is.'

The good feeling didn't last. Why had he done it? Too embarrassed to say no? Not wanting to appear mean? To impress Cordelia? How would he have responded if he'd been with Dodds, or Linda? He wasn't sure, but when he remembered his first impulse had been to reach into his pocket, he felt a little better.

He looked around for Jinx and saw him with the tramp, who shook his head and hurried away. Jinx came back grinning. 'I told him, Danny.'

'What, Jinxy?'

'What day it is. Told him, told him it's Tuesday, Danny.'

'Well done, Jinx,' said Cordelia, exchanging a smile with Danny. It didn't matter that it was Wednesday.

On reaching the lake, Jinx stumbled over the low, hooped fence. Fleeing ducks beat the water with their wings to a safe distance.

'Now you've frightened them. You're not supposed to cross the fence,' said Danny.

'He's all right,' said Cordelia, 'no need to be so law-abiding.'

Fair enough. What harm could Jinx do on the dried mud bank? She'd spoken with a smile and he could see she had not meant to hurt. So why did it hurt? Did she think him a goody-goody, like mates thought him a swot, like Ron thought him an arse-crawler? Until last Saturday night he'd had no run-ins with the law. Law-abiding?

His mother on the low stool by the coal fire.

Big men bending down, touching her shoulder as they speak.

Women with plates of sandwiches, filling glasses with beer from an enamel jug.

So many people in their little home.

Ah, here's Danny, the man of the house now.

Be good for your mummy.

Your daddy would want you to be strong for her.

Where is Daddy?

He's with Jesus, darling.

You've got to look after your mummy.

But Mummy looks after me!

Yes, but be good for her, won't you.

Will it stop her crying?

On his mother's lap, pressing against her red, wet face, he whispers, I'll be good.

Or law-abiding.

He'd never even pinched from Woolworths. He'd been tempted, but wouldn't risk being thought less than the fine young man he wanted to portray. He'd become a passive good guy but envied the more daring, lovable rogues, like Dodds, who some girls, not least Linda, seemed to find attractive. He was dull Tony in *West Side Story*, not exciting Riff.

The ducks returned warily. Jinx held out a whole slice of bread.

'Not like that!' said Danny. He caught Cordelia's smile and relented.

Jinx ignored him anyway and waited calmly as the ducks did their best to pull the slice from his hands. But only as they nuzzled the last bits from his fingers, did he let go – as good a way of feeding ducks as any.

'Can we get any more bread, Danny?'

'No, but we could get an ice cream.'

'Ice cream! Not for ducks!'

Pleased with his joke, Jinx stepped back over the fence.

Lunchtime in the park on a summer's day. Hundreds enjoying the illusion of fresh air, only slightly tainted with a whiff of stale water and duck shit. Older loungers slumped in deck chairs in zigzagging rows and broken circles. Well-equipped picnickers sat on plaid rugs eating off paper plates. Others were on park benches, with tea cloths on their laps, brushing crumbs to waiting sparrows. On the grass, men sunbathed in shirtsleeves and braces, using folded jackets for pillows. Women, propped on straight arms, legs out in front, some with dresses spread like fans, some with them hoiked excitingly high up their thighs to let the sun at their legs. Those in tighter skirts sat side-saddle. One or two lay on their backs with their knees up, inviting a furtive glance. And a pair of lovers stretched out on the grass, the man on his back, the girl lying on top, between his legs, kissing him.

'They look fond of each other, don't they,' said Cordelia. Would Cordelia do that? Would Linda? Would he?

They bought ice-cream cornets and sat on the grass with Jinx between them.

A few yards away, a tramp-like character put down a duffle bag from which he took breadcrumbs in handfuls and held out his arms. Soon sparrows were squabbling on his upturned palms. Jinx got up for a closer look but went too near. The birds flew off. However, instead of complaining, the man invited him forward and eased him into position. He gently pulled one of Jinx's arms straight out, put crumbs in his hand and spoke to him softly as he backed away. A cock sparrow was the first to land, followed by others. In his delight, Jinx swung round to show Danny and Cordelia and launched a feathered squadron into the air. From his other hand, the cornet dropped to the ground. His upset was brief as, once more, the man whispered something to settle him and this time filled both his hands with crumbs. A small crowd stopped to watch the unlikely pair, while a score of birds circled and fed. For once, Jinx was standing perfectly still, grinning, arms outstretched like a lanky St Francis.

Danny and Cordelia finished their ice creams and lay back, propped on elbows, squinting at the sun. She took off her cardigan and, in her sleeveless dress, rolled on her side into the space left by Jinx. Doing the same would bring Danny face to face, and close. He stayed on his back for a minute, then, shielding his eyes to make it look as if the sun had prompted him, he turned to her and laid his head on the inside of his arm. When she mirrored this move, their elbows touched and excitement fizzed in his chest.

'He thinks the world of you,' she said.

'Who?'

Why did he find it so hard to respond graciously to compliments?

'Who do you think?'

'Oh, yes. He's easy enough to please. All you have to do is everything he wants.'

Her smile invited him to say more but he could think of nothing.

'You're kind, Danny Byrne.'

Instead of what would feel like an immodest thank-you, he replied, 'He can be a right royal pain in the arse, you know.'

'But you give him a lot of time.'

'So, you can imagine how big a pain I get,' he said.

The sun went behind a cloud. Their faces were inches apart and while they spoke, he saw only her green eyes and the golden flecks.

'This is nice, isn't it?' she said.

Did she mean the weather? The park? Or being with him?

The sun burst through the clouds and, a second later, its heat reached their faces.

'Yes, it is,' he said, thinking of her but in case she realised this, he added, 'You know, in the middle of the week, when everyone's at work.'

She began opening and closing her eyes. He found this gently mesmerising and felt he could fall asleep if he watched long enough.

On a nearby bandstand, uniformed soldiers struck up their bang-toot-crash music. Cordelia opened her eyes and they shared a smile at the corny sound.

'It's good to get away from the estate,' she said.

'Sure is,' he said, Steve McQueen style.

'Even better to get away for good.'

So, Cordelia, as well as Linda. He had an image of two lovely plants around whose roots the soil was loose, while his remained stuck in home-clay. His mother had often said that, like most sons, he'd be off as soon as he could, whereas daughters tended to stay close. Was he an exception? A mummy's boy?

'Would it?' he said.

'Oh, I'd miss it, of course, and Mum, but I don't want to stay longer than necessary. I'd miss you, too.'

'Would you?'

She gave a little nod.

He closed his eyes.

'Are you tired?' she said.

'Not really, but I like the sun. Don't you think it would be nice to sleep a bit in the afternoon, like they do in Spain?'

'You can sleep if you want to.'

'Not now,' he said, but he kept his eyes closed for a while. When he opened them, her face was closer, revealing how much prettier she had grown, more bone and hollow, freckles either side of her nose. He wanted to tell her this but wasted time thinking of how to say it without sounding like a boyfriend.

'You are kind though, Danny,' she said, as if he'd denied it earlier.

Was he? Kindness was certainly one way of getting people

162

to like him. He was kind, he thought, because being kind works.

'Really?' he said.

'Really. And not only to Jinx. What boy shampoos his mum's hair, let alone admits it?'

He'd had no choice. His mother had mentioned it to Nobby's mum, and Nobby had broadcast it immediately, prompting Dodds to suggest his true vocation could be in the company of poofters.

'I like washing hair.'

'Would you wash mine?'

'Yes, I would.'

'See, that's what you're like.'

She reached for her cardigan and drew it over their heads. In the filtered light, he sensed the beginning of something exciting – and worrying.

'That's better,' she said, so close that, between them, a single daisy quivered in their breath. He pulled back to take in her smile. He squeezed her bare arm, eased her closer and kissed her. Later he wasn't sure whether it was she who kissed him. They didn't repeat it but continued looking and smiling under their cotton canopy that covered whatever was blossoming between them.

He wondered if he should pull her on top of him, like the nearby lovers. But in broad daylight, even with their faces hidden? And then what? And what if she resisted? And what if she didn't?

He thought of Linda but wanted to kiss Cordelia again. He held back, not for Linda's sake but for the confusion spreading in his head.

'Danny!'

Jinx! They sat up. The sparrow man had gone but Jinx

was nearby, slumped low in a deckchair. The park-keeper stood beside him, while Jinx held out a handful of bread-crumbs.

'He frightened the birds away, Danny.'

The attendant replied apologetically, 'It's threepence if he wants to sit there.'

Jinx shook the remaining crumbs onto the grass. The three of them waited as the sparrows finished them off before Danny took Jinx's hand and led him away.

As they passed Cordelia, Danny put out his other hand to help her up. Minutes later Jinx spotted a squirrel and broke away to circle the tree it had climbed. Now that he wasn't holding Jinx's hand, he wondered about holding on to Cordelia's. She squeezed his fingers to help him decide. But they were out from under her cardigan – and there was Linda to think of. He let go.

20

As they neared the estate, a voice behind them said, 'Well, if it isn't the Three Musketeers.'

Linda, in a white blouse, dark jacket and skirt, and black high heels. Hardly summer clothing, but office-smart. Relieved that Jinx was between him and Cordelia, Danny took in Linda's sharp, sparky attraction. 'Yes, Milady.'

The frown was instant.

He realised that she hadn't got the reference. Cordelia, who had, smiled.

Linda glared at her. 'Supposed to be funny?'

Seeing Cordelia taken aback, Danny said, 'Yes, it was.'

Jinx's head drooped. 'Can we go now, Danny?'

Linda's angry glance told Danny what she thought of his intervention and silenced Jinx. She switched back to Cordelia. 'Think I'm a puppet?'

Cordelia shook her head. 'No, Linda. Not *Thunderbirds*, there's a "Milady" in *The Three Musketeers*.'

Linda's hands went to her hips. 'Well, aren't you two the bright little bookworms.'

'Really, we weren't trying to—' said Cordelia.

Linda, eyes shining, said, 'We, eh?'

'Well, yes,' said Danny. '*We* took Jinx to the park and, yes, *we* have both read *The Three Musketeers*. There's no need to—'

'Well, very nice for you,' said Linda.

With no more to say, Danny shrugged. 'Look, we've . . . I mean I've got to get Jinx back.'

'Don't worry,' said Cordelia. 'I'll see him home. Come on, Jinx.'

Jinx stayed put. 'I want to go home with you, Danny.'

Danny held onto Jinx's hand. 'Thanks, Cordelia, he can stay with me.'

'I'll be off then,' said Cordelia. 'Bye, we had a lovely afternoon, didn't we?'

The tension between the two girls became palpable. Sensing that all was not well, Jinx looked to Danny for an answer.

'Bye, Cordelia, yes, it *was* a lovely afternoon,' said Danny.

When Cordelia had left, he said to Linda, 'So, how was work today?'

She started to walk past him. 'Fine.'

'Wait a sec. Look, I'm sorry about the Milady stuff.'

'Oh yes?'

'Yes, are you sorry about the Musketeers stuff?'

'I was only joking.'

'And I wasn't?'

'But you both guessed I hadn't read it.'

He hadn't, but that would have been his guess.

'Anyway, I didn't like her sharing your little joke,' she said.

'What do you expect her to do if she finds something funny?' said Danny.

He wished he'd resisted the chance to be clever. Cordelia's appreciative smile had been no match for Linda's infuriated glare.

'Who said it was funny? It made me look thick.'

It didn't, but was this the time to tell her that – on the contrary – wide-eyed irritation had sharpened her beauty?

'No, it didn't. Look, I'm sorry, sometimes I don't think enough before I say things.'

'I didn't like seeing you two together, with or without Jinx.'

Jinx had stayed mute during the harsh exchanges but, on hearing his name mentioned, tugged on Danny's hand. 'Can we go now, Danny?'

Danny had heard only Linda. 'Really?'

'Well, what do you expect me to think, Danny?'

Her jealousy, if that was what it was, shocked and pleased him. In defensive mode until now, he bit down on a spontaneous reply that would have said, in her place, he wouldn't have been jealous. But he remembered how spontaneity had betrayed him in the Wimpy Bar.

'Well?' said Linda.

'I expect you to think there was nothing in it.'

'OK, let's forget it,' she said, with the calm of someone who would be filing, but not forgetting.

Jinx tugged at him again and they all set off in silence. In the estate, Danny ushered Jinx towards the playground. 'Now play here, Jinxy, till Crockett shows up.'

'I thought you were taking him home,' said Linda.

'No, here is fine. His family know where to find him.'

Jinx hesitated and glanced warily at Linda. 'Danny?'

'Yes, Jinxy.'

'We did have a lovely time, didn't we?'

'Yes, we did, it was great.'

With a shy lift of his head he said, 'Bye Linda.'

Linda's face softened. 'Bye Jinx.'

They walked together into her block. She pressed the button for the lift. 'You're a funny one, Danny Byrne. I don't think you understand what's actually going on when it comes to girls – or maybe you do!' She gave him a peck on the lips, too quick for him to return it. The lift doors opened. 'Anyway, let's see if we can work it out. How about a coffee at the Regency tomorrow? I've got a day off.'

Before he could say yes, she stepped into the lift, 'About eleven o'clock . . . then?'

The 'then' thing was no longer funny, if it ever had been but, although he didn't like the meeting sounding compulsory, he couldn't wait.

'Yes, great.'

She pressed the button for her floor but seconds later the doors reopened.

She cocked her head to one side and smiled. 'Forgot to say, we did have a lovely few minutes, didn't we?'

The doors closed before he could answer.

21

When agreeing to meet at the cafe, Danny had forgotten that Cordelia might be working there. On arrival, he pushed the door ajar to check and was relieved to see someone else behind the counter. He wondered if Ellen Hill was 'unwell' again.

He bought a tea and waited at a table by the door. Linda arrived soon after in black slacks and a sleeveless white polo-neck; tight-ribbed, it accentuated her breasts, which were smaller, more separated than Cordelia's but equally striking.

She sat opposite him. 'Oh, you're having tea. I prefer coffee mid-morning.'

'Would madam like something to go with her coffee?'

She smiled at his retort. 'No, just coffee, thank you.'

Danny returned with the coffee and sat opposite her.

'Is your leg still painful? It seemed OK when you were at the park yesterday.'

'It was only cramp, you know.' His only pain now was one of embarrassment for what happened during their date.

169

But, unlike with Cordelia, he felt no need to apologise for what he'd said in the Wimpy Bar.

Dodds threw open the door and strode past their table without seeing them, but he spotted them as he came away from the counter holding a mug of tea and two door-step bacon sandwiches on a plate.

'Mind if I join you?'

'Yes,' said Danny with the half-serious, half-joking response that was normal banter between the boys. On this occasion, despite his smile, Danny meant it. Dodds wouldn't care either way.

Linda shrugged but didn't look too put out.

Dodds sat beside her. 'Budge up! Don't often see you in here.'

'Day off,' said Linda. 'We have coffee about this time in the office.'

Dodds began wolfing down a sandwich.

'Hungry then?' said Linda, smirking at Danny.

'Busy morning at the market, no time for breakfast,' said Dodds, his mouth a washing-machine churn of bread and bacon. 'So, what are you going to do on your day off?'

'We haven't decided yet,' said Linda.

Danny was pleased to hear the 'we' and hoped Dodds had taken note.

Dodds shrugged and carried on munching. Behind him, Jinx's face appeared at the window, bobbing up and down above the strip of pink gingham curtain. Danny pretended not to see him, but Jinx began banging on the glass with the palm of his hand.

Dodds and Linda turned around.

'It's his mate,' said Dodds.

'He's not my mate,' said Danny.

'What is he then, your ward, like Bruce Wayne's Robin?' On rare days, Dodds's taunts could be almost funny.

Jinx carried on waving. 'Danny! Watcha Danny!'

Danny gave Jinx a not-now shake of his head and didn't look at him. 'It's OK, he'll go soon.'

When Danny looked seconds later, Jinx had left.

Linda reached across and tapped his arm. 'So, what is it that makes you Jinx's favourite?'

'Am I his favourite?'

'Looks like it to me. He wasn't calling out to Dodds, was he? Why do you spend so much time with him?'

'He shares Danny's love of books,' said Dodds, pleased with what he thought was a funny comment.

'Don't be a dick, Dodds,' said Linda. 'What is it about Jinx, Danny?'

'Yeah, what exactly?' said Dodds.

Any mention of his friendship with Jinx, however innocent, brought heat into his face. 'What do you mean?'

Linda leaned forward on her elbows. 'He's basically a little kid. Isn't he?'

'He's not a little kid, it's just that . . . well, he seems fond of me, and I don't like being tough on him.'

'Seems very clingy'

'Clingy?' said Dodds. 'Jinx used to follow him everywhere, drove him mad before the accident; nothing's changed since.'

'I guess he is, a bit,' said Danny.

'Is it because you were with him when he fell?'

It hadn't taken long for someone, probably Dodds, to tell her. 'Perhaps,' he said.

'And you feel bad about it?' said Linda.

He couldn't quite control the force of his reply. 'Why should I feel bad about it?'

Startled, Linda said, 'Look, I didn't mean . . .'

'I know but I really don't remember much more,' he said, wishing he could remember nothing.

'Poor you,' said Linda.

'Poor you,' said Dobbs in a girly voice. Linda gave him a playful, disapproving punch.

'There was nothing I could do,' said Danny, sensing a familiar flash of self-doubt.

'I'm sure, but at least he doesn't know he used to be, you know, normal,' said Linda.

'But he *does*, sort of. He knows his life changed after he fell. What he doesn't get is what he's missing . . . how his life could be.'

She shrugged, as if running out of sympathy. 'Anyway, he enjoys being with you,' she said.

'Best mates,' said Dodds.

Taking her cue from him, Linda smiled and, as if trying to bring the subject to an end, said, 'He should be happy you're so nice to him.'

'You're such a nice boy,' said Dodds.

'Piss off,' said Danny.

'What? I'm agreeing with Linda, he *is* happy, isn't he?'

'Maybe, some of the time.' He caught them exchanging a smile and grew angry. 'Would you be happy that you dribble a lot? That you wet the bed? That picking your nose is a favourite pastime? Happy how long it takes to realise children half your size and age are taking the piss? Happy that people smile at you but won't linger in your company?'

Linda sat back, in wide-eyed silence.

Realising he'd overdone it, he said, 'Sorry, but his life isn't so simple.'

172

Unabashed, Dodds carried on. 'I don't know, Crockett says Jinx cries most mornings but suspects he often puts it on to get attention.'

'Crafty devil,' said Linda.

'How would you wake up in soaked sheets? Laughing?' said Danny.

'All right, Danny, take it easy,' said Dodds.

And who are you, thought Danny, to be looking out for her?

'Why are you so touchy? It's not as if he's family,' said Linda.

Unable to resist his usual jibe, Dodds leaned sideways to jog Linda. 'Could be. He's tall and dark like Danny. Crockett's family are fair-haired midgets. Apparently, back then, women thought Danny's dad was a bit of all-right.'

Danny got to his feet. 'Fuck you, Dodds, can't you change the record?'

Dodds stood too. 'Can't you take a joke?'

'Not when it's the same one, every time.'

He hadn't sworn in front of a girl before. He caught surprise on Linda's face but no sign of her taking offence.

She turned on Dodds, but without irritation. 'For Christ's sake, Dodds, I thought I was the one with a big mouth.'

No longer smiling, Dodds said, 'Why does he spend so much time with a spastic, then?'

'Maybe he's a nicer person than you,' said Linda.

'Or maybe he feels guilty about Jinx falling.'

Danny's heart lurched. He kicked back his chair and clenched his fists.

Linda screamed, 'Stop it!' The cafe fell silent until Jinx put his head inside the door. 'Danny! Come and play with me, Danny!'

'What'll it be this time? Invisible football or Would Ya?' said Dodds.

'Sometimes, Dodds, you can be a right . . .' said Linda.

'What?' said Dodds, grinning, hands up in defence.

Danny moved to the door to see Jinx. Linda followed him. Seeing them together, Jinx moved away and waited.

Linda waved at him and on getting no response, said to Danny, 'Not too sure of me, is he?'

He's not the only one, thought Danny.

She sighed. 'I guess he's the way he is and it's not going to change.'

'Guess not, but he's not so bad to be with, you know. If you could have seen how wonderful and gentle he was when feeding the ducks and sparrows in St James's Park. All I do is give him a bit of time, it's the least I can do.'

'Why, though?' said Linda.

Why?

Go on, show me, Danny.

No.

I'm going to try, Danny.

It's too dangerous, go and play with your mates.

Aren't you my mate?

I'm off. Wait for Crockett if you want to do it.

He won't let me. Show me once more, please.

Jesus, Jinxy. Like this, you look ahead and jump down to the pavement if you lose your balance.

Will you stay and watch me do it?

OK.

Hold me until I start.

Ready?

No, don't let go yet.

Get on with it or I'm going.

174

It's a long way down, Danny.
For God's sake!
OK, here I go.
Go on then!
Not so hard, Danny!
Jump down!
Danny!
Jinxy!

'Danny, what's the matter?'

'Nothing, why?' he said, angry that his feelings must be showing.

'Because . . .' Linda said no more but took his hand.

'It's when I remember him falling,' he said.

'It must have been terrible.'

'I thought he was dead.'

'But he didn't die, and you did what you could, got help.'

'A woman in a pinny heard me screaming for help.'

He didn't tell her that he'd also been screaming, 'It wasn't me!'

'I couldn't help him, didn't dare touch him.'

He cleared his throat. 'Look, I've got to go.'

'Do you have to?'

He pointed to Jinx. 'Yes, there's him for a while and, later, the off-licence.'

'See you soon?'

'That would be nice.'

She touched his arm. 'Instead of going out for a meal, why don't you come around on Sunday for some tea, at about four?'

He wouldn't have much of an appetite; his Sunday dinner didn't start much before three o'clock.

'Are you sure?' He envisaged balancing a cup and saucer

and a plate while her mother scrutinised him. 'I'm not so sure . . . you know, about tea and cake.'

'Who said anything about cake?' With a smile, she added, 'Oh, and my parents won't be there.'

Was he that transparent? 'Really? Where will they be?'

'Does it matter?'

It did for him and, especially, how far away.

'No, but I'd rather not . . .'

'. . . be there when they get back? Don't you like them?'

'No, yes. It's just that they're . . . parents.'

'If you must know they're going to Ripley, in Surrey, for tea with my mum's sister. She has a nice house with those lovely Austrian blinds in the bedroom windows.'

Austrian blinds? He didn't ask in case she started describing them.

'Although it's in a village on the Portsmouth Road, there are country lanes and a little river close by.'

'You sound like an estate agent,' he said.

'What do you mean?'

'Giving details of the place and not the relatives.'

She frowned. 'You say the nicest things to a girl. I was actually trying to reassure a nervous boy that my parents won't be coming back suddenly to frighten him.'

'You say the nicest things to a boy.'

Jinx came closer. 'You coming or not, Danny?'

Having got their attention, he turned shy and swivelled around looking at the ground.

Linda smiled and repeated Jinx's question. 'You coming or not?'

'Yes, please. I'd love to.'

22

Ellen and Cordelia Hill emerged from their block and came towards him. Two blondes in high heels, Cordelia in a loose-fitting white dress and her mother in a tight cream skirt that forced a slightly pigeon-toed walk.

Cordelia put an arm through her mother's and slowed down, but it was Ellen who spoke. 'Hello, Danny.'

She had her hair piled elegantly high, although it was a little less lush in the backcombed bits on top. Make-up emphasised her good looks and, apart from a bit of puffiness under her blues eyes, she was still a bit of a stunner.

Danny thought women looked better with their hair up. It signalled special occasions, when they could wear more make-up, more revealing clothes and perfume. At times of contact with the opposite sex, such as at dances and parties, this enhancement widened the attractiveness gap between male and female – and made approaching girls more daunting. All Danny could do to sharpen up would be to wear smarter clothes and, perhaps, risk splashing on a bit of after-shave – 'perhaps', because he didn't shave that much and, according to Dodds, unnecessary after-shave was perfume. As for the occasional spot, make-up wasn't an option.

Ellen's open-necked blue blouse framed the V between breasts that had pressed against him on the staircase. The camera in his head kept running and, before answering, he took in the swell of Ellen's stomach under her skirt, indicating a soft absence of corsetry, what his mother laughingly called her 'shaper'. Ellen's white sling-backs may have been right for summer but the red nail varnish couldn't disguise ugly toes.

Cordelia's pale yellow shoes were high-heeled, closed and classy. Her blonde hair fell shining to the round neckline of her dress. No cleavage on show, only the invisible push of breasts that brought a catch to his throat.

'I said hello, Danny!' said Ellen, jerking him from his reverie about their physical attributes. How long had it lasted? Did they mind? Or did their smiles display a learned female tolerance for clumsy male behaviour? Did they expect this kind of reaction when they dressed up? He hoped so, but couldn't help feeling he had been rude. Blushing, he said to Ellen, 'You look nice.'

Disappointment flashed across Cordelia's face at not being included, before her smile returned and she gave her mother a see-I-told-you nudge.

Freshly flattered, Ellen pushed back an imaginary strand of hair from her temple. 'Why thank you.'

Much too late, he added, 'You both look nice.'

'We're off to a wedding,' said Ellen with a wink. 'Who knows, there might be a few eligible chaps there for us.' She laughed and jogged her disapproving daughter. 'By the way, congratulations on passing so many exams.' A small, vain link between eligibility and exam success crossed Danny's mind.

'O levels, Mum.'

'Yes, I know, you told me.'

Pleased that Cordelia had told her, Danny said, 'Thank you, it was a bit of a surprise.'

With irritation in her voice, Cordelia said, 'Oh, I don't think so. He's staying on at school, might even go to university.'

'I see,' said Ellen. She didn't but, like others, she had no follow-up to 'congratulations'. 'I always said Cordelia should have stayed on too.'

But what, Danny wanted to ask, had Ellen done about it?

Ellen frowned. Had his disapproval shown? 'I did, didn't I, Cordelia?'

Cordelia turned away, like a boxer avoiding a jab. 'Yes. Mum.'

This response, tolerant in a way he could not understand, appeared to reassure her mother. For the first time, Danny understood the mini-tyranny that the needy can exert over those who love them. He had no time for Ellen's delusional recasting of their life together.

'She's too good for Angelo's. It's not as if she even earns tips. You'd be better off, love, in a full-time job,' said Ellen.

But not at school, where she would be now if her mother wasn't a drunk, thought Danny.

'The cafe's all right, Mum, it's local and Angelo's flexible.'

Not to mention making it easy to cover her mother when she's incapable of doing her job.

Ellen appeared to sense what he was thinking and changed the subject. 'Where are you off to, Danny?'

'To the gym, at the boys' club.'

'The gym, eh?' She winked at him. 'Well, you're certainly looking fit, isn't he, Cordelia?'

Cordelia gave an embarrassed shrug. 'We must get on, Mum.'

'See you, Cordelia, have a nice time, Mrs Hill.'

Danny picked up his kit bag. When Ellen noticed it, her face froze and a red flush rose in her neck.

He prayed she wasn't about to remember.

'Mum? What's the matter?'

Ellen shook her head, 'Nothing, it's nothing, love.'

'But there is something, what is it?'

Nothing except that she might be standing in front of a boy whose memory hadn't been fogged by alcohol, who had seen her at her most wretched. Others on the estate had witnessed her being drunk but none had held her while she peed herself.

Danny recalled her flirty comment about his 'big bag'. Had seeing it again revealed him as the Good Samaritan she didn't want to remember – and who didn't want to be remembered?

She took a deep breath. 'It's nothing. Come on, Cordelia, we've a wedding to go to.'

As they passed, he inhaled Ellen's perfume. Had she smelled and looked this good on the staircase, would he have been more tempted? Had he, as Dodds had said, missed an opportunity? Watching her walking away with her daughter, Danny was certain that he would have done no such thing. This brought a surprising mix of relief and an unfamiliar sense of maturity – it also reminded him that Dodds could be a dick.

At the top of the street, Ellen and Cordelia Hills paused

to greet Crockett. At the same time the sun came out. It showed through the back-combed parts of Ellen's hair and projected Cordelia's body in silhouette against her linen dress. As if she knew what was being thrillingly screened for him, she turned and gave a little wave.

Maybe his session at the gym should start, not finish, with a shower.

Crockett came towards him with his unmistakable who-gives-a-fuck walk: toes flipping up from his ankles.

He crossed his eyes. 'God, there's gold in them thar Hills. And Cordelia, blimey!'

Danny saw the joke but a surprising possessiveness stopped him smiling. 'Do you think so?'

'Oh, I do. So does Dodds; he's just been telling me how hot she is and how she's up for a bit of tit, and more.'

Danny was surprised by a wish that this wasn't true.

As if tuned into Danny's thoughts, Crockett's smile disappeared. 'He's lying, of course. Don't believe what anyone around here says about the sex they've had, other than with their own hands.'

'But I should believe you?'

'Yes, 'cos I don't tell lies.'

Danny had never heard Crockett lie, except when trying to pull girls who weren't local by claiming he played on the wing for Fulham reserves – and his only pretence was to raise his height with Cuban-heeled Chelsea boots. Others would react to doubts about claimed sexual exploits with, 'you're only jealous' or, more aggressively, 'calling me a liar?' Crockett would simply say, 'Believe what you fucking like.'

He was in full flow. 'Even if what he says is true, remember if girls don't do it, we can't do it. So, who's he to grass up any girl he's been with? Anyway, it's the sort of claim put about by those who don't get as far as they want with birds.'

Yes, unfair, thought Danny, to divide girls into those who do – good but sort of bad, and those who don't – bad but sort of good. And worth waiting for? But for how long?

'Anyway, aren't you trying to get into Linda Bain's knickers?' said Crockett.

'Am I?'

'Nuts if you're not.'

Danny nodded, thinking of the immediate future with Linda, in which only promised sex would feature.

As if he were a mind-reader, Crockett said, 'Look, if you ask me, it's not the girls who keep their hand on their ha'penny who are special, it's the ones who don't. Question is, do they stay special afterwards?'

23

At a quarter to four on Sunday, Danny called Linda from the phone box on the estate. 'Just ringing to say I might be a few minutes late.'

'It's OK Danny, they've gone,' said Linda.

Stung at being sussed, he said, 'I was only trying to be polite.'

'Oh, no one could say that you're not polite, Danny Byrne.'

Or, as Cordelia had said, law-abiding.

'Glad you think so,' he lied.

In the silence that followed, he hoped she was thinking that trading clever comments wasn't how girlfriends and boyfriends behaved.

'Well, come as soon as you can,' she said.

She opened the front door, wearing blue slacks and a white blouse. She glanced along the balcony and surprised him with a kiss on the cheek before leading him inside.

'Sit down, tea's nearly ready,' she said, and went into the kitchen. He chose the sofa; it looked comfortable and, unlike cinema seats, had no separating armrests.

Linda came in and put the tray down on the glass coffee table. Teapot, cups, saucers, cutlery, plates, and a fat Victoria sponge. A red rose pattern smothered the china teacups, whose handles looked as if just holding would snap them.

'Blimey, this is genteel.'

'What?'

'I mean, nice.'

'I made the cake,' she said.

'What, yourself?'

She closed her eyes. 'No, the cook and the maid gave me a hand.'

Although stung, he was impressed that someone so sharp, so trendy, could also be so domesticated.

'No, I meant it looks so good.'

'Why shouldn't it?'

He gave up. Why indeed?

He pointed at the cups. 'They're nice. We use mugs, this is like being in a restaurant.'

'I suppose so,' she said, less in agreement, more to confirm their differences.

She sat close to him and poured the tea. Her proximity had his scrotum tightening and his appetite for cake diminishing. Next would come the balancing of teacups on their laps but he couldn't wait. He took her shoulders and swivelled her towards him.

She pushed him away. 'Do you take milk?'

He didn't know anyone who didn't.

'Yes, please.'

She poured the milk in second. Was this posher than putting it in first, as he did at home?

'Sugar?'

'Please.'

'Help yourself.' He spooned in two heaps from the bowl and stirred in the sweetness. Only then did he notice the unused teaspoon in his saucer. Flustered, he hoped he'd retrieved matters by putting the dry one in the sugar bowl.

'Don't worry,' said Linda kindly but her look of 'surely you can do better' made him feel no better. Next, she cut a large wedge of sponge and handed it to him on a plate. He put his tea back on the tray, waited till she'd served herself, picked up the cake and bit into it.

'This is delicious,' he said, with his mouth half-full, hoping a compliment might compensate for etiquette failure.

'Thank you,' she said, and began eating her slice with one of the small forks that sat on the tray. Danny was grateful that her mother wasn't there to witness such a lack of refinement. Linda said nothing but he sensed she was too much her mother's daughter not to be tutting inwardly.

He grew irritated at being made to feel as socially inadequate in a council flat much like his own, as he had been by the inhabitants of Warwick Square. He gave Linda an apologetic shrug but continued eating without the fork.

Linda put down her plate and took his hand. He kissed her but the moment their tongues touched, she sat back, smiling. 'We taste of cake.'

He kissed her again and, remembering Crockett's advice about taking time with girls, fought to control himself. But the energy that arrived with his erection proved hard to resist. He pushed her down as gently as he could. She didn't object and even put her hands behind his neck to draw him to her. His hands began travelling her body but she tracked them effectively, pushing them away when they lingered too long in sensitive areas. Then she surprised him by kissing his ear and exploring it with her tongue: something new, warm and shivery that had him making the mistake of reaching for her breasts. Everything stopped and she shoved him off with more force than he felt necessary.

She stood in front of him with her hands on her hips. 'Are you going to behave, Danny Byrne?'

'Yes, sorry.'

She rejoined him on the sofa and let him kiss her, but this time his tongue failed to make it past a wall of teeth. Running out of ideas, he turned and pulled her onto his lap, forgetting about his erection. He gasped and lifted her while he tried to rearrange things. She gave him a startled glare of disapproval, as if getting this excited in her presence was something he could control. But her look softened as she sat again, facing him with her legs either side of his, and put her arms around him. It was all he could do to resist thrusting upwards. He cupped a breast and she allowed his hand to rest there, until the faintest squeeze had her slapping it away. Meanwhile, what began as slow, shallow and, he hoped, barely noticeable thrusts grew more vigorous until he was bouncing her on his lap like a baby. This, he imagined, could be a fully dressed rehearsal for what might one day happen for real. The vinegar strokes soon followed but, as he was losing control, Linda got up and skipped into the kitchen. He sat back, his mouth fish-gaping, while everything finished without her.

The front door opened.

'Linda?' Mrs Bain followed her loud 'cooee' into the front room.

'Oh, Daniel Byrne!' She struggled for composure but couldn't help herself, 'What are you doing here?'

He stood up, as his mother had told him to do when a lady comes in. But instead of looking polite, he saw from

Mrs Bain's face that it served only to confirm his surprise and guilt. She looked him up and down and paused for a microsecond on his crotch, where he feared the outline of his disappearing erection might have been visible. He swivelled towards the kitchen, where Linda stood horrified, lipstick smeared around her mouth. 'Danny came around for a cup of tea and some of my cake. Didn't you go to Auntie Clare's then?'

Mrs Bain looked to her husband, which Danny interpreted as, 'well-what-do-think-of-this-then?'

Mr Bain, embarrassed, took a breath and said the wrong thing, 'Hello, lad.' He coughed and carried on, 'No trains at Vauxhall, something about weekend works. No choice but to come back. We managed to call Clare to let her know we weren't coming.' He turned to his wife. 'Bit of a disappointment, eh love? What with no lunch and all.'

Mrs Bain's deep frown stopped him talking. 'I'll get you something to eat in a minute.'

Danny relaxed at this switch to the mundane. Mrs Bain picked up the teapot and cupped her hands around it. 'Stone cold,' she said, staring like Miss Marple at Linda, to let her know it must have been quite a while since they were drinking tea.

Mr Bain broke the silence. 'Maybe, I'll just have a bit of cake for now.'

'Please yourself,' said his wife.

Unspoken irritations hung in the air; not all directed at Danny.

With a fierce glance at Linda, who glared back, Mrs Bain picked up the tray and took it out.

Danny checked his groin and thanked God for black jeans.

187

'The cake is really good, Mr Bain. Linda's a good cook.'

'Yes,' said Mr Bain and followed his wife into the kitchen.

Danny moved towards the door, 'I think I'll be off now.' Mrs Bain reappeared. 'Not going already are you, Danny? Won't you have some more tea?' No mention of cake.

'No thank you, I'm working this evening. I've got to get home and change.'

'Working on a Sunday? Where's that then?'

'The off-licence.'

'An off-licence?'

Was the disapproval in her voice for his selling alcohol or for working on the Lord's Day?

'Yes, I'm putting in extra shifts to pay for a holiday in Devon next week.'

'With that boys' club?' She made it sound like a borstal. Ernest's club was for all boys, not only the kind Mrs Bain approved of. Some of its members may have been rascals, not least Dodds and Crockett, but Danny didn't know what he'd do without it, and he wasn't going to have it slagged off. Now that he was certain he didn't like Mrs Bain, he found it easier to stand up to her. 'It's great. I go whenever I can.'

She sensed his diminishing respect and switched to another topic to re-establish the upper hand. 'Devon. We've had lovely times in Devon, haven't we Linda? Mainly Torquay. Do you know Torquay?'

'I've never even been to Devon.'

Her pursed lips, conveyed, 'no, I suppose not.'

Mr Bain came out of the kitchen. 'What'll you be doing there?'

'We're camping, and we'll be doing some canoeing and rock climbing.'

As Danny edged towards the door, Mrs Bain said, 'Climbing over rocks?'

'No, climbing up rock faces, cliffs.'

'Funny thing to be doing on a holiday.'

'But you're not a young man, love,' said Mr Bain. 'It sounds exciting, just take care of yourself, lad.' Relieved, Danny felt this was a kind way of saying cheerio.

Linda came alongside. Face wiped; composure regained. 'Of course he's going to take care, aren't you, Danny?'

Pleased as he was to hear this, it sounded too much like an order, an echo of how Mrs Bain might speak to her husband.

'Anyway, thanks for the tea, and the cake.'

Mrs Bain turned her back and made for the kitchen. 'Goodbye Daniel.'

Mr Bain flicked a finger of farewell at his temple.

Out on the balcony, Linda took both his hands. 'Well, Danny Byrne.'

'Yes, Linda Bain?'

'That was embarrassing.'

'Yes,' said Danny, unsure whether she was referring to his earlier loss of control or her parents' untimely return.

'Mum's not very happy.'

'Guess so.' He couldn't care less and it must have shown.

Her tone became chilly. 'When is it you're off?'

'Friday.'

'Will I see you before then?'

'I'm working every night till we leave.'

'Will you miss me?'

He hadn't thought about it but imagined he would.

'Of course I will,' he said.

'I expect at least two postcards.'

189

'Two! We'll be in the middle of the country.'

As he leaned forward to kiss her goodbye, she smothered a yawn and put a hand on his chest. 'Two.'

'OK.'

At least when he wrote, he wouldn't see her yawn.

Her lips opened in a half-smile and her face clicked into the sharp beauty that stirred him again. She shook her head, as if dealing with a naïve boy who didn't yet understand what she needed from him. As he gazed into her lovely face, he wondered what that might be and then, if he found out, whether he would be able to give it to her.

'Take care, Danny Byrne.'

She gave him a quick kiss and went inside.

24

After four evenings at the off-licence, Danny had enjoyed a good run with delivery tips which, together with his wages, had given him enough cash not to need the promised spending money from his mother. He'd also deepened his taste for illicit Babychams when working in the cellar.

He turned up on Thursday to see, as usual, Ron's nostrils closing in a sniff as he looked at his watch. 'Get your overall on, quick smart, there's lots to do.' A greeting as close to a bollocking that he could reasonably apply, given that Danny was five minutes early.

Danny hauled up several crates containing quarts of cider from the cellar and got down on his knees to shove the bottles one by one under the counter. As he pushed the last one into place, a dull note replaced the usual clink against its neighbour. A soft explosion followed that blew the bottle apart in his hand. Cider streamed across the floor and blood spread over his fingers.

Ron was beside him in a trice, hissing and shaking his head.

'Sorry Ron, they just touched . . .'

'Touched eh, well this'll come out of your wages. Go and get the mop and bucket.'

As Danny got up, he put a hand on the stack of brown wrapping paper by the till and smeared it with blood running from a curved gash between his thumb and forefinger.

'Jesus, get your hand off there and go and fetch a plaster!' said Ron. He snatched the bloodied sheet and thrust it at Danny. 'Wrap it in this for now. I suppose I'll have to clear this lot up.'

Danny was at the first-aid box when Mr Braden returned from the Conservative Club. 'What's happened?'

Danny lifted the brown paper to reveal blood seeping from the cut.

'That's going to need more than a plaster, lad.' He went to the small kitchen, fetched a clean tea towel, unfolded it and bound it tightly around the wound. 'Grip this and don't let go.' He ushered Danny back into the shop. 'Ron, you're going to have to take this young man to the hospital, that cut needs a stitch or two.'

Ron shook his head. 'He'll be all right. Teach him to take more care when stocking up. I'll find a big plaster.'

He went towards the first-aid box, but Mr Braden held up his hand. 'Ron, take him, now, please.'

Ron eyed the mess on the floor.

'Leave that, I'll sort it,' said Mr Braden.

Furious, Ron made for the door. Danny followed. His 'transport' stood outside: an ancient Morris van that smelt of stale beer and bare metal. Ron climbed in and started up. 'Get a move on!'

Danny had barely made it into the passenger seat when Ron's impatience surged into his right foot and they roared away. The sliding door screeched back along its rusty runners.

'Close that door!' said Ron.

With his left hand out of action, Danny twisted around to pull the door closed with his good one. At that moment, Ron swung the van into an angry right turn and Danny followed his outstretched hand out of the open door. He hit the road and rolled till he came to rest with a thud against the large, spoked wheel of a market barrow. He lay still, eyes closed, assessing if he was hurt. He wasn't.

'Impressive, my son: eight, maybe eight point five. You a stunt man or what?' Danny opened his eyes and saw a beefy barrow-boy, grinning under his flat cap, who reached out a hand. 'Come on, up you get.'

Minutes later, the van roared back towards them. Ron was leaning out, holding the door pillar. 'What are you fucking playing at?' He hit the brakes, which brought the van to a squealing halt. It also propelled the sliding door forward to smash his fingers.

Ron's eyes rolled up into his head. He gave a yelp followed by a series of hisses as he sucked air in and out of his teeth. For a minute, he sat doubled up with his mangled hand tucked in an armpit, tapping his head on the steering wheel. 'Oh, god fucking hell, oh my good god fucking hell.'

'Ron? Are you OK?'

'Are you all right, mate?' said the barrow-boy.

Ignoring him, Ron leaned back and croaked at Danny, 'Get in!'

Danny climbed into the passenger seat to the sound of cars honking at them to move. Forgetting his injury, Ron flung an indignant hand out of the door to deliver an imperfect V-sign from a clump of bloody fingers. He snatched the hand back with a yelp of pain. After taking several deep breaths, he managed to get the van going again, using his left hand to change gear and steering with his right forearm.

'Would you like me to change gear for you, Ron, so you can steer with your good hand?' said Danny.

'Don't be so fucking stupid.'

They turned into the hospital approach, where an ambulance was coming towards them, taking up most of the road. Ron, in his agony, decided that his was the emergency vehicle. Instead of letting the ambulance pass, he cruised for the gap. Wing mirrors met with a bang, followed by a sickening scrape as the two vehicles came alongside. The attached ambulance prevented Ron's door from opening. He shooed Danny out of the passenger side and followed him. He began remonstrating furiously with the ambulance driver, but when he raised a bloody fist to emphasise a point, he realised how much damage he had done to his hand. He took a closer look, swivelled and passed out in the road.

Ron was carried into Casualty on a stretcher from the damaged ambulance. His bleeding hand had been wrapped in a temporary bandage and one of the ambulance men asked Danny to hold it up to help stem the flow. An elderly woman said to Danny, 'I hope your dad will be OK.'

Ron threw his good arm over his eyes, revealing the bloodstain in the armpit of his brown shop coat. 'If I was his dad, darlin', I'd get these blokes to take me back and lay me down in the middle of the road.'

Danny and Ron didn't speak to each other while being treated and, once they were patched up, they sat in silence in the waiting room, holding their bandaged hands up for relief.

Mr Braden arrived, stern-faced. 'Well, the van's going to

be out of action for a while. And so will you two by the looks of it.' He thought for a moment then, pointing at their bandaged hands, began chuckling helplessly as he compared them to a pair of fiddler crabs. Still smiling, he added, 'With only one useable hand each, maybe you can work together, you know, carrying crates between you.'

Neither of them thought this funny.

Out of the corner of his mouth, Ron said, 'At least we won't get through so many Babychams.' Danny stayed silent as Ron got into his stride with muttered curses about 'useless Jonahs, who shouldn't be allowed within a mile of decent working people.'

'Now, Ron, these things happen,' said Mr Braden.

'Not to me they don't,' said Ron, 'but with the likes of him around . . .'

'It wasn't me who crashed into the ambulance!' said Danny.

Mr Braden held up both hands. 'Look, chaps, we must go, I've had to shut the shop for a while. Come on, my car's outside, let's get you both home.'

'Thanks, but I live just up the street,' said Danny.

As he opened the door to his Jaguar, Mr Braden winked and waved him goodbye. Considering that Danny would be away on holiday and that Ron, as well as the van, would be out of action, Mr Braden was being remarkably decent. Ron may have been right about most bosses, but he was wrong about Mr Braden.

On the way home, Danny's hand throbbed and his heart sank at the prospect of a now inactive, active holiday. Uncertainty about Linda deepened his gloom and he decided that even though Friday night was now free, he would wait until he got back from Devon to see her. He thought, too, of Cordelia, which added more confusion and, as ever, when his head filled with worries, they were joined by reruns of Jinx's fall. He put off going home to the certain fuss his mother would make about his hand and carried on walking. With night falling, he found himself close to his old street and the night-watchman's hut.

25

Liam sat by the glowing brazier on a wooden kitchen chair. Finnegan dropped his head between his paws and growled, daring Danny to come closer. Liam silenced him with a single 'whisht' and eyed Danny's bandaged hand.

'How's the other fellah?'

'It wasn't a fight; I had an accident where I work.'

Liam studied his face this time. 'Is it painful?'

'Sort of.'

Liam pushed a stool forward with his foot. 'Sit, boy, agin I get ye a cup of tea.' He shook a battered kettle to confirm it contained enough water and bedded it into the brazier's hot coals.

'Ye seem troubled, boy. By more than your painful hand?'

Danny didn't answer.

'Is it about that fine girl, with the name from *King Lear*?'

Danny shook his head. 'No, although, yes, a little. Her . . . and another girl.'

Liam's eyes widened. 'Two girls? And ye think that's a problem?'

Danny smiled but shook his head and nervously broached his older, deeper burden: Jinx and the fall. 'Funny how one problem can shrink the size of others, isn't it?'

'It is, so.'

In the silence that followed, Danny resisted the pressure to speak, until Liam opened a door for him. 'So, this other problem?'

Danny took a deep breath. 'Have you ever done something, something bad that only you know about?'

Liam struck a match and let it burn close to his fingers without flinching as he lit the tobacco in his pipe and puffed it into life. After flicking the match into the brazier, he remained silent. Danny sensed that Liam understood that his 'something' was important.

Liam eventually took the pipe from his mouth. 'In answer to your question, God, yes, I have!'

'And does it bother you whenever you think about it?' said Danny.

'It? I'm afraid I have more than one. Some continue to bother me, as ye say, and others don't. Time rubs some away altogether.'

'And what did you do about it when . . . you know?'

'There was a time when I'd have told a priest. Shared it, if ye like, with him and, who knows, possibly, God.'

'Did it help?'

'Hard to say, especially with the tough memories, those that weaken a body whenever they come to mind. They're with me yet. For those, ye just have to find the strength to carry them with you through your life.'

'So, telling a priest didn't work?'

'Who knows, boy. Life might have been worse if I hadn't. I did receive a little comfort, though, when whispering through the grille.' He fell silent again. 'But a priest's forgiveness, even on behalf of the Almighty, isn't the same as forgiving yourself.'

'And did you forgive yourself?'

'For some things but for others, not at all. They're with me yet.'

Liam sat back, silent, and stared at the glowing coals as if they held his memories. He leaned forward and put his fists on his knees. 'Now, if you were to tell someone, would it help? I mean, would it make things better?'

'I don't know, it's not as if I stole something and could put it back.'

'I don't have ye down as a thief, boy.'

'And I didn't do it deliberately, and if I did, it wasn't meant to hurt, you know, like shouting "boo" behind someone, not knowing they're holding a valuable vase.' The analogy pleased Danny, not because it was fitting but because it had come to him spontaneously.

Liam smiled. 'Ah, the pain of unintended consequences.'

'Yes.'

'Ye are a decent boy, Danny, or whatever it is wouldn't be making ye feel so bad. Has it been a long time since?'

Was this the moment to force his guilt out of hiding? He felt himself moving towards revelation.

'Five years ago, and I was with—'

Liam held up his hand. 'No, don't tell me. But if, and I say if, ye tell someone, it should, at the very least, be a person who needs or deserves to know.'

Maybe, thought Danny, but what about my need to tell?

He sighed, feeling as if a bridge he was about to cross had been barred.

'All I'd say is, think carefully before revealing something

important if it relieves only ye but passes the burden of knowing to others.'

Danny shook his head. 'But if everyone knew, it would so be hard. I'd want to get away from here.'

'Maybe, but our troubles tend to get into our suitcase wherever we go. Are ye sorry for what you've done?'

'Oh yes.'

'Contrition, as priests call it, can be a spur to avoid making the same mistake again. Would letting on undo what has happened?'

'No.'

'Would it hurt those you tell?'

'Yes.'

'And would it hurt you, once you told them?'

'Not sure I could bear it.'

Danny closed his eyes. Out of the puzzled and frustrating thoughts swirling through his brain, he was certain of only one: whether he confessed or not, he'd be living with the consequences of his actions on the bombsite wall for the rest of his life.

Liam put a hand on his shoulder. 'Be a little easy on yourself, boy. And remember it can be a sin to tell an untimely truth.'

The kettle steamed on the coals.

'Would ye like that tea now?' said Liam.

'Thank you, I would.'

That night Danny lay in bed, knowing that his part in Jinx's fall would continue to gnaw him from within and, if revealed, would smash him from without.

If it was time to tell someone, who? Who, as Liam asked, deserved to know? His mother? She would love him and offer comfort, but he could envisage the agony in her face.

Crockett? His friend, whose brother's life, and that of his family, had been blighted? Jinx, whose heart would break if he were to lose Danny's friendship? And what would telling them do to Danny Byrne?

Was he worrying too much? After all, wasn't his story of Jinx's fall accepted on the estate and the details largely forgotten? Most of the time he forgot that the story wasn't quite true until, at moments like these, he remembered. A lead weight formed in the pit of his stomach. He stayed awake till the early hours and finally fell asleep while thinking of Jinx the way he was before the fall.

26

Ernest stood inside the deep roof rack on top of the minibus, chunky legs apart like the Jolly Green Giant. Beneath him, boys in holiday mood milled around laughing and shoving.

'Morning Daniel, give me your rucksack.'

Danny tossed it up for him to slot among other bags, folded tents, pots and pans, and Calor gas cylinders.

Dodds turned up with a suitcase.

Crockett winked at Danny. 'I'd put that inside if I were you, Dodds, rain spoils imitation leather.'

Dodds gave him a threatening look and hurled the case up to Ernest. To transfer the piss-take to someone else, he tapped Danny's bandaged hand. 'Wanker's cramp?'

It was holiday time, so Danny kept things light as he told them what had happened and with a grin held up his good hand. 'This one's OK.'

'Fucked up your week, though,' said Dodds.

'I'll manage.'

Physical activities may have been off the agenda, but Danny was looking forward to the free time, extra reading and laughs with mates. And he'd be away from the estate, from Ron, from Gasping George, even from Linda, about whom he needed time to think.

Ernest climbed down and threaded a rope through the eyeholes of a tarpaulin and tied it down over their gear with arcane knots.

Nobby came out of the club. 'All set for your "ging gang goolie goolie ging gang", and porridge?'

Danny bit his tongue at the boy-scout jibe. 'For a moment, I thought you might have changed your mind.'

Nobby, pale and more gaunt than usual, gave him a pitying look. 'No chance, I only came to take back my deposit from Ernest's bird. Is she going too?'

'Yes.'

'Dodds'll be pleased.'

'It's only for five days, Nobby, getting away could do you good. You look like shit.'

Nobby shrugged.

'Seriously, you're white as a ghost.'

'It's my night-time colour, helps me to be seen in the dark.'

'Are you sure you're all right?'

'Everything's sweet, Danny boy.'

'You might even enjoy coming with us.'

'Joking, aren't you?'

'You'll be with mates.'

'I've got other mates.'

'What, up-West mates?'

'They're OK, at least they don't sing around campfires.'

'It's not too late. Ernest would wait for you to get your gear.'

Nobby gave a wistful smile. 'Nah, I've got stuff on. I'm not a schoolboy, remember.'

'How can I forget?' said Danny.

From behind his curtain of patronising banter, Danny's oldest friend peeped through. 'Sorry, look, have you got enough dosh?'

'Yes.'

"Cos you're welcome to the couple of quid I got back from Ernest.'

'No thanks.'

'Suit yourself, but if—'

'Really, I'm OK for money, thanks.'

'Sweet.'

He looked disappointed and fragility replaced his bravado. Fearing that he had become unsteady, Danny reached out to support him, but Nobby stepped back, raised a hand. 'I told you, it's all sweet, see ya.'

He slouched away. Danny watched, seized by sadness and a sense of loss for his misfit friend, who was steadily cutting himself adrift, and trying to convince himself it was what he wanted.

Ernest came over. 'No change of mind for Alan, then?'

Danny couldn't speak and shook his head.

'Pity,' said Ernest and turned to the boys. 'All aboard, lads, I'll just go in and get Valerie.'

'Oh yes, Valerie!' said Dodds, as if she was going to be one of the week's physical activities.

Valerie, in tight red slacks and yellow blouse, climbed in and Ernest got behind the wheel. She threw an elbow over the back of her seat. 'Hello, boys.'

From the far end of one of the two facing bench seats, Dodds asked in a Leslie Phillips voice, 'Hello, Valerie, looking forward to a good time?'

Danny cringed as embarrassment reddened Valerie's face.

But was there also a suggestion of a smile? She turned and stared through the windscreen. Ernest said nothing but drove away, crunching more aggressively than usual through the gears.

Ernest and Valerie's straight-backed discomfort was palpable. In the quiet that followed, Danny contemplated that hint of excitement in Valerie's reaction and felt angry that Dodds's outrageous behaviour may not have been entirely misplaced. Had her blush been for what Dodds said, or because she found it exciting, or because Ernest had heard it too? Could Dodds be getting closer to what he was after by behaving badly? Much as Danny believed in the importance of doing the right thing, he knew it didn't always pay off – something he discovered as a small boy when, for a time, he'd believed that if he was good, Arsenal wouldn't lose.

He could see that his friend's obsession with Valerie was likely to be a spoiler in the days ahead and his irritation escaped into speech. 'Can't help yourself, can you?' he whispered.

'What do you mean?' said Dodds.

Crockett weighed in too. 'Yeah, can't you leave it out for once?' His eyes flicked towards Ernest. 'He's given up a week's holiday to take us lot away and you start sniffing around his fiancée.'

Dodds looked about him, sensing this was how everyone felt. His smile was defiant. 'I'm only being nice.'

'No, you're not, you're being a moron,' said Crockett.

Dodds made a grab for him but Danny and the others restrained him.

'All right back there?' said Ernest.

They all sat back. 'Fine,' said Danny.

205

One of the other boys held up a pack of cards. 'Brag, anyone?' Everyone settled down to play – and to lose some of their holiday money to Crockett. They lifted their heads only when they reached Stonehenge, where Ernest thought it important that they stopped for a closer look.

'No one's completely sure of its purpose,' said Ernest, as they walked among the stones. Danny found it fascinating but kept quiet when the others, as was their habit, opted for piss-take about anything with which they didn't want to engage: 'Stone-Age skittles?' 'you'd think they'd have finished it', 'made a right mess of the field'. The holiday mood was set, and when Ernest told them Stonehenge was built three thousand years before Westminster Abbey, Crockett said, 'Around the last time Dodds opened his wallet.'

Deep into Devon there were calls for another break and the need to pee. When Ernest resisted Dodds pleaded, 'Come on, Ernest, I need to go so badly, I can taste it.' Ernest glanced at Valerie and blew out his cheeks in disapproval. 'And enough of language like that, thank you, Stephen.'

A little later, they reached a village and pulled in beside public toilets. 'OK lads, fifteen minutes. Don't go too far,' said Ernest.

Crockett spotted a newsagent on the other side of the road and, newly flush with cash, said, 'OK, the Milky Bars are on me.'

They piled into the poorly lit shop that smelled of news-print and sweets, with a hint of Jeyes Fluid rising from the old lino. A man was being served by an old woman in a wrap-around pinny. She eyed the boys with instant hostility. Crockett nudged Danny and pointed to a sign behind the counter: NO WHISTLING IN THE SHOP. Dodds pursed his lips to disobey but Crockett put a hand over his mouth.

'This needs to be done properly.' He shooed them outside. On the pavement, he took charge. 'OK, line up. Now, "Colonel Bogey", please.'

'Colonel Bogey?' said Dodds.

Crockett whistled a few bars.

'Oh, "Hitler has only got one ball". Why didn't you say so?'

Crockett's eyes rose into his head. 'Sorry, Dodds.'

The man came out of the shop. 'Right,' said Crockett, 'after me.' He led the whistling marchers back in. The woman's face contorted in fury. Within seconds, laughter rendered them incapable of keeping their lips together, all except Crockett, who kept blowing from a straight face.

The woman screamed, 'Get out!' Crockett turned to the others, waving his hands like a conductor, urging them to complete the tune. Behind him the woman started swinging a broom handle. 'Out, out of here, you scum!'

Crockett stopped whistling when she caught him on the head and, from across the counter, aimed a couple of surprisingly deft blows at the others. Her stick became a grisly flail when it caught one of the flypapers that dangled from the ceiling. It detached and caught in Dodds's hair. 'Shit, shit!' Get this off me!' he shouted.

Like Dodds himself, no one wanted to touch the fly-encrusted strip. When a couple of bluebottles fell into his open-necked shirt, he whipped it off to shake them out and dipped his head among his circle of mates, 'Get this thing off!' No one made a move to help.

Meanwhile, the woman dropped her stick and, panting, picked up the receiver of an old Bakelite phone to make what Danny guessed would be a regular call to the local police. The boys made for the door.

Outside, Dodds yanked the flypaper from his hair but couldn't get it off his fingers. He trod on it to pull it free, but it stuck to his shoe and, in a Chaplinesque hopping sequence, transferred it from one foot to the other. Finally, he scraped it off against the kerb and grabbed Crockett. 'Are there any left on my head?'

Crockett made a show of looking thoroughly. The corpses of at least three bluebottles were visible in his hair. 'Nope.'

After going to the Gents, they got back in the minibus. Everyone but Dodds was laughing, but they all regretted not buying before whistling. While Ernest was checking something under the bonnet, Valerie returned from the Ladies and climbed into her seat.

Dodds, shirt off and happy for his muscular torso to be on show, said, 'Hi Valerie, I hope you didn't get up before you finished.' He grinned at his audience but they reacted only with silent embarrassment.

'Don't you be so horribly rude, Stephen Dodds,' said Valerie. She thought for a second and added, 'And so crude.' This time there was no hint of amusement. Dodds had gone too far. Would she tell Ernest?

Her smiling fiancé got behind the wheel. 'Everyone on board?'

'Ernest,' said Valerie, putting a restraining hand on his shoulder. The boys held their breath. She said nothing but sat back to let the policeman standing by her open window speak to Ernest.

'Just a minute, sir,' which sounded like 'seurr'.

Ernest fired a look of suspicion over his shoulder before getting out to speak to the policeman. The boys watched them talking, nodding, and occasionally pointing towards the minibus. After some details were recorded in the policeman's notebook, the two of them came over and Ernest opened the back doors.

'Listen carefully, boys, the police officer has something to say.'

'Now, I understand you're on holiday' – the 'you're' was a rich 'yeurr' and Danny knew this accent would now be part of their holiday banter – 'and I don't want to spoil it, but I do want you to know that the lady in the shop, Mrs Moran, is extremely distressed by your conduct.'

Crockett mouthed the word 'yokel' at Danny and, with lips pursed in a silent whistle, crossed his eyes. Caught off guard, Danny failed to stifle a laugh.

The policeman glared at him. 'You may think it's funny, lad.' Danny's face burned. 'It may be, I'll allow, a somewhat strange sign, but it's her shop and the least you can do is show an old lady some manners.' He looked slowly around the boys. 'Do you agree?'

They took their cue from Ernest and copied his affirmative nodding.

'Well, I hope you'll show a bit more respect in future.' They were nodding again. This time he realised they were not taking him seriously and shook his head in disappointment. He said no more but grasped Ernest's proffered hand and left.

'Not so bad for a country plod,' said Crockett.

'Now David, what did he say about respect for people?' said Ernest.

'Yeah, respect,' said Dodds and led everyone in vigorous nodding, which turned to helpless laughter. Ernest gave up and started the engine.

27

As they rolled through the village near to their campsite, Crockett called out, 'Hold on, Ernest!' The minibus came to a halt. 'Could you back up a bit, please, there's a poster on a tree about a disco tonight.'

Ernest's shoulders hunched as he put the minibus, and his plans for a quiet night, into reverse.

Saturday 21st August
Village Hall Youth Club
DISCO
8 p.m. to 11 p.m.
Entrance – 1 shilling

'Yes!' said Dodds, 'and it says Disco, so no Jim Reeves! How far's this from our camp, Ernest?'

Ernest turned around wearily. 'Not far, about two miles.'

A chorus of Cockney voices chirped up, 'Two miles!' For Londoners a distance requiring a bus or Tube ride.

'You'll give us a lift, won't you Ernest?' said Dodds.

'I don't know, there's a lot to set up.'

After much teenage moaning, Ernest looked at Valerie and shrugged assent.

'Great,' said Dodds, 'local yokel birds.'

On Crockett's side of the minibus, a woman was standing patiently while her whippet was shivering and straining on the grass verge. Crockett slid open his window. 'Excuse me, madam, would it help if I squeezed its head?'

The boys roared with laughter and expected outrage, but she floored them when she said in a rich Devon accent, 'You might as well, my lovely, I've tried everything else.'

Lesson learned, thought Danny: quick wits aren't the preserve of city dwellers.

When they arrived at the camp, Dodds pushed the favour further. 'If there's a pub in the village, maybe you and Valerie could go – and pick us up later.'

With a resigned shake of his head, Ernest started unloading.

In barely controlled chaos, they managed to set up the kitchen tent and those for the boys. Danny shared with Dodds and Crockett. On the other side of the kitchen, away from the boys, Ernest set up his and Valerie's single tents.

Ernest called them together. 'Who wants to go to this disco tonight?'

Vigorous nodding.

'OK, now who wants to help me set up the Elsan toilet and dig the latrine trench?'

Silence.

'And what if it were to be a case of no dig, no disco?'

Still no response.

'I need only two of you.' He looked to Danny as his bell-ringer for the others. Danny held up his bandaged hand.

'Sorry Daniel, I forgot.'

Crockett, mumbled, 'OK then, Ernest.'

'Thank you, Matthew,' said Ernest.

Dodds patted Crockett on the back. 'Crockett's your man, Ernest, he knows all about shit and what to do with it.'

Crockett winked at Ernest. 'True, thanks to a lifetime of friendship with Dodds.'

'Looks like that qualifies you to help, too, Stephen,' said Ernest, handing Dodds the spade.

Danny followed them to the far end of the field. Near a hedge, Ernest marked out a three-foot square and asked Crockett and Dodds to dig down about eighteen inches, while he erected the small tent that would cover it and set up the chemical toilet. The only digging Dodds and Crockett had done was in sand at the seaside. The real thing, in dry soil, was difficult. They took turns with the spade and, for all his strength, Dodds was as glad as Crockett each time it was handed over.

Ernest inspected their work and smiled. 'Thanks lads, tough job, isn't it? But more pleasant than what others will have to do when it comes to emptying and filling in.'

Back in their tent, Dodds took a quarter-bottle of Smirnoff vodka from his case. 'I brought this livener along, didn't think we'd need it so soon.'

'Powerful stuff,' said Danny, noting the blue label of the much stronger version.

'You should know,' said Dodds. 'Bought it at your off-licence, from that miserable git in the brown coat who talks to himself.'

He half filled a plastic beaker with orange cordial and topped it up with vodka. He took a gulp, then added more vodka. He offered the beaker to Crockett, who shook his head. 'No thanks, don't need it.'

Dodds held it out to Danny. 'You do, though, don't you?'

Danny wanted to say 'No', remembering the last time he'd drunk to boost confidence at a dance. Yet he did need it and, at Dodds's urging, took a long swig of the sharp, sickly mix. Dodds emptied the beaker and drank nearly all the neat vodka left in the bottle. He passed the last inch to Danny, who had to dab his watering eyes after draining it in one.

'Should you be on the pull tonight, chaps? Haven't you already got birds?' said Crockett with a grin.

Dodds gave him a pitying look but Danny felt a twinge of guilt – not about being potentially unfaithful, but at realising he hadn't thought about Linda since leaving London.

'Who says I'm on the pull?' said Danny.

'Come off it, we're always on the pull, aren't we?' said Dodds.

At eight thirty, the boys climbed into the minibus in what, for a camping trip, were their best clothes: cotton trousers, Fred Perrys and Ben Shermans of differing colours, and Hush Puppies. Crockett stuck to his high-heeled boots.

Dusk was falling when they arrived at the village hall. Music boomed through its open doors.

'No sign of any birds,' said Dodds, eyeing a group of surly local lads, milling around the entrance.

'They'll be inside,' said Crockett, 'dancing already.'

'Well, there's going to be a bit of competition for their boyfriends tonight,' said Dodds, eyes shining with vodka-fired aggression.

Although warmed up by the vodka, Danny worried about the possibility of aggro but, as usual, Dodds and Crockett didn't appear to give it a thought.

'Let's go,' said Dodds, and led them past the hostile locals.

From behind a desk, a vicar beamed a wary welcome and took their entrance fees.

'Where are you from, boys?'

'London,' said Dodds, sticking out his chest.

The vicar fought hard to hold on to his smile. 'Well, I hope you're enjoying yourselves down here.'

'So far so good,' said Dodds.

Ernest and Valerie joined them at the desk. 'I'll be here at eleven o'clock on the dot. If you don't want to walk home, be ready.' The boys mumbled agreement and went in, while Ernest stayed to chat with a fellow Christian.

Inside, stackable metal chairs were arranged around the walls. The lights were off, save for a couple of spotlights picking out a mirror ball. Children's paintings hung every-where and a large notice board displayed details of a monthly quiz, cricket fixtures and bridge evenings.

The local boys came in, pretending not to look at the girls but not holding back on stares for the Londoners.

There was little action early on, as town and country boys alike waited for the slow tunes; except for Crockett, who was showing a group of girls his big-city dance moves. Some laughed but a couple were impressed and began to copy him. One of the local boys mocked Crockett's size by getting down on his knees to dance next to him. Crockett had seen it all before and, undeterred, moved closer to a small slender girl, who clearly thought him cute.

During the slow sessions, boys from both groups made hesitant forays onto the dance floor and most retreated as soon as the music speeded up.

Danny danced with a couple of girls, who were friendly but kept looking over their shoulders at boys who weren't. Since he'd arrived, he had been exchanging glances with a girl with bright blonde hair, wearing a short cotton dress. Twice he'd set off to ask her to dance but had been beaten to it by a brawny local with slicked-back hair and farmer's sideburns.

For the last dance, Danny got to her first. As they moved around the floor, the local lads' aggressive gestures and increasing piss-takes began to worry him. The girl wasn't bothered. She danced excitingly close and, when he said he came from London, pressed her body against him from thighs to face. 'I know,' she said, as if agreeing to sex there and then. Before Danny could enjoy the prospect, the farmer came over and shoved him away. The girl shrieked at him to sod off, but he stayed, palms up, fingers curling, inviting Danny to fight. Two other locals joined him and, with back-up in place, he aimed a punch at Danny, who threw one in return with his good right hand. Both punches missed and clumsy, upright wrestling followed. Crockett leapt on one of the two mates and tried to choke him. As Danny struggled to get free to throw a decent punch, Dodds threw an extremely decent one that dropped Danny's opponent to the floor. In full cry, Dodds went for the third boy, only to be thrust violently aside by Ernest who, arms wide to separate the combatants, shouted, 'Lads! Enough!'

He helped the stunned boy to his feet and yanked Crockett back to the Londoners' side of his imposed line. The lights went on and Ernest was joined by the vicar, who was content to leave the talking to him.

'OK, my lads, out, now!' said Ernest. He turned to the vicar. 'I'm so sorry about this.'

The vicar nodded nervously.

Back in the minibus, Valerie asked. 'What happened, Ernest?'

'Boys being boys but, sadly, forgetting that we are guests around here.'

'We', not 'they'. Ernest was nothing if not loyal, thought Danny.

The boys grumbled that he wasn't being fair, as the locals had started it. But this was about as unfair as Ernest got.

Danny sat on the bench seat between Dodds and Crockett. He turned from one to the other. 'Thanks, you know . . .'

Crockett shrugged.

'Mates, aren't we?' said Dodds.

Danny nodded, contemplating the strange and imperfect thing that is friendship.

28

Ernest leaned out of the driver's seat and called back to Danny. 'You'll be OK, won't you Daniel? We'll be back at lunch time.'

'Fine, see you later.' Danny raised his good hand as the minibus pulled away. Dodds and Crockett responded with V-signs. No point going with them, as they would be canoeing and out of sight for the day, leaving him at the boating centre with only Valerie for company.

With the morning to himself, Danny took the torn-out last quarter of *The Adventurers* by Harold Robbins and went for a walk. At the top of a meadow that sloped towards a nearby village, he stretched out against a gate post that was missing a gate. Facing the sun, he inhaled the morning air, and although the gentle breeze carried a whiff of farmyard, it put the so-called fresh air of St James's Park in its place. He began to read, hoping for at least one more of the sex scenes that had featured with satisfying regularity throughout the story. An hour later none had appeared, but he was gripped by the final pages and the impending death of the hero.

'Hello.' A girl's voice.

He looked up. About twenty yards away, silhouetted against the sun, a girl raised a hand in greeting as she walked by. He waved back and said, 'Hi,' which he thought more cool. She stopped, as if waiting for him to say more. Uncertain what to do next, he decided to concentrate on his book, but not before he'd taken in her short red frock that flared from the waist: the kind to follow upstairs on a bus, and easy lifting for gusts of wind. These images removed all sense from the words on the page.

The girl's dog, a small, black mongrel, made a beeline for him. Danny gave it a click of his tongue which he hoped conveyed, 'hello, now piss off'. The dog ignored him and dipped its snout, bite-close to Danny's crotch. He pulled up his knees and shooed it away; undeterred, the dog cocked its leg and peed over one of his basketball boots before scampering off.

'Freddie, no! Oh, I'm *so* sorry,' said the girl, who looked familiar.

'It's OK.' He returned to his book and flexed his toes as damp warmth spread into his sock.

'I thought this would be where you'd all be camping. Recognised you when I saw your bandaged hand. Where are all your friends?'

'Gone canoeing.' He held up the bandaged hand, 'Not for me at the moment.'

'So, all alone then?' said the girl, in a way that added sudden excitement to their conversation.

Still between him and the sun, she came nearer and stood, hands on hips. He held up his good hand to shield his eyes. When she turned side on to shout at the dog, the silhouetted outline of her breasts elevated his natural interest to Barbara-Windsor focus.

However, he had never initiated *Carry On*, innuendo-led conversations with girls in the way that Dodds found so easy, partly because he didn't have the nerve but mainly because he didn't want to. He aspired to being like Steve McQueen, not Sid James.

She came alongside and without the sun behind her, he recognised the girl with whom he'd had the last dance the night before.

'I'm sorry about last night.'

'Yes, pity it all ended like that.'

'Our boys aren't used to competing with you lovely London lads.'

Danny nodded, marvelling at the idea of being 'lovely' solely for being from London.

'We got that impression.'

'And now, Freddie peeing on you like that.'

'It's OK.'

She pushed a hand through what looked like genuinely sun-bleached hair. 'I wish I could make it up to you in some way.'

A small catch in his throat seemed to release heat into his face.

'No, it's OK, no harm done.'

'Really?'

She came closer. In daylight, she wasn't as pretty as he remembered when the lights were low, and the vodka was working. But with those beautiful breasts, Medusa would have been attractive, and part of him might already be turning to stone.

'How . . . how could you make it up to me, then?' said Danny.

'Well, for a start, I could feel in your pocket for change.'

219

Blimey! Losing control of his thoughts, he tried to focus, to no avail, on being relaxed, and cool. But instead of bringing laconic Steve McQueen responses to mind, all he could hear in his head was a Dodds-like voice shouting, *this could be it, Danny boy!*

He put his book aside and went to get up. She reached down to help, assuming that, with his injured hand, he needed support. They stood face to face and his nervousness began dissolving in the sugary scent of her breath. Here was a moment to say something mildly suggestive in return, as if he were used to this kind of situation, but a whoosh of groin flare rendered him dumb.

She came even closer, her large brown eyes dreamily roving back and forth between his face and her breasts. She shrugged as if to say, 'well, what are you waiting for?'

He wasn't waiting; more that, for a moment, he couldn't move.

'This is what we might have done after the dance last night. Guess I should've known that Billy Chase would spoil things. He thinks that being a tough guy is more attractive than being nice looking.'

She was saying all the right things.

'Anyway, he got his comeuppance from your beefy friend. Serves him right.'

Harsh as she was being about Billy Chase, Danny sensed that once he left for London, he would be the one she'd dance with at the next disco. Had she been trying to make poor Billy jealous?

'Hope you didn't injure your bad hand in the fight,' she said.

'No.'

'How did you hurt it?' Before he could answer, her eyebrows rose. 'I hope you hadn't been over-using it.'

Blimey, he thought, you could be related to Dodds.

'I cut it on a broken bottle.'

'Silly boy.'

At the bottom of the meadow, a figure had appeared. He stepped back. The girl turned to look and sighed. 'Don't worry, no one can see nothin'. Come on, let's go over there.'

She took his hand and led him behind a hedge that offered only shoulder-high cover.

She put her arms around his neck and pressed her breasts against him. 'What's your name then?'

'Dan,' he said, remembering Linda's mother's comment about it sounding more grown-up.

'Well, Dan, I'm Geraldine.'

She thrust a hand into his jeans pocket. He resisted his instinct to pull away.

'Ah, I think I've found some change already,' she said.

The figure in the distance, a woman, was definitely coming their way.

'What's the matter, Dan? Don't you want me to?'

Yes, he did! But there, in the open air? He tried to speak and wondered how a pulse thumping through his groin could constrict his throat. He nodded.

She backed into the hedge. 'Now, let's see.'

The woman was getting closer behind a golden retriever that was quartering the field ahead of her.

Feeling time was against him, he pulled her to him and said, 'OK, can I . . . please?' He wasn't sure what exactly

'Aren't you a polite boy! Just a minute.' Assuming he wanted to see more, she stood back and lifted her dress to reveal red knickers above suntanned legs. With his heart pounding, he reached up inside to her thin white bra, stretched by breasts that rose and fell as if she were breathing through them. Trying to give each equal attention, his good hand moved urgently and clumsily between them.

'Slow down, Dan, gently.' Once he'd forced his hand from 'squeeze' to 'caress' mode, she pulled down the zip of his jeans. He groaned as she took gentle but firm hold and steadied herself by putting her other hand behind his head. Then came the sliding collar of her fingers as her hand moved up and down inside his jeans, and his breathing began to match her rhythm.

From the corner of his eye, he saw that the woman, head-scarfed and cardiganed, was beginning to take an interest.

Was it this that began to slow his breathing? Or was it because what had initially had him gasping with pleasure was now generating images of Geraldine squeezing an udder? He backed away, shocked that the exhilaration of a girl doing this for him hadn't lasted. And that she couldn't do it as well as he could.

'What's the matter?' she said.

'Someone's coming.'

She whispered in his ear. 'Not yet they're not.'

He'd never heard a girl talk like this.

She caught him looking behind her. 'Don't worry about her, it's only Ma Johnson. She's done what we're doing often enough in her time.'

Ma Johnson *was* worrying him, and time was running out.

He reached down to feel the softness between Geraldine's legs. She let out a moan that startled him. God, he thought, if she could be this loud with his hand outside her knickers, how high would the volume go if he went further?

By now, Freddie had decided the retriever was too close and began growling. Ma Johnson had stopped to stare in their direction, near enough to guess what was going on. He stepped back.

Geraldine sat down and pulled at Danny to join her. 'Come on Dan, please, keep going.'

'Jasper, heel!' said Ma Johnson.

Flustered, Danny stayed on his feet.

Geraldine stood up, 'Oh sod it, sod her!'

The retriever appeared beside them, sniffing Danny's groin. Geraldine's dog growled and snapped at its arse.

'Bugger off, go on,' said Geraldine. And to Ma Johnson, 'Take your bloody dog out of it.'

'Who do you think you're talking to, Geraldine Archer?'

Jasper switched groins and shoved its nose up her dress; this was too much for Freddie, who buried his teeth in the retriever's ear. A row ensued with much growling and shrieking as Geraldine and Ma Johnson struggled to drag their dogs apart. Danny pulled up his fly and started backing away. As the conflict continued, he decided to leave and broke into a jog.

When, from a distance, he heard Geraldine calling, 'Don't go, Dan, Dan!' he didn't turn around.

29

At the campsite, everyone had returned. Canoeing had been abandoned, as the river was too shallow to tackle rapids. Danny checked the tent for Dodds and Crockett, but no sign. In the field behind the tents, the other lads were kicking a ball around. They hadn't seen Dodds, but told him that Crockett had gone with Ernest to find a supermarket twenty miles away in Exeter.

In his tent, Danny's frustration deepened when he remembered that those eagerly awaited final pages of *The Adventurers* were lying unread in a Devon field. He took another book from his rucksack, rolled his sleeping bag into a pillow and stretched out on the camp bed, hoping for some second-hand sex in James Hadley Chase's *No Orchids for Miss Blandish*. It had been recommended, with a knowing wink, by the second-hand bookseller in Rochester Row. Danny begrudged the man's assumption that it was his kind of book, even if he was correct. He bought it anyway and resisted the urge to explain that he also read the kind of books that the winker *didn't* sell.

The early pages gave little indication of an imminent erotic scene and, after skimming fruitlessly to find one, his thoughts turned to Geraldine and how, when it came to the first grown-up act of his life, he had failed to be a grown-up. How, in front of a woman who was only an adult version of Geraldine, and whom he would never see again, he had let embarrassment put him off. Geraldine might have stampeded him a bit, but these excuses couldn't ease the knowledge that, somehow, he'd let her down, as well as himself. More experienced than he, she had probably guessed it was his first time, and been prepared to show him how. He could blame the arrival of Ma Johnson and the subsequent dog fight for ending his chances, but in truth he had lost all momentum before they got close. His gloom was complete when he recalled his mother urging him to observe proper standards of behaviour with girls and how, at the time, they hadn't entered his head.

He tossed the book aside and lay back to run an edited version in his head of what had happened. This time, without Ma Johnson and the dogs, it featured only Geraldine, on her back, legs raised, her red knickers hanging off one ankle. To his relief, his erection returned, strong as ever, so soon after wilting in her hand in real life.

'Danny!'

He spun onto his stomach and reached for the book.

This time it wasn't Ma Johnson spoiling things but Ernest, who stuck his cheery face inside the tent. 'Would you like to give me and Matthew a hand to unload? It's mainly carrier bags, so even with your injured hand it will help.'

Danny looked over his shoulder and squeaked, 'Sure, Ernest, give me a minute.'

Focusing on football league tables, a favourite erection

225

eradicator, he zipped up and went to help. With Crockett, he carried the bags to the kitchen tent where Ernest unpacked them.

'Thanks lads, that should see us through the rest of our stay,' said Ernest.

Danny and Crockett wandered away as Ernest finished up.

'How come you're back so soon?' said Danny.

'We saw a supermarket on the way that had all we needed. Seen Dodds?'

'Not in our tent,' said Danny.

'He was sniffing around Valerie when we left. God she's thick, doesn't see how acting a bit friffy at Dodds's flattery hurts Ernest – but, of course, he says nothing.'

True, thought Danny; between Ernest's decency and Valerie's stupidity, Dodds would find a way in.

'Guess it's hard for Ernest to show he feels threatened by a club member,' said Danny.

'Well, Dodds is Dodds,' said Crockett, 'and I don't think Valerie's as innocent as she makes out. Either way, Ernest needs to sort them both. I would.'

Ernest caught up with them. 'Cup of tea, lads?' They shrugged assent. 'Hang on, let me get Valerie.' They followed him to her tent.

'Hello love, we're back,' he said, pulling back the tent flap, which opened like a curtain on a scene, more a tableau, as – for what felt like an age – those on view didn't move.

Valerie lay on top of Dodds between his legs, frock-up, white knickers rolled down below her buttocks on which Dodds's hands were clamped. Ernest froze and forgot to let go of the flap. Danny's gaze jumped between Dodds's firmly closed eyes, Crockett's wobble-lipped smile and Valerie's bare arse. Ernest finally came to and let the curtain fall on his future wife's betrayal.

Ernest turned around, facing the boys but, they were certain, not seeing them. The flesh on his normally benign face set hard, as if he'd been seized by a sudden loss of faith. He walked off and stopped a few yards away with his back to them, hands on hips.

After whispers and a scuffling inside the tent, Dodds emerged. 'Fuck. Fuck!'

'You didn't?' said Crockett.

'Would've, if Ernest hadn't come back so early.'

'That all that's bothering you?' said Danny.

'What do you mean?'

'I mean, what about Ernest?'

'What about him?' But his aggression eased as their faces told him that this was about more than a thwarted shag. From the tent came the sound of Valerie sobbing. They moved out of earshot.

Against their silent disapproval, Dodds stuck to his 'so-what?' guns 'She was up for it.'

'You were in her tent!' said Danny.

'She invited me in.'

Crockett shouted in his face. 'Oh yeah? So, she said, "why don't you come and see me in my tent and I'll get my knickers off for you?"'

This scene flashed up in Danny's mind before his anger got him shouting too. 'Sod who invited who, she's Ernest's fiancée! What about that? You've ruined things for them.'

'Ruined? I only had hold of her arse.'

'Oh, only that, and in front of Ernest.'

'I told you, she was up for it!'

'That's not the point!' said Danny.

'Piss off! Who the fuck do you think you are, anyway?' said Dodds.

Always a tough question for Danny, but this time his answer was, with his good hand, to punch Dodds in his defiant face. The blow caught his cheekbone. Seemingly unaffected, Dodds dived forward to grab Danny around the waist. Winded and instantly aware that he was tackling a stronger opponent, Danny lurched back and brought them both to the ground, where they grappled, snatching at each other's wrists to stop punches being thrown. When Dodds forced himself on top of Danny, Crockett jumped on his back to pull him away. 'For fuck's sake, pack it in!'

Dodds bucked like a bronco and sent Crockett sprawling. Dodds finally wrenched his right hand free of Danny's bandaged left but, on the point of delivering a clean punch, he was lifted and thrown back on his arse by Ernest.

'Lads, lads.'

Ernest stood over Dodds, who must have thought he was about to take revenge because he leapt to his feet and stood back.

'There's no need for this, boys.' Here was Ernest, no longer the betrayed fiancé but their club leader again. Dodds stared at the ground.

'You're good friends, so I want you to shake hands.' It sounded comically old-fashioned. Had it been anyone else, they would have laughed, but it was Ernest. Danny and Dodds faced each other sullenly.

'And look at each other! Mean it!' Surprised to hear Ernest shouting, they stepped forward and shook hands.

'Good,' said Ernest.

Calm descended and they stood not knowing what to say

until, behind Ernest, Valerie emerged from her tent, head down, carrying her small suitcase. 'I want to go home.'

Ernest turned around to see his fiancée's red-rimmed eyes and mascara-smeared face. In the gentlest tone, he said, 'Of course, let me take your case.'

Danny and Crockett left, tugging Dodds with them. Back in their tent, Dodds started packing his own case.

'Too late to get a lift to the station with Ernest and Valerie,' said Crockett, with a wink at Danny.

Dodds saw it. 'I'll hitch. You don't think I'd go with them, do you?'

'Dunno. Seems you're capable of anything,' said Danny.

Dodds clenched his fists.

Crockett stepped between them. 'Short holiday, though. But if you must go screwing around with the club leader's fiancée.'

'Look, once we got started, she got as carried away as me.'

'Yeah, but who started it?' said Danny.

Dodds threw up his hands. 'Do you know what? Do you know what I think?'

'Think? Steady on, Dodds,' said Crockett.

'She's not good enough for him.'

After a short silence, Crockett surprised Danny by nodding agreement.

'OK, I was out of order but . . .' said Dodds.

'But she's going to be his wife, for God's sake,' said Danny.

'Not now she's not,' said Crockett.

Danny recalled Ernest's haggard face and his struggle to keep control, and how he had been a model of dignity in dealing with both Dodds and Valerie. But Dodds had a point.

Crockett threw up his hands. 'Maybe it's best. I mean, if she could do this with you, she could do it with anyone.'

229

Dodds couldn't help smiling. 'Oh, thank you very much!'

Danny picked up Dodds's case and handed it to him.

Dodds shrugged but looked cheered that things weren't so bad between them after all. 'No more boys' club for me, though. Time to do other things.'

'Too grown up now, eh? What with your new car coming and all,' said Danny.

Dodds frowned. 'See you in a few days.'

As he headed out to the road, Crockett shouted, 'And if you see Valerie on the train, keep your fucking hands to yourself.'

Dodds didn't look back.

Crockett shook his head. 'That Valerie, soppy cow. However, Dodds might just have saved Ernest from an unhappy marriage.'

'But he didn't do it with that in mind,' said Danny.

'Dodds doesn't have much in mind about anything, except . . .'

'So, because things turn out all right in the end, he gets away with doing wrong.'

'Bother you, does it?'

'Yes, it does.'

'Has it really turned out OK? No more club for him,' said Crockett.

'He'll have the front to return and Ernest will welcome him back. It's what Ernest does,' said Danny.

Crockett stretched and put his hands behind his head. 'At least we've something to be grateful to Dodds for.'

'Oh?' said Danny.

'That arse! The flash of that amazing arse. Boy, is Ernest going to miss it.'

Danny grinned. It was, indeed, an image, along with Geraldine's breasts, to keep in mind for future reference.

'Oh well, some Dodds-less days to go. It might make a pleasant change,' said Danny.

It didn't. It rained for a couple of days and they spent long hours in their tents. Danny's hand healed enough to need only a plaster, which allowed him to go canoeing on the river that was finally deep enough. But they missed Dodds and his central role in their friendship; a troublesome totem around which banter formed and grew hilarious, or heated.

When told of Dodds's departure, Ernest simply nodded. That evening he insisted on driving Danny to the village phone box to call and find out if Dodds had got home OK. He had. For the rest of the week, to everyone's relief, Ernest behaved as if nothing had happened, but he was less than his usual joyful self and was seen more than once at the edge of the camp, hands on hips, staring into the distance.

The day before they were due to leave, Danny remembered the postcards he'd promised Linda. In the village post office, he handed over the money for two.

The shopkeeper gave him an extra one. 'Here you are, love, it's three for two this week, as we're getting near the end of the season. All you need to do is buy an extra stamp.'

He didn't want to, but she was already holding up three stamps. He moved to a small shelf by the counter and wrote, *Dear Linda*, but struggled to find enough words to fill the space. In extra-large writing, he mentioned only the weather and the canoeing and, knowing her mother would be reading it, closed not with 'love' but with *looking forward to seeing you soon*. He saw no point sending two clumsy greetings

231

on the same day. For the second card, he thought first of his mother, who had told him not to bother, and then of Cordelia.

Crockett, who had been waiting outside, came in. 'What's the hold-up?'

'Thought I might send one to Cordelia, too.'

Crockett grinned. 'Two-timing eh?'

'No.'

Was he? He couldn't be sure.

'Go on,' said Crockett, 'it'll make her happy, birds like that sort of thing.'

Writing to Cordelia, like talking to her, proved easier. He wrote about an 'eventful week', in which Ernest had proved to be a fine bloke and, after hesitating, that it would be good to see her again.

'Do you think it's OK for blokes to put kisses under the messages?'

'Not unless you're a poofter,' said Crockett.

Outside, Danny popped the cards, kiss-less, into the postbox.

Crockett pointed to the third card. 'Who's that one for?'

'It was a free extra. Linda asked for two but I couldn't think of anything more to say.'

'No one else to send it to?' said Crockett.

'How many girls do you think I know?'

'Bit of a waste not to send it.'

Then Danny remembered Nobby, pale and gaunt, walking away after offering him spending money for the holiday. He'd probably never had a postcard in his life.

'I won't be a sec, Croc.'

Danny returned to the shelf.

Dear Nobby,

Had a good time. You wouldn't have enjoyed it, too much fresh air and daylight! You also missed one of the best renditions ever of 'ging gang goolie goolie . . .'

Dodds blew it with Ernest and went home early. Hope you're taking care. If you're not, give my regards to your new mate, Giles.

Danny

PS Thanks for the offer of dosh for the holiday, it was kind of you.

30

On returning from Devon on Wednesday evening, Danny went to the phone box and called Linda. After the pips, her mother answered. 'Tate Gallery 4211.'

'Hello, Mrs Bain, it's Danny Byrne, could I speak to Linda, please?'

'Oh.' In the pause that followed, he envisaged her adding another item to the blacklist on her daughter's prospective boyfriend: 'doesn't have a phone at home'.

'Just a moment, she's not long in from work.'

Unlike Danny, who had been gallivanting around in Devon with roughs from that boys' club.

She put her hand over the speaker. A muffled exchange ensued, comprising much more than 'It's for you.'

'Hello, Danny. I haven't got your postcards yet.'

'I had a great time, thanks.'

'Don't be sarky.'

'I only managed one.' He nearly added, 'sorry' but no longer felt apologetic. 'We were out in the wilds and I only got to the post office yesterday and there didn't seem much point sending two . . .'

'I see.'

He guessed she'd stopped listening after 'managed only one'.

'So, you had a good time,' she said.

'We did.'

'Dodds didn't, he's been back a few days. What happened exactly?'

He resisted the temptation to tell her. 'Oh, you know Dodds, always taking things a bit too far.'

'He said he'd fallen out with the club leader.'

'Yes, pity that.'

'And he had a mark on his face. Didn't get violent, did it? He wouldn't say.'

'With Ernest, of course not!' said Danny.

'In that fight with the local boys, then?'

Danny was surprised that Dodds had mentioned only one bust-up, and annoyed that she wanted to know so much about it. 'So, you've seen him, then.'

In the silence that followed, he thought she was on the point of telling him something important. Whatever it had been, it wasn't what she said next. 'I'm glad you're back.'

'Me, too. When can I see you?' said Danny.

'Last time, you mentioned going out for something to eat.'

'Yes, where would you like to go?'

'There's a nice Italian restaurant in Victoria.'

'Sounds fine.'

'How about Friday?' she said.

'Yes. Would you mind if we met in your courtyard this time?'

'Oh, why?'

'It's just that . . .'

'Doesn't matter, half past six?'

'I'm looking forward to seeing you.'

'I'm looking forward to seeing you, too,' she said.

He was pleased to hear this but wished she'd said it first.

As if sensing his need for reassurance, she added, 'Really, I've missed you.'

Spirits only partially lifted, he said, 'Half past six, then.'

'Bye . . . then,' said Linda.

It felt like the wrong moment to ask her to pack it in with the 'then' mimicry.

31

Next day, Danny and Crockett came out of the Regency and were startled by a long blast of a car horn. A blue Ford Anglia pulled up beside them. Dodds stuck his head out of the window and waved a vigorous V-sign. 'Fucking pedestrians!'

'Sorry, we didn't order a minicab,' said Crockett.

Dodds, finally in his new car, the belated seventeenth birthday present, only a couple of months after passing his test. But he didn't look happy. 'Well, do you want a ride or not?'

'No thanks, unless you want to give us a lift to the club,' said Danny.

'The club, haven't you had enough of it for a while?' said Dodds.

'At least we have a choice whether to go or not,' said Crockett.

'We didn't unload yesterday, said we'd help Ernest sort everything out this morning,' said Danny.

'Aren't you good boys.'

Crockett winked at Danny and stuck to mates' law, which allowed nothing to impress. He pointed to the Anglia's inverted rear window. 'Looks like your rear window's had a nasty karate chop.'

Dodds glowered at him. 'Fuck the window, just get in will you!'

Crockett was undeterred. 'Mummy told me never to accept lifts from strange men.'

Dodds sat back, breathing deeply, fighting to stay calm. 'Come on! We've waited long enough for this fucking car.'

True. Danny and Crockett were always going to be his first passengers. They'd looked forward to heading out 'on the pull' and had plans to drive to the coast at weekends. Yet now the car had arrived, envy was elbowing out the pleasure Danny had expected to feel.

'When did you get it?' said Danny.

'Waiting for me when I got back.'

'And you haven't pulled a bird yet?' said Crockett.

Dodds looked ready to explode. 'OK, I'll drop you at the fucking club.'

Crockett grinned and opened the door to let Danny climb in to sit behind him.

While getting in, Danny said, 'Isn't this the wrong way round, Croc, given your shorter legs?'

'No,' said Crockett and gave Danny's arse a shove. Once seated himself, he turned to Dodds and tapped the dashboard. 'Thank you, my man, off you go.'

Dodds floored the accelerator.

Crockett grabbed the back of Dodds's seat. 'Take it easy, this is how you drive *after* we've robbed the bank!'

At the end of the road, Dodds swung the car in the

opposite direction to the club and roared along the embankment.

'What's up?' said Crockett.

Dodds stayed silent and stared straight ahead. At Lambeth Bridge, he took the roundabout so fast that the car came close to keeling over. Crockett turned to Danny, attempting a grin but looking worried. Approaching Vauxhall Bridge, the lights turned red. Dodds kept going. Danny closed his eyes. Amid the sound of horns and squealing tyres, they made it unscathed through the junction.

'What the fuck are you doing? You mad bastard!' said Crockett.

'What? What did you call me?' said Dodds.

'A bastard, are you trying to get us killed?'

Dodds turned right around to say to Danny, 'The short-arse is right.'

The lights at the approaching Chelsea Bridge junction were also red. Danny slapped at Dodds's face to get him to look at the road. 'Stop!'

'Dodds, for fuck's sake!' said Crockett.

Dodds revved harder. Danny gripped the seatback and Crockett jammed his feet against the dashboard. The lights turned to red and amber. Unharmed, they sped on to the Royal Hospital Gardens, where Dodds braked hard and wrenched the car across oncoming traffic. To the sound of more blaring horns, the car came to a jarring halt in the lay-by in front of the large gates.

'Fuck you, Dodds,' said Crockett, reaching for the door.

Before he could get out Dodds said, 'How's this for being a bastard?'

Eyes closed, he hit the throttle again. The car roared forward, bounced up the pavement and smashed into the boundary wall. Danny toppled forward over Crockett's seat. Crockett banged into the windscreen and bounced back. The engine stalled and steam hissed from under the crumpled bonnet.

As Crockett straightened up, Dodds caught him in a headlock. 'That's what bastards do, you short-arse.'

When Dodds let him go, Crockett punched him hard in the side of his head. 'This is what short-arses do!' He paused and added, 'You bastard.'

Danny dived between them. This time, Dodds didn't retaliate and simply stared ahead.

'What's going on, Dodds?' said Danny.

'It's true,' said Dodds.

'What's true?'

'The "bastard" bit.'

'We could have told you that,' said Crockett.

'My mum and dad aren't my parents.'

Crockett refused to get serious. 'Whose are they then?'

Danny grabbed his shoulder. 'Button it, Croc.'

Dodds put his hands over his eyes.

A man standing astride a pushbike tapped on his window. 'Everything OK?'

Dodds didn't move.

'Yes, thanks, we're fine,' said Danny.

'Made a right mess of your car.'

'You don't say!' shouted Crockett.

'Only trying to help,' said the cyclist and pedalled off.

Crocket and Danny got out and went around to Dodds's side. Danny opened the door and said, 'Come on, get some air.' He grabbed Dodds's arm and was surprised how easily he complied. On his feet, Dodds was shaking his head, as if saying 'no' pre-emptively to whatever Danny might say.

He began taking deep breaths. Danny feared they might be about to turn to sobs and put a hand on his shoulder.

'What do you mean, they're not your parents?' said Danny.

'They've just told me that they adopted me as a baby.'

'Sorry, Dodds,' said Crocket, 'that's bastard news . . . er, I mean . . .'

After shaking his head at Crockett, Danny said, 'I'm sorry, too, Dodds. What a shock.'

'I'll say, it's turned him into Stirling Moss,' said Crockett.

'No wonder you feel bad,' said Danny.

Dodds, getting his breathing under control, shrugged. 'Dunno, right now, more angry.'

'What about your real parents? Did they tell you? Do you know where they are?' said Danny.

'Dead? Abroad? In jail?' said Crockett.

Danny shoved him. 'Jesus, Croc.'

Dodds pulled away and pointed at the car. In a mimicked high-pitched voice he said, 'Sorry we're not your parents but look at the new car we bought you!'

'They didn't really say that?' said Danny.

'Something like it,' said Dodds.

'That would do it for me,' said Crockett.

As if he hadn't heard him, Dodds said, 'Now, I'm wondering who they were, these people who gave me to a butcher, who spouts the fucking Bible all the time.'

In the silence that followed, Danny tried to put himself in Dodds's place but couldn't get there.

'But why tell me at all?' said Dodds.

'Would you sooner not know?' said Danny.

'Yes. No. Well, not like this.'

'How then, for fuck's sake, with semaphore?' said Crockett.

Dodds closed his eyes. 'I come from the kind of people who give their baby away.'

'Could have been only the mother . . .' said Danny, and immediately wondered if he should have said, your mother, or your real mother. 'Maybe she was a young girl who got into trouble and the father legged it.'

'Yeah, look at our estate, three mums for every two dads,' said Crockett.

'At least you've got two parents. OK, your old man can be a pain in the arse but your mum's a diamond,' said Danny.

'After all their Christian crap, they've been lying to me.'

'Seems to me, they've done a pretty decent Christian thing for seventeen years,' said Danny.

Crockett threw his arms up in exasperation. 'Look, I was born months after my parents got married. I'm a bit of a bastard myself.'

'Don't we know it,' said Danny.

Dodds showed the beginnings of a smile.

'You're just a poor, deprived kid with parents who were thoughtless enough to buy him a car for his birthday. Fucking unforgiveable,' said Crockett.

'So, the car is supposed to make everything OK, is it?'

'It's a fair old try, don't you think?' said Crockett.

'They're still your mum and dad, aren't they?' said Danny, 'You may be upset but you must know they love you – and you've got a new car, for God's sake!'

'I'll have it if you don't want it,' said Crockett, 'but you'll have to get it fixed first. Speaking of fixing, there's a phone box by the bridge – shall I ring Moon's?'

Moon's was the garage on Horseferry Road that serviced Mr Dodds's Rover. Dodds paused to think, then, in a telling acknowledgement that, for now at least, he would need his adoptive father's help, he nodded. 'OK, thanks Croc.'

Crockett set off and Dodds started inspecting the damage.

'Let's get it off the pavement,' said Danny, 'the police will notice this if they drive by.'

He pushed from the front while Dodds pulled and steered with one arm through the driver's window. With the engine no longer steaming, the car simply looked parked. They got back inside.

'So, what now?' said Danny.

'I don't know.'

'Maybe you should see it from their—'

'Don't! Right now, I want to see it from *my* point of view. OK?'

'OK, but why does it make you so angry? Don't you like them any more?'

Dodds shrugged. 'Not sure. I don't know them like I thought I did. And now I have real parents that I don't know.'

'Do you want to find them?'

'Dunno, it's got me wondering. I can understand a girl getting put up the duff and not being able to cope, but not a father legging it. He must have been an arsehole.'

Danny was glad Crockett wasn't there to make a comment about inheriting characteristics from your parents.

'It happens, quite a lot,' said Danny.

Dodds sat back. 'I don't want to think about it, but I can't stop.'

Danny pointed at the crumpled bonnet. 'How will they take this?'

'The usual. They'll say how disappointed they are and point to lessons that can be learned. Then, after a couple of days, they'll behave as if it had never happened.'

'And you don't like them!'

'Dunno.'

'But they've given you so much, and they're going to give you more.'

'I'm going to be a butcher, Danny. Thing is, I'll never know if that's worse or better than what might have been, if I hadn't been dumped.'

Danny felt pretty sure that it wouldn't have been better.

'What's wrong with being a butcher, in a business that'll be yours one day?'

Dodds didn't answer and Danny had run out of reassurance. The more he thought about it, the less sympathy he had for Dodds's reaction.

Dodds got out of the car and leaned, straight-armed, head-down, against the driver's door. After a couple of minutes, he popped his head through the open window and, nodding, gave a sheepish smile that indicated he was over the worst.

Seconds later, he stood back and confirmed it. 'Anyway, fuck it.'

'Language, please!' said Crockett, coming up behind him. He grinned and pressed his hands to his cheeks like an excited child. 'Moon's will be here soon, and we're going to get a ride in their big red truck!'

32

At six o'clock, Danny waited in the courtyard of Linda's block. Movement on her balcony drew his eye and, looking up, he saw Mrs Bain. She made no gesture of recognition but turned away, no doubt to tell Linda that the boy who couldn't be bothered to come to her door was waiting, like a cab driver, in the courtyard.

Feeling nervous as he waited, he recalled that she hadn't been overly enthusiastic to his suggestion that they go out for a meal. Was this to be their 'last supper'?

Linda came skipping down the stairs and greeted him with a hug and a kiss on the cheek. Standing fifty feet below Mrs Bain, Danny could feel her disapproval for a daughter who wasn't going to modify her behaviour or the company she kept for anyone, even her mother. Danny hoped Linda was also signalling that she was pleased to see him. As they left the courtyard, Linda turned to wave to her mother. Danny waved too, which was as close as he dared to the V-sign he'd like to have given.

'Not keen on me, is she?' said Danny.

'Does it matter? I'm the one going out with you.'

'Well, no but . . .'

'So, the holiday was OK?'

He nodded, 'Devon's nice, I can see why your parents like it. It was good to get away.'

'From what?'

'Not *from*, why can't it be good just to get away *to* somewhere?'

She shrugged. 'How's your hand?'

'Fine, thanks. Only this little plaster now.'

He held up his hand, but she wasn't looking. He feared that her greeting in the courtyard might have been the highlight of their date.

On the way to the restaurant, Linda alternated between brittle – walking apart – and benign – clutching his arm. The effort to be benign seemed just that, an effort, and she gave off none of the warmth that had raised his own temperature during teatime at her flat. Once, when she linked arms and came close, he tried to kiss her, but face radar moved her lips out of range.

'Not in the street, Danny!' she said, as if the street was only one of a long list of settings in which a kiss would be inappropriate.

In the restaurant, they sat either side of a scrubbed table, and on wooden chairs like those in his own kitchen. She took off her short white jacket to reveal a black ribbed polo-neck with no sleeves. It occurred to him that if this did prove to be their 'last supper', it could be a long time before he sat opposite a girl as beautiful as Linda Bain. The waiter, who seemed equally impressed, lit a candle in a Chianti bottle that sat on the table between them. He offered to hang up Linda's jacket. She refused and put it over the back of her chair. Danny would have declined the offer, too, but the waiter didn't ask him.

As it was the first time he'd been in a restaurant that wasn't a chippy or a Wimpy Bar, he'd been happy for Linda to choose their meals. She had shrugged and gone for 'her favourite'. The shrug left him thinking that, like with dancing, letting a girl lead wasn't the thing to do.

The meal arrived in oval earthenware dishes. Danny waited for Linda to start and, following her lead, began eating only with the fork.

'Never had this before,' said Danny.

'Never had cannelloni?' she said, in the same way her mother had said, 'never been to Devon before?'

Linda realised it. 'Sorry, I didn't mean. . .'

When asked about the wine, she asked for two glasses of Chianti. He had never had wine before either, and wondered if it would taste like the Harvey's Bristol Cream his mother bought at Christmas. It didn't, and he was surprised by how much he liked it. He stopped himself taking another swig when he noticed Linda was only sipping.

'Nice, isn't it?' she said.

'Yes,' he said, bridling that, like her mother, she couldn't help making a virtue of knowing or having done something he hadn't.

'Cannelloni isn't that common, is it? I mean not like fish and chips,' he said.

'No, it's Italian.'

'You don't say. Well, now I can add it to the other Italian things I know about: Spaghetti Bolognese, Alfa Romeo, Sophia Loren, ice cream . . .'

'No need to be sarky.'

'Well, don't be snobby. Do you think I didn't know?' he said.

'No.' A weary concession, as if the subject, or he, wasn't worth any more bother. Yet she gave an apologetic smile that had him regretting the way he'd reacted.

'Sorry,' he said, and soon wished he hadn't, as it did little to warm her chilly demeanour. Maybe apologising had been a mistake and caused her to think him a bit of a wimp not prepared to hold his own against her? Whether she did or not, he decided that saying sorry had been wimpish.

He emptied his glass of wine on only the second time he picked it up. Linda's was barely touched. Flustered, he said, 'Would you like some more wine?'

She shook her head. 'No thanks, but have another if you want.'

He had brought what he thought would be more than enough money but, having looked only briefly at the menu prices outside, thought it best to go cautiously. 'No, that'll do me.'

Almost finished, he found difficulty eking out the last of the cannelloni from the curved sides of the dish. He deliberately used the dessert spoon to scoop up the remainder and waited for Linda to comment. When she showed no hint of disapproval, he felt a little ashamed.

'Are you going to have a sweet?' he asked.

'A pudding? No thanks, I think I'll go straight to coffee. Fancy a cappuccino?'

He did, and he told her that cappuccino had converted him to coffee. How, at home, he'd occasionally risked the chicory brown liquid of Camp Coffee, in the belief that, like beer, it was an acquired taste. It wasn't. And how the smell of instant coffee bore no resemblance to the heady aroma of beans roasting in the big spinner at Cullen's grocer's.

Linda gave the smiling nod of someone who hadn't been

listening. Danny sipped through the froth to the scalding liquid, while she waited, spooning the brown-speckled mousse into her mouth.

'So, Dodds didn't have much of a holiday in Devon,' she said.

'He decided to leave, no one forced him.'

She showed no sign of wanting to know more. 'Still, he came home to that nice new car.'

'Have you seen it?' said Danny.

'Yes, he gave me a ride in it.'

An image of Dodds driving her away from him came into his head.

'Me, too, with Crockett yesterday. The car's not so nice now, unless Moon's can complete the bodywork in twenty-four hours.'

Her face tautened and her sharp, beautiful features were for a moment only sharp. He hoped he hadn't sounded too pleased in telling her, but he pushed on. 'He smashed it up deliberately.'

'Really? Is he all right?' she said.

'Really. He's fine, physically at least. You might want to ask him why he did it. Oh, and Crockett and I are all right too.'

She frowned and their words dissolved into silence. Danny watched her finishing her coffee, his stomach churning with the knowledge that things were ending, that Linda was in another league, peopled by those who were beautiful but impatient. At the same time, there came a growing realisation that it might not be a league he wished to be in.

The waiter put the bill on the table in a small saucer. Linda reached for her handbag and picked up the bill to check it. Another thing she thought Danny wasn't up to?

249

He took it from her fingers, he noted the total, reached into his pocket and put down enough cash, including a ten per cent tip, and got to his feet.

'Aren't you going to check it?' said Linda.

'No,' said Danny. 'Ready?'

She smiled and he wondered how many smiles he was away from the final one. Outside the restaurant, she took his arm. 'Thank you.'

'It was nothing,' he said.

'It wasn't "nothing". You can't earn very much at the off-licence.'

'I do all right.'

'Not all right enough to pay for both of us when we go out.'

Was she suggesting going halves in future? But what future? Behind her talk of him not having enough money, he had heard a different message: that it could be he who wasn't enough. They walked along Victoria Street, arms linked, but neither applying any pressure of affection.

'Do you think much about the future, Danny?'

This threw him, mainly because he didn't.

'Not really, until now, except for the obvious: A levels, university maybe. I think more about the present – and a lot more about the past.'

'Oh?'

'Well, there's so much more of it.'

'Well, yes,' she said, and asked no more questions.

On reaching the estate, she began looking in her handbag for her key. In the lift, she stared at her shoes. At her door, she put the key in the lock before turning to him. Surprised how tenderly she was looking at him, he went for what he feared would be a last kiss on her beautiful mouth. She

ducked to one side and pecked him lightly on the cheek.
'Thank you, Danny Byrne.'

She opened the door and went in, leaving him feeling
that they had been carrying something heavy between them
and had just set it down.

In the courtyard, he wondered if this was how you end it
with someone: by not mentioning it and closing a door? He
considered going back and ringing her bell to make sure he'd
understood things right. But he had no idea what he would
say. He thrust his hands in his pockets and started walking.
At the river, he crossed Lambeth Bridge, walked along the
Albert Embankment and came back over Vauxhall Bridge,
turning over in his mind what he'd done, or not done, to
turn Linda off. By the time he reached the Tate Gallery, he
had come to the painful conclusion that it wasn't about what
he had or hadn't done; it was about who he was – or wasn't.

He had, though, briefly flourished in her affection, and
for a while had felt like an improved version of himself. But
Linda hadn't noticed this, or she had noticed and realised
he wasn't what she wanted. Either way, he had learned that
when it came to liking or even loving, control lies with the
one who cares least.

He wouldn't contact her again. She had been kind enough
not to say it was over. She hadn't dumped him but he had
been dumped.

Back in the estate, Cordelia, dressed to the nines in heels
and a red miniskirt, emerged from the Tap House. She put
a pack of Rothmans in her bag. 'Hello, Danny, just picking
up cigarettes for Mum.'

'You've been out then?' he said.

She fell in beside him. 'Yes, pictures.'

'Dodds?'

She nodded. 'And you?'

'We went for something to eat.' He regretted it sounding as if it was more grown-up than 'going to the pictures'.

'Oh?'

'One of those Italian restaurants in Victoria.'

'Sounds nice.'

'It was OK. I had cannelloni for the first time.'

'Lovely.'

Was he the only one who'd never eaten it before?

When they reached the bench outside Jones's, she put down her bag, sat beside it and tucked her hands under her thighs.

He stopped but remained standing. 'So, pictures again?'

'Yes, and not in the back row,' she said.

'That can't have pleased him.'

'Do you know, I don't care.'

'Oh.'

Much as Danny didn't like to admit it, Dodds was a catch for girls, especially now that he looked like Charles Bronson's younger brother. There was also the extra attraction to others, like Linda, of his uninhibited behaviour. For a moment, he saw himself and Cordelia as a couple of second-division teams that had missed out on promotion.

It was time to shut up, but his thoughts made it into his mouth. 'That didn't last long.'

She sat back and closed her eyes. 'Too long,' she said.

She might have said the same to him, if she knew. He felt an urge to offer comfort but went only as far as sitting beside her.

It was growing dark. A streetlight came on. She lifted her face to it, as if sunbathing, and pushed her hair up. Seeing her bare neck brought a catch to his throat.

'Really?' he said.

'Dodds is OK. You know, clear about what he wants.'

Now he was Dodds again, not Stephen.

Danny recalled the stout resistance she had to put up while watching *Moll Flanders*, but her face told him it wasn't about that.

'He talks about himself a lot, and what he's going to do,' she said.

Danny nodded agreement, while knowing that he was no different, except that instead of talking, he was forever *thinking* about himself.

'It's as if whatever he's doing, whoever he's seeing, it's only something to do, someone to be with until he gets away,' she said.

'Did he tell you about his mum and dad, then?'

'No, what about them?'

'Oh, nothing.'

'He says he plans to leave home as soon as possible. And now he has a car, he'll be doing more of what he wants; even asked me if I felt the same about still living at home with Mum.'

'Do you?' said Danny.

'Now and again, but it doesn't last.' She took her hands from under her thighs and stretched out her legs. Her mini-skirt rose a little. 'And you two, how are you getting on?'

'I don't know. . . things change.'

'For the better?' she said.

'No. Strange, isn't it, how you expect things to get better when you're with someone you like, but . . .'

'Yes,' she said.

A car rolled towards them. He looked up. Dodds was at the wheel of the Rover that belonged to his father. Despite crashing the car he'd been given, he must have extracted maximum recompense from his father for the news of his adoption. 'Getting away' may now have been put on hold at the prospect of having a butcher's shop with a budget for posh cars. Next time Danny saw Ron, he'd point out that secondary-modern kids can become one of the bosses, too.

Danny waved, but when Dodds saw them, he accelerated. The car sped past, but not fast enough to prevent a fleeting sight of Linda, staring from the passenger seat, her face a picture of regret, with no hint of the triumph Danny might have expected. He gazed up the street long after the car had gone.

So, final confirmation, with no time wasted, that it was over. The difference between what he had been expecting and it finally happening brought a soft thud of sadness to his stomach. But, almost immediately, it began to fade against a growing feeling of acceptance, even relief.

He'd forgotten Cordelia was with him until she squeezed his hand.

'Well, there it is,' he said.

Cordelia didn't reply. Minutes passed, as they sat in silence.

Eventually, Cordelia stood up. 'Mum will be gasping for her cigarettes. I'd better go now,' she said.

'Me too,' said Danny.

'You, OK?'

He was beginning to think he was. 'Fine, thanks.'

33

As Danny got home, Nobby was coming out of the door.

'How goes?' said Nobby.

'All right. Had enough to eat?'

'Don't be like that, your mum invited me in. Can't get enough of her sausages and mash.'

'No, don't suppose you can.'

'So, did you get your leg over a yokel?' said Nobby.

'What's it to you?'

He grinned. 'Nothing, but it's a lot to you, isn't it?'

'You still look like shit, Nobby.'

Nobby shrugged and, as if Danny's description had reminded him, said, 'Do you fancy coming up West with me tonight?'

'Why would I want to do that, after last time?'

'Oh yeah, a bit of bad luck that, blown out by the blonde bird, and getting nicked.'

'I wasn't blown out, she had to leave.'

'Well, she was back last week. Didn't see her with anyone.'

'Really?'

'Yeah, might be there tonight,' said Nobby.

'Doubt it, last time was a Saturday. Today's Friday.'

'It's still the weekend, and there's bound to be other birds. Come on, if you need dosh, I've got plenty.'

'No thanks.'

Danny tried to push past him, but Nobby held his sleeve and pulled him face to face. His cheeks had become more concave, his eyes bloodshot. 'Look, it would be good if you could come tonight.' He was pleading, not asking.

'Why's that?'

'Oh, you know, a bit of company.'

'Yeah, right!'

Then, for the first time in ages, Danny was caught out by Nobby saying, 'Please.'

Would it be so bad to go again? Danny thought of Jackie and the buzzing excitement of his last visit. He had nothing ahead of him but a gloomy night indoors. 'OK, what time?'

'Around ten?'

'See you there.'

'Sweet,' said Nobby.

Danny went in. His mother was in the kitchen, washing up Nobby's plate. 'My, you've a face like a wet week, what's the matter?'

'Nothing.'

'Lover's tiff?'

'God you can be irritating, Mum.'

She smiled. 'Especially when I'm right?'

He ignored this and, so soon after cannelloni, turned down her bangers and mash.

Later, washed and changed, he popped his head around the front-room door. 'I'm off out now, Mum.'

'Bit late, isn't it?'

'For what?'

'Going to make it up with her?'

'No, I'm not, will you mind your own business!'

She raised her hands, smiling. 'OK, OK, keep your hair on.'

On his way out, she said, 'Be careful, and get home at a decent time.'

He felt in no mood to do either. As he closed the front door, she shouted, 'And keep out of police stations!'

He knew she was worried but guessed she'd also be chuckling in the hall.

34

Giles stood on the doorstep of La Discotheque, plying his mine-host banter to those passing, which changed depending on whether he was addressing males or females. To older couples he offered no welcoming smile, indicating with a slight shake of the head that La Discotheque wasn't for them. Maybe Giles wasn't such a hard-bitten Soho sleazer, after all.

Once more displaying zero recognition, Giles said, 'On your own, son?' Without waiting for a reply, he added, 'Don't worry, you'll find some nice company here.' Danny took his change and thought of adding, 'Giles' to his 'thank you', but Giles's lifted eyebrows said, 'well, are you going up or not?'

Danny pushed open the door. A blast of smoke-laden air and sound whooshed past him. While his eyes grew accustomed to the dark, he waited and watched dancers silhouetted by the white glow from lights framing the small stage.

Nobby came over to him. 'Lively tonight. Oh, and that bird you were with last time is here.'

He pointed to the dance floor, where Jackie was in a clinch with a worryingly good-looking bloke. Danny raised a hand in greeting but received barely a nod of recognition. With little prospect of repeating their previous intimacy, he reflected that, when it came to girls, he kept having to start again.

A slow session began and couples came together with little attempt at dancing beyond 'hold on and shuffle'. Jackie and her partner moved like conjoined twins.

'There are other birds here,' said Nobby. 'Do you want to get a drink?'

'At those prices?'

Nobby glanced around before pulling the edge of a small brown envelope from his jeans pocket. 'Dubes instead?'

'Not this time, thanks.'

'Please yourself.'

The music stopped and, over Nobby's shoulder, Danny saw Jackie and her partner stand apart. He regretted that tonight he'd taken no Dutch courage, but this might be his only chance. He took a deep breath and stepped onto the dance floor.

'Would you like to dance, Jackie?' he said, making it clear to her partner that he wasn't a stranger.

The guy moved between them. 'This isn't an "excuse-me" dance, mate.'

'You weren't dancing.'

'Don't get fucking clever with me.'

Danny stood his ground on legs that were less than steady. From behind her partner, Jackie shook her head. Not a complete 'sod off', more what Danny hoped was a 'not now'.

He decided that what might come next wasn't going to be worth it and, trying to affect an air of indifference, he went back to Nobby.

'Blown out, again?'

'Guess so. Give me some of your sweeties and let's see if I can find someone else.'

In the toilet, Danny knocked back five purple hearts. Sober this time, he noticed the stink of urine and took in his surroundings: the sticky lino, the shit-coloured stains below the sink's single tap, the lone, naked lightbulb and, in the ruined mirror, how his face looked diseased. What the hell was he doing in a place like this?

Two men came in, stocky, with who-you-looking-at? faces. Nobby followed them. Instead of going to the urinals, they stayed by the door, silently encouraging Danny to leave. Nobby looked worried but avoided eye contact. Danny wondered why he spent time with people who frightened him.

As Danny left, one of the men closed the door behind him. He must have kept his weight on it because for the next few minutes, it wouldn't open for anyone who tried to go in. Danny made for the padded bench near the DJ and waited for the pills to do their stuff. When the men came out, they made for the exit by going straight across the dance floor, rightly assuming that any dancer in their path would get out of their way.

Nobby emerged and came over. Even in semi-darkness, Danny could see that whatever happened in the toilet had rendered his face paler. Nobby's hand shook as he held out a couple of sticks of Wrigley's. 'Want some?'

Danny declined. Nobby shrugged and went to the bar and returned holding two bottles of beer by their necks.

'If you don't want gum, these'll help with the dry mouth.'

'What's the matter, Nobby?'

'Nothing's the matter.'

'Yes, there is, what is it?'

'A bit of business has become urgent, something I could do without tonight.'

'And?'

'I have to go out to pick up something. Will you wait till I get back? I won't be long.'

Alarmed by Nobby looking so scared, Danny agreed to wait.

From inside his jacket, Nobby took out a small bundle of tiny brown envelopes bound by an elastic band and handed them to Danny. 'Hang on to these for me. It's getting late and I don't want to get rolled in the street.'

Before Danny could answer, Nobby had left.

Scared too, now, Danny shoved the bundle into his pocket. It was well past midnight. He returned to the bench to drink his beers. The pills had yet to kick in and he felt tired. He looked over at the mattresses and smiled at their being available for anything but rest. He sat back, taking in his dark, sordid surroundings and decided that he hated La Discotheque and everything in it.

By one o'clock the pills had kicked in and Danny was on his feet, swaying to the music.

Nobby returned, still looking worried. Danny wasted no time in returning his bundle of envelopes. 'So, what now?' said Danny.

'Didn't get that bit of business completely sorted.'

'For fuck's sake, why do you keep calling what you do "business"? Do you think it sounds more important?'

'It's what it is and I've got more to do tonight.'

'Why are you doing this shit, Nobby?'

'Well paid, mate. One good night and I earn more than you do in three months at the off-licence.'

261

'Well, good luck with your "business",' said Danny.

The purple hearts had raised Danny's pulse to top speed and blood thumping in his ears was matching the volume of the music. Across the floor, Jackie and her new boyfriend waited to take the place of a couple who were getting up from a mattress.

In his heightened, if agitated state, he thought he'd have one more try and set off across the dance floor. Jackie saw him coming, pulled her partner close and kissed him. Danny walked straight past them towards the exit.

Nobby caught up with him as he reached the door. 'Leaving?'

'No point staying.'

'There are other birds here.'

'Not for me there aren't. I've had time to check.'

'Well, if you're going, maybe you can do me a favour,' said Nobby.

'What?'

'Here a minute.' He ushered Danny back against the wall and took a large white envelope from his jacket. 'I've got to get this to George. Take it for me, will you?'

'At this time of night?'

'George doesn't sleep much, and he'll be expecting it. You don't have to see him, just stick it through his letterbox.'

'What's in it?'

'Some dosh.'

'Do it yourself.'

'I need to stay here. Please, be a mate.'

'No.'

'Look, I've bought my supply. Leaving now will mean customers going without, and they can get nasty. There'll be something in it for you.'

262

'Oh yeah, how much?'

'How much do you want?' said Nobby.

Because Danny had said 'no' before money was mentioned, Nobby's question was a stab of shame.

With desperation in his white face, Nobby said, 'Please, Danny.'

'Give it here then.'

'Sweet.' Nobby handed him the envelope. 'Keep it safe, whatever you do.' Danny folded it in half and put it in his back pocket. Nobby offered him a couple of pound notes.

'Keep your money,' said Danny.

At the bottom of the stairs, Giles held up his re-entry marker pen. Danny walked past him.

'Not coming back then?'

'Not in a million years.'

'Wise lad,' said Giles.

Surprised, Danny turned around. Giles had his back to him, as if he'd said nothing.

In Lower Regent Street, Danny took out the envelope. If, as he suspected, the wad of notes inside were fivers, he was holding more money than he'd had in his life. When putting the envelope back, bumps under the crease stopped it folding. His stomach churned. Money and drugs! At the same time, the sound of sirens chasing each other around the London night reminded him that he was out again, illegally, on the streets of the West End. He shook the pills to one end of the envelope, folded it and shoved it back in his pocket.

Jogging down the Duke of York Steps, he noticed, too late, that he was about to overtake two policemen. If they stopped him, tell-tale signs of drug-taking were bound to show in his eyes. And if they asked his age? Or searched him? Should he turn back or carry on? One of them looked back and saw him. He tapped his partner's arm. Danny passed them, looking straight ahead. At the bottom of the steps, he slowed his walk to what he hoped was an innocent pace, but as he crossed the Mall, he heard, 'Hold on a minute, son.'

They were about ten yards away. For once, fear didn't turn his legs to jelly; in his drugged state, it gave him wings. He sprinted into St James's Park and soon put a hundred yards between himself and the one policeman who gave chase. Terror and purple hearts, what a combination! He felt he could run forever, but his chaser – although not as fast – hadn't given up. As Danny crossed the bridge over the lake, his racing brain debated whether to keep or chuck the incriminating evidence. Panic made up his mind. On the other side, he flicked the envelope into the water. Instead of sinking, the white oblong floated on the surface and shone in the light of a lamppost.

'Sink, fuck you!' he said, through gritted teeth.

At the other end of the bridge, the panting policeman was walking towards him. 'OK son, stop there. What did you throw away?'

Danny considered giving up, and claiming he was only delivering something for a friend, but started interrogating himself: to whom? from whom? and, why throw it away? After what felt like an age, the envelope slipped out of sight and he sped away. The policeman gave chase as far as Birdcage Walk and gave up.

Danny kept going until he'd crossed Victoria Street, where he slowed to a walk, trying to calm down. By the time he reached Regency Street, fear of being caught had been replaced by terror at how George would react. He badly needed to pee. He crossed to the hexagonal urinal on

Horseferry Road, known locally as the 'scent bottle'. Having no doors and available night and day, it was a favourite halt for cab drivers – and for locals coming home from a night on the beer, a last-stop lifesaver that saved them from pissing themselves on their doorstep while fumbling for the key. It was also a venue for late-night assignations and, although the four urinals had chest-high separators, after dark it took nerve to stand next to an occupied one.

On his way in, Danny came face to face with a young policeman doing up his fly. He made way for Danny but hung around outside and said, 'Out late, son, aren't we?'

We? Yes, he thought, 'we' were in that shithole Discotheque, we took a few pills, we couriered some drugs and money – and we outran two of your colleagues.

Although the policeman sounded unthreatening, Danny wasn't going to risk being asked more questions. When he'd finished peeing, he flew out the other side of the urinal and raced into Vincent Square.

This time his chaser was fit enough to stay in close pursuit. On reaching the estate, Danny kept going rather than betray where he lived. Once he'd crossed Vauxhall Bridge Road into Pimlico, he began to feel tired and looked for a place to hide.

At the end of his old street, the brazier glowed red in front of Liam's hut. Out came Finnegan, barking.

'Whisht boy.' Liam emerged and, on recognising Danny, realised something was up. Gasping too hard to speak, Danny pointed back over his shoulder. Liam grabbed his arm and dragged him to the far end of the hut, lifted the lid on the big metal trunk and shoved him down into it.

'Quiet now,' he hissed. Danny flinched as he tried to calm his breathing and to get comfortable on a mattress of pickaxe handles. The lid came down, followed by a groan of metal under pressure as Liam sat on it. Finnegan was barking again.

'Whisht,' said Liam.

In premature-burial dark, panic drove Danny to bang on the lid to be let out. Liam gave a couple of responding thumps which, Danny guessed, were to disguise his own. The metal trunk flexed and creaked as Liam got up. The policeman was inside the hut. 'Seen a young lad go by here?'

Danny screwed his eyes shut, hoping that self-imposed blackness would be less scary than that with his eyes open.

'Ah, he must have been the one who set the dog barking,' said Liam.

'Don't know which way he went, then?'

'I don't. To tell ye the honest truth, it woke me from a bit of a doze, but I trust ye'll not be reporting me for dereliction of duty, officer.'

'Guess I've lost him.'

On the edge of hysteria, Danny clenched his teeth and breathed through his nose.

The trunk groaned as Liam sat down.

'Would ye like a cup of tea, officer?'

Danny groaned. Jesus, what was Liam doing!

'No thanks, good night.'

Danny held out until arrest became a better prospect than dying of panic. He banged on the lid again. Liam lifted it and whispered, 'Quiet now, he might be close yet.' He went to close the lid again.

'Not on your life,' said Danny, and scrambled out.

'Don't like confined spaces then, boy?'

'Who the hell does?'

'Still, any ould port in a storm, eh?' said Liam.

Danny rubbed his back where the wooden handles had dented it.

Liam smiled. 'But not the most comfortable hideout.'

Danny pointed at the trunk. 'Thanks . . .'

Liam thought for a moment. 'I hope you can tell me you're not after doing anything bad.'

'Not really bad, but illegal.'

Liam waited; head cocked.

'It's because I'm not old enough to be out overnight. I was caught recently . . . this time it would have been the courts,' said Danny.

'Not a hanging offence then. I doubt ye've much to fear from the police.'

'No, but . . .'

'Ye seem, nevertheless, troubled, boy.'

Yes, and the more Danny thought about things, the more troubled he became. How much money and how many pills were lying in duck-shit sludge at the bottom of the lake? He leaned over, holding his churning stomach.

'How about some tay? A little earlier than I usually take it but still . . .' Liam poured water from a large enamel jug into a battered kettle, shoved it into the brazier's coals, and livened them up with a poker. 'So, what is it, lad?'

Without looking up, Danny told of Nobby's request, the envelope, the chase and how he'd panicked. And how someone scarier than the police was about to be seriously pissed off.

Liam lit his clay pipe and his full, whiskered cheeks caved in a couple of times as he got it going. 'Now who's this George fella?'

'He's a big bloke that my friend Nobby works for.' As I do, he thought. 'Everyone's scared of him,' said Danny.

267

'I see,' said Liam, 'so his reaction won't be too civilised.'
'No.'
'Will you let your father know?'
'I don't have one.'
'No father? A hard absence for ye and your mother.' He took a few more sucks of smoke. 'I guess that on your estate everyone knows where everyone lives?'
Danny nodded.
'Well, this may be a good place to hide but not to stay. This friend of yours, will you be able to warn him?' said Liam.
'Yes.' Bowel-swilling fear gripped Danny as he imagined George's retribution and, although he wasn't scared of Nobby, he dreaded having to tell him what had happened.
'A good friend?'
'Does "old" mean the same as "good"?' said Danny.
Liam filled a brown teapot with boiling water and stirred in several spoons of tea.
'I suppose it depends.'
'He was, once.'
'And now?'
'Now? Not so much. I see him around.'
Liam handed him a mug of tea and poured in milk from a bottle. 'Sugar?' Shaking a little, Danny nodded, and three heaped spoonfuls went in.
'Few friends stay good, or bad for that matter, all the time.'
Danny sipped the scalding tea and considered the ups and downs of his lifelong friendship with Nobby.
'I suppose so,' said Danny.
'I imagine ye'll be warning him?' said Liam.
Along with tea and sympathy, Liam was easing him towards responsibility.

'Yes, I'll call around first thing. He won't be home yet and I daren't go back up West now.'

'A good start, boy.' He paused. 'And look, now, if there's any help I can give ye . . .'

Danny couldn't see how he could and, less shaky now, got to his feet. 'I don't think so, but thanks for hiding me, and for the tea.'

'Any time, Danny Byrne. Keep your head up.'

35

'In late last night?'

'Mum, why do you ask when you already know?' said Danny, groaning as he emerged from dreams that had tormented him since the purple hearts finally released him into sleep around five o'clock.

She stood over his bed, holding a mug of tea. With his first sip, the events of the previous night returned. He hunched up. 'Jesus, what time is it?'

'Nine o'clock, what's the matter? You weren't up West again, were you?'

'No, just with the others.' Then, the supporting lie. 'At Dodds's.'

'Didn't see that Linda Bain, then?'

'No.'

'Oh, thought you were . . .'

'Look, I've got to get up now.'

She left and, as Danny pulled on his clothes, his stomach went into fast spin. In the hall, he shouted, 'No breakfast for me, Mum. I have to go. Work.'

'Didn't you tell me it was this afternoon?'

Every dodgy answer was letting her know that something was wrong. Best to get out.

'Bye, Mum.'

He banged on Nobby's front door. Jean answered in her nightie under an open, quilted housecoat.

'My, you're early! Not able to sleep?' She called over her shoulder, 'Alan!'

No answer from Nobby's room. Jean shrugged and went into the kitchen. 'See if you can rouse him.'

Nobby lay face-down on the bed wearing only his boxers. Danny shook him.

He turned over and squinted. 'What is it?' His focus improved and realisation grew that something was up. 'You did get it to George?'

Danny shook his head. 'Sorry.'

'Fuck.' Nobby leapt out of bed and got dressed. 'Let's go.'

In the street, nerves sped their walking close to running. 'What happened?' said Nobby. Danny told him.

'Fuck, fuck, fuck.' He crossed the street to the cafe.

'We should go somewhere else,' said Danny.

'He's never about this early. I need to think.'

They sat facing each other with two mugs of tea. Danny had no appetite but watched in admiration as Nobby, with retribution looming, devoured a bacon sandwich.

Danny broke the silence. 'I'm really sorry about this.'

Nobby looked at him without blinking. He shrugged, finished his tea and said, 'Don't worry, it's sweet.'

Nobby got up, but Danny's relief to be leaving vanished when Nobby went instead to the pinball machine, shoved in a sixpence and fired off the first ball.

Danny joined him. 'What are you doing? We need to go!'

271

Nobby had already trapped the ball on a flipper. 'In a minute, this helps me relax.'

'Relax? Here? What kind of weirdo are you?'

With a rueful smile, Nobby said, 'One that's fucked, I guess. Unless you've got fifty quid handy?'

Danny shook his head. 'So, what can we do?'

'When you're fucked? Not much. I could run away and hide, but where to, and for how long? No, this is where we live, Danny boy – our manor. Trouble is, Gasping George lives here too.' He thought for a second. 'I suppose I could threaten to tell the rozzers what's in his old aunt's lock-up over the river, and about the drugs and money he hides in her flat – I've picked up there for him a few times.' He paused. 'But that could get me killed.' He gave an ironic grin. 'Which is a bit worse than getting a kicking.'

Unnerved by Nobby's fatalistic calm, Danny was struck most by his switch to the first person: 'I' could run, not 'we'; Get 'me' killed, not 'us'. Danny eyed the door and tried to ignore the growing pressure in his bowels.

Nobby fired off another ball and, even in his heightened state of anxiety, Danny found his friend's skill temporarily captivating. With imperceptible touches on the buttons, he took his time to capture the ball on a flipper, let it slide gently towards the end and launch it from the right spot every time. In this manner, he hit the target repeatedly until, with the first ball still in play, replays began racking up. All this while, George could arrive at any minute.

With Nobby showing no sign of wanting to leave, the notion of leaving him to his fate flashed through Danny's mind. It was followed instantly by shame at his cowardice, which stirred up a little courage. He swallowed hard. 'Look Nobby, I'm going to tell George it was me . . .'

The cafe door opened and Banger trotted in. Nobby didn't turn around but, shoulders hunched, waited like a condemned man. Reilly stayed in the doorway. George ambled up red-faced to stand behind Nobby.

'Where is it?'

Still with his back to George, Nobby said, 'Don't know, George. It's lost, I'm sorry.'

In a throat constricted by dread, Danny's confession stayed unspoken. Nobby glanced at him, flicked a finger to his lips and gave a small shake of his head. George grabbed him under his arms, swung him around and hurled him towards Reilly. Danny broke free of his fear and moved to help him.

'Stay where you are, Pages!' said George, and shoved him hard against the pinball machine. The lights went out and a ding indicated 'tilt'.

Reilly dragged Nobby out backwards. George ambled after them and slammed the door behind him, leaving Banger inside.

Through the window, Danny saw Reilly shove Nobby towards George, who seized him by the throat and dipped his head brutally into his face. Nobby's legs buckled but George held him up with his left hand. Nobby, face bleeding, leaned close and said something in his ear, to which George responded with a brutal right cross and let him drop to the ground.

Shaking, Danny forced himself to pull open the door. Banger darted out. George turned to Danny with a snarl. 'It's what happens to those who lose what belongs to me.' A warning but nothing more. Whatever Nobby had said to George, he hadn't grassed on him.

On the ground, Nobby came to and through bloodied teeth said, 'Fuck you, George.'

273

George gave the nod to Reilly, who stepped forward and kicked Nobby in the stomach.

Nobby curled up. 'Fuck you, too, Bloodnut.'

To silence him, Reilly toe-poked the side of his head and turned, blinking hard with excitement, to give Danny a mocking grin. Then he crouched down to taunt Nobby while patting his cheeks. Danny's anger boiled over. He rushed forward and with all his strength punched the side of Reilly's face. Reilly wobbled on his haunches and collapsed on top of Nobby.

At the sight of Reilly and Nobby in a heap, Banger rushed to join their game. He bounced and yelped around them before fixing himself to Reilly's leg.

Hands on hips and gasping from his exertions, George said, 'You're gonna be sorry for this, Pages.'

All Danny could think of was what white-hatted cowboys would say, 'But he kicked him when he was down!'

George shook his head in disbelief.

Like a scene from Laurel and Hardy, Nobby struggled to untangle himself from the stunned Reilly, who couldn't shake off the randy Banger. Danny pulled Nobby to his feet and began dragging him away.

'Banger!' said George.

The dog let go and Reilly made his way towards George on his hands and knees, which only reignited Banger's affection.

'No point running, Pages,' said George.

Danny led Nobby around the corner. They'd gone about a hundred yards when Banger came into sight behind them, followed by George. He moved with the slow, scary certainty of Frankenstein's monster, while supporting the unsteady Reilly. To keep them out of sight, Danny dragged a bewildered

Nobby around every corner. In Monck Street, they ran into Crockett outside the municipal yard where road sweepers stored their barrows, and sewer men changed and showered.

'What's happened to you two?' said Crockett. Danny, who hadn't been hit, wondered if being shit-scared had changed his appearance, too, but on looking down saw that Nobby's blood covered his Fred Perry shirt.

'George and Reilly,' said Danny. 'They're after us.'

'That's enough, I'm not running any more,' said Nobby.

Nor should he, thought Danny. Nobby had received his beating, now it was his turn.

Crockett took control. 'This way.'

In an adjacent cul-de-sac, he stopped beside a large manhole cover, patterned with raised squares that looked as if they could be spannered. He took a small T-bar from his jacket, inserted it and lifted the heavy iron cover a little.

'Get your hands underneath, Danny!' said Crockett. Together, they pushed it up till it was vertical. 'Now, down there!'

'Down there' was a shaft out of which came the sound of rushing water, and a sickening smell. On one side of the hole, a rusting ladder disappeared into the dark.

'You first, Danny,' said Crockett.

Danny hesitated. 'It's a bloody sewer!'

'What did you expect, a wine cellar? Don't worry, it'll be fine, as long as you don't fall in – and hold the sides not the rungs because of shit from shoes.'

Danny got on the ladder and, with Crockett's help, Nobby followed. Danny descended while steadying Nobby by the arse of his jeans.

Still woozy, Nobby said, 'What the fuck are we doing?'

'Hurry, I can hear them!' said Crockett.

About eight feet down, they arrived on a concrete platform that was a foot above the moving sewage. They stood in slime left by a recent overflow. Danny clutched the ladder with one hand and held Nobby with the other. Nobby was shaking his head, mystified but hazily acquiescent, until a heavy thud from above turned everything black.

'Christ,' said Nobby, 'he's shut us down here. Crockett!'

For the second time in twenty-four hours, being trapped in total darkness brought Danny close to panic. He tried to steady his nerves by reassuring Nobby. 'He's hiding us, that's all, we won't be here long.'

Nobby calmed down. 'But the fucking smell.'

In the dark, the stink of diluted shit running beneath got stronger but at least it was moving. Crockett had once told Danny that if you could hear running water down a sewer, the smell is bearable. If you couldn't, you needed to be careful, as the fumes could be overpowering.

The stench proved too much for Nobby and Danny heard the pre-vomit convulsions in his stomach, followed by the sound of lips bursting. The first volley, containing bits of what had to be bacon sandwich, splattered Danny's chest.

'Whoa!' said Nobby. Danny sensed him falling away and pulled him closer.

'Crockett! Let us out!' screamed Nobby.

Danny found Nobby's mouth and covered it with his hand. 'George and Reilly are up there!'

Nobby pulled Danny's hand away. 'But he's already done me,' he whispered, between spits to clear his mouth. Danny thought of admitting it was he who they were after now, but didn't.

From above came a mumbled exchange of voices. Danny strained to listen. Not hearing clearly and being in the dark with the whooshing sound of the running sewer reminded him of nights in bed, listening to Radio Luxembourg through the static.

They must have come closer to the manhole, as he could now hear Reilly. 'Course you've seen 'em. You blind or what?'

'Nope, now fuck off.'

A scuffle followed. Danny assumed Reilly had gone for Crockett. Banger barked and, another voice, George's, said something indecipherable.

'But the little shit knows where they went,' said Reilly.

'Oh yeah? Even if I did, the answer would still be, fuck off,' said Crockett.

'This isn't over, you short-arse cunt.'

'Better than being a big one.'

No more from Reilly but a parting shot from Crockett, 'Any messages? I'm sure they'll be in touch.'

'Christ, Crockett, don't prolong this! said Danny under his breath.

'Prolong what?' said Nobby, who could wait no longer and started screaming to be let out.

A crescent of light appeared above as Crockett lifted the cover and strained to push it up. While climbing, Nobby lost his footing and his arse thumped onto Danny's head. They both held on. Momentarily stunned, Danny followed him up and forgot Crockett's warning not to hold the rungs that Nobby's shoes had smeared with whatever they'd been standing in. Once they'd crawled out, Danny rubbed his stinking hands on the pavement until they were dry. Nobby stayed on his knees to puke into the hole.

'That's it, Nobby, saves time if you go direct,' said Crockett. 'Now, out of the way.'

He eased the cover down halfway and let it bang into place. Nobby flinched and rolled onto his back. They got him up and propped him against the wall. Crockett pointed to the lump under Nobby's eye. 'Judging by that, I think he needs the hospital.'

'No way,' said Nobby, 'I'm going home.'

'First place George will look,' said Crockett.

'But why? Why does he want to do me again?' He thought for a moment. 'He's not after you, is he, Danny? You didn't tell him that you . . .?'

'Tell him what?' said Crockett.

'Later,' said Danny.

Crockett shrugged.

'Maybe I can come to yours, Danny?' said Nobby.

'Jesus, Nobby,' said Danny, 'see what working for George does? It puts us all in the shit.'

Crockett grinned. 'Well, pretty close.'

Nobby turned his head, revealing his swollen cheekbone and blood dripping from one ear: the battered face of a friend who hadn't been a grass.

'We'll go to my house, Mum will fix him up,' said Danny.

Crockett scouted ahead until they made it safely into Danny's block. 'I'm off. Take care, chaps. Oh, and welcome to my underworld.'

36

Danny's mother was on the balcony, bringing in washing.

'Hello boys . . . Alan! Your face! And your shirts! Have you two been fighting?'

'No,' said Danny.

'Look at you, Alan! What happened?'

'Fell over.'

'Bollocks! You'll be telling me you walked into a bloody door next. Who did this?'

Danny had never heard her say bollocks before. Nobby wouldn't look at her.

'This is George, isn't it?' she said.

Nobby kept his head down.

'That bullying, fucking bastard!' She pushed open the front door and directed them indoors. Danny missed what she said next, as he was taking in the fact his mother had said, 'Fucking'.

Nobby hesitated. 'Maybe I should be getting home now.'

'Home? God, if you had a proper home this wouldn't have happened.' Nobby's head dropped. Instant regret had her gently taking hold of his face. 'Oh, I'm sorry, Alan, love.'

She turned to Danny. 'It's time that bastard was sorted out.'

In rare moments of anger, he'd heard his mother say 'bastard'. Today it sounded no more shocking than 'bloody'.

'OK, both of you, inside and get those shirts off, I'll put them in to soak.' She noticed the damp patch and the bits on Danny's shirt and pulled him close. 'Have you been sick?' Danny shook his head. 'And what's that other smell?'

Danny looked at his hands and remembered where they'd been. They both eased their shoes off before going inside. In the bathroom they took turns at the sink and went into the kitchen. They sat at the table, bare-chested. Nobby's visible ribs revealed that it wasn't only his face that had become gaunt. Danny's mother rinsed a flannel under the cold tap and, with her finger in it, rubbed away the dried blood that Nobby had missed, as if she were using a licked hankie to wipe a smudge from a child's face. Next, she banged out half a plastic tray-full of ice cubes on the draining board and wrapped them in a tea towel for Nobby to hold against the swelling.

Lips pursed in anger, she opened a pack of sausages, laid them in the frying pan and jabbed them with a fork as if they'd offended her. She chopped an onion while holding the fork between her teeth – which she swore stopped her eyes watering – and put half a dozen potatoes on to boil. The boys stayed quiet throughout her preparations, during which she stopped to refill the tea-towel ice pack.

She dished up bangers and mash, the Byrnes' comfort food, but Nobby couldn't face it. She didn't press him. When

Danny finished eating, she said, 'Weren't you supposed to be at work this morning?'

'Got it wrong, it's this afternoon.'

'Thought so. What time?'

'One o'clock.'

'Better get going, then. Get a shirt on, and find one for Alan.'

In clean shirts, the boys looked at each other in silence until Danny said, 'See you later.' Nobby got up to go too.

Danny's mother put a hand on his shoulder. 'You're staying here for now. At least you can drink a cup of tea.'

'I need a bit of air, Aunt Cora.'

The old jealousy for Nobby's place in his mother's affection welled up in Danny but, once they were out on the balcony, he put it aside. 'Look, it was me they were after. While you were on the ground, I clocked Reilly.'

'Really? Wish I'd seen it.'

'Slowed down his blink for a while,' said Danny.

'Ha! Now you're in for it, too.'

'Guess so,' said Danny. 'By the way, what was it you said to George after he nutted you?'

Nobby gave a painful smile. 'I resign, you fat cunt!'

Danny laughed out loud but Nobby winced when he tried to join in. They leaned on the balcony wall and didn't speak. Small children were playing hopscotch in the courtyard. Danny's thoughts turned to making amends for what Nobby had suffered on his behalf, and resolved to treat him more like the brother he'd wished for as a small boy.

After a while, Nobby said quietly, 'That's the last time he's gonna do that to me without paying for it. Time for me to hurt him.'

'Oh yeah, how?'

'I've got an idea. That's the last kicking I'm gonna take.'

Danny inspected Nobby's face. One eye was barely visible above the swollen cheekbone. The other held Danny's gaze.

A shiver ran down Danny's spine. Jesus, he thought, he means it!

37

Coming out of his block, Danny saw Linda across the street. A buzz ran down his spine as he wondered what to do. Before he could decide, she came over to him.

She had on white slacks and a dark polo-neck jumper contrasting with her wan face.

'So, you saw us,' she said.

'Did I?'

'Come on, Danny, why pretend, for god's sake?'

Why, indeed?

'Nice car, a Rover,' he said.

She lifted her chin, eyes blazing. 'Yes, it is, isn't it?'

'I have to go . . . the off-licence.'

'I'm glad you saw us; it makes things less difficult.'

'Really?'

He was taken aback to see her eyes glisten with a film of tears. 'I'm sorry, Danny.'

She swallowed and he sensed she needed his help to keep going, to say what must be said. How should he respond?

Was he angry or sad, or not surprised? He waited, not to make it hard for her but because he couldn't decide.

'It's just that Stephen, he . . .' she said.

Now Dodds was her Stephen, a day after being Cordelia's.

'What?' said Danny.

'He's more . . . we're . . . he's . . .'

'Got more money?' said Danny.

She closed her eyes but not before he'd seen the flash of anger. When she opened them, it had gone. 'Please don't.'

She turned to go.

'I'm sorry, I didn't mean . . .'

He *had* meant it, but he had also meant the apology.

She clasped her hands behind her neck. 'Me and Dodds, we've, I don't know, more in common, at this time. Can you see that?'

'Guess so.'

'We want similar things, sooner rather than later. He wants to get on.'

'He hasn't talked of getting away then?'

'Yes, to a place of his own.'

'Not too far from Daddy and the shop, though.'

She sighed. 'You don't have to be like this, Danny.'

She was right, and he felt ashamed. 'Well, if that's what's important: getting away and getting on.'

'It's part of it. I like him, he makes me laugh.'

'He makes me laugh, too,' said Danny.

'Maybe if we'd been older . . .' she said.

'You mean if I was older. But then Dodds would be older too.'

She looked down. 'I suppose so.'

'Not much point in waiting, then.'

'I really am sorry, Danny.'

For a moment, he wanted to be that older Danny, ready to measure up to what she wanted. 'And if I'd left school, took the job offer at the off-licence?'

She was suddenly her old self. 'Bollocks! You mustn't do that, and you know it. You've got the chance to do other, better things.'

I have prospects, he thought, but she doesn't have time.

'Things that take time?' he said.

'Yes. Look, do you really want to go to work now, like Dodds or Crockett, or me?'

'Would that be so bad?'

'Yes, because it's the easy bloody option! Anyone can get a job, but you've got a choice. If I thought a job was what you really wanted, things might have been different. But you never have!'

Linda Bain: certain about herself and what she wanted, and unnervingly accurate about him. He was listening to a grown-up.

He shrugged. 'Well, there it is,' he said quietly.

She took his arm. 'Are you OK, Danny?'

Surprised that he *was* OK, he said, 'Yes, why?'

'Because I'm not,' she said.

He wanted to say something harsh, so that their parting wouldn't feel only one way. But he had nothing harsh to say, at least nothing that would be true.

She dabbed away a couple of tears with the insides of her wrists. He wanted to hold her, tell her he understood, that she was right, but it was she who pulled him close, kissed him on the cheek and walked away, pulling a hanky from her sleeve. A girl his own age but much older – and not as tough as she made out.

For a brief time, he'd been on the edge, ready to fall in

love. But Linda, with whom love might have been possible, had pushed him away from the edge and prevented him from falling.

He wasn't sure whether the hurt he felt was due to losing Linda or to his ego being dented? Both, he thought, but it was a relief to know that, even combined, he could accept them.

At the end of the street, Crockett stood to attention to give Linda a mocking salute. She shook her head at him and turned the corner without looking back.

'What have you said to upset her?' said Crockett.

'Said? Nothing.'

'She was crying. Haven't dumped her, have you?'

Danny shook his head.

'But it's all off?'

'I guess it was never really on, Croc.'

'Dodds?' said Crockett.

'Yeah.'

'Thought as much. Coming back early from holiday gave him the chance to get in there.'

'It would have happened anyway. I think he was always her front runner.'

'Not upset, are you?'

Danny smiled, ruefully. 'Abandoned by a girlfriend for one of my best mates? Honestly? Yes, but I'll get over it.'

'Good, plenty more fish in the sea,' said Crockett.

'For God's sake Croc, next it'll be, "Better to have loved and lost than never to have loved at all."'

'Haven't heard that one. Not bad though, is it?'

'I despair of you, Croc.'

'What are you going to do now?'

'Get on with things, it's not the end of the world, is it?' said Danny.

'I meant today, not your bloody life!'

'Oh, going to the off-licence. Said I'd think about the permanent job offer while I was away. I'm off to see Mr Braden now.'

'Always "*Mr* Braden", isn't it? Can't say you haven't got the manners for it.'

'Part of the job, being polite to everyone, just like you, Croc!'

'A career in the booze trade? You know what I think of that idea.'

'Thank God your opinion doesn't matter,' said Danny.

'You're not going to accept? Don't you fucking dare!'

'You haven't been talking about this to Linda, by any chance?'

Crockett looked puzzled.

'Don't worry, Croc, how could I ignore five feet three inches of career advice?'

Crockett grinned. 'No charge.'

38

'Good holiday, Danny?' said Mr Braden.

'Yes, thanks.'

'And your hand's better?'

Danny held it up. 'Fine now. How's Ron?'

'He's OK too.' He put a finger to his lips and pointed down the cellar stairs. 'Now, how about that training post? It's open till the end of September. Have you discussed it with your mother?'

'Yes,' he lied. He hadn't mentioned it to Cordelia, Ernest or Liam either but felt sure their advice would be similar to – if more polite than – Linda's and Crockett's. Truth was, they would all push him towards the decision that he had always had in mind.

'And?' said Mr Braden.

'I'm going to stay on for A levels, maybe go to university, if I can.'

Mr Braden gave a small frown and laced his fingers across his ample stomach. He grinned. 'That's the spirit, lad, if not the kind you could have been selling.'

Ron came up from the cellar carrying a crate of Blue Bass.

Mr Braden put a hand on Danny's shoulder. 'I'm pleased for you, lad, not that you wouldn't have made a good career with us.' With a wink at Danny, he added, 'Isn't that right, Ron?'

Ron muttered something indecipherable.

'And we'll still be happy to have you working here evenings and Saturdays, won't we, Ron?'

Ron gave a little shudder at the prospect. Another wink from Mr Braden emboldened Danny to say, 'There's one thing that might make me change my mind.'

'Really, what's that?' said Mr Braden.

'Well, if I thought that Ron would miss me too much . . .'

Mr Braden let out a huge guffaw. Ron emitted his hall-mark hiss.

Mr Braden shook Danny's hand. 'OK lad, off you go, see you soon.' Cheered that at least one of the wrinkles in his life had been ironed out, Danny put out a hand to Ron, who thrust his own into a pocket of his brown coat and said, 'Tomorrow evening six o'clock – and don't be late!'

Mr Braden's conspiratorial light-heartedness had lifted Danny's mood, and with it came a benign feeling for Ron.

'Looking forward to it, Ron. You and me against the Armitage-Shankses, eh?'

Mr Braden looked bemused. Ron shook his head and Danny caught an unfamiliar contortion on his face that might have been a smile.

39

Turning into the estate, Danny found himself close behind Ellen Hill. His heart sank to see her tottering on white high heels, back and forth between the railings and parked cars. Each change of direction seemed to increase her speed, which she found hard to control. She managed to bring herself to a halt by grabbing a railing and stood looking out of mascara-smudged eyes, catching her breath, wary of setting off again.

Not again, thought Danny, but as he went to slip past her, she let go and veered across his path. After a few more wobbly steps, an ankle gave way and she tumbled to the ground. She sat back against a car, knees up with her legs too far apart, revealing white knickers between the pale flesh above her stocking tops. One stiletto lay beside her, its heel sticking out at right angles like a broken finger.

What were the odds, he wondered, of his being present to witness for a second time Ellen's plunge into revealing vulnerability?

As if she'd caught him looking, she stretched out her legs,

pulled her handbag onto her lap, tried to push into place her blonde bouffant that had collapsed over one ear.

He looked around and, once more, there was no one else to give Ellen the assistance she needed. 'Can I give you a hand, Mrs Hill?'

She looked up blearily and tried to focus. 'Mrs Hill, eh? Blimey, young man, we must stop meeting like this. What's your name again?'

Danny didn't answer.

His mother had told him that heavy drinking reveals your true personality and that there were three kinds of drunk: happy and silly, morose, and nasty. Sitting on the pavement, propped against the wheel of a Morris Minor, Ellen was a smiling, happy drunk – even if she was likely to be less happy later.

Not a nasty one like Danny had been at the boys' club dance.

He reached down to her. 'Let me help you up.'

'Okey-dokey. Blimey, I've ruined these nylons.' Once on her feet, she took a deep breath and waved him away. 'OK now, darling, thank you.' With that, she lifted her chin, and Danny couldn't help admiring how she kept her head up in a situation where others might be inclined to lower theirs. Off she went again, broken shoe in one hand, handbag in the other. For a couple of yards, all went well, until she tripped and stumbled forward into the arms of a man coming towards her. Ernest held her tight.

'Goodness,' he said, putting down a carrier bag, 'I thought you were about to fall.'

'Already have, love, just now, came a right cropper, back there.'

'Oh dear, do you have far to go?' said Ernest.

She pointed vaguely down the street with her broken shoe. 'Along here.'

'Looks like this lady needs a bit of help, Danny,' said Ernest, sounding like Batman talking to Robin.

'Danny! Of course.' She grinned. 'I recognised those strong arms.' She turned to Ernest. 'My knight in shining armour, you know.'

Danny cringed. Had alcohol erased only the most shameful part of her memory of what happened the time he'd helped her?

'And what a polite knight.' She found the rhyme funny and chuckled.

She clung to Ernest, who said, 'Where are you going, Danny?'

'Home, via Jones's for milk.'

Ernest held up the carrier bag. 'I've just been – bread and cornflakes.'

'Well, I can't stand here all day while you blokes talk about shopping,' said Ellen.

She stooped to take off her one good shoe but lost her balance.

Ernest saved her. 'It's OK, Danny, I'll see she gets home.'

Why was he doing this? A Dodds assumption came fleetingly to mind. But no. Ernest's open face revealed only a decent man relieving a boy from having to escort a grown, drunk woman to her home.

'Are you sure, Ernest? I know where she lives.'

'I know where I live too,' said Ellen.

As they set off, arm-in-arm, she said to Ernest, 'Nice boy that . . . strong arms. I think my Cordelia's sweet on him.'

When Danny got home, Nobby had gone.

Clearly worried, his mother said, 'He wanted to get home.'

'Why would he want to go there?'

'Don't start, Danny, not now! Where else would he go?'

There was only one other home Nobby frequented these days.

'I've got a good idea,' said Danny.

40

In the post office, Jinx leaned on the marble counter, watching Danny buy a postal order and stamp for his mother's football pools coupon.

'Can I post it, Danny?'

Danny gave him the stamp to lick and stick but, before he could stop him, Jinx shoved the envelope into the postbox with Her Majesty's head upside down. Could this lack of respect stop his mother's coupon reaching Littlewoods? Worse, what if this time she had found enough draws to win? He rejoined another queue.

'What's up, Danny?' said Jinx.

'Nothing, I want to check something.'

'What for?'

Good question. Why would his mother win this time, after years of failing to find eight draws each week? She had asked him to kiss the envelope for luck and he had obliged, knowing it made no sense. But now he couldn't help envisaging a different scenario next Sunday morning, as she checked the results: the routine hopeful smiles, followed not by the usual philosophic shrug but by her hands flying to her face in disbelief at winning. He had to ask about the stamp.

The woman behind the counter smiled at him from under blue-rimmed flyaway spectacles. 'Don't worry, love; a bit disrespectful maybe, but it'll get there.'

'Where we going now, Danny?' said Jinx.

'Home, Jinxy.'

'Why, Danny?'

'Because your mum wants you back before teatime.'

He gripped Jinx's hand and they walked along Vauxhall Bridge Road, looking for a gap in the traffic to cross over.

'There's Banger!' said Jinx.

On the other side, Banger lay beside George at one of the tables in front of the Surprise pub. Reilly sat next to them, legs stretched out, hands in pockets, chewing, as usual, the pulpy remnants of a Swan Vesta.

Jinx waved, 'Banger!'

Banger lifted his head; Reilly stood up and alerted George, who aimed an index-finger gun at Danny but motioned Reilly to sit down. Before obeying, Reilly pointed first at his chest, then at Danny and shouted, 'See you later.'

Relieved to hear 'later', Danny gave him a V-sign. Jinx giggled and did the same, with both hands.

Reilly shouted, 'Out with the spaz again?'

Jinx knew the term well and the hurt in his face drove Danny to shout, 'Now, if you like!' The exchange was interrupted by Nobby, zigzagging towards them along the pavement. On catching sight of George across the road, he came to a halt, swaying and staring.

'What are you doing?' said Danny.

Nobby didn't answer. As Danny got closer, it was clear

why: he was drugged to the eyes, one of which was now completely closed from his beating.

Danny tugged his arm. 'Come on, Nobby, you shouldn't be here!'

Nobby shook him off. 'His turn now.'

'Whose turn?'

'His, the fat bastard!' he shouted, loudly enough for Reilly to notice something was up.

Danny moved between Nobby and the road. 'Come away.'

Jinx, eyes fixed on Nobby's smashed face, said, 'Yeah, Nobby, come with us.'

Danny grabbed Nobby's shoulders. 'Haven't you had enough?'

Then, as if it explained everything, Nobby shoved a grease-proofed paper bag under Danny's nose. It contained three cooked sausages, laced with congealed fat and spotted with burnt-on onion. Danny's mother must have given them to him to eat cold.

'Mum's sausages?'

'What's it to you?' said Nobby.

What's it to me, thought Danny, that my mother treats you like some prodigal son? That you come and go at our place as if it's yours? That I'm supposed to treat you like a brother?

However, inches from the smashed face that Nobby had suffered because of him, Danny remembered his debt and whispered, 'I don't want you to get hurt again. Please, come away.'

Nobby ignored him and moved from side to side, to see across the road. When Danny looked for himself, he saw George get up and go inside the pub. His departure spurred Nobby to take out a sausage and begin waving it. As if by magic, Banger got up. Nobby shoved Danny away and hurled the sausage across the road. It landed on the opposite pavement, where Banger leapt forward and swallowed it in a couple of snaps.

Now he had the dog's attention, Nobby held up another. 'Here Banger, here boy!'

Danny shouted, 'Nobby, don't!'

Reilly saw the danger, too, and shouted, 'Stay!'

Banger obeyed only George. He padded to the kerb but crouched back when a lorry rumbled past.

Nobby tossed the sausage into the middle of the road. 'Look, Banger!'

Banger dashed forward and gobbled it down. Traffic passing behind him cut off his return and, as car horns blew, he crouched again, ears flat to his head. Nobby waved the last sausage back and forth. The dog waited, expecting the sausage to be thrown, but Nobby got down on his haunches and held it out. 'Here, boy.'

Banger trotted forward. Had he kept going, he might have made it, but George emerged from the pub, and in his rasping master's voice roared, 'Banger!'

The dog froze. A thud followed a screech of brakes as a van sent Banger somersaulting through the air. He landed on all fours and stood for a moment before keeling over, legs twitching as if he were dreaming. The van didn't stop.

Jinx shrieked and lolloped towards the dog. Yards away, a bus closed in. Danny dived forward, grabbed Jinx by one wrist and swung him around, hammer-thrower style. Jinx tumbled back onto the pavement. The bus juddered to a halt but clipped Danny's shoulder, sending him sprawling onto the tarmac.

Danny got to his feet and the bus driver slid back the window of his cab. 'What are you playing at?' he shouted.

'We weren't playing!' said Danny and pointed at Jinx. 'He could have been killed.'

'Yeah, and you, too.' The driver looked around at people gathering on the pavement and changed tack. 'You all right?'

Danny nodded. The driver nodded, too, and the bus pulled away to reveal George, on the opposite pavement, rooted to the spot, until his mouth opened in a howl of despair that got him moving.

From his side of the road Nobby answered by screaming, 'See, see what happens! You bastard!'

George strode into the road, oblivious to Nobby's screams, screeching brakes and blaring car horns. He sank to his knees beside Banger, whose blood, spreading from a wound in his neck, had put a shine on his black coat. Gasping for air, George began passing the flat of his hand back and forth along the length of his dog, as if a one-inch force field prevented him from touching.

All traffic had stopped. In an eerie quiet, drivers got out of their cars to look.

Reilly joined George and knelt beside him. Banger's legs had stopped moving but his ribcage still rose and fell. Eager to help, Reilly slipped his hands under Banger to lift him. The dog yelped and George felled Reilly with a single blow. 'Don't you fucking touch him!'

With his great hands trembling with the effort to be gentle, George picked up Banger. He rose to his feet and – blind to everything around him – carried his dog past Danny, Jinx and the now silent Nobby. With another yelp of pain, the dog wrenched itself around and savaged his wrist. George didn't flinch. 'Easy Banger, easy boy.' Banger

298

bit him again, this time on the chin, but George only held him closer. He carried on, stopping every few yards, shoulders heaving to catch his breath and to press his face against Banger's bloody neck and whisper comfort. Danny found himself on the verge of tears not only for Banger, but for the brute he reviled who, distracted and disoriented by grief, walked away with his dying dog in the opposite direction to where he lived.

Reilly got up and staggered to Danny's side of the road. The traffic got going again.

On the pavement, Jinx was hugging himself. 'Banger's hurt, Danny, really hurt!'

Danny put his arms around him. 'It's OK, Jinxy. George has got him, he'll be OK.'

Close by, Nobby began shouting again, as if George were still there. 'Only fucking thing he cares about!'

Reilly moved unsteadily towards Nobby. Danny left Jinx to get to Nobby first. If anyone was going to hit Nobby, it would be him. He made a grab for him. 'You cruel bastard!'

Whatever drugs Nobby had taken, they hadn't impaired his reflexes. Before Danny could get a grip, Nobby nutted him. Jinx screamed. Reilly stood back, nonplussed. Nobby squinted at Danny, seeming only vaguely aware of what he'd done. He turned and lurched away. When Danny put his hand to his nose, it came away bloody.

Reilly, holding the side of his head said, 'I was only trying to help his dog and the bastard hits me!'

Danny reached out to steady him.

'And you can fuck off,' said Reilly.

Danny shoved him hard. Reilly fell on his arse and sat on the ground with a bewildered look on his face and his blink in overdrive. It was the second unsatisfying outcome to their feud. The first time Danny had felled him, he hadn't been expecting it, and today he'd already been hit by George.

Jinx barely glanced at Reilly as he shuffled past him and clutched Danny's arm. 'Is Banger really going to be all right, Danny?'

The truth could wait. 'I'm sure he will, Jinxy.'

They left Reilly sitting on the ground, swearing vengeance.

At Jinx's front door, Mrs Murphy lifted Danny's chin for a closer look at his face. 'Who did that?'

Danny pushed Jinx into the hall. 'Not Jimmy?'

'No, course not,' said Danny.

'Well, you know what he can be like, without meaning to . . .'

'No, it wasn't him.'

Jinx started crying. 'Banger got run over and Nobby hurt Danny!'

She pulled Jinx to her and he circled her waist with his arms. She lifted her pinny to wipe his face and with wide eyes, silently asked Danny if this was true.

He nodded.

'Alan?'

'He'd taken stuff,' said Danny. 'I don't think he knew what he was doing. But he's hurt George much more.'

'How?'

Danny mouthed, 'Banger.'

Jinx pulled away from his mother. 'George carried Banger, even though Banger was biting him. But Banger's going to be OK, Mum.'

Danny closed his eyes to tell her he wasn't.

'Who'd have thought Alan could do that to you, Danny, of all people.'

'Yes, who'd have thought it.'

'Poor Alan,' she said, 'now he's for it.'

Jinx began rotating his body from the waist up. She held his hands, sat him at the table, took a packet of custard creams from the kitchen cabinet and shook some onto a plate. 'Your favourites, Jimmy, and now I'll make you a nice cup of tea.'

After putting on the kettle, she beckoned Danny into the front room. He told her how George and Reilly had beaten up Nobby and what had happened on Vauxhall Bridge Road. 'I don't think George knows Nobby was responsible – but Reilly will tell him, even though George clumped him.'

Danny cleaned himself up as best he could in the bathroom. The bleeding had stopped but the swelling on the bridge of his nose had him feeling boss-eyed.

Back in the kitchen, Mrs Murphy offered Danny tea.

'Thanks, but I'd better get to work.'

'Bye, love. I'll tell Crockett what's happened when he gets in.'

Danny ruffled Jinx's hair. 'Bye, Jinxy.'

Calm now, with a mouth full of biscuits, Jinx said, 'See you later, Danny.'

At the off-licence, Ron was serving behind the counter. Once the customers had left, Ron took a close look at Danny's face. 'Right, get stocking up.' Danny checked the shelves and the space under the counter and found only one or two gaps. Once he'd filled them, he offered to work on the counter.

'You'd better go and ask Braden,' said Ron.

Mr Braden stood up behind his desk. 'I know young men get into scrapes, lad, but I can't have you serving customers looking like that. That will have to be all for today. Best if you go home. Come back next week when you look more presentable.'

41

George's Ford Zodiac was parked outside the entrance to Danny's block. Rather than go in and be trapped, Danny walked on. George climbed out of the car. 'Wait there, Pages.'

This sounded more like, 'don't you fucking move!' Danny took more safety paces and waited. 'Look, George, Reilly had it coming. Nobby was already out of it when Reilly kicked him.'

'Not talking about that.'

Danny eased backwards to match George's surreptitious steps towards him.

'What then?'

'Banger.'

Danny guessed the worst but asked in hope. 'How is he?'

'What do think? You saw what happened.'

'Yes, I'm sorry, George.'

'Banger's gone,' he said, the catch in his voice unrelated to his emphysema. Danny felt a stab of sympathy; it didn't last.

'Why didn't you stop him?' said George.

Why indeed? Hadn't he just watched as Nobby waved the sausages?

'If you hadn't hurt him so badly, he might not have . . .'

George took another step forward. 'Where is he?'

'Don't know, and I don't care!' Danny pointed to his swollen nose. 'You didn't see him do this to me.'

George gave a shrug. 'Fuck your face. He killed my Banger, lost my money, so . . .'

'So what? Beat him up again? Is that all you can think of?'

'Oh dear! Upset, are we?' said George, with the sickening smile of a bully that detonated Danny's fury.

'He didn't lose your money!'

George's smile disappeared. 'Oh yeah?'

'I did.'

'How's that?'

'I was bringing it to your place for him and got stopped by the police.'

He came closer. 'So, where's the money?'

'In the lake in St James's Park.'

'You useless toerag!' George lunged for him. Danny jumped back and jogged away. He stopped, out of reach, for now.

'Think you're some kind of gangster, George Kelly? You're just a nasty bastard who likes frightening people, a big fat bloke in hilarious half-suits who thinks he's Al Capone!'

Even with his anger in full spate, Danny had time to think, Christ, what am I saying?

Panting from his effort, George said, 'I should have known better than to trust a poncey bookworm.'

'Who you needed to write your pathetic, threatening little notes because you're so thick.'

George's smile returned as he walked back to his car. 'See you soon, Pages, very soon.'

304

Danny's anger was fading but enough remained for a parting shot. 'And you can tell Reilly that he can come and see me anytime.'

'Oh yes, I'll tell him.'

As George drove off, the last adrenalin-fuelled drops of courage drained away at Danny's feet, leaving him shaking at what might happen next.

Should he risk going home now? He doubted whether George would come to his door but would be patient, with menace, and let Danny worry about 'when'. However, going in now would let his mother know he'd been sent home early, and there'd be the smashed nose to explain. He walked away.

At Harry's, Crockett came out holding a bag of chips. He straight to the point. 'Mum told me what happened. Boy, is Nobby in the shit. George's dog. Fuck me!' He grinned. 'If only Nobby had waved fivers instead of sausages, he could have got George run over instead. Want a chip?'

'No thanks.'

On seeing that Danny wasn't smiling, Crockett said, 'Scary times.'

Danny shuddered at how serious things had become for him, and Nobby.

Crockett pointed to Danny's nose. 'Growing a trunk? Try a bag of Birdseye on it. See ya.' He went into his block but paused in the entrance. 'We're going to have to be careful, now.'

'We're'. This was his friend, Crockett.

42

Although not yet dark, the brazier in front of the hut was lit.

Finnegan scooted out, barking, but stopped on seeing Danny. Inside, Liam lay, knees up, on the big trunk that was too short for his stretch. He swivelled slowly off his creaking bed. 'What's up, boy?'

Danny shrugged. 'Nothing.'

Liam came out with a rag in his hand. He grabbed the poker embedded in the brazier, stirred up the coals and shoved it back in.

'Is that right? Nothing?' Danny stayed silent. Liam pointed at Danny's nose. 'And how did that come about?'

'It was Nobby.'

'Not the one ye carried the envelope for?'

'Yes.'

'Revenge?'

Was it? Nobby had been badly beaten because of him. But then he recalled Nobby's demented satisfaction as George held his dying dog. Hurting his oppressor had been the priority. Nutting Danny hadn't been part of the plan.

'No, he didn't know what he was doing. He was so blocked,' said Danny. Liam raised a questioning eyebrow. 'High on drugs that made him mad enough to pay George back for hurting him.'

'And now this George is after ye for losing his money?' said Liam.

'No, not at first. I thought it was because I punched his mate, Reilly, but it was Nobby he was after.'

'A lively old time ye've been having.'

'Nobby didn't tell him it was me who lost the money and took a beating for it.'

'Stout lad.'

'But George knows now because I've just told him,' said Danny.

Liam's lips blew out a silent whistle. 'Why?'

'I got really angry and for a few minutes it stopped me being scared.'

'Ah, sure 'tis often the way.'

'I nearly shat myself afterwards.'

'That, too,' said Liam.

'But I went further, slagged him off, told him what I thought of him. I was buzzing, like I'd taken Nobby's pills. I even hoped George might feel bad for hurting the wrong person and leave Nobby alone.'

Danny gave a rueful smile.

'I suppose your man is not the regretting type?' said Liam.

'No, but, do you know, for a while I felt better about myself – that I had some bottle after all? It didn't last.'

'Few bodies can stay brave all the time, boy.'

Danny paused. 'But Nobby did a terrible thing, he killed his dog. And now it can't be long till George—'

307

'Killed his dog? Mother of God!' Liam stooped to pick up Finnegan. 'Come in, Danny, and sit down.'

They sat on the big trunk. Finnegan nestled between Liam's feet.

'A rare mess altogether, boy. But like all problems, t'will pass.'

Danny drew little comfort from this but made a stab at being cheerful. 'At least I won't have to write his nasty little notes any more.'

'Notes?' said Liam.

'What he called polite threatening letters to those who owed him money, and other stuff. On top of what I get from working at the off-licence, his money made it easier to keep up with my friends who work.'

'Not exactly a career though.'

'I know. Anyway, I've decided to stay at school.'

'Well, I'm delighted to hear it.'

'But I wish . . .'

With his thumb, Liam pressed tobacco in his pipe, lit it and waited.

'For a start, I wish I could feel more grown-up.'

'Now why is that?'

'To be more sure of myself, worry less, stop thinking about myself so much.'

Liam's eyebrows rose. 'And ye think that growing up, as ye call it, will achieve this?'

'I hope so,' said Danny, unsettled by Liam's reaction.

'And your girlfriend, Cordelia?'

'She's not my girlfriend but she is a friend. I had a girl-friend, Linda. Well, sort of . . . I didn't do so well at being a boyfriend.' Danny blew out his cheeks. 'And neither is a girl who . . .'

'Who what?'

'You know, would let me . . .'

Liam took the pipe from his mouth. 'I'm pleased to hear it. So, I assume sex, too, is high on your agenda?'

Danny nodded. 'My friends say they've done it already and I . . . well, it's something I'd like to get out of the way.'

He groaned silently at having said too much – and for making losing his virginity sound like passing a driving test.

'So that's what your friends say, is it? Let me tell you, Danny Byrne, sex is unlikely ever to get out of your way, as ye put it.' He paused and drew on his pipe. 'So, your friends have more money *and* more sex!'

'Sex is quite important, isn't it?'

'God it is,' said Liam. 'But without love it's not worth so much.' He shook his head. 'But try telling that to young men who wake each morning with glory in their fists.'

As Danny absorbed the shock of hearing this, Liam continued. 'I may be giving ye an old man's wisdom. Nevertheless, I believe it to be true. All the sex in the world won't compensate for a lack of love, though a man might go for years thinking it will.' He stopped as if this had jogged something in his memory. 'But sure, isn't it better altogether to go for the right girl and not for those who might accommodate your carnal desires?'

Disappointed by Liam's question, Danny plunged on. 'I'd like to go for both.'

'Wouldn't that be unfair to each kind of girl?'

Another reasonable, if unwelcome, question. Before Danny could find an answer, Finnegan leapt, growling, from between Liam's feet.

'He's in here, George.'

Reilly, squinting and smiling, stepped back to let a larger shape block the entrance.

'Here!' said Liam. Finnegan trotted back and sat by the trunk.

George ducked his head inside and, as if Liam wasn't there, said, 'Outside, Pages.' He stepped back and waited.

Shaking, Danny got to his feet, but as he went to move forward Liam stood, flung an arm out across Danny's chest, and walked out ahead of him. Outside, Reilly bounced around, ready for action. Liam ignored him and turned to George. 'Good evening.'

George, his eyes on Danny, said, 'Yeah, never mind all that. Go for a walk, old man.'

'Now where would I be going?' said Liam.

Still looking at Danny, George said, 'Anywhere. Just fuck off for a while, will you.'

'I will not.' This got George to look at Liam, who continued, 'This is my place of work. T'would be a dereliction of duty to, as you say, go for a walk.'

George tried to shove him aside, but Liam leaned into him, forcing George to take a backward step, and then he picked up one of the sledgehammers that stood inside the entrance. He held it up vertically: at the top, one hand held the fourteen-pound head, the other gripped the wooden shaft halfway down.

'Ha!' said George, 'so that's how you Paddies swing a hammer? I won't tell you again, out of my way!'

When Liam shook his head, George went to throw his favoured right cross but, in a flash, Liam switched his hold and rammed the end of the hammer's wooden shaft into George's midriff.

Eyes wide and mouth gaping, George let out a huge gasp,

worthy of his nickname, and sank to his knees. Reilly measured up to Danny, who rushed to meet him.

'Back!' Liam roared. Danny and Reilly froze.

Liam pointed to George, who was still on his knees, gulping for air, and said to Reilly, 'Would ye like some of what your pal, who appears to be at prayer here, is after receiving?'

Not completely cowed, Reilly saw what he thought was a weapon, and grabbed the poker in the brazier. He let go with a howl and bent double, blowing on his hand and shaking it. 'Fuck, fuck, fuck!'

George, now on all fours, said. 'I'll kill you for this, Paddy, and you, Pages.'

Liam let the head of the sledgehammer drop on his back. 'I think not. I hear ye take yourself for a big fish around here, is that right?'

George didn't reply.

'Listen now. If any harm comes to this boy, or to his friend, a number of my younger, wilder Irish acquaintances from Kilburn will be down here for a visit . . . the whole clan. And I promise ye, they can really spoil a nice afternoon. Do ye get me?'

Still no answer.

This time, Liam dangled the hammer in front of George's face. 'For the love of God, will ye speak up!'

George, breathing easier now, rose to his knees. 'I get you.'

'Now, will ye be gone.'

George struggled to his feet and glared at Liam. He opened his mouth as if about to speak.

'Yes?' said Liam.

George decided to say nothing and stumbled away, shoving the wincing Reilly ahead of him.

'Now boy,' said Liam, 'where were we?'

Which, in the same circumstances, Danny thought John Wayne would say.

Back inside the hut, Liam unscrewed a pint bottle of Guinness and poured the stout carefully into an enamel jug. He took the rag from his overalls, wrapped it around his hand and pulled the poker out of the fire.

'That young fella, the poor creature, has a fierce amount to learn about conductivity.' With that he plunged the poker into the Guinness and watched it hiss and froth. He took two tin mugs from a shelf and filled them with the warmed stout. He rammed the poker back in the brazier and gave one of the mugs to Danny. 'Cheers, boy.'

'Cheers,' said Danny. It tasted foul but he took another swallow to pretend it was OK. They sat down on the large trunk.

'Why do you do that with the poker?'

'Habit, I suppose. My father used to do it to his porter in winter, but it's become an all-year practice for me. The heat softens it, makes it less bitter.'

Danny couldn't imagine how it could be more bitter.

'Be of good cheer, boy. I hope he won't be bothering ye any more – or your unfortunate pal.'

Danny wasn't so sure. George had been humiliated on his own manor and wasn't likely to let it go. However, the threat of wild Irish navvies descending on him did seem to have had an impact.

'If he did, would your Irish friends really come down here?'

Liam smiled. 'What friends?'

43

As the lift in his block was out of order, Danny took the stairs. On the final flight, he found Nobby splayed across the steps, resting his head on his arms. He straightened up. 'Danny!'

Danny pointed at his swollen nose. 'Well, you can fuck right off.'

'Danny, I'm sorry. I didn't mean it.'

He *had* meant it at the time. But who had he been at the time? Not the Nobby Danny knew. Had the drugs revealed who he really was? Or had they changed a quirky but kind loner into someone who could kill a dog and attack a friend?

'I can't believe I did it. His dog!' said Nobby.

'Why did you then?'

'Couldn't think how else to hurt him. He cares about no one, nothing, except that dog.' Nobby grabbed the banister and pulled himself slowly to his feet, but his legs gave way and he sank down. This was the moment for payback, but Danny couldn't bring himself to land another blow on that puffed and bruised face.

'Can I stay at yours?' said Nobby.

Here was something Danny *could* do. He climbed the stairs past him, leaned down and shouted in his ear, 'No!'

Indoors, Danny's mother pulled him close to examine his face. 'Why would Alan do that to you?'

Danny told her what had happened, but kept mention of losing George's money for another time.

'Where's Alan now?'

He told her.

'Why, for God's sake? Of course he can stay here, especially if that bastard's looking for him. Get him in here, now! What were you thinking?'

'I was thinking about this!' Danny's hand flew to his damaged nose. 'In fact, I was also thinking about beating the shit out of him.'

'Don't you use that kind of language with me!'

She took his head in her hands to look closer at his injury and sighed. 'OK, but he needs to be somewhere safe, not out on the streets. Go and get him, Danny.' She ruffled his hair to mollify him. 'Please?'

Danny left, giving the door an unmollified slam. He jogged down the staircase. No sign of Nobby. He went to both ends of the courtyard to check the streets. Nothing.

His mother was waiting on the balcony.

'He's gone,' said Danny.

'Better get around to Jean's.'

'Really? Why do you think he wanted to stay here? You know Nobby hates being at home. Anyway, George could find him there.'

'Jean might know where he's gone.'

'Really? Why would she start now? She's never cared before.'

'Just go, will you!'

*

314

Jean opened the door; the smell of cigarette smoke escaped around her. She wore a nylon nightie, covered in faded red roses. Danny wondered if she was dressed for an early night, or unchanged from the night before?

'No, I haven't seen him, love.' The outline of a tall man moved behind the kitchen window. She saw Danny had noticed. 'Alan wasn't home last night.'

Of course he wasn't, thought Danny. Why come home to her and another uncle?

Danny walked away. She called out, 'How's your mum? Say hello for me.' He ignored her.

'Well?' said his mother when he got home.

'Surprise, surprise, Jean had no idea where he was.'

'Was she OK?'

'Well, if she wasn't, there was someone in the kitchen who might have been looking after her.'

Her face became stony. 'So, where do you think Alan would go?'

'Don't know,' he lied.

That evening, Danny joined his mother on the sofa to watch the telly. After a few minutes, she got up to turn down the sound and sat closer to him. She put a hand on his knee. 'Don't be too hard on Jean, love.'

'Oh, why not?'

'She's had a tough life. There are those who it breaks and those who manage to bend and bounce back. Jean broke.'

He had no wish to talk about Jean but he waited to hear more.

'We were friends as girls in the old street. After I met your dad, we saw less of each other but kept in touch. Then she found Bert and thought he was the bee's knees. He wasn't much cop, but she couldn't see it. He used to knock her about, and she'd often have bruises on her face and arms, and there were times when she had to hold her ribs when she coughed.

'When your dad went around to confront him about it, Bert just stood there smiling. Worse still, she said it was nothing really, that they'd only been larking about. He was always "my Bert", even after he walked out on her. But she fell apart. Lost her job in the offices at the Art Metal. Paying the rent got difficult, and when she was threatened with eviction, she took in lodgers on the QT. Not long after, she got pregnant with Alan, and a year later I had you. We got close again, especially,' she gave Danny's knee a squeeze, 'when we were with our little boys. After your dad died, she was a good friend and, for a time, the only friend I wanted to see.

'With Bert gone, she complained about being lonely, despite the blokes she saw, and the lodgers. When we moved to the estate, I thought things would improve; we might have been on our own, but we had our sons. Strange, but having Alan didn't help her like you've helped me.'

She stopped and looked at him. 'You have, you know, don't know what I'd have done without . . .'

Pleased as he was to hear this, Danny was also embarrassed. 'It's OK, Mum.'

'She hated the flat being empty and talked of needing a man around, as if Alan didn't count.'

Hearing this, any new-found sympathy Danny was feeling for Jean began to dissolve.

'But what about Nobby?' he said. 'What about *his* loneliness among all those lodgers and "uncles"?'

'I know, love, he hasn't had it easy but I've . . . we've always tried to do our best for him, haven't we?'

'Maybe, but wasn't that Jean's job?'

His mother fell silent, as if her thoughts, too, had switched to Nobby: forever at their place, especially at mealtimes, and staying late because he didn't want to go home.

Tonight, he'll have gone up West to another kind of home, worse than the one he had. Danny thought of going to the West End to look for him. But where? Nobby went to other places than La Discotheque and to meet up with other so-called friends.

Emboldened by his mother having opened up, he asked, 'Which one of Nobby's "uncles" was his dad then?'

Her face froze. 'Don't be cruel, Danny, it doesn't suit you. Who are you to judge?'

'Not judging, Mum, asking.'

She sighed. 'Who knows? She saw quite a few blokes at the time.

'Who, then?'

'Does it matter now?'

'It might matter to Nobby.'

She shrugged. 'I don't think she knows.'

44

Danny sat opposite his mother in the kitchen. She took a sip from her mug of tea and put it down. 'I said too much last night. Promise me you'll never tell anyone.'

'Who would I want to tell?'

'Just promise, will you!'

'Don't worry, Mum.'

There was a bang on the front door.

'Now who could that be this early? Can't they see we've got a knocker?'

'I'll get it,' said Danny.

He could see no one through the glass panels, but opened the door to check along the balcony. When he released the catch, something heavy shoved the door open against his shins. He stepped back and pulled it wider. Nobby rolled across the threshold and curled up at Danny's feet.

His mouth hung open, a small echo chamber for the sound of his breath fighting through whatever was clogging his lungs. Danny reached down and shook his shoulder. 'Nobby!'

Nobby's eyelids flickered, revealing only the whites of his eyes – like Jinx's, after the fall.

Danny's mother came into the hall, pulling closed her dressing gown that had lost its cord.

'Oh God, Danny! What's the matter with him?'

Danny sat cross-legged and lifted Nobby's head into his lap. 'Come on, Nobby, wake up! Mum, I think we need an ambulance.'

'An ambulance? Really?'

'Really, Mum. Knock on the Smiths' door.'

'I'm not properly dressed!'

'As if they'll mind!'

She stepped over Nobby and hurried two doors along to the neighbours who had a phone.

Nobby shifted his head against Danny's knee, as if it were a pillow.

Danny's mother returned. 'They're on the way.' She went to the bathroom and came back with a wet flannel. She knelt beside Nobby. 'Alan? Alan love!' She leaned closer to smell his breath. 'It's not drink.'

Danny wished it was.

She wiped Nobby's face. He groaned, opened his eyes and struggled to focus. Through a gurgling in his throat that had Danny willing him to cough, Nobby said, 'Sweet . . . got home.'

Danny's mother closed her eyes but tears squeezed out. 'That's right, Alan love, you'll be OK now.'

Danny winced. He hadn't let him in last night. But Nobby had nearly broken his nose! But this didn't matter now, and the lines from the Robert Frost poem he had studied at school came back to shame him: *Home is the place where, when you have to go there, they have to take you in.*

Danny rocked back against the wall. 'I'm sorry, Nobby!'

Nobby lifted his head and tried to speak, but his chest heaved and he coughed up phlegm laced with blood. Danny's mother wiped it away.

Had that been a nod, an acknowledgement of Danny's apology? He wished with all his heart that it was. Danny's mother reached across to hold his hand. 'Don't worry, Danny, we'll get him looked after.'

His mother looked from one boy to the other, then closed her eyes, as if praying. Two ambulance men arrived at the open door with a wheelchair.

'Fine time for the lift to be out of order,' said one, catching his breath. 'Now, what's happened?'

Danny waited, deferring to his mother, but she shook her head and went into her bedroom.

One ambulance man squatted to attend to Nobby and put an oxygen mask on his face. He looked at his colleague and pursed his lips in a silent whistle.

'Right,' said his colleague, 'we need to get a move on.' Danny answered his questions.

'He got here on his own.'

'Slumped against our door.'

'About twenty minutes ago.'

'No, his breathing hasn't changed.'

'Yes, long enough to say bits, maybe nod his head.'

Danny wanted so badly for it to have been a nod.

'Nobby. Sorry, I mean Alan, Alan Clarke.'

'No, he doesn't live here.'

'No, I wasn't with him.'

With this answer Danny choked up. The ambulance man put a hand on his shoulder.

'He lives with his mum, Twenty-Three Thorney House.'

'Don't know . . . but he might have been taking drugs.'

'Don't know, purple hearts, maybe, or other stuff.'

Like the 'serious syringe' stuff he might have moved on to.

Danny's mother emerged from the bedroom, dressed now. 'Well, what do you think?'

'Hospital for this lad,' said the man at Nobby's side.

'Can I come with him?' she said.

'It's only at the end of the road, you know.'

The one who'd been asking Danny questions, shook his head. 'Course you can, my dear.' Then, to his mate, 'All set for those stairs?'

They lifted Nobby into the chair, covered him in a red blanket, buckled a leather strap across him and set off. Danny and his mother followed.

Another friend on his way to hospital – and who was to blame?

Before they loaded Nobby into the ambulance, Danny felt for his hand through the blanket. He squeezed. No response. No forgiveness.

He turned to the ambulance man. 'Will he be all right?'

The man frowned. 'The best thing you can do is go and tell your friend's mum.'

Had he been Nobby's friend?

'Go on,' said his mother, 'you'll be quicker than me.'

'No, you get her! I'm going with Nobby.'

His vehemence surprised them all. Hurt, and looking suddenly small beside him, his mother acquiesced and hurried off.

Eyebrows raised in disapproval, the ambulance man said, 'You can get yourself to Casualty.'

Danny ran the three hundred yards to Westminster Hospital. In Casualty, they wouldn't tell him anything. He waited outside on a long wooden bench, rocking forward to ease an ache of regret, unsure how much of it was due to Nobby's plight or his own.

His mother arrived with Jean, who was wide-eyed and smiling dumbly. She gave a hysterical little laugh. 'Now what's he been up to, eh? Always up to something, isn't he, Danny?'

With a shake of her head, his mother warned him to say nothing. After nearly an hour, a doctor came out. 'Mrs Clarke?'

Jean clutched Danny's mother. 'Oh God, come with me, Cora?'

His mother took her hand and beckoned Danny to come too. They followed the doctor through the swing doors, down a side passage to a room where they were offered seats in small armchairs.

'We did all we could, Mrs Clarke, but Alan's heart failed. He'd—'

With her membrane of delusion finally rent, Jean screamed. Danny's mother got up and bent to hug her.

Jean pressed her fists into her cheeks. 'Alan, Alan, what have you done? What have you done to me?'

Danny got to his feet. 'To you? What has Nobby ever done to you?'

Joan turned her blank, puzzled face to him. His mother gasped and pulled her friend close. 'Danny! No, please!'

'Look, Mum, not even a tear!'

His mother stood up and whispered, 'How can you say such things? Everyone reacts differently.'

Jean seemed oblivious to what he'd said. He may not have hurt her, but he *had* hurt his mother.

The doctor broke in. 'Would you like to see him?' His mother caressed Jean's face to encourage her to her feet. The doctor led them both through the door.

'Are you coming, Danny?' said his mother.

'No, Mum.'

Then, as on the morning after his nan died, she said, 'If you don't, you might regret it.'

He took a deep breath and followed them.

In a private ward, Nobby lay on a bed, covered to his chin with a blue sheet. The lighting had been turned down but Nobby's gaunt white face almost shone, except for the livid swelling from George's fist.

Standing behind the two women, Danny said, 'The bastard!'

Jean turned to him, perplexed. His mother whipped around. 'You should go, now!'

'I wasn't talking about Nobby!'

Neither woman appeared to hear him. The doctor took his arm. 'Shall we give them some time?' Outside, Danny said, 'I was talking about the man who gave him those bruises.' Still holding on to him, the doctor said, 'He didn't die from whatever caused his bruises.'

'But his mum must have thought so when she saw his face.'

The doctor sighed. 'I can see that but he actually died from whatever he'd taken.' He was quiet for a moment. 'Are you Danny?'

'Yes.'

'Ah, only at one point, Nobby, as you call him, said your name.'

'Did he?'

Danny's head began to spin. The doctor reached out to steady him.

'Nothing else?' said Danny.

'Not really, the next word was barely audible – but it sounded like "sweet".'

45

News of Nobby's death rumbled around the estate in a mix of sorrow and speculation: Not much of a life. Got a bit flash lately. Hadn't he become a junkie? Up West. Wrong crowd. Dealing drugs. Poor Jean. Poor Nobby, you mean! Worked for George. Didn't Nobby kill his dog? George beat him up. Still, if you hang around with the likes of George . . .

Danny received lots of sorries and are-you-all-rights, some genuine, some from those only joining in the strange communal excitement that follows a local death. Everyone assumed Danny would be most affected, as they thought him Nobby's best friend. A status he no longer merited, as Nobby would still be alive if he had said yes to his plea to stay with him. Yet the estate resisted revision of its collective memory that went back years to when friendships were first formed, nicknames allocated and reputations established. Their good wishes only added to Danny's guilt at letting down his friend. He cut short those who wanted to stop and talk more about Nobby.

At the kitchen table, Danny's mother topped up his mug of tea and pushed the milk bottle towards him. 'Do you want to go and see Alan at the funeral parlour?'

'Not sure, Mum, do you?'

'No, love. It was the last place I saw your dad. I don't know what those undertakers do to faces but the man I saw bore little relation to him.' She took his hand. 'He's the man in our photos, Danny, just as Alan, whatever they do to him, will always be this blond rascal you grew up with.' From her handbag, she took out a black-and-white photo of two small boys, in short trousers, holding a toy bus between them. 'Jean wanted me to have this, said it reminded her of happier times.'

What it reminded Danny of was how he had envied Nobby his toy bus and its battery-driven headlights – as well as what the photo didn't show: how much tighter had been his grip on that toy. And how Nobby, with no prompting from his mother, had decided – on the very day he'd received it – to lend his Christmas present to his younger friend.

He would go to see Nobby.

'Are you sure?' said his mother. He could only shrug, as his reply was held up by a jumble of reasons: to say goodbye, as he hadn't when Nobby was loaded into the ambulance; or in the hospital where he'd behaved badly; above all, he felt a need to repeat his apology. Shamefully, he was also curious, after what his mother had said, to see how changed Nobby might be after the undertakers had done with him.

The receptionist at the undertaker's asked for his relationship to the deceased.

326

'I'm his . . . was his friend.'

'A moment, please.'

She disappeared into the back office and re-emerged to lead him into a windowless room lit by one lamp stand with a beige, tasselled shade.

She closed the door behind him. The coffin rested on dark wooden trestles on the far side of the room, as if to give visitors a chance to say that they had been in to see him without having to look into the coffin. He resisted an impulse to wave Nobby cheerio from where he stood. He remembered his nan's dead face, and being encouraged to kiss her. He wondered if his mother would want him to kiss his friend goodbye.

The receptionist gave a soft knock on the door, which banged into him as she opened it. 'Are you OK?'

How long had he been standing there?

'Yes, fine thanks.'

When she left, he went over to the coffin. In the soft lighting, there was little contrast between Nobby's waxen skin and the cream sheet tucked under his chin. Danny's mother was right. His friend looked more dead and less like Nobby than he had in the hospital: eyes closed; lips sealed with a thin line of wax and mouth stuffed to make his hollow cheeks convex. The thick make-up hadn't quite concealed the bruise on the swollen cheekbone, but had thickened the blond hairs above his top lip: Nobby's attempt at a grown-up moustache that would never grace a grown-up face.

Danny leaned over him and said, 'God, Nobby, I hope you know I'm sorry.' Suddenly self-conscious to be speaking out loud, he turned to check if he was still alone. Then he took hold of one of Nobby's hands and, momentarily stunned by how ice-cold it was, whispered, 'See ya mate.'

As he stepped back, he jogged the coffin, causing a small shake of Nobby's head. Alarmed at first, Danny began to smile, as it reminded him of something that never happened to Nobby, the pinball maestro: tilt!

46

Jean went to ground until the day of the funeral. It was left to Danny's mother to keep an eye on her and to organise everything with the Co-op. As Jean didn't have enough money to pay for a car to follow the hearse, a whip-round was organised, and Angelo put a collection tin on his counter. When he brought it to George's attention, his donation was a scowl. The pinball machine's lights continued to flash but no one played. Eventually, Angelo switched it off. 'We give it a rest for a while, eh Danny?' He smiled. 'Maybe, at last, it starts to make me a bit of money.'

At the boys' club, training for the coming football season started. When the first session was over, Ernest asked the boys to observe a minute's silence in Nobby's memory. They shifted about, examining the ceiling, but the quiet force of Ernest's presence sustained their co-operation. He closed his eyes and clasped his hands in silent prayer, and after a minute added a spoken one, 'Dear Lord, look after Alan.

Amen.' The boys appreciated the brevity and joined in the 'Amen' with gusto.

'Think kindly about Alan, boys, and what you might learn from this tragedy.'

They nodded but Danny guessed that, like him, they'd already learned all they needed to.

On the morning of the funeral, Danny's mother stood on the balcony outside Jean's flat, while he waited downstairs for the hearse. Small crowds gathered on each side of the street to see Nobby off. Most stood silently, arms folded; a couple of men removed their hats. Danny and his mother got into the car with Jean. There was room for more, but Jean could think of no one else to ask. She wore a black skirt and blouse, and a navy-blue shawl Danny's mother had lent her.

The two women sank back in the plush leather seat. Danny perched opposite on the pull-down and savoured the appropriate hush inside the Austin Princess.

By the time they were rolling through Wandsworth, Jean had fallen asleep and slumped against his mother, who said,

'She didn't sleep much; told me she took extra sleeping pills at about five o'clock this morning. I had the devil's own job to wake her.'

Danny feared that after being absent for much of Nobby's life, Jean might now be out of it at his funeral. Danny's mother was gently stroking Jean's face. When she stopped, she looked long and hard at Danny.

'God, her only son,' she said, and wept.

Danny reached forward and squeezed both her hands in one of his, but could think of nothing comforting to say.

The two-vehicle cortege glided up to the Putney Vale

Crematorium. Outside, about twenty people had split into small groups. Danny was surprised to see some of the older mourners smiling, even laughing, until the hearse pulled up. Crockett and Dodds, for whom this was a first, stood apart, serious, silent. They had on their blue-serge suits, bought at Christmas from Burton's. Danny admired the fashionable sloping jacket pockets, with one above for tickets, and knew they would contrast sharply with his dark blue jacket and grey school trousers. On days like this he felt most keenly the limitations of a schoolboy budget. Crockett and Dodds wore open-neck white shirts. At least Danny had the black tie his mother had found for him.

They woke Jean and helped her out of the car. Danny wrapped an arm around his mother's shoulders. She straightened up, dabbed her eyes with a hanky and, as she took firm hold of Jean's arm, said, 'That's it, no more tears today, Danny.'

They were greeted by a vicar, eyes watering and face puce from a streaming cold. After shaking hands, he took out a hanky to blow his nose.

As they waited for the funeral director to get everyone else into the chapel, Dodds walked over, head lowered in what would, in other circumstances, be fight mode; but he wanted to talk.

Danny moved away from his mother and Jean to meet him.

'Look, about Linda,' said Dodds.

'It's OK, really, it's OK,' said Danny.

'Sure?'

'Sure.'

Dodds gave a nod. 'All right then, good.' After a few seconds, he added, 'Still mates?'

'Still mates,' said Danny.

The funeral director called them over to the hearse to join Crockett and three more boys who had agreed to carry Nobby's coffin. Danny was paired at the front with Crockett in a lopsided arrangement that would have been the same for whoever Crockett partnered. They lined up while the funeral attendants rolled the coffin back and invited them forward to take over. When they grabbed the gilt handles, the funeral director panicked, 'Not the handles! Underneath! Lift from underneath!'

'Handles you can't use, what's the fucking point?' whispered Dodds.

'It's all going to burn with Nobby, that's the point,' said Crockett, 'and mind your language, we're nearly in a church.'

'Are we ready, boys?' said the vicar, before turning away to cough.

Danny could see only the top of Crockett's head, but he could visualise his grin as he chanted, 'It's not the cough that carries you off, it's the coffin they carry you off in!' The vicar gave him a weary glance and led them in.

Crockett was wearing his Cuban heels but, to compensate further for his lack of height, pushed the coffin up on his hands to bring it to the level of the others. He couldn't sustain it and, halfway down the aisle, let it drop to his shoulder. The coffin tilted down and sideways. To maintain balance, Danny found himself imitating a Groucho Marx walk and, to the sound of Dodds choking back laughter, they carried Nobby, head down, to where the funeral attendants took over and slid the coffin onto the rollers between the four-poster surround.

Danny joined his mother and Jean in the front row. Most people had filled the back pews, leaving those between empty.

At the back, he was pleased to see Cordelia and, among more people than he expected to attend, Mr Jones, Bill from the Tap House and Harry from the chip shop. Dodds passed to the end of the second row, followed by Crockett's mum, Crockett and, finally, Jinx. Ernest rushed in, late, and they moved along to make room for him behind Danny.

'Hello, Danny!' said Jinx, with his usual absence of volume control. Shushed by his mother, he put his hand through the back of the pew to Danny, who squeezed it but didn't turn around.

After brief words of welcome and an opening prayer, the congregation's pitiful effort to sing 'The Lord's My Shepherd' was mercifully drowned out by the loud music produced by someone who sounded like they were learning to play the organ. Next, Danny's mother read from the New Testament, the bit in St John about 'eternal life'.

Earlier that week, she had asked Danny if he would like to say something about Nobby at the funeral. He had refused, partly out of fear but mainly because of guilt about the night Nobby overdosed.

Had he agreed, he would have mentioned how Nobby had to become tough, tricky and independent, because life with his single mother was a struggle; how he had no one else to look out for him, except Danny's mum; how he could play a pinball machine like a concert pianist; and how working for George Kelly had been a big mistake; and, if any wisdom could be gleaned from Nobby's untimely death, it was that living somewhere you don't mind going home to, and belonging to a boys' club, can save your life.

So, it was left to the ailing vicar to cough his way through a short homily that could have been about anyone and made only cursory mention of the information Danny's mother had given him: 'Born in 1948; his mother's only son; life cut short; missed by his friends; promise unfulfilled, and who knows what he might have gone on to?'

Danny had a fair idea and a sigh from the second row told him that Crockett agreed.

The vicar stumbled to the end of his tribute. In the short silence that followed, Jinx pointed at the coffin and, in a loud voice, said, 'Is Nobby in there, Danny?'

Crockett yanked his brother's arm back and shushed him. Danny turned and whispered, 'Yes, Jinxy.'

'Thought so,' said Jinx. 'He used to give me fag cards and marbles, you know. Still got 'em. Oh, and cakes from the cafe.' He grinned, 'I ate them though!'

Muffled laughter broke out but, embarrassing as Jinx's outburst might have been, it said more about the Nobby that Danny knew than what they had just heard.

The vicar moved across to the coffin for the final committal.

Danny looked around at Crockett, eyes wide, asking, Was that it? Crockett shrugged.

Heart pounding, Danny rose to his feet. 'No, there's more than that . . .!'

The vicar stopped, open-mouthed. Blood thumped in Danny's ears as he struggled to find the words he wanted to say, but they wouldn't come. His face burned and, mute, he sat down. His mother clutched his knee and whispered, 'It's OK, love.'

Then came a firmer grip on his shoulder and Ernest said, loud enough for everyone to hear, 'Would you like to say something about Alan, Daniel?'

Danny wasn't sure. Ernest was. He got Danny to his feet and ushered him forward to stand facing the congregation. He squeezed his arm and smiled. 'Go ahead.'

The expectant faces before Danny blurred and his head swam in the heady scent of lilies in a nearby vase. And he had no notes to refer to! But this time he could not face the humiliation of sitting down again. He gradually got control of his breathing and, as everything came slowly into focus, he cleared his throat.

'I've been friends with Nobby, it's what we've called him since we were little. Our mums were – are – friends too. He was older than me, which sort of gave him the right to be bossy, but he was kind. He once let me borrow, on Christmas Day, a special present he'd looked forward to getting all year.

'I didn't see so much of him as we got older because I spent a lot of time at the boys' club – and Nobby hated sport. But he could play pinball machines like a genius. Whether it was the one at the cafe or in those arcades up West, he cracked them all. But we'd often see him at Harry's chip shop after football training, when he would take the pi . . . mickey out of our exertions. We'd hang around chatting for a while before going home. However late you stayed, you'd always have Nobby for company.'

He was on the point of saying why when Jean's eyes closed against what might come next, and his mother shook her head. He took a deep breath instead.

'I saw even less of him recently, except in the cafe or at our place, where he had the knack of turning up at mealtimes.'

Jean's eyes remained closed.

'The sort of work he'd started doing, and the man he worked for, made him happy at first – and a bit big-headed. But in the end, what he was doing made him unhappy, and frightened.'

Dipped heads and whispers told Danny he'd publicly slagged off Gasping George. But, with anger now augmenting his nervousness, he added, 'Nobby's business, as he called it, took him to the West End. I . . . I mean we, went with him a couple of times . . . but it wasn't for us.'

His mother's slight frown said, 'so, more than once!'

'He claimed he'd made new friends, but they weren't real friends – anyway, none of them are here today. I guess Nobby took a few wrong turns . . . and because he had no one, including me . . . us, to support him, he kept going.'

Danny sensed a fidgeting in the pews and wondered if it had been fair to say, 'us'.

Panic rose in his throat and stopped him speaking. In the excruciating silence that followed, most heads bowed in embarrassment, but Ernest was nodding encouragement and Jinx, grinning, gave him a wave.

As the bonds of their early childhood came back to him, Danny took another deep breath. 'Nobby was a good friend to me – better than I was to him. When I was in trouble, he stuck by me. And when I let him down recently, he let me off . . . He had a favourite word. Instead of saying, OK, or good, or thank you, he would just say, "sweet". Well, I think Nobby was OK, and good, and if I could say anything to him today it would be "sweet".'

Choking back tears, Danny forgot to move until Ernest beckoned him back to his seat. Desperate to sit down, he was thwarted by the vicar asking everyone to stand for the committal.

As the curtains began to close around the coffin, Crockett called out, 'Yeah, sweet, Nobby!'

'Sweet, Nobby!' said Jinx, delighted to copy his brother.

'Sweet!' roared Dodds.

Stifled laughter and more 'sweets' broke out behind them before the curtains finally hid the coffin from view. The vicar gave the blessing and stood as if he were a magician waiting for them to re-open with a 'taddah!' to prove Nobby had gone.

Danny and his mother stepped into the aisle to let Jean leave first. Everyone followed, after pausing to shake the vicar's damp hand.

47

Outside the chapel, in a paved area bounded by a low box hedge, two wreaths and a few bunches of flowers lay on the ground in front of a small sign bearing Nobby's proper name. Danny couldn't face talking to anyone and took the chance to make his way past scores of headstones to where his father was buried.

He stood beside the grave. The scent of freshly cut grass made it hard to recall the one he'd been expecting: the smell of drying cement that always brought him closer to his father than any headstone or photo. He stood with his hands clasped behind his head and wondered whether there was an afterlife. If there was, would his father be proud of him, even if he knew what his son was really like?

'What you doing, Danny?' said Jinx, standing behind him.

'Hello Jinxy, thought I'd get away for a bit, my dad's buried here.'

'Are they going to bury Nobby now?'

'No, he's being cremated.'

'What's that?'

'It's like being buried but . . . different.'

'Oh.' Jinx closed his eyes for a moment. 'Wanna play Would Ya, Danny?'

'Not now, Jinxy, let's sit over there for a minute.' Danny led him to a nearby seat on which a dull brass plaque remembered a Violet, 'Vi', Brown.

'I want to ask you something, Jinxy.'

'I'm not good at questions, Danny.'

'Do you remember that day. . . when you fell?'

He screwed up his eyes. 'I remember the hospital after.' He paused. 'And before, when we were playing, Danny . . . on the wall.'

Danny's back stiffened. 'Oh.'

Jinx leaned in close and whispered, 'I think you were angry with me.'

'I wasn't angry, Jinxy, but . . .'

'It's OK, Danny.'

'I shoved you forward. Do you remember that?'

'Think so.'

Danny groaned. Self-preservation framed the next question. 'Have you ever told anyone?'

'No, Danny, I remember best when I'm with you.'

'I'm so sorry, Jinxy.'

Jinx buried his face in Danny's chest. 'I'm not.'

'Why?'

''Cos I'd have to go to my brother's old school . . . and you wouldn't be my best friend.'

'Wouldn't you like to go to school?'

'No. Don't want things to be different, Danny.'

'OK, Jinxy.'

Liam had asked him who would benefit were he to confess. Would he? Could confession rid him of the guilt that chewed his insides? He envisaged what would follow if it became general knowledge on the estate: Danny Byrne, who ruined Jinx's life, then broke his heart by admitting what he'd done; who drove his friend, Crockett, and his parents to the point of hatred; who brought heartbreak to his own mother. Shame drove him to his feet.

Jinx stood up, too, and as if the conversation had never taken place, said, 'Are we going now, Danny?'

Looking into Jinx's devoted, unjudgmental face, Danny's shame began to drain away. In its place came relief and a surprising sense of indignation, a need for self-defence. As if standing in his own dock, he pleaded out loud, 'I was twelve years old, for God's sake!'

Jinx flinched. 'What's the matter, Danny?'

'Nothing, Jinxy, nothing.'

Danny hugged the boy who would never grow up, whose best friend was the one who had damaged him, but whom he could not bear to lose. Jinx wrapped his arms around him. This might not have been forgiveness but, as with Nobby's final 'sweet', Danny felt forgiven. Jinx and Nobby, bound together in his heart by his sins of commission and omission. Their forgiveness, if that's what it had been, was for him alone. It would ease his guilt but not absolve him. However, he would no longer feel guilty about keeping his secret to himself.

From outside the chapel, Danny's mother waved to him.

Feeling lighter, Danny said, 'Let's go, Jinxy.'

As they walked back, the sun came out. Cordelia, in a black dress that set off her blonde hair, walked towards them. 'Well done, Danny.'

'Yeah, well done, Danny,' said Jinx. Then, puzzled, he said, 'What have you done?'

'Not much, Jinxy.'

'Cordy, Nobby is being cremated, you know.'

She gave Danny a brief smile. 'I know, Jinx, it's very sad.'

'Yes, sad. We were talking about when I fell off the wall, Cordy.'

'Oh, can you remember it?' said Cordelia.

Jinx looked at Danny. 'No . . . can't.'

The loyal response had Danny wondering what Jinx would have been like today, if he hadn't fallen. It brought him close to tears.

Cordelia cocked her head to one side. 'Danny? Are you OK?'

'Yeah, are you OK, Danny?' said Jinx, taking his hand.

'You did Nobby proud. You must miss him,' said Cordelia.

'Yes, I do.' He wiped his eyes. 'Sorry.'

'Sorry for being upset at your best friend's funeral? Don't be silly.'

He couldn't tell her his tears were not for the Nobby that was, but for the Jinx that could have been.

Jinx tugged at his hand. 'Yeah, don't be sad, Danny.'

Cordelia put her hand on his forearm. 'Oh, and thank you for your postcard, it was nice of you to think of me.'

Still poor at handling compliments, he managed to stop himself admitting that there had been free extra cards. He smiled instead and guessed that Linda's card would have arrived too, but he doubted there would be a place for it on her mantelpiece.

'I like your Ernest,' said Cordelia. 'He saw my mum home the other day.' She put a hand through her hair. 'I think they might be meeting again.'

'He's a good bloke,' said Danny, hoping she hadn't noticed his surprise at such an unlikely pairing.

She smiled. 'A good Samaritan, like you.'

'Samaritan?'

'You helped her, too, didn't you?'

'A bit, it was mainly Ernest.'

'Maybe, but although she had suspected it before, it was then she knew for certain it was you who brought her home the first time.'

His face burned. 'Oh, I see.'

'It couldn't have been pleasant for you. Thanks.'

Her matter-of-fact reference to her mother wetting herself dissolved his embarrassment. This, he thought, is how adults deal with difficult subjects. He gave a grateful shrug.

Cordelia noticed Danny's mother walking towards them. 'Look, I'd better get going. See you later.'

'Yes,' he said.

'Well, doesn't Cordelia look lovely in that dress?' said his mother, as she came up to him. Without waiting for a reply, she said, 'I'm glad you went over to the grave, love. I don't have time, today. And how are you, Jinx?'

Jinx lowered his head. 'I'm OK.'

She looked back to where Jean was untangling herself from some well-wishers and said, 'Time to go. The cafe's doing tea and sandwiches.'

'Can I come in the car with you, Danny?' said Jinx.

Danny shook his head. 'Sorry, Jinxy.'

'Don't see why not,' said Danny's mother. 'Without you two in there today, it wouldn't have be̶e̶n̶ . . . you wouldn't have been right.' D̶ . . . . well, it about to cry, b̶u̶t̶ . . . Danny thought she might be b̶o̶t̶h̶ . . . , but she took a deep breath and held them ̶b̶o̶t̶h̶ by the hand. 'Anyway, you'll cheer us up on the way home, won't you, Jinx?'

48

Angelo's handwritten sign on the door of the cafe said, *Close – Its Private Reseption.*

Danny's mother chuckled. 'That'll do.'

She settled Jean in the window seat favoured by George, and fetched her a tea with a quartered sandwich. Jean was ready for tea but didn't want to eat. Angelo brought over a cup for Danny's mother, who began eating Jean's sandwich. She beckoned Danny over, but he declined. He had nothing to say to Jean.

Jinx went straight to the switched-off pinball machine on which there were plates of sandwiches. He turned and called out, 'The lights are off, Danny.'

Rather than explain why, Danny said, 'I think it's broken, Jinxy.'

Jinx shrugged and crossed to the counter, where a more appealing layout of Battenberg slices, chocolate fingers and London cheesecakes awaited.

Dodds and Crockett arrived. 'Fuck me, that was weird,' said Dodds.

'Weird?' said Danny.

'I mean, new.'

'New?' said Crockett

'What is this, Twenty fucking Questions? I mean one of us, dying, being dead. Isn't that weird, and new?' said Dodds.

'New for Nobby,' said Crockett.

'What *was* new,' said Dodds, 'was allowing a short-arse to carry the coffin. I swear I could hear Nobby's head banging about when your end sagged. Maybe you should have carried it on your head, then Danny wouldn't have had to walk like he'd shit himself!'

Danny laughed and Crockett had to smile at this rare example of Dodds humour, but when Dodds gave them a puzzled look, they realised he hadn't meant it to be funny. However, he was right about death: it *was* new, and it had been weird carrying their friend during the last moments in which he still had a body. Now that Nobby would soon be ashes in an urn, Danny hoped, with Sunday-school logic, that if he had a soul, it had left before his coffin rolled into the furnace.

Other mourners were setting about the sandwiches and waiting for the right moment to offer Jean their condolences. The early respectful hush disappeared in a hum of conversation, broken by the odd burst of laughter, which confirmed Danny's assumption that funeral solemnity prevailed only when the corpse was present.

Cordelia came in with Ernest. He shook hands with the boys in turn, saying their name at the same time. He held Dodds's hand a fraction longer and gave a warm smile that had Dodds looking down at his feet. The boys exchanged puzzled glances. Was this shaking-hands stuff another 'done thing' at funerals?

'A sad loss, boys, let's pray that Alan's now in a place where he'll be well, and happy,' said Ernest.

The boys didn't reply, hoping Ernest wasn't going to say another prayer, and certain that Nobby would rather be there in the cafe, even if unwell and unhappy.

Instead, and to everyone's relief, Ernest put a hand on Danny's shoulder. 'Well done, Daniel, Alan's send-off wouldn't have been the same without your words.'

'No, it certainly wouldn't,' said Cordelia.

Uncomfortable in the presence of flattery, Crockett and Dodds eyed each other and responded with embarrassed grunts. Danny shared their embarrassment but, in the glow of Ernest's praise, he began to regret they had not heard everything he had wanted to say.

Ernest detached himself to go on a smiling, handshaking tour of the cafe; engaging people he'd not met before and dissolving their natural reticence. Danny watched him in admiration. This was the way to meet the world: head-on, open-hearted, with everything you are on show. No wonder most people on the estate found Ernest hard to work out. With admiration but not entirely with approval, Crockett said, 'Something else, isn't he?'

'Yes, he is!' said Danny.

Crockett held up his hands. 'OK, keep your hair on. We like him too, you know. Anyway, I'm off.' He went over to Jinx and grabbed his hand. 'We're going.'

'Me too,' said Dodds.

Danny pointed to the food. 'Nothing to eat?'

'Nah, not the kind of food I want to eat in the cafe, not enough grease. Anyway, the Tap House will be open soon.'

'I want to stay with Danny,' said Jinx.

Crockett held tight. 'Not today.'

As he was being dragged away, Jinx waved a cheesecake. 'Bye, Danny!'

At the door, Dodds and Crockett remembered to give Jean a sympathetic wave, but she barely noticed, as she was listening to Ernest. He was holding her hands like a vicar – a good vicar – might, and she smiled for the first time that day.

When Ernest left, Cordelia said, 'I think he's off to see my mum. She talked of them going to Hampstead Heath. I bet she's spent the afternoon getting ready.'

Danny knew how attractive Ellen could make herself, but he couldn't see her as Ernest's girlfriend.

'Really?'

She frowned. 'Why not, aren't they about the same age?'

Why not, indeed? Still, it felt a little strange for their club leader to be going out with a local mum.

Stumped for a suitable answer, he was grateful when Cordelia changed the subject. 'Have you been to a funeral before?'

'No, I was too young for my dad's and my nan's funerals. I found it all a bit strange.'

'So did I, and when the curtains started closing, I got scared for Nobby.'

'Me too, I wanted his spirit or soul, whatever you want to call it, to make its getaway before the coffin went into the flames.'

'Goodness, I hope it did,' she said.

They fell silent, as if imagining Nobby's escape. Remembering his visit to the funeral parlour, Danny said, 'I went to see him after he died.'

'Oh?'

'My mum reckons that going to see a dead person isn't

only a chance to say goodbye, it makes it easier, later, to accept they've gone.'

Cordelia's shoulders twitched in a shiver. 'I think I'd rather take someone's word for it.'

They were now the only ones in the Regency who weren't of Jean's generation. Danny crossed to the counter where his mother was helping Angelo. Cordelia went with him.

His mother wiped her hands on the teacloth. 'Off now then, love?'

She added a smile for Cordelia. 'Did Danny tell you how lovely I think you look in that dress, Cordelia?'

'Thank you, Mrs Byrne.' She smiled at Danny. 'No, he didn't.'

'Men, eh?'

'Can I help? This is normally my job,' said Cordelia.

'No, thank you love, you two get along.'

You two? Was his mother assuming, or encouraging?

'Say goodbye to Jean, won't you, Danny . . . please. And be, you know, kind.'

'OK, Mum.'

She relaxed and smiled. He went over to Jean, not only because his mother wanted him to, but because of Ernest's example.

'I'm off now, Aunt Jean, I'm really sorry about Alan.'

Jean took his hand. 'You and your mum were good to him, Danny. Thanks for what you said at the funeral – and not saying what you could have. I know you don't think much of me . . . I could have been a better mother, wish I had.' Danny shook his head but she ignored his denial and pulled him closer to whisper in his ear, 'No one can say anything to hurt me, now, except your mum, but she never does, and you . . . well, you were a chip off the old block today.'

Liam was right. He would have been wrong to mention an untimely truth.

He tried to straighten up, but she held on. 'By the way, your postcard arrived yesterday.' She shook her head and gave a half-smile. 'Couldn't tell what you were on about: all that ging gang goolie stuff, and who's Giles, for God's sake? You were right to tell Alan he was kind, though. He was, especially to me, although I wasn't always kind to him.'

Danny remembered Nobby pleading to stay at his home. 'Nor was I.'

'Don't believe that for a minute,' said Jean. She finally let go of his hand. 'Anyway, I'm sorry he didn't get your card, it would have meant a lot to him.'

Danny choked up and could only pat her shoulder by way of goodbye.

Cordelia was waiting by the door.

'What's the matter?' she said.

'Nothing, Jean's upset.'

'So are you.'

Embarrassed, he replied sharply, 'Am I?'

She put her hand on his chest. 'Don't be such a bloke, Danny Byrne! It's a sad day.'

'I'm going now.'

'Shall I come with you?'

'If you like,' he said, without thinking.

When her shoulders slumped, he held out a hand to her. 'I mean, yes, I'd like you to.'

49

On their way through the estate, Cordelia stopped at the bench near the children's playground. 'Would you like to sit down for a bit? How about this one? It's in the sun.'

There was something about Cordelia and sunshine.

They sat but didn't speak. He hoped she wouldn't want to talk about Nobby. As if she could tell, she said, 'So, what have you been reading?'

'*Tess of the d'Urbervilles*.'

'Ah, poor Tess, so sad . . .'

'Hang on, I haven't finished it yet.'

'Sorry, well, all I can tell you is that Tess *is* poor and . . .'

'Did you know it's one of my A level books?'

She lowered her eyes and gave an apologetic nod.

He nudged her gently. 'Look, that's OK by me. I miss how we used to read the same books – and talk about them.'

Her face lit up. 'Really?'

'Yes, and you saw things in them that I didn't. They helped a lot with my essays.'

'They did?'

How selfish he'd been not to tell her at the time.

'Yes, and do you remember how we'd move on to other stuff, things we couldn't really talk about to the others without them taking the piss?' Should he have said, 'mickey', instead? It was a doubt that wouldn't have crossed his mind in Linda's company.

'Such as?' said Cordelia.

He could see in her face that she remembered only too well but wanted to hear it from him. 'You know, the world beyond the estate, what life would be like when we grew up, what it might be like to fall in love.'

'Or to lose a friend . . . like poor Nobby,' she said. 'Remember how upset you were about Oliver in *My Son, My Son*?'

'You remember that?'

She nodded and, as they both stared straight ahead, added, 'Pity we stopped talking about things like that . . . but without the books to start things off . . .'

He wondered how different those 'things' would be now if she, too, had stayed on at school.

'Shame you had to leave school,' he said.

'Yes it was,' she said quickly, as if irritated that he had changed the subject. 'It was the love stories that meant most to me. It didn't matter if the endings were happy or sad – *Jane Eyre* or *Wuthering Heights*, *Little Dorrit* or even *Romeo and Juliet*.' She paused and took a deep breath. 'Do you know, I used to imagine they were . . . us.'

'Oh? You didn't say.'

She blushed. 'Silly, really.'

'Not silly, but . . . surprising.'

How different to Linda. Cordelia read books; Linda read magazines. Only now did he recall that she had never asked what books he'd be studying for A level, let alone try to read them. Yet he had found her so attractive, and exciting in a way that books and reading could never be. Maybe they weren't as important as he thought.

'I sometimes wonder if I read too much and *do* too little,' he said. 'After all, books are about people living, going places, doing something – not reading. I feel I should have got more from the books I've read.'

'Oh, but you have! They've made you much more interesting.'

'Than who?'

She came closer. 'Than everyone.'

Her face was near enough to kiss. But here, on the estate, between two high blocks from which, as his mother would say, 'anyone could be looking'? She stayed close and, in what he would later think of as a Dodds moment, he kissed her anyway. She held his face in her hands to keep the kiss going a little longer. They sat back, breathing deeply, heads up to the sunshine and anyone who might be watching.

Cordelia held his hand. 'Would you like to come to my place?'

'But your mum . . .'

'She'll be out with Ernest by now.' She smiled. 'Anyway, she won't mind, she thinks you're a bit of all-right.'

Good to know, but it was the 'she'll be out' that got him to his feet.

The flat smelled of cigarette smoke, laced with perfume, which Danny guessed Ellen had squirted on for her date with Ernest.

Cordelia took off her shoes, something that Danny didn't

do at home. 'Shall we go in my room; it's less smoky and we could listen to some music?'

Her bedroom?

His shock must have shown.

'I didn't mean . . . look, it's just that my record player's in there.'

Heart thumping, he removed his shoes and followed her into a well-lit bedroom brightened by wallpaper flecked with tiny yellow flowers.

A Pye record player sat on one end of her dressing table. Next to it, a silver frame held a black-and-white photo of her handsome blond parents, clutching ice-cream cones. As Danny took in the man's high forehead, accentuated by his fair hair, he was startled by sudden recognition. Nobby would never have become that good-looking, but the resemblance was strong. Danny had never heard the estate's often expressed and often justified aspersion: who does he look like? about Nobby. Was it because so little had been seen of the actor who had always been away on one tour or another? But why, when home for such short periods, would he have found time for Jean when Ellen was so much more attractive? Hadn't she, or Jean, or Cordelia ever noticed? But even if they had, why ever would they mention it?

While he pondered these questions, the girl who might be Nobby's half-sister picked up the photo frame. 'I wish I'd known my dad. He hurt Mum terribly, but I've rarely seen her look as happy as she is here.'

Seeing Ellen's once beautiful young face, Danny said, 'It's easy to be hurt by those who make us happy.'

'Yes,' she said, with a wistful smile, and put down the photo.

He fell silent, sorry that he might have brought Linda

and, possibly, Dodds into their conversation. Finding nothing to say and, alone with a girl in her bedroom for the first time, he stood waiting for direction. She invited him to sit on the bed, while she placed a handful of 45s on the record player's stacking spindle and pushed the lever. The first dropped. Clack! 'Wishing and Hoping' by Dusty Springfield. Neither of them could suppress awkward smiles.

She sat next to him, propped herself on straight arms and stared at the floor. When she finally looked up, he put his arms around her. Her kiss was softer than Linda's, and ready to continue. Linda had possessed a kind of in-built timer that soon brought kisses and embraces to a halt. With Cordelia, breaks were likely to be breathers, not 'that's enough' signals.

She got up, flustered. 'I'm really sorry but I must go to the toilet.'

Danny reflected that during romantic moments like this in books and films, no one ever needed to go, but that it must happen all the time in real life. According to Dodds, it was less of a problem for blokes because, once the blood was up, it effectively shut down male plumbing.

Had she really gone for a pee? Surely, she wasn't preparing for sex. If she was, could it be a cue for him to get ready? Should he have brought a condom? Difficult, as he'd never had one and would rather die than, as Dodds had done with a smile on his face, buy a packet of three in Boots. Dodds ostentatiously carried a Johnny in his wallet, just in case. Danny didn't even have a wallet.

Rattled, Danny noticed that some of the little raised squares on the candlewick bedspread had tufts missing, making the pattern annoyingly uneven.

Clack! He thought the next record should be, 'She's Not

There' by the Zombies, but it was Elvis Presley singing 'Wooden Heart'.

Cordelia returned. 'Sorry about Elvis, one of Mum's records has got mixed up in mine . . . Danny! What are you doing?'

Nothing, except speculating about having sex.

She began brushing away bits of lint from a bare, perfectly picked square.

'Oh god, I'm sorry, I didn't realise I was . . .' he said.

'Destroying my bedspread?' She sighed. 'Don't worry, it's an old one.'

Clack! 'You Really Got Me' by The Kinks. She sat close to him. When he lifted her hair to kiss her neck, the small charge that went through him seemed to pass to her because she gave a shiver. He tried to slip his hand inside the top of her dress, but it was too tight. She surprised him by unzipping the back to let it come away at the front. But on trying to unhook her bra, there was no more help. He settled for caressing her breasts through the silky black material. When she covered his hands with hers and pressed them against her, he could feel her heart beating and, when her nipples grew hard, he had to force himself to breathe.

They turned to lie lengthways on the bed. He pulled her on top of him and she lay between his legs. Under her skirt, he discovered she was wearing black stockings and suspenders: appropriate for a funeral and amazing for him. As his hands lingered above the stockings on what Dodds called the super six inches of bare flesh, he sensed she wanted him to stop but she didn't resist.

Instead of taking his time and savouring this marvellous moment, the image of Valerie, in the same position – with her naked bum on view – flashed into his mind, and

354

reminding him that to have sex, he needed to be between *her* legs, not the other way around!

Losing control, he eased her – he hoped he hadn't pushed her – onto her back. When he moved one hand higher, she clutched it and whispered, 'Please stop, Danny.'

He rolled away, embarrassed. 'Sorry.'

She sat up. Clack! 'Help!' by the Beatles. His own selection would have been, 'I Can't Get No Satisfaction' by the Rolling Stones, but on reflection decided 'Help!' was about right.

He sat up too and, expecting disapproval, was surprised to find her regard full of affection. They lay down again, facing each other, and settled for holding and kissing, which was enough to get his erection surging back to life. When she pulled him close enough to feel it, an involuntary heave in his groin had him panicking that he would be unable to hold back.

A Dodds-like voice in his head shouted, 'go for it!' but his mother's quieter, more insistent voice, said, 'the girl, Danny, think about the girl'. It was too late to go for it but was it too late to stop? And he wanted to stop. He scoured his brain for boring distraction and began silently reciting: *German Bight, Rockall, Dogger, Humber, Finisterre, Biscay* . . . But even these locations were sounding irresistibly exotic and erotic. He finally resorted to repeating Pythagoras's Theorem. Cordelia held his face between her hands and slowly closed and opened her eyes, as if trying to help him slow down. But he was beyond help. A whooshing filled his ears as the scent of her hair and closeness of her hips brought him to a shuddering finish.

He sat up, mortified at this happening again, yet wishing she could know how hard he had tried to stop.

She reached up to rub his back. After a while, she said, 'I've never, you know, done this before.'

'Really?' he said.

Christ, he'd said it out loud!

Her face froze at hearing the surprise in his voice. 'Dodds?' she said. He couldn't answer. 'You don't believe what he says, do you?'

'No, I don't. Really, I don't,' he said forcefully, because it was true.

Here was a moment for a timely truth, although given what had just happened, it would come as no surprise to Cordelia.

'I've not done this before either.'

She waited, as if making up her mind, and then pulled him down to kiss him. 'And best we don't, not yet.'

Clack! 'I Got You Babe', Sonny and Cher.

Maybe they would in time when, like his parents had, they became certain of each other.

'Have you ever been in love, Danny?'

'No, I haven't.'

'Have you imagined what it would be like when it came along?'

Until recently, he'd imagined only what sex would be like when it came along and had managed his ever-present urge for it in the most satisfying (during) and unsatisfying (after) way.

'Not really,' he said.

'I used to wonder what you have to do to get someone to love you, or at least to give yourself the chance of love.' The records had finished; the silence amplified her words. 'And how far you should go to spark love in someone, or in yourself for that matter.' She lifted her head. 'I don't believe you can get someone to love you by making love. Do you?'

God, he thought, she has really been thinking about this!

Even though he hadn't thought about it, he agreed. 'No, I don't.'

She came close and took his face in her hands again. 'Would you have carried on just now . . . if I had let you?'

Blimey!

'Yes, I think I would have . . .' he said, surprised how easy it was to be honest with her. 'Although it probably wouldn't have been right, would it?'

'No,' she said.

He should have stopped talking at this point but didn't. 'After all, it should be with someone you're in love with, shouldn't it?'

'Well, we might be getting close because I already love you, Danny Byrne.'

A choking fizz rose from his chest into his throat. Only his mother had ever said she loved him.

'You do?' he said, but remembering his mother's counsel added, 'But, I mean, don't you think it should be . . . that you deserve it to be, with someone who loves you?'

She put her hands on his shoulders and pushed him away to look at his face. Tears beaded her eyelashes. 'And it's not you?'

Could he love her? He fell silent, as thinking and feeling jammed his head. The sensation was different to that he'd felt with Linda. But would that have grown stronger if Linda had felt the same? Linda, whose affection had been conditional on his being the kind of person she wanted him to be. For Cordelia, he seemed to be that person already. Cordelia, who had time for him, with whom he could talk so easily, who kissed like he'd imagined a beautiful girl would, who knew he wasn't always the nice person he pretended to be? And hadn't she just said she loved him?

Before this summer, he'd had a boy's idea of what it would be like to be a boyfriend. Then along came two girls to show him how difficult it could be. Girls, so different: in looks; in what they said and how they said it; in what they saw in him, and in what they expected from him. Similar only in that they were much more grown-up than he was.

Cordelia moved closer, waiting for an answer.

He shook his head, uncertain what to say but sure that he didn't want to hurt her. 'I don't know, Cordelia.'

A tear ran down her cheek. 'Well, at least one of us does.'

He lay back, hands behind his head, mind racing, words unavailable.

She leaned over him. 'Danny, you're only sixteen, for goodness' sake!'

This wasn't the moment to say, nearly seventeen.

'I know,' he said, 'there are times when I feel a bit young for . . . all this.'

She shook her head. 'I don't mean that! What I mean is you've got time, that there's no rush. Why should anyone expect more of you? Why should you expect more of yourself?' She turned away, as if shy of him seeing her say, 'There's no one I'd like to be with more than you, Danny Byrne. But you can take your time with everything, including me.'

He hadn't been enough for Linda, and he certainly wasn't enough for himself. Yet Cordelia was accepting all of him – and asking no more than he could give.

Her face came into soft focus as she came even closer. 'Do you think you could love me, Danny . . . one day?'

Should he say yes, if only to stop the tears she was blinking away? Her eyes didn't move from his, driving home her question. He didn't know what to say but slowly, in the absence of words, came the thrilling, and troubling, realisation that if he kept returning her gaze, he might well love her.

'Could you?' she said.

He didn't know, but he couldn't look away.

50

Next morning, Danny and Crockett sat in the cafe at a table close to the counter where Cordelia was serving.

On hearing what had happened at Liam's hut, Crockett nodded slowly, as if reflecting on the seriousness of the situation. 'Are you telling me that George was on all fours and, with a red-hot poker to hand, neither of you thought of giving him the old ring-singe?' Danny burst out laughing. Maintaining a straight face, Crockett said, 'Missed opportunity. Still, at least Bloodnut got his fingers burnt.'

It was hard to feel down for long in Crockett's company, and Danny's mood lightened further as, nursing his mug of tea, he reflected that despite a summer of turmoil and tragedy, some things had got better: guilt about Jinx's fall and Nobby's death remained but no longer gnawed his stomach; he had opted, with relief, for education instead of work; his friendship with Crockett and Dodds had, if anything, deepened even though their lives were on different tracks; and the relationship with his mother had shifted up to a new level that pleased them both. If he hadn't become much more mature, he knew better what being mature meant – and that it wasn't necessarily brought about by having sex. And, he had a girlfriend.

His remaining worry was that, despite Liam's warning, Gasping George would follow through on his threats. As if on cue, George came in, alone, provoking the usual hush. Danny and Crockett tensed for action, but George ignored them as he lumbered between tables and chairs to his favourite spot. Once seated, he signalled for his tea, settled back and lit the stub of a cigar. Danny eyed the door, comforted that, in Reilly's absence, he could get to it first if George made a move. However, George's only move was to say to the boys, 'So, your mate's nicely smoked then.'

Cordelia had arrived with his mug of tea.

Barely acknowledging her, he said, 'Thank you, darlin', now get us a bacon sandwich, will ya.'

She stared at him, as if waiting for a 'please'.

'What?' he said.

'You're a horrible man, George Kelly.'

Momentarily taken aback, George recovered. 'What you think means fuck-all to me, darlin'. Now get my sandwich, will ya.'

Tears rolled down her face but she stood her ground. George looked about him with his smug smile, refined over years in the company of those he frightened. Danny's resentment boiled over. He got up and went to Cordelia's side.

George did no more than raise an eyebrow. 'Now, what can I do for you, Pages?'

'Nobby would be here today if it wasn't for you.'

'What, that toe-rag? Nothing to do with me. Killed my dog! Remember?'

'You think more of a dog than a human life?'

'Too fucking right, he wasn't worth a leg of my Banger.'

361

Danny put his hands on the table. Despite his throat constricting with fury, he squeezed out,

'You're a cunt, George.'

Cordelia gasped. Danny stepped back, stunned as much by what he'd said as by the danger that might follow.

Instead of lunging for him, George smiled again and in a snarling whisper said, 'Don't fuck with me, Pages. This is my manor and if you want to live safely in it, watch your mouth. Now fuck off.'

Crockett came over. 'Come on, Danny.'

'Take the dwarf's advice,' said George.

Turning to leave, Crockett swivelled a hip to jog the table. George's mug turned over and tea steamed into his lap. George struggled to his feet, tugging at the crotch of his trousers to prevent groin scald. Crockett moved out of range and said, 'Please, George, no need to get up.'

'You're next, you short-arsed shit!'

Angelo came over to wipe the table and gave George a dry tea towel. 'I get you another tea, George.'

'And my bacon sandwich,' said George, rubbing his crotch with the towel.

'OK George, but it's the last time. From tomorrow, please, you come to the counter like everybody.'

'We'll see about that, Angelo, my son.'

'I'm serious, George. No more special service.'

George glared at him. 'Oh yeah? Anything else?'

Angelo's hands shook as he looked George in the eye. 'No, but what I say, George, I mean it.' Danny believed him and, given his shocked expression at yet another person defying him, so did George. Lost for what to do next, Angelo put his arm around Cordelia's shoulders. 'Maybe best if you go home soon.' He led her back to the kitchen.

As Crockett and Danny reached the door, George called out, 'Oh, by the way, Pages, why don't you check on your Paddy friend – maybe take a few bandages.'

'What?'

'Think I wouldn't come back on that old bastard?' George looked slowly around him to take in everyone present. 'Like I said, best not to fuck with me.'

Outside, Crockett said, 'Hang on a minute.'

He took out a black felt marker and crouched down at the driver's door of George's white car. With an artist's flourish, he drew the image he'd perfected over the years: a large pair of hairy balls, beautifully shaded and spiked with pubic hair – and an equally immaculate but minuscule dick that pointed up to the window.

'Jesus, Croc. It's so good, he'll know it's you.'

He grinned. 'I won't bother to sign it then.' Suddenly serious, he added, 'Want me to come with you?'

Crockett, his mate.

'No thanks, Croc, see you later.' Danny went to offer him an Ernest-style handshake, but Crockett was already on his way.

Liam's hut now stood isolated in the flat, rubbled terrain that was once a street. The men and their bulldozers had gone. Fearful of what he would find, Danny ducked inside. Finnegan came forward to greet him without barking. Liam was sitting on the trunk, head down, arms wrapped around his chest. Through laboured breathing, he said, 'I think my little fellah's getting used to ye, Danny.'

'What happened? Was it . . .?'

'Yes, a bit more business with our friend, George, although he wasn't with the lads who are after visiting me.'

'Do you want me to get help?'

'God, no.'

Lines of dried blood descended from his nostrils and his teeth were tinted pink. 'But your face,' said Danny.

'The face will be OK. 'Twas the old body that took the hefty belts. Yet I think those young fellas weren't too hard on me, thank God, on account of my age and all. I hope that that will be enough for George now, and that he'll not bother you, or your friend.'

'My friend is dead.'

'Mother of God, your man didn't . . .'

'No, no, but he was partly to blame . . . as was I,' said Danny.

'I'm sorry, boy.'

'Thank you, Nobby was . . .' He couldn't continue.

'Are ye all right, boy?'

He wasn't, but he took a breath. 'Fine, but what about you?'

'I've suffered worse. It was George's tit for my tat. Let this be an end of it. I'll not keep the feud going. Anyway, he'd soon have a job finding me.'

'Oh?'

'As ye can see, 'tis all finished here, save for me and the hut. I'll be away in a day or two.'

'Where?'

Liam gave a painful shrug. 'Not sure and, at my age, a man can't be picky about locations.'

Danny swallowed hard. 'I'm sorry you're going.'

'I am too, boy. I've enjoyed getting to know ye.'

'Are you sure you'll be OK?'

'I'll be fine, in a while. Sure, doesn't recovery take me a little longer these days.'

'Is there anything I can do?'

'Thank ye, boy, no.'

Remembering George's smile at the cafe, Danny didn't repeat the word he'd called him but shook his head. 'He's a bastard.'

Liam straightened up and winced as he clutched his ribs. 'See here now, Danny Byrne, sometimes ye have to accept that there's no more to be done. Call it a draw and don't look for a rematch – which means no more messing with your man, there.'

George had given Danny the same advice. It made sense. However, accepting it would only confirm George's status on the estate, unless . . . For a moment, Danny envisaged a braver version of himself taking a blunt instrument to George in the dark, but the thought was soon followed by frustration at knowing that he would do no such thing.

Liam noticed. 'Let it go, boy. Not easy, I know, but for the best. Now, I'm going to lie down for a bit. Few things hurt as much if ye can sleep.'

He went to lie back but struggled to raise his legs. Danny bent and lifted them for him. Too tall to stretch out, Liam pulled up his knees. Finnegan jumped up to lie under them. Liam held out his hand; Danny took it and, as on the first day they met, he managed little purchase inside it.

'Thanks, boy. Away now, and God between ye and all harm.'

Danny had little faith in God's ability to help, but it occurred to him that he might have been helped already, via two very different Christians.

Liam raised an arm in farewell and closed his eyes. Danny was used to having 'boy' added to his name but he'd miss hearing Liam's, 'by'.

Outside, surveying the barren waste of his old street added to Danny's sense of loss at Liam's imminent departure. He found it hard to imagine what kind of man his father would have been, but he hoped he would have been a bit like Liam, – and Ernest: willing to listen, to take him seriously, and to stand beside him whenever the sky darkened. He felt weak and terribly young.

He looked over to where his old house once stood and recalled life as a small boy with his mother, and the times spent with the friend who had lent him his precious, long-awaited toy on Christmas Day. Nobby's death and now Liam's injuries reignited a desire for revenge, but it soon faded into familiar frustration at the hopelessness of doing anything about it.

On his way home past the cafe, two painters in white over-alls emerged, and with them came the sound of the pinball machine in action again. Then, as if Nobby had nudged him, Danny thought back to the perfection of his friend's final, unfinished game, during which he had mentioned the one option that might have warded off George's vengeance: a threat to tell the police about what was kept in his old aunt's flat and lock-up. George had promised to kill him if he told anyone. But Nobby had told Danny. Now, out of George's grasp, Nobby could grass him up from beyond the grave. Fired up but frightened, Danny made for a telephone box. Inside, he took a deep breath and dialled the local police station.

'Rochester Row Police.' The voice was formal, no nonsense. With his determination dissolving, Danny blurted out, 'I want to report someone who steals stuff, sells drugs, beats people up . . .'

The voice sounded interested but unimpressed. 'Please slow down.'

'OK. I know where he keeps stolen goods and where he hides the drugs that people sell for him.'

'Hold on, who am I speaking to?'

'Who?'

'Let's start with your name.'

'My name?'

'Yes, these are serious allegations.'

Danny slammed down the receiver and his hands shook as he envisaged George exacting his revenge on a grass, even from prison. 'This is my manor, Pages, and if you want to live safely in it . . .'

He left the phone box, legs betraying him, heart thumping. As he entered the estate, coming towards him were Cordelia, accompanied by her mother and Ernest.

Cordelia's face lit up. Here was his girlfriend

As she came closer, her smile faded. 'Danny? What's the matter?'

'Nothing.'

'What did George say to you at the cafe?'

Having no wish to talk about George, Danny said, 'Oh, you know, the usual.'

'Hello, Daniel,' said Ernest, looking a little shy to be with Ellen, who put her arm through his, hoping to make him more comfortable. It didn't quite work but he managed to smile and said, 'We're off to St James's Park.'

Ernest, now an honorary inhabitant of their estate.

'Want to join us?' said Cordelia.

Still shaky and needing to think, he said, 'I'd like to,' which was true, and 'but I have to get home,' which wasn't.

'Pity,' said Ellen, her face already under repair with

happiness. 'And thanks, I hear that you've been a knight in shining armour for my Cordelia this time.'

'This time?' he said.

She smiled and a little nod told him her thanks were also for what he'd done for her.

'Not really,' said Danny, 'she was the brave one. Anyway, enjoy the park.'

Cordelia took his hand. 'Are you sure you're OK?'

He was feeling better already. 'Fine, see you later, maybe.'

He watched them walk away, Ellen in the middle linking arms with her daughter and Ernest.

Passing through the estate, Danny got a wave from the lady in the launderette as she folded the clean clothes. It was to her he took his washed Levis to dry when he needed them in a hurry. Next, he received a smile from Mr Jones as he stacked milk crates. Behind his shop, small children were shrieking in the playground while their mothers chatted on the benches. Danny stopped and turned full circle to look up at the high sides of the estate blocks. Behind the rows of identical windows were homes that were anything but identical. And inside, families and their neighbours: good and bad; easy and difficult; quiet and noisy; comfortable and skint. Living their lives on their estate, his estate. During the last game of pinball he'd ever play, Nobby had called it 'our manor'. George may have been its most dangerous inhabitant, but it wasn't *his*.

In his own courtyard, Danny walked around the abandoned hopscotch, chalked by kids in their block, on their estate. And it *was* 'theirs', in its most important sense: of belonging, not, as Gasping George saw it, of owning. With this simple revelation, Danny's resolve flooded back. He started walking and, remembering Liam had said that no one can stay brave all the time, speeded up in case his determination didn't last. Yesterday, he wouldn't have dreamed of what he was going to do; tomorrow, he would surely regret it, but today . . .

Light-headed and struggling to control his breathing, he entered the phone box and picked up the receiver.

'Rochester Row Police.'

'Hello, my name is Danny Byrne.'

Acknowledgements

Sincere thanks, again, to my super-supportive agent, Broo Doherty and my ever-patient and understanding editor, Kate Bradley.

As usual, I needed all the help it could get. When I felt like giving up, my writing group kept me going. I am indebted to Diane Chandler, Wilma Ferguson, Joy Isaacs, John Elliott, Judith Evans, Peggy Hannington, Catherine Hurley, Janice Rainsbury, and Jana Sheldon. I had great help from writing pals, Martin Cummins, Keven Kelly, Michael Ray and Nick Thripp – and Jim Sinkinson.

Finally, I'm grateful to writer friends, Susan Chadwick and Bernard O'Keeffe – insightful and invaluable readers.

Inspirations

St Andrew's Club, Westminster – because a good youth club can save your life.

My Irish uncle, Michael Walsh, without whom there'd have been no Liam Marnell.

THE
PIMLICO
KID

One boy. One street.
One summer he
will never forget

Barry Walsh